RETURNING

A COLLECTION OF STORIES

Jo Lauer

www.jolauer.com

For all the people who've enriched my life. You know who you are.

Also by Jo Lauer

Best Laid Plans

Table of Contents

Acknowledgements

Thank you to Nancy for engaging with my characters as though they were mutual friends; to my writer's group: Anne Marie, Dmitri, Nancy, Gayle and Kimberly, who provided hours of support and feedback; to Andy Bauer who once again took my internal vision and produced a superb cover; to Kathryn Marcellino for formatting assistance; to Trudy, Margie, Joan, Sus, and Sara for their indispensable input on cover choice; and to my grandsons Lincoln and Everett who inspire me to be my best self.

Paddle

Prologue

"Leastwise you'll be cooler down there," seven year old Paddle whispered to her Aunt Seraphine as the grave diggers slowly lowered the polished oak casket. The smell of musty earth, like a basket of mushrooms, wafted up from the dark hole as she knelt by the edge of the grave.

With her dirt-encrusted knuckle, Paddle wiped at a trickle of sweat mixed with a tear or two as it slid down her cheek. A handful of mourners, as wilted in the Louisiana mugginess as the flowers placed at the head of the grave, gathered around the small family plot. Preacher Marcus, Doc Lester, Ginny and Benji Hawk, Deputy Sheriff Higgins, and four old women from Aunt Seraphine's quilting group sang the last refrain of "Amazing Grace."

Paddle knew about planting people. It started when she was just a little kid, four years old, when her momma and daddy got killed by a logging truck run amok. Then Grandma, who'd taken her in, died of the bad lungs. Aunt Seraphine had moved in to take care of Paddle and Grandpa until he shot himself in the head out in the timber while hunting rabbits. Paddle never could wrap her thoughts around that one.

Three days ago, she went into the kitchen for a glass of water and found Aunt Seraphine crumpled on the floor looking sort of gray. Heart just gave out, Doc Lester had said.

"It's all right. I'm a big girl now—I can take care of myself," she'd said to Doc, who had pulled her into a big old bear hug, then driven her over to Ginny Hawk's just down the bayou.

"'Course I'll take her in," Ginny said, her voice all gruffed-up with love and sadness. "She'll be the big sister Benji's never gonna get any other way." And that had been that. She was officially part of the Hawk family.

"Benji, don't you touch those cupcakes in the display case. I mean it," Ginny admonished Paddle's five year old new brother a week later. "Paddle, grab that coffee pot over there and fill up Deputy Sheriff Higgins' cup, will you?" She shooed Daemon the cat out of the puddle of sunlight where he'd curled up right in the middle of the Blue Hawk Diner.

It was good to feel useful and earn her keep. Paddle got all saucer-eyed when Sheriff Higgins left her a quarter and said she'd make a right-fine waitress.

Ginny spread her arms wide to take in the whole café and said in a voice that made the Deputy Sheriff chuckle, "Some day all this will be hers." She nodded in Paddle's direction.

"Benji, stop spinning on that stool, it's going to make you hurl," Ginny shouted back over her shoulder. She laid out some paper and crayons at one of the booths and settled him there. "Thanks, Mike," she called to Mr. McPherson who'd left a handful of bills next to the cash register for his Southern Comfort Breakfast Special.

This is how life went, year after year—daily chats with the locals, catching up on the latest gossip, a few foreign visitors from out of state with their funny accents who used words like *quaint* and *delightful*. On the first of every month, Ginny would sit down with Paddle and make up a "special" and show her how to price it out so they wouldn't lose their shirts on it.

Calendar pages kept turning and a decade passed. To Paddle, it looked like this was the life she was destined to live. It wasn't a bad life—working at the diner after school—but when those foreigners talked of places like the Rocky Mountains with their deep canyons, or the lake in Utah that was so salty you couldn't sink, or even the gold coast of California that sat right there on the Pacific ocean, the travel bug bit at her like a swarm of mosquitoes. "Might as well put that dream to rest," Paddle would tell herself as she moved from booth to booth refilling the salt and pepper shakers.

Then Lucas arrived.

Chapter 1

The first time I saw Lucas Plum, she was perched on a spinney-stool at the counter of the Blue Hawk Diner, listening to Ginny yammer away about Benji, and how one day he'd be a famous musician. Benji couldn't play a penny whistle for a dollar, but his mamma believed in him.

Copper red curls sprung from Lucas' head like a clock maker's bad joke. Her eyes were as muddy as the water of the Mississippi, and she could turn on you with a gaze as intent as spawning trout. She had no eyebrows. I'd never met anyone without eyebrows. Her voice was gritty, like beach sand flecked with specks of burnt tobacco. And her smell reminded me of a dusty hay loft in mid-summer where a patch of sun has found its way through the broken barn boards.

Elbows propped on the green Formica counter, she was saying, "Mm-hmm, person's got to have a dream, all right," nodding her head, making those springy curls bounce just above her bowl of Blue Fire Chili.

"Hey, Marie Antoinette," Ginny called to me, motioning me out of the middle of the doorway where I stood, backlit by night, transfixed by the sight of Lucas. I'd just gotten back from delivering a freshly-baked pie to Miz Hatcher's guest house.

Marie Antoinette isn't my real name, of course—it's just what Ginny calls me. Says I'm quicker to lose my head than just about anybody she knows.

I shuffled up to the counter, unable to stop looking at the place where there should have been eyebrows.

Daemon, Ginny's mangy cat, black as the night sky, smelling of bright chips of stars, moist dark earth, hearth fires and mystery, padded his way in behind me, slunk to the back of the diner, turned a disdainful rump on the whole affair, and settled next to the radiator diffusing damp cat throughout. He was allowed.

"This here's Delta," Ginny threw a freckled arm around my shoulder. She cocked her head toward the stranger on the stool. "And this here's Lucas—Lucas Plum," she said, bouncing her own eyebrows at me, and smiling all lopsided.

"Call me Paddle," I said, hoping not to have to go into the long story about being named after the Delta Queen, biggest danged paddle boat on the Mississippi. Paddle suits me just fine. We shook hands. Mine was cold and wet, like a trout pulled out of the river. Hers was warm and dry like an old flannel nightie hanging on a clothesline in the sunshine.

"You look like a girl with a dream," was all she said. A slow, easy smile softened her parted lips. The muddy brown of her eyes shifted slightly like sludge settling on the river bottom.

I glanced away for a moment. The neon glare blinked iridescent green and pink through the plate glass up front, causing those in the prime window seats to glow like radiated cadavers. I looked back at Lucas.

"Where you from?" I asked, shifting my weight from one foot to the other. I wasn't sure what to do with my hands all of a sudden, so I stuck them in my coat pockets along with damp, wadded up Kleenex, a crumpled gum wrapper, and a tube of Chapstick.

"Not many places I haven't been from," she said. "Just passin' through, like a change of weather." Again, that slow, easy smile.

Ginny left us to go fill Deputy Sheriff Wilt Higgins' coffee cup at the far end of the counter. He appeared to be trying to listen without appearing to be trying to listen, as he casually stirred sugar into his coffee, glanced our way, sort of bored like, then back at the swirling steam from his cup.

"Take a load off," Lucas motioned to the empty stool next to her.

"Thanks," I said, even though it was like having company come in to your own home and say to you, hey, make yourself at home.

"So, what do you do around here for Equinox?" Lucas Plum spoke softly and leaned towards me, the Blue Fire Chili all but forgotten. Her

7

eyelashes were so pale, I almost thought she didn't have those either until I saw her blink up close.

I guess she could tell I didn't know what she meant because she said, "You know, tonight? The time when the day and the night are equal and life is suspended in perfect balance? It's exciting, isn't it?"

A twitch of that excitement sprung her curls into action. The sludge shifted once more, and shone slightly with the promise of sunrise.

I wasn't sure what she was talking about, but I like that she was talking.

"There's that moment when beginnings are as likely as endings, where the visions of dreamtime slip away and sleep turns to wake as you open your eyes to the first rays of morning light, to the hopes and dreams of a new day." She paused, stretched and yawned as if she'd just crossed over the threshold.

"Can't you just feel it, Paddle?" The air around her seemed to crackle and glitter for just a second.

Yes, I think I was beginning to feel something.

"We should be celebrating the harvest as well as the barren times ahead. It's all part of the cycle of life, you know?"

Her eyes had taken on a misty quality as if she were relaying stories told by her ancestors, sitting in a circle around a fire out in the woods on a clear, starry night just like this one.

For a moment, I was there with her, in the woods, around the fire, listening, knowing.

"Equinox is the moment of no return, Paddle, the momentum that brings life forth, like a chick beginning to peck its way out of the egg," she said.

For just a minute, I imagined myself with my old brown leather suitcase in my hand, stepping onto the Greyhound heading west…

"There's no turning back," Lucas said in almost a whisper.

… handing the driver my ticket…

Lucas turned the full focus of her gaze on me, and time slipped away. I felt all floaty and light, held in place only by those eyes fixed on mine.

"It's a time of letting go, Paddle—letting go of all those self-imposed limitations, fears, the 'shoulds', all the stuff that hibernates deep within," she said.

... settling into the seat by the window and looking out through the smudged glass one last time on this sorry excuse for a town...

"There's only this moment and the next, Paddle. It's time to step into your Destiny." Her voice, full of urgency and in command, called from somewhere on the outer edges of reality.

... the door sliding shut. I'm traveling down the highway. I'm flying through space. There are no boundaries. I'm free...

I felt a mixture of exhilaration and fear—exhilaration that there is only this moment and the next, fear that there is only this moment and the next.

"Take that bowl for you, Lucas?" Ginny's voice sent my flying spirit careening to the earth like a blown-out comet.

"Looks like it could rain," Lucas said, turning slowly on her stool to stare out of the plate glass the next day. A milky glow haloed the streetlamp outside the diner. The late afternoon sky and the sidewalk were the same chalky gray. She wiped a smear of catsup from her chin with her crumpled paper napkin and tossed it over her shoulder. It landed on the counter with a soft *thip*. Ginny swept it away along with a few cold fries.

"You staying at the Dew Drop Inn?" I asked, knowing that it was the only place in town to rent a room except for old Miz Hatcher's place, and that's haunted.

"Stayin' in my bus, right out back of the diner. Ginny said I could use the facilities since I'm taking all my meals here," she grinned. "Yes sir, nothing like rain on the roof when you're living in a bus."

At that moment, I wanted nothing more than to be vagabonding around the country in an old beat-up bus, pulling in to strange burgs, checking out the locals, sleeping with the sound of rain pelting overhead. Happy as an ant on a cupcake, I'd be.

"I've been thinking of journeying tonight, Paddle. Care to join me?" Lucas leaned against the back of her stool and stretched out legs that seemed to go forever. It occurred to me, I didn't know how tall she was since I left first last night and never saw her upright all the way.

Before I could answer, Ginny returned with the milk, set it down with a splash. A white puddle smirked up from the counter. "Leavin' already? You just got here," she said with a whine in her voice. My own heart took a brief time-out.

"Not that kind of journey, Ms. Hawk. I'm talking about a shamanic journey, where you look for your spirit guide. You know, drums and all," she said, as if we had any idea of what on earth she was talking about. "Maybe you'd like to join us?"

Lordy, I thought, and shook my head.

"Only drums we got around here are the set Pepper Frank plays over at the Moose Club for the annual Winter Wonderland Ball," Ginny chuckled.

"Oh, I travel with my circle drum, made by a shaman down in Santa Cruz, California—special elk skin, since Elk is my power animal," Lucas said.

I was reminded of those tent meetings that come to town every couple of years where the Holy Spirit fills the preacher who starts talking in tongues, babbling away so you can't understand a word he's saying. Shamans, spirit guides, power animals—what the? I had to admit, I was more than a little curious.

At ten o'clock, Ginny hung the Closed sign on the door. I straightened the chairs and swept up while she did the deposit. We turned off the lights and followed Daemon out the back door.

There was an eerie glow coming from Lucas' old bus, and a funny smell, kind of like burning mattress. We looked at each other, then back at the bus door.

"Well, go on," Ginny whispered and gave me a little shove, "knock or somethin'."

"Hey, Lucas," my voice cut through the quiet of the dark alley. "It's Paddle and Ginny, come to journey," I said, as if I knew what that meant. I could feel a knot in my stomach, and my armpits were starting to odor up on me.

Lucas' face appeared in the window. She slid the side door open and stepped out into the night, surrounded by that pungent smell.

I covered my mouth and coughed through my nose as quietly as I could. I knew Ginny was uneasy. She had a mean grip on my elbow.

"Welcome," Lucas said, all serious. She was holding something that looked like a smoldering bunch of weeds bound with string. "First we'll smudge, and then we'll enter," she said, as she fanned the smoking bundle up and down, head to toe, and all around first my body, then Ginny's.

"This is sage," she said, "to purify you, to open your consciousness up to receive the gifts of Spirit. May you be blessed."

Ginny sneezed, and then giggled. "Bless me, indeed," she said. I tried to look solemn for the occasion so Lucas wouldn't think we were making fun of her.

"Come on in and find a place to stretch yourself out. There are some pillows to rest your head on," Lucas said.

Was this like a slumber party, I wondered? There was one candle sitting on a wooden box that cast enough light to see that all the seats, except for the driver's, had been removed. It was like a little room on wheels.

"Well, isn't this just cute," Ginny babbled.

A big mattress covered most of the floor. Toward the back, there was a collection of feathers, rocks, dried flowers, more candles and some pouches arranged on top of a silky scarf. Long, orange colored curtains were drawn over all the windows, and when she slid the door shut, the rest of the world just disappeared. Must be what being inside a mother's belly was like—quiet, and soft, and warm.

Lucas was sitting propped up by several big pillows that leaned against the back of the driver's seat. A circular drum as wide as her body rested on her lap. A light colored animal skin stretched real tight covered the drum and reflected the candlelight.

"You both comfy?" Lucas tamped out the smudge bundle in a big mother-of-pearl seashell next to her, and picked up a stick with a thick padded end covered in soft leather. The candles flickered shadows that danced quietly along the curtains.

Lucas told us that she was going to keep a steady beat on her drum for a while, and we were to close our eyes and imagine finding a place in nature where we could enter the earth.

"Like a rabbit hole, or a tree stump, or maybe a pond," she said, her voice soft and far away. And we were to imagine ourselves just letting go and falling down, down, down, farther and farther into the earth until we landed somewhere.

"What if we wind up in Hell?" Ginny said with a nervous giggle.

"You're perfectly safe," Lucas assured her, with what I thought was a great deal of patience. "Just listen to the drum and let it guide you."

She instructed us to look around and ask whatever we saw if it was our power animal, and when the drum beat quickened, to bring that being back with us in the palm of our hand.

"They put people in the funny farm for things like this, don't they," Ginny joked.

"Ginny!" I hissed at her. Honestly, sometimes she acts so dumb, she embarrasses me.

Lucas didn't seem to mind though. She picked up her drum and began a regular beat with her padded stick. I closed my eyes, shutting out the warm glow of the bus, and looked around behind my eyeballs for that place where I could go down into the earth. The drumbeat made my whole body feel heavy, like it was sinking.

A picture came to my mind of a tree stump I found while hiking in the timbers outside of town. Good a place as any, I figured, and I imagined myself throwing a leg over and easing down into the burned out hole. I could hear the drum, soft and regular, like an anchor so I wouldn't get lost. I worked my way down past old roots, climbing down farther into a tunnel that just seemed to go forever. Funny, I thought, it's light enough to see down here under the earth.

When the soles of my feet landed on soft ground, I looked around me for a clue as to where I might be. Sand—warm, soft, and creamy-colored—spread as far as I could see. In the distance, the dunes swept up to meet a robin's-egg blue sky. Not a cloud in sight, or anything else. So quiet, all I could hear was a faint drumbeat from another land.

I squinted my eyes and scanned as far as I could for any sign of life, let alone a power animal. Getting kind of discouraged, I drug my toe through the sand leaving a lazy trail next to my foot. I looked around behind me wondering how I was going to get back, feeling kind of lonely and edgy. I turned back around to see grains of sand start to shift and scatter, like something was trying to come up from under. I stared at that spot, watching the sand rearrange itself, not sure I wanted to see what it was, the only other living thing in this strange place.

Then the head of a snake, the size of my foot, came poking through the sand, followed by a long sleek body that just kept coming. It was about as long as two broom handles. This was no normal snake, no indeed. It was the color of sunset, all coral and pink with slices of gold and purple wound through it. It glowed in a way that made the sand shine all round it. Two dark beady eyes turned themselves on me and a golden tongue flicked in and out, tasting for my fear.

We just stared at each other. I tried to blink, but couldn't. Then I remembered Lucas' words, and though I couldn't even move my little toe, I managed to croak out, "Are you my power animal?" *And please don't kill me if you're not*, I added silently. My throat felt as dry as the sand I was standing on.

Without breaking eye contact, the snake began a slow slither my direction, and just before reaching my feet, began to coil around and around on itself, making a swirling sunset in the sand. Long beams of color shot out in all directions, splashing me, and the dunes, shooting rays up into the sky.

From the center of the coil came the words, *Step into your Dessssstiny*. I swear that snake smiled at me.

My jaw hung open like a broken screen door. Then I heard it, the drumbeat, quickening, louder, insistent. Come back, come back, it called. How was I going to bring the sunset snake back with me in the palm of my hand? Surely, I'd die trying.

I bent my knees slowly, quietly as I could, and leaned forward, bracing myself with my left hand in the fine grainy sand, and reached real careful-like toward the snake. Swirls of color splashed over my hand and arm and up my body making me tingle.

Just as my hand touched the coiled body, there was a *poof* and bright sparks of color shot every which way. Then there were only glistening embers of color, a glowing coil of ash where the snake had been.

The drumbeat was louder and more insistent now, demanding my return. I reached out and grabbed a handful of cool, colorful ash mixed with fine grains of sand.

When I turned around, the tunnel that had deposited me here reappeared. I followed it through the dim light, forward and up, finding footing on roots and rocks embedded in the dark, rich earth. Sky, laced with overhanging tree branches and leaves, came into view as I poked my head back up through the stump.

Just then the drumbeat stopped. I blinked and looked around me. The candlewick flickered and sputtered quietly. The smell of sage lingered in the orange glow. I heard a long, low snore coming from

Ginny, stretched out, mouth open, just to my left. Lucas sat still as a goddess, a beautiful smile on her face, drum resting in her lap.

"Welcome back," she beamed at me. "What do you have in your hand there?" she asked, nodding at my right hand, all balled up and resting on my chest.

I rolled over on my left side and pulled up to a sitting position, my right hand still curled, guarding my treasure.

"Sunset snake ash," I said, not knowing what else to call it.

"Well, Paddle, if Snake came to you, that's powerful medicine, all right," she said in just above a whisper, nodding her head. Her coppery curls bobbled and dangled, and reflected the candlelight.

Then she said, "And if she left her skin, that's a sure sign a new beginning is on its way." A tingle shivered my body like a draft of cold air on the back of my neck.

Just then, Ginny snorted, sputtered, coughed, and woke herself up. She rubbed her eyes with her knuckles and rolled over on her side. Through a huge yawn, she said, "D'I miss the party?"

I swear, some people are just hopeless.

"Nope, you're just in time," Lucas grinned at her, as she pulled out a round chocolate cake from next to the driver's seat, and a bottle of red wine with the cap already unscrewed.

"To the ancestors," she said as she tossed some cake crumbs on the floor of the bus. "To the Mother of us all," she said as she added a drizzle of wine to the crumbs on the floor. Then she passed the cake and bottle around. We each took a big hunk of cake followed by a swig of port.

"If this don't beat all," Ginny said, through a mouthful of chocolate.

The rain tapped out a steady rhythm on the metal roof of the bus as the bottle of port made another round, and then another. I don't know when I'd ever felt so pleased with myself.

The sun was shining in a cloudless blue sky when I slammed the front door of the diner the next morning. Along with a backpack stuffed full of just about everything I owned, I wore a grin so wide my ears hurt. I had a roll of bills stuffed in the back of my pack, two more piles folded neatly in each pocket of my jeans, and some small bills tucked in my socks. Nothing in my way, I was ready to see the world. Well, nothing except maybe Ginny, but I figured I could explain it in a way that she'd just have to be happy for me.

Dee Dee Combs and her toddler brat sat at one of the window tables, fussing about cold cereal and hurry up, do you want to be late? Deputy Sheriff Higgins sat at the far end of the counter sipping his morning coffee and reading the sports page of the paper. Ginny was back in the kitchen yelling at the dish washer to get those cups on the shelf, she'd need them soon enough.

Lucas must be using the facilities, I figured, as I heaved my pack onto a stool and set myself in the one next to it. Ginny came out looking like hell, red-rimmed puffy eyes, a speck of tissue lint on her upper lip from blowing her wet nose. Her bottom lip quivered.

"She's gone, Paddle," she choked out before the tears started running down her cheeks. Ginny turned and leaned heavily against the counter and sobbed. Deputy Sheriff Higgins raised an eyebrow but never took his eyes off the sports page.

The blood leaked slowly out of my head and my body felt like it was moving through thick syrup as I made my way to the back door of the Diner. I stuck my head out to see an empty alley—not a trace of bus or person. *Passing through like a change of weather*, she'd said.

My lips went numb as I looked at nothing parked where my life had been rerouted just hours earlier. A swirl of color caught my eye. I stepped out onto the asphalt and bent down to put my finger in a puddle of oil-soaked rain. The rainbow colors rippled as I pulled my finger slowly through the water. Somewhere in the far reaches of my mind, I heard *Dessssstiny*. I heard Lucas saying, "There's only this moment and the next, Paddle."

The last thing Lucas had said to me before I called it a night was, "Sometimes you've got to pull up anchor, Paddle, and flow with the river, just like your namesake."

There's only this moment—I stood up slowly, shrugged, and walked back into the diner—and the next.

"I'll write to you; I promise," I called over my shoulder to Ginny. I picked up my backpack and headed out the front door.

Chapter 2

Dear Ginny,

Hope you're over being mad at me. Sometimes you just got to do what you just got to do. I'll be home again one day.

Hitchin' is easier than I thought. I'm somewhere in Missouri right now sitting under a big old shade tree munching on a fried chicken leg that Mrs. Barstow gave me. She and her husband, Ollie, dropped me off and headed east to a family reunion. Nice people so far. It's a long way to California. I'll be in touch. Hey, to Benji and Daemon. Yours, Paddle

Paddle licked a stamp and stuck it on the postcard. She carefully wedged the card and pen back in her pack, and picked up the chicken leg that rested on a big green leaf. She took a satisfying gnaw and chewed slowly as she leaned back against the oak. This was life on the road. This was America, and Paddle was seeing it.

Maybe she could forgive Lucas for running off on her like that. In one of their deep philosophical talks, Lucas had said that people come into your life for a reason, a season, or a lifetime. "Guess it took Lucas to get me out of that backwater town," she mused out loud to a crow perched on the bough above her, eyeing the chicken bone. The crow bobbed its head in agreement.

Paddle tossed the bone over her shoulder. The crow abandoned its perch. "Bone appetite," Paddle chuckled. It was an inside joke she and Ginny shared back at the diner.

She wiped her fingers carefully in the thick green grass, then stood and stretched. It was mid-day and the sun was toasty. She settled her pack on her back, brushed the twigs and debris from her jeans and headed back toward the highway, leaving the lush meadow of wildflowers behind her. She hauled herself carefully over the split wood fence, and paused a moment, her left ear straining for any hint of vehicle coming from the south. Two robins were chatting it up and a horse neighed in the distance, but nothing that sounded like a motor rode on the airwaves.

Paddle turned up road and walked in a slow steady rhythm, lost in thoughts of people, places, and things unknown. She was so lost that she forgot to stick out her thumb as an old Chevy sailed by. A scrawny kid with a mop of blonde hair waved at her from the back window.

Paddle set her pack by the side of the road and hauled out her canteen. She took a long, deep swig of water and wiped her mouth with the back of her hand. The sun was at a forty-five degree angle and the trees cast shadows across the highway.

She heard before she saw the rusty old pick-up truck of undeterminable color rattling up the road. On top of it this time, she stepped up close to the side of the road, grinned real friendly-like, and stuck out her thumb. A scraping sound and a high pitch squeal signified a down shift as the pick-up lumbered to a stop a few feet short of where Paddle stood, still grinning, thumb still akimbo.

"You stuck or something?" a querulous voice called from the rolled down window on the driver's side.

Paddle squinted into the sun toward the voice. She shook herself out of her position, picked up her pack, and walked up to the source of the question.

"Hey," she offered, sticking out her hand, "I'm Paddle."

"Arizona Pancake," the young woman said, proffering a hand out the window. She was a vision of pale blonde hair that haloed out from under a battered straw hat. Her face was liberally sprinkled with freckles and her eyes were blue as the cornflowers that grew wild in the fields. She wore faded overalls and a well-worn, once-white-now-gray tee shirt.

They shook hands. Paddle felt a low voltage current of energy pass through her hand. The two stared at each other for a moment.

"Where you headed?" Arizona asked.

"California," Paddle said with a shrug. It sounded more like a question than an answer.

"Goin' the wrong way," Arizona replied sociably.

"I'll get there eventually," Paddle smiled. "Where you going?" she asked, noting the pick-up bed filled with a poorly folded tent, a sleeping bag that diffused a musty scent on the afternoon breeze, an old camp stove, and assorted pots and pans.

"Iowa," Arizona offered. "Got friends living on the land there. Said I should come see them sometime."

Paddle nodded.

"So, you want to ride along, or what?" Arizona jerked her head toward the passenger's side.

Paddle nodded. She threw her pack into the pick-up bed, walked around to the other side of the truck and creaked the door open. After several slams, it stuck shut. Paddle slid herself toward the middle of the seat.

The two vagabonds talked and sang their way north as the sun slid lower in the sky. When they sang "Amazing Grace," Arizona sang *that set my spirit free*, instead of *saved a wretch like me*. She said she just couldn't think of herself as wretched. Paddle didn't know you could just up and change the words to a song to suit yourself.

Night was settling in as Arizona pulled off onto the side of a country road.

"Got plenty of food to share," she nodded toward the bed of the pick-up behind her. "Figured we could stop here for the night. I'll show you how to do truck camping," she offered as she hauled herself from the driver's seat and stretched her arms to the early evening stars.

Paddle rammed against the passenger door a few times until it gave way, and then stepped out into the cool air. The night before, she'd unrolled her sleeping bag next to a cow pasture fence and fell asleep to the lowing of cattle in the distance. This felt a lot less lonely.

Arizona emptied out the truck bed and erected the tent over the frame while Paddle set up the tin cook stove on a patch of earth she'd cleared of debris. They worked in companionable silence. An owl hooted nearby and the moon peeked at them between the treetops.

Over bowls of red beans and rice, Arizona told Paddle about the commune in Iowa, how they could live off the land, work in the garden, weave blankets from sheep wool dyed in berry and herb juices. How there was singing and dancing every night to guitars and harmonicas and flutes and drums. How everyone loved and looked after each other and cooked their meals together in a big yurt.

As Arizona's voice droned in the background, Paddle's mind drifted back to the diner, to Ginny and Benji, the only family she'd known for a long time. A tear formed in the corner of her eye and left a snail track down her cheek.

When the pots and pans had been wiped clean, the food put away and the stove cooled off, Paddle and Arizona unfolded their sleeping bags inside the walls of the tent. The last sound Paddle heard as she drifted into a deep sleep was a slow zip sealing them safely in their cocoon.

Paddle opened her eyes to the sun pounding on the canvass. The smell of fresh brewed coffee and oatmeal wafted through the unzipped flap. Outside the tent, Arizona sang "You Are My Sunshine," in a husky alto.

"Guess I don't have to ask how you slept," Arizona chuckled as Paddle climbed out of the truck tent and wiped the sleep from her eyes with her two fists like a toddler just waking from a long nap.

She poured herself a cup of coffee and sat down next to Arizona on an old patchwork quilt spread by the side of the road. A ragged map sat at its center. A thick purple line ran from New Orleans to approximately where they sat.

"I figure one good day of travel and we'll be in Iowa," Arizona tapped her teeth with the capped end of the purple pen, "unless you want to take a little side trip up to Chicago?" she ventured. "See the big city?"

"I don't know," Paddle said warily, "isn't that where they have the Mafia and all that crime? And Al Capone?" she tried to remember what she knew of urban life up north. She reached over and filled a bowl with oatmeal.

"Nah, that was a long time ago," Arizona reassured her. "Guess I'd rather just get us to The Land as soon as possible," she said. That's how she'd begun referring to her final destination.

Somewhere outside of Hannibal, Arizona made a wrong turn that took them onto Highway 72. As they crossed a large muddy river, Paddle asked, "Isn't that the Mississippi?"

"I guess it is," Arizona exhaled an elongated cloud of smoke that reminded Paddle of the night she and Ginny went journeying with Lucas.

"You're going the wrong way then," Paddle ventured.

"Guess I am," Arizona giggled and coughed. She handed the smoldering paper-wrapped tube to Paddle who rolled it gently between her fingers, examining it like a curio.

"Go on," Arizona urged, "take a toke. It'll loosen you up."

"I think one of us ought to stay tight enough to read the map." Paddle handed the joint back to Arizona and unfolded the map that was stuck under her seat. "Looks like we can turn north at Springfield, follow 74 west and come into Iowa through Burlington," she said as she ran her finger in a slow horseshoe.

"I guess I'll be ready for some lunch by then," Arizona laughed hysterically. "Maybe a herd of cattle," she said with a foolish grin on her face and tears rolling down her cheeks. Paddle didn't get the joke, but she nodded anyway. She looked out the window, watched the timberland go by in the distance, and wondered if this had anything to do with her *Dessssstiny*.

"Regale me with your life story," Arizona said and yawned hugely. "You running away from something?"

"Naw. Maybe running to something, but I don't know exactly what it is yet," Paddle mused. She wasn't used to talking about herself and didn't know where to begin. "How about you? You running away from something?" she glanced sideways at Arizona.

"Not that anyone would notice," Arizona heaved a sigh. "I'm a trust-fund baby with time on my hands and money in my pocket. Folks are in Europe, or maybe it's Argentina this month. Figured I'd go find me a family that stays put, if you know what I mean." Paddle nodded, although folks she knew didn't wander any farther than the next city for groceries on a Saturday morning. Paddle knew staying put.

They stopped outside of Springfield for lunch, and Paddle watched with fascination as Arizona packed away two greasy hamburgers, a large order of fries, chocolate malt, and a slice of pecan pie to Paddle's burger and medium coke. The mid-day sun heated up the cab of the truck as they headed north toward Peoria.

"Next time we cross the Mississippi, let's stop for a swim, okay?" Arizona burped, patted her chest, and grinned.

"If we can make that the last time we cross the Mississippi, you got yourself a deal," Paddle smiled. They rode on in silence, sated with food, hair flying in the warm breeze. Paddle's eye lids were heavy and she gave over to the weight of sleep.

Before her eyes, crusty with sleep, squinched open, Paddle was aware of sweat sluicing down the side of her face. Her hair was matted against the window sill and a crick held her neck in check. She let out a groan. No response.

Paddle opened her eyes to an empty truck. It must have been one hundred degrees in the shade. She stretched slowly, and used the tail of her shirt against the heat of the door handle to let herself out of the truck and into a dusty parking lot. Paddle glanced up and down the street. A market, gas station, hardware store, a generous sprinkling of liquor stores, and a handful of wooden summer cottages made up this bleak rest stop.

A few dusty old crows flapped slowly overhead and a waft of wet mud lingered in the heavy air. Paddle made out the top of a bridge span through the pine trees. Every now and then, a motorboat, like an overgrown mosquito, would buzz lazily by not far away.

Before she could work up a good worry, Arizona came skipping out of a liquor store with a brown paper sack full of supplies, if you could call cold beer and potato chips supplies. Arizona did. The girl managed to look perky even in this heat, Paddle mused.

"Picnic time," Arizona said with a wink. "This is Gulfport, and that," she gestured grandly toward the end of the street, "is the Mississippi River. Just across the bridge is Iowa," she grinned. "Figured we'd have us a picnic down on the levee to celebrate our arrival."

"I could use a dip in the river," Paddle added, aware of the odor wafting from her body.

"This way," Arizona pointed. "The guy at the counter told me how to find the path down to the water." She hitched the sack onto her hip and sauntered down the sidewalk with Paddle in tow.

They spread themselves out in the shade on a grassy patch just next to the muddy bank. The smell of fish, algae, wet earth, heat, and pine mingled with malty beer as Arizona popped the tops of two cold cans and handed one to Paddle. Arizona gulped noisily and wiped foam from her mouth with the back of her wrist. She smacked her lips. Paddle opened a bag of chips and munched thoughtfully.

"Not thirsty?" Arizona asked in amazement.

Paddle examined a blade of grass, watched an ant hover over a crumb of chip. "I've never had beer, exactly," she stammered.

"Well, Lordy," Arizona shook her head, "if that doesn't beat all. Guess I'm just a bad influence on you all the way around. Cheers," she said, lifting her can.

"Cheers right back at cha," Paddle grinned. They clicked cans and Paddle took a long, deep swig of the golden liquid. She burped and took another swig.

"Whoa, there partner. You might want to pace yourself," Arizona advised. "We have two six packs here." They munched and drank companionably. The cold beer cooled them, quenched their thirst, and sent them into a relaxed stupor.

"Does beer make you hear things?" Paddle asked.

"Like hallucinations, you mean?" Arizona sat up and looked at her traveling companion with concern.

Paddle shrugged her shoulders, a silly grin on her face. "Like I thought I heard someone crying," she said.

"Oh, no. Don't go getting maudlin on me," Arizona frowned. But just then her ears perked as she heard it too, some distance off, but definitely sobbing.

The two staggered to their feet, abandoning the bag of chips and tipping over a can of beer as they braced each other upright.

"This way," Arizona whispered and nodded her head toward a marshy trail that led through the water rushes.

"Why are we whispering?" Paddle whispered back.

"I don't know," Arizona whispered again then erupted in giggles. The two of them chortled as they wobbled down the path through the mud.

As they rounded a bend, the sobbing was closer and louder. It had a sobering effect on the girls.

"Hey," Arizona called out. "Hey, you need some help, or anything?"

Paddle shrieked when a visage, dressed in a soaking wet muddy leather tunic, arose from the banks just ahead of them. The girl's black hair hung in two soggy braids, and a murky strand of algae dripped from her shoulder. She wore one moccasin and her backpack leaked muddy water at her feet.

She wiped her tears with her forearm, sniffed, took a step forward, mustered up a shred of dignity and offered her hand. "I'm Kiowa Su Lafner," she said in a cultured voice.

Arizona shook her hand and made the introductions. Paddle nodded her greeting from behind Arizona, her eyes wide, taking in the sight of Kiowa Su.

"My canoe capsized and the current took it on down the river," she sniffed. "I managed to save myself and my backpack, but I lost my food, some provisions, and…" She puddled up again. "My map. It was an antique." Kiowa Su burst into sobs that shook her shoulders.

"There, there," Arizona reached over and gingerly patted her on the arm. She glanced at Paddle who shrugged.

"I'm an anthropology major," Kiowa Su choked out, "and I was recreating a native canoe trip to New Orleans. I even made my own canoe." The thought of the loss was more than her legs could bear, and she slumped down on the bank once again, in utter despair. Head in hands, she cried, "I can't even get home."

Arizona brightened. "This is perfect!" she bubbled.

Kiowa Su looked up at her in disbelief. Paddle scratched her head and looked doubtful. She had a hunch they'd just picked up another traveling companion.

"You don't want to go home," Arizona said.

"I don't?"

"No. You're an anthropologist, and adventurer, a cultural observer, right?"

"Uh…"

"Okay, so maybe it's not an Indian trek down a river with an antique map in a handmade canoe, but we're headed to a real live commune. Back to the earth, and all that."

"Commune?"

"Come with us." Arizona was grinning and nodding her head like a rattle.

A radiant smile broke out on Kiowa Su's face like sunshine after a storm. Perfect white teeth twinkled and her big brown eyes shown with gratitude.

"In fact, Kiowa Su—" Paddle was about to explain how she was an add-on to Arizona's plan, when she was cut short.

"Call me Ki, please."

"Okay, Ki," Arizona took up. "We were just having a picnic when we heard you crying. If the bugs haven't finished it off, there's plenty left. You must be hungry after all that..." she paused to find the right word, "excitement," Arizona spun a new take on the tragedy.

It's funny how fate brings people together, Paddle thought, as she led the trio back through the marsh grass to their picnic spot. For just a moment, she thought she heard Lucas say something about "destiny." "Must be the beer," she muttered.

They consumed the remaining food and three more beers, packed up the truck, and crossed the muddy Mississippi.

"Still want to go for that swim?" Arizona grinned at Paddle who looked down over the bridge rail at the water below.

"I'd strongly advise against it," Ki offered.

They spent the next many hours hop-scotching across Iowa following highway and interstate numbers on the map—34, 35, 80, and 71. The sun was low on the horizon, a deep red-orange slashed with lavender and gold behind a field of corn, as they pulled onto a badly marked dirt road. A hand-lettered sign tacked to a tree hung at an odd angle.

"Morningsong Ranch," Arizona read the sign as she turned off the engine. "This is it," she said in a hushed voice, the kind you use when you enter a church. "We're home."

"This is in the dead center of nowhere," Paddle offered, squinting ahead down the tree-lined lane. "The last farm must be fifty miles back. Haven't passed a grocery in hours."

"You sure it's okay just to drop in? I mean, they don't know we're coming, right?" Ki asked.

"Listen to you two," Arizona chuckled. "This is a commune—back to the land—everyone is welcome, no such thing as a stranger. I'm telling you, we're home." She turned the ignition on and eased the truck down the rutted path. As they rounded a hairpin curve with a shuddering of gears, the three gasped in unison at the sight before them.

The charred remains of log cabins, thatched shacks, hay bale hovels, a smattering of rusted farm equipment, and burned vegetable stubs in the garden greeted them. A wooden outhouse lay on its side in a murky puddle that was afloat with debris. There was no life at Morningsong Ranch.

Paddle's mouth hung agape. Ki's knees buckled. She fell with a dusty thwump onto the ash-covered ground and burst into tears. Arizona emitted a low wheezy sound like a death rattle. Her head turned slowly from side to side as she took in the wreckage.

"What do you suppose happened?" Paddle spoke the words over an acrid, smoky taste in her mouth.

"I aim to find out," Arizona said. "Let's go."

Paddle glanced down at Ki, frowned, shook her head and extended her hand. "C'mon."

Ki wiped her runny nose with the back of her sleeve. Muddy tears streaked down her cheeks. She sniffed loudly as she took Paddle's hand and struggled to her feet.

"I'm tired, and hungry, and hot," she whined.

"And you look like hell, and you don't smell so good, either," Arizona added. Paddle chuckled.

"Couldn't we just stay here for the night?" Ki pleaded.

"Look, we don't know why the commune was burned to the ground. In the off chance that it might have been intentional, we'd be sitting ducks to camp out here," Arizona reasoned. Her voice had an edge to it.

"Intentional?" Ki gasped. "You think someone burned them out? Who'd do a thing like that?"

"I propose we drive back to the last farm house and ask some questions." Arizona turned on her heels and headed for the truck. Paddle shrugged and followed silently.

"It's almost dark," Ki said in a worried voice. She dusted herself off as best she could and followed the others back to the truck, glancing over her shoulder every few steps at the second catastrophe of this very long day.

Arizona blew dust from under the tires as she swerved back onto the road. She gunned the engine from frustration as much as a race with the onset of night.

"Might want to switch on your lights," Paddle ventured, as dark shadows crisscrossed the road in front of them.

"You going to start telling me how to drive?" Arizona spat. Paddle looked straight ahead. A moment later headlights cut through the shadows. "Sorry," Arizona muttered.

The moon was just visible when Arizona turned left onto a deeply rutted dirt road and slowed to a crawl. Ki emitted a squawk each time a tire dropped into a groove and the bottom of the truck scraped earth. Just ahead a whitewashed, two story farmhouse lay surrounded by a rickety picket fence. A pen of sheep rustled about to the left of the house. A scattering of free-range chickens ambled around in the dusk, some roosting near an old shed. A tractor, a pick-up, and a faded black Ford coupe occupied a rusted metal lean-to. There were lights on in the front of the house.

Arizona killed the headlights, switched off the engine, and looked at Paddle who looked at Ki who looked back at Paddle who looked at Arizona.

"I'm not doing this by myself," Arizona said.

Both doors opened and the three stepped gingerly into the night air. Crickets and katydids sang full throttle from the darkening fields.

Arizona cupped her hands around her mouth and hollered, "Hello—is anyone there?"

A moment later a floodlight lit the whole front yard and the farmhouse door opened a crack. An old man with a shock of white hair stuck his head through the opening, and then leaned farther out to get a good look. His plaid flannel work shirt hung open over a white tee.

"Lost?" he hollered back.

Mustering her courage, Arizona walked toward the door, followed at a short distance by Paddle. Ki stood with a death grip on the handle of the pick-up.

"Evening," she offered a smile. "Sorry to interrupt. We've been traveling for days to reach our friends at Morningsong Ranch just up the road. Place looks burned down. I was wondering if you could tell me where everyone went."

The man withdrew his head, slammed the door loudly and turned off the floodlight, leaving them with only the rising moon to help them find their way back to the truck.

"Hey!" Arizona shouted her indignation.

She turned just as Paddle reached the truck. Ki had crawled into the middle of the seat and was gesturing wildly to Arizona. Arizona heard the low-throated growl as a German shepherd rounded the corner of the farmhouse and stood in a slice of moonlight with teeth bared.

"Run!" Paddle shouted as she climbed in and slammed the truck door. It bounced open and she slammed it several times in succession, muttering under her breath until it caught.

Arizona shot through the night, jumped in behind the wheel, and slammed the door. With lightning speed, she threw the truck in reverse and backed down the rutted road. The three bounced about the cab of the truck. Paddle clung to the door and Ki clung to her.

"Damn," Arizona wheezed as she shifted back into first gear on the main road.

A deep rumbling laugh started in Ki's belly and filled the car. Paddle began to chuckle. Arizona shook her head as the truck filled with hysteria. Unable to suppress a grin that distorted her face she gave over to laughter. Ki doubled over and held her stomach. Tears cascaded down her face. Paddle held her head in her hands as if trying to get a grip on herself and rocked back and forth. Gasping for breath, Arizona pulled to the side of the road. She cut the engine.

"Okay, on to Plan B," she said weakly.

"We don't have a Plan B," Paddle chortled.

The three laughed themselves into exhaustion. They took turns peeing behind a tree. Arizona opened and passed around the remaining can of beer, nicely warmed by the heat of the day.

"Well, we can't stay here," Ki stated the obvious.

"I say we head for California," Paddle remembered her original destination. "The gold coast, palm trees..."

"Sunshine, the ocean, freedom..." Arizona sighed.

"And movie stars," Ki added.

"Ever the anthropologist," Arizona chuckled.

Chapter 3

Dear Ginny,

Hi to you and Benji. Met up with some traveling companions, Arizona and Kiowa Su. We were headed for a commune in Iowa, but it didn't exactly work out. So, I guess it's on to sunny California like I'd originally planned. Having lots of adventures along the way that I know you'd be raising your eyebrows at. Your worldly traveler, Paddle

The three took turns driving, navigating and sleeping throughout the night. By flashlight, with the map like a blanket over her knees, Ki guided Paddle south on I-29 and west on I-80 while Arizona snored loudly with her head wedged against the passenger door. Just outside of Omaha, Ki nudged Arizona awake at an all-night gas station and convenience store while Paddle went in for coffee and donuts. Spurred on by caffeine and sugar, Ki slipped into the driver's seat and Arizona rode shotgun.

Halfway through the first verse of "Red River Valley," sung quietly by Arizona, Paddle slipped into a murky sleep disturbed by images of charred wood on a bleak landscape, and vultures circling low.

At sunrise, mid-Nebraska, they changed places once again. It became their pattern every four or five hours throughout the day—eat, pee, change places, drive, sleep. No one spoke of the commune or ventured a guess as to the fate of its inhabitants.

"Nothing but miles and miles of more miles and miles," Ki grumbled as she scanned the flat horizon. Conversation was sparse. The sun beat down on the hood of the pick-up and hot air blew dust through the windows. They drove on.

Outside of Laramie, the terrain changed. Foothills, outcroppings of craggy rock, tumbleweed and range cattle dotted the landscape. They pulled into town and parked in front of a diner.

"We deserve a real meal," Paddle said, "and a place to wash up." No one argued with that. The three grungy travelers spilled out of the truck, groaning and stretching legs and backs under a canopy of stars against a pitch-black sky. The cooling night air was deliciously breathable and Paddle filled her lungs.

The customers at this hour were mostly truckers. Weighed down by their cowboy hats, they sat at the counter hunkered over white mugs of coffee. Patsy wailed about love gone wrong from the corner jukebox. Paddle and Arizona settled into a red vinyl booth while Ki slipped into the Ladies Room for a spit-bath at the sink. The wooden fan blades hummed lazily overhead. Paddle leaned her head back against the booth and her eyes slid shut. She was startled awake by a nasal twang.

"Hey girls, what can I get 'cha?"

"Ginny?" Paddle said; disoriented, she blinked and looked around to get her bearings.

"Nope. Name's Star," the woman offered.

Paddle knuckled away the tears that brimmed her lashes.

"You okay, honey?" Star kept one eye on Paddle as she slid the menus onto the table.

"Just a little homesick, I guess," Paddle said. Ki rejoined the table, damp hair brushed back in a long ponytail.

"Where y'all headed?" Star leaned one hand on a hip; the other held an order pad and pencil. It reminded Paddle of the song, "I'm A Little Teapot." Paddle began to chuckle.

"California," Ki offered. She glared at Paddle who was now laughing so hard she fell over sideways in the booth. She hooted and held her stomach.

Star raised her eyebrows and shot a glance at Arizona and Ki who both shrugged. She took their orders.

By the time Star got to Paddle, she had regrouped and sat wiping tears from her face with her napkin. "Travel weary, I guess," Paddle explained.

Revitalized with food, cleaned up and ready to roll, they forged ahead. The sun rose behind them somewhere in Utah casting a ruby haze over the asphalt. They drove on. And on.

"I'd just about kill for a real bed tonight," Ki said, knuckling the crick in her neck.

"Money's tight. Gotta get all the way to California. Food, gas, you know," Arizona held the voice of reason.

"Back home there're traveler's missions, like the Salvation Army, where you can stay for free. They even feed you, I think," Paddle offered.

"No way," Ki piped up. "They make you pray. Maybe even promise to convert or something. And you sleep in a big room with everyone else on cots. Eeeuuw. A bunch of dirty, homeless strangers."

"You mean like us?" Paddle added.

"For an anthropologist, you're pretty narrow-minded if you don't mind my saying so," said Arizona, not caring one whit if she minded.

"They'd have real showers, I bet, and pillows on the cots," Paddle moaned at the thought.

Outvoted, Ki frowned as they pulled up in front of a Quonset hut at sunset. The Angels of Mercy shelter sign read You Are a Child of God and You Are Welcome Here. Ki snorted when Arizona turned off the engine and a chorus of "What a Friend We Have in Jesus" wafted through the early dusk.

"Couldn't be any stranger than journeying," Paddle said as she slid across the seat after Ki.

The screen door creaked as Arizona tugged on the handle. The door was pushed open from inside and a round-bodied woman with apple dumpling cheeks and sparkling blue eyes greeted them in a whisper.

"Welcome, my children. You're just in time for Vespers. Come in, come in." She latched onto Arizona's elbow and ushered her, followed closely by Paddle and Ki, to a row of empty folding chairs at the rear of the room. They shuffled into their seats exchanging uncomfortable glances and embarrassed smiles as the flock turned to acknowledge them.

An elderly man as tall and thin as the woman was short and round began reading Scripture in a wobbly voice. When he said, "Let us pray," Ki stared straight ahead, Paddle dropped to her knees and clasped her hands in front of her, and Arizona crossed herself and bowed her head.

"Amen," the gentleman finished after a long beseeching prayer for the souls of all gathered. "Now, if you'll all join us at the table, I think Mother is ready with grace and fried chicken," he chuckled.

"I'm about prayed-out," Ki whispered loudly to Paddle as they moved the chairs they were sitting in around a long wooden table filled with bowls of mashed potatoes, gravy, and green beans, platters of chicken, dishes of broccoli and glazed carrots, and three pies with steam escaping from slits in the golden crusts.

"You'd better pray they don't throw us out of here before we eat," Paddle shot back.

After dinner, Mother read the House Rules regarding use of the facilities and sleeping arrangements. "Men on one side, women on the other—and no crossing over," she wagged her finger, "and morning prayers before breakfast." Ki groaned.

A faint shimmer of moonlight filtered through the screen door at the end of the Quonset hut. The three had found their cots and snuggled their weary bodies onto bleached sheets and pillowcases. The rough Army surplus blankets scratched the soft skin under Ki's chin. Arizona sneezed at the smell of mothballs that wafted up from the blanket each time she turned on her cot. Paddle snored deeply and moved not a muscle.

The night was filled with rustling sounds, squeaking coils, occasional throat clearings, whimpering, snoring in a variety of pitches, and the regular flushing of the toilet followed by the opening and closing of the bathroom door.

Arizona lay on her back and stared at the ceiling. She pushed the light-up button on her watch and groaned softly when she realized it was only two in the morning.

"You awake?" Ki whispered from the next cot.

"Yup."

"This place gives me the creeps. I say we hit the road."

"Now?" Arizona turned onto her side. She could make out the dim outline of Ki, sitting up with legs dangling over the edge of her cot. Ki squatted onto the floor and duck-walked over to Paddle's cot. She shook the edge.

"Huh? What?" Paddle braced herself up on one arm, face to face with Ki. "What's wrong?" she asked.

"Oh, I don't know," Ki huffed. "I lost my canoe, I'm a million miles from home or civilization, I can't sleep, I'm captive in a religious cult, and I think my cot has bedbugs—other than that, not much."

Arizona snickered. She had pulled on her shoes and was fishing around under her cot for her pack.

"And if I have to say one more prayer, I'm going to puke," Ki finished.

"Did she say 'puke'?" Paddle giggled quietly, getting into the spirit of this turn of events.

Like robbers stealing away in the night, the girls crept along the side of the Quonset, past slumbering bodies, to the screen door. Arizona gently pushed at the wooden frame. An ungodly creak cut through the night.

"Run for it!" Ki stage whispered. The three shot out the door letting it slam in their wake. They tumbled into the truck dragging packs and bags in behind them. Arizona gunned the engine and they peeled out of the gravel lot like a great escape scene in a B-movie, laughing hysterically, and punching each other playfully.

On the road again, they passed a café and gas station closed for the night. Stars began to fade, and on the horizon was a strip of translucent light that squeezed beneath the endless blanket of night.

"There," Ki pointed at the flashing neon light announcing Open 24-Hours. "No more grace with our grits or prayers with our pancakes," she grinned.

As they approached the diner, a man, woman, and small child, all looking like cadavers under the glow of the green neon, turned blank eyes to watch the trio.

Paddle stopped short at the door. "Whoa, this is feeling like Night of the Living Dead or something. Maybe we should go on up the road a way."

"Don't be silly," chided Arizona. "What could possibly go wrong?"

They overstuffed themselves on heavy country breakfasts of eggs, ham, potatoes, gravy, biscuits and some pale fruit that tasted suspiciously like cantaloupe. As the coffee cups were being refilled,

Arizona reached in her pack for her wallet. They had pooled their money back in Iowa to make the details of traveling simpler.

She fished around blindly for a moment, and then pulled her pack onto the table. One object at a time she emptied the contents onto the Formica.

"Housecleaning?" Ki joked.

"Ummm, I don't know how to tell you this exactly..." Arizona's eyes darted back and forth and her voice was pitched a notch higher than usual.

"Oh, God!" Ki exclaimed, looking at Arizona.

"Thought you were done praying," Paddle quipped. She looked at Arizona and her own smile faded like madras on a clothesline.

"My wallet's gone," choked Arizona. "I had it back at the Angels of Mercy, I know I did."

"Must have fallen out in our rush to pack," Paddle offered. "Guess we're going to have to go back and see if someone found it."

"You're kidding," Ki leaned forward in disbelief. "We can't go back there, we're fugitives. That would be so humiliating."

Just then, the waitress appeared and asked if there was anything more she could get them. Sheepishly, the three shook their heads and the bill was left on the edge of the table.

"One humiliation at a time," Arizona mumbled. "How're we going to pay for breakfast?"

Ki dropped her head and stared into a trickle of egg yolk slowly congealing on her plate. Paddle picked up her coffee cup and swirled the cold contents for a moment.

"Would ten dollars cover it?" Paddle asked, red faced.

"Almost, but we don't have ten dollars," Arizona said moving the bill around on the Formica.

Paddle bent down so that her head was just beneath the table for a moment. She fished around in her sock and came up with a neatly folded ten-dollar bill.

"I'm sorry," she muttered as she placed the bill on the table.

"A hold out?" Arizona said, incensed. "What happened to all for one and one for all?"

"Oh, lighten up," Ki grumbled as she reached into her blouse and pulled a five dollar bill from the padded lining of her bra. "If we hadn't held out, we'd be in a peck of trouble right now." She smacked the bill next to the one Paddle had put down.

"Well, I'll be," Arizona said, astonished.

"Me too," Paddle offered. "I didn't know you wore a padded bra," she said, looking wide-eyed at Ki.

Awkward glances and embarrassed smiles were exchanged. All was forgiven.

"We still have to go back to the shelter," Arizona sighed.

Heading east, they sang a rousing chorus of "You Are My Sunshine" as the sky turned a pale peach, then crimson, then gold. They chatted nervously, made silly puns, and laughed louder than was called for to buoy themselves up for the unpleasant task ahead.

"Do you think they'll call the police?" Ki asked.

"We didn't do anything illegal. We just left before prayers," Paddle reassured.

"I'm thinking they might consider that illegal," Arizona joined in. More nervous laughter.

Fifty miles back down the road, the Quonset hut sat to the left. The gravel parking lot was empty. As Arizona neared, the screen door opened, and Mother stepped out onto the porch. She shook the head of a mop vigorously into the morning air. Arizona scrunched down in the driver's seat, peering over the wheel only enough to keep the truck on the road and sailed on by the shelter.

"What'd you do that for?" Paddle shook her head.

"I just can't face that sweet old woman," Arizona whined.

"Oh for heaven's sake," Ki tsked. "Turn around, go back, and park around the side. I'll go in," she offered bravely.

Arizona eased the truck around and crept up on the shelter. She pulled off the road just short of the entrance and was going to cut the engine, when Paddle shouted, "There it is!"

Lying in the gravel covered with dust was the rawhide wallet that held their combined fortune, their ticket west.

Arizona put the truck in neutral alongside the wallet and Ki jumped out of the truck, grabbed the wallet, wiped it against her pants leg, and was climbing back in the truck when the screen door opened once again. Father stepped out into the sunshine and squinted their way.

"Hey," he hollered and took a step forward.

"Go! Go! Go!" Ki yelled at Arizona who gunned the engine as Ki swung her body into the cab and held the door shut. Paddle held onto her.

The engine died. The trio groaned. Father tottered forward shaking something in his hand at them.

"You three…" His voice was gobbled up in the trail of gravel, dust, and exhaust as the engine caught and the tires made contact.

"Faster," Ki urged, "he's going to shoot us."

Paddle glanced over her shoulder out the cab window. "Not with a Bible, he's not."

"Gee, this is as much fun traveling as I've ever had," Arizona said. She wiped sweat from her forehead with the back of her hand.

"Me too," grinned Paddle.

"She was being sarcastic," Ki frowned.

Chapter 4

It was dusk when they pulled in front of a small casino at the end of the Strip in Reno. A bow-legged cowboy wearing a big hat and a disheartened look stepped through the door and stood staring dismally at the dusty parking lot.

"This is the land of broken dreams," Ki quipped.

"Guy looks like he just lost his mortgage," Arizona added.

"Or his dog," Paddle said.

The trio had agreed to stop for dinner only, and to use the facilities. Arizona had negotiated an extra five dollars each to play the slots or whatever they chose.

"What if we lose it all," Paddle wondered.

"What if we win, big," Arizona argued.

They watched the cowboy remove his hat, scratch his head, kick at the dust, and wander off down the street and into the next casino. They gave a collective sigh before piling out of the truck.

Inside the casino, the garish lights removed all sense of time. There were harsh sounds of clicking, whirring, and beeping from the machines, shouts and cries from players, the slap of cards, and the blaring of a game that had gone into overtime on the television over the bar.

On one of the bar stools sat a woman worn down by life—she could have been forty or seventy—dressed in a paisley jumpsuit. She stirred a steady stream of sugar into a coffee mug as she stared vacantly at the image of herself reflected in the bar mirror.

"We better eat first," Ki suggested, "before we lose our appetite."

"Oh, come on. This is Reno. Just one slot machine first, please," begged Arizona. "Then we'll eat, I promise."

Since the fiasco back at the shelter, Paddle had been keeper of the collective finances. She reached in her pack and pulled out the money envelope.

"We're into the big bills now. I'll go get change. Can you at least get us a booth?" she nodded to Ki and Arizona.

When they had come into the casino, Paddle had noticed patrons getting change from the scantily uniformed young women with big money belts who wandered through the casino. She saw one such woman a few feet away. The shape of her body and the mass of hair struck a familiar chord somewhere in Paddle's mind, but never having been in a casino before, she disregarded it.

"Excuse me miss," she lightly tapped the woman on the shoulder. The woman turned slowly.

"Looks like Destiny has brought us both to Reno," smiled Lucas Plum, as if they'd just run into each other at the diner back home.

Paddle, frozen in time, mouth hanging open, twenty dollar bill dangling between her thumb and forefinger, made a squawking noise from the back of her throat.

Lucas grabbed her for a quick hug. That seemed to release the spell. Paddle tumbled back into the present.

"Lucas!" she gasped. "What on earth are you doing in Reno?"

Lucas turned those slow muddy eyes on her. "I might ask you the same thing." She smiled broadly. "Listen, Paddle, I get off in about an hour, we can talk then. Where're you sitting?"

Paddle pointed toward the booth where Ki and Arizona were staring at the scene unfolding across the room. Ki gave a little finger wave. Lucas handed Paddle her change and promised to meet them as soon as she could get free.

"Wow," Arizona shook her head slowly as Paddle, knees buckling, dropped into the booth, "you know a casino girl? Gosh, she's gorgeous."

"That's Lucas Plum," Paddle said, transfixed on Lucas as she moved across the casino.

"The famous Lucas Plum with the VW bus and the journeying and all that?" Ki asked, breathless. "What's she doing here?"

"Don't know. Guess we'll find out in an hour." Paddle looked as if she were in a fog.

"Well, I'm going to go play a slot. If the waitress comes, order me a burger, fries, and a chocolate malt, okay?" Arizona slid out from the booth and vanished.

"I thought you said she was a redhead?" Ki stared across the room at Lucas who was laughing with a patron. The springy curls cascading down her back and over her shoulders could only be described as champagne blond.

"Used to be," mused Paddle.

"She has no eyebrows," Ki observed.

"Yeah," Paddle said with a smile, remembering her first encounter with Lucas back at the diner a million years ago.

Arizona returned, chagrined. "It's like going to a coin laundry. Darned thing gobbles up your quarters but you don't even get clean clothes." She squeezed in next to Paddle.

"Oh here, let me try," Ki sighed and grabbed a quarter from the table. "When in Rome, and all that."

"It's Reno. We're in Reno," Paddle corrected as Ki disappeared into the crowd.

The waitress who took their orders was nonplused by the cacophony of rattling coins, flashing lights and gleeful squeals from across the room. Both Paddle and Arizona craned their necks to see who hit the jackpot. A swarm of humanity had encircled the lucky winner and swallowed him from view. They shrugged and returned to their menus.

Moments later, Ki scrambled through the crowd, grinning hugely.

"I won two hundred dollars," she gasped. "Can you believe it? Just one quarter and all this money came pouring out. I've never had so much fun." She wiggled into the booth. "I'm famished," she said as she gleefully dumped a bucket of change onto the wooden tabletop.

Arizona rolled her eyes. "Seeing as how that was a community quarter you invested, I think it's only fair that you split the win."

Ki regarded Paddle. "And what do you think, Paddle?"

Paddle pulled the stub of a pencil out of her pocket and made a quick notation on her napkin.

"Comes to about sixty-six dollars each. That'd be mighty generous of you, given as how it could have been your quarter that won," Paddle said reasonably.

"You two are amazing," Ki shook her head. "I thought we were in this all for one and one for all after that fiasco back at the restaurant in Utah. I'd planned to donate the whole mess to the kitty."

Arizona and Paddle exchanged guilty glances across the booth. With a shy smile of apology, Paddle put her fist on the table. Arizona stacked hers on top, and Ki capped the tower with her own fist. In unison, they chanted, "All for one and one for all," just as the waitress unloaded a cafeteria-style tray piled with burgers, fries, malts, and apple pie.

"Now, that's what I like to see," she said, "best friends, close as sisters."

Each of the three sat in silent reflection as the food was being distributed. None had had a best friend, or a sister, until now.

"Got room for one more?" Lucas' lips bowed into a slow smile as she stood by their booth. Her blonde curls swung gently as she cocked her head.

Paddle, with a big grin on her face, scooted over and motioned Lucas into the booth. Arizona and Ki scrunched to the right. "Everyone, this is Lucas Plum," Paddle said, her voice full of awe and wonder. "Lucas, meet my friends Arizona Pancake and Kiowa Su Lafner."

"Call me Ki," Ki said extending her hand across the booth.

"Well, the legend lives," Arizona said, giving Lucas a hardy handshake and a chuckle.

Lucas nodded to each one in turn. "Well," she said as she slipped off her shoes, folded her legs Yoga style on the cool vinyl seat and massaged her feet, "what brings you all to Reno?"

"Long story short," said Paddle, "I was headed to California, Arizona was headed to a commune in Iowa, and Ki here was rowing a canoe down the Mississippi headed for New Orleans."

"Fate sort of threw us together," Arizona took up the tale. "And someone burned down the commune, so here we are."

This seemed to make perfect sense to Lucas whose curls bobbled as she nodded her head.

"We decided we might as well go on to California, since that's where Paddle was headed to begin with," Ki offered.

"The gold coast and palm trees" Paddle said with a twinkle in her eyes.

"Sunshine, the ocean, and freedom" Arizona smiled.

"And movie stars," Ki added with enthusiasm. All three broke into giggles at what had become their California-or-Bust motto.

"Last person I ever expected to see working in a casino in Reno, Nevada, is you," Paddle smiled over at Lucas. "A post card would have been nice," she chided.

"Ah, Paddle, I knew you'd find your way. But it had to be your way, your destiny," she smiled fondly at her old friend. "That morning after our journey, I pulled a Medicine Card and it pointed me west. So I moved on," Lucas said with a what-can-you-do shrug of her shoulders.

"Like a change of weather passing through," Paddle remembered out loud, "like flowing with the current."

"Mmmhmm. Earth, Air, Fire and Water. I'm a water sign. West is the direction of water," Lucas said with a nod.

Ki, entranced by this strange conversation, held a forgotten French fry that dripped catsup between her fingers. Arizona, chin in hand, elbow resting in a smudge of apple pie on the tabletop looked mesmerized.

"So, Reno? Is this where you were headed?" Paddle asked, still somewhat bewildered.

"I wasn't really headed anywhere, like a destination," Lucas explained to all three, "just west. The bus threw a rod outside of Reno and I couldn't afford to get it fixed. Milo here, he's the boss, offered me a job." She winked at Paddle, "Long story short."

"Hey," Arizona came out of her trance, "I've got a great idea." She pulled her arm out of the pie smudge and swiped at her elbow with her napkin. "Why don't you come along with us?"

"Yeah," chimed Ki, "we're going to San Francisco—that's west. There's lots of water there—a whole ocean of it," she grinned.

"How are we going to get the four of us in the pick-up?" Paddle said, feeling miserable about being the wet blanket of reason.

"We'll sell the truck and use the money to repair Lucas' bus. There'll be more room for all of us," Arizona said brightly.

"It's a win-win all around," Ki chirped. "Are you in?" she beamed at Lucas.

There was a moment of silence at the table, a sense of time suspended. Paddle leaned forward. Ki's hands were clasped at her throat in anticipation. A grin froze on Arizona's face.

"Okay," Lucas broke the spell, "I'm in!"

"Whoopee!" Paddle shouted. She slammed her fist on the table followed by Ki then Arizona. Lucas topped it.

"All for one and one for all," they chanted.

The woman in the paisley jumpsuit they'd passed on their way in shuffled by just at that moment.

"Yeah, right, until one of you hits the jackpot," she muttered and shook her head.

The girls grinned at one another.

The next morning, Fate was on their side. The bar girl, Merilee, Lucas' former roommate who had just married Thornton the English teacher at the high school and moved into a ranch house on the outskirts of town that Thornton's rich Granny had gifted to them, bought Arizona's pick-up truck for more than it was worth. Spread the good, she had said as she laid a stack of green bills across Arizona's palm over breakfast.

Lucas cashed in her paycheck and added it to the kitty. She gave Milo a big hug and said goodbye to this chapter of her life. The foursome walked the six blocks to Bubba's Garage to liberate the bus.

Bubba, who prided himself on personal service, had washed and polished the bus, replaced the windshield wipers, and cleaned the interior as best as he could, working around a cluster of bird feathers, bunches of dried flowers, melted candle wax, carved wooden figures, a pile of Native American blankets, and an assortment of odd looking instruments that made a variety of strange sounds.

"Good Goddess, I think he even starched the curtains," Lucas exclaimed as she opened the side door.

Chapter 5

Dear Ginny and Benji,

Whoa, you're not going to believe who we ran into, in Reno, Nevada no less! Three guesses. Okay, it's Lucas! She was being a blonde casino girl. Her bus broke down, we fixed it, and we're all going to California together. Wish you were here. Stay tuned. Love, Paddle

Paddle dropped the card into the mailbox on the corner and whistled her way back to the bus.

It took less than half an hour to empty out Arizona's truck, find a place for everything, and put everything in its place.

"It looks just like a little home, doesn't it?" Ki admired her arrangement of camp stove utensils in a pottery vase snuggled into a corner.

"Shotgun," cried Paddle, climbing into the passenger seat. Ki and Arizona arranged themselves on the mattress that padded the floor in the back of the bus.

As they chugged away from the curb and lumbered down the street, a quartet of voices left a chorus of "California Here I Come," floating from the open windows.

Ki studied the map while Lucas drove. There was a sense of excitement in the air. The girls chatted and joked as the miles flew by.

They gave a collective *whoopee* as they crossed the California state line not far from Reno, and all four craned their necks from side to side, and bobbed their heads to take in the scenery.

"Doesn't look all that different to me," Ki said. "Where are the palm trees?"

"Let's go as far as Auburn then stop for gas," Lucas suggested.

"And ice cream," Paddle added.

"And pop," Arizona chimed in.

"They don't call it pop out here," Lucas admonished. "It's soda."

Arizona wrinkled her nose. "Soda's something you scrub bugs off the fender with."

"And I heard they don't say paper sacks out here—it's paper bags," Ki offered.

"And they don't have supper at night, they have dinner. Lunch is what you have in the middle of the day," Lucas instructed.

"Geez, sounds like a foreign country," Paddle mused. "Where's the ocean?"

Ki handed the map over the seat to Paddle who poured over Route 80, using her finger to trace the connecting highways that would carry them across the state right to the water's edge.

"Do we know just where in California we're heading?" Arizona asked no one in particular.

"I have a friend in San Francisco," Lucas said. "She lives in an area called the Tenderloin and volunteers at this big church called Glide Memorial. We could look her up, probably stay with her a while."

"Yeah, unless it's been burned to the ground," Arizona said quietly.

An uncomfortable quiet settled over the four. They rode on in silence.

In the hilly burg of Auburn they refueled car and body, stretched the kinks out of muscles, and breathed in California summer air.

"I think I can smell the ocean," Arizona filled her lungs.

"We're nowhere near the ocean," Paddle said as she unfolded the map on the picnic table at the gas station/rest stop. Again, she ran her finger along Interstate 80. "Might be the Sacramento River; that's coming right up."

"No, it's the ocean. Definitely the ocean," Arizona declared.

"Sacramento?" Ki chimed in. "Can we go see the Capitol building? Maybe the Governor will be there. I've always wanted to meet a Governor."

"I don't think you just drop in on the Governor," Paddle said.

"Maybe there will be a protest on the Capitol steps," Ki tried again. "I've always wanted to join a protest," she grinned.

Lucas shook her head, climbed back in the bus and started the engine. The other three tumbled in, scrambled and jockeyed for positions. "Next stop, Sacramento," Lucas announced into her cupped hand, a bad imitation of a tour bus guide.

For the next hour they took turns playing Tour Guide.

"On your left, please notice a real live California cow."

"If you'll look up please, you'll see a real live California sea gull."

"If you'll open your window, you'll notice a whiff of California ocean air." This began a debate about whether California ocean air smells different from Oregon or Washington ocean air that lasted until they pulled into Sacramento at dusk.

Punchy from days on the road and giddy at having arrived in the Golden State, they treated themselves to a night at a rundown motel just outside of Sacramento's Old Town.

The evening desk clerk was a weasely man with a thin, greasy handlebar mustache which if you squinted could easily pass for rodent whiskers. Paddle knew if she met his beady eyes, she would lose it. She slipped the collective treasure pouch to Lucas. "Here, you check in," she said with a lopsided smile that threatened to grow into an uncontrollably goofy grin.

Arizona and Ki explored the rack of postcards and chatted animatedly about places to go and things to see.

"Stairs are around to the left," said the clerk. "Your room is 305."

Lucas leaned on the counter, suddenly overcome with fatigue. She stifled a yawn. "Surely you have an elevator."

"Only goes down," the clerk said, bored with the conversation.

"If it goes down, then it has to go back up to the floors, right?"

"Yup."

"Then why can't we just ride it up?"

"Only goes down for passengers."

Lucas rubbed her temples. Paddle stood nearby, head averted, shoulders shaking silently.

"Let's go," Lucas said, resigned, as she grabbed her bag and headed for the stairwell. The others followed like goslings after Mother Goose.

As they passed, Paddle examined the wall next to the elevator door. Sure enough, there was no call button. "Weasel Man says it only goes down," she chortled, weary tears of exhaustion sliding down her cheeks.

The next morning, after a continental breakfast of withered orange slices, dried Bear Claws, and cast-iron coffee in Styrofoam cups, they set off to see Old Town, the Capitol grounds, Lavender Hill, and a large mall on the west side of town. The Governor was not in, nor was there a protest in progress. Having done Sacramento sufficiently, the foursome headed south on I- 80 to San Francisco.

"Should we call ahead or something," Arizona worried, "to let your friend know we're coming? I mean, just in case."

"I thought we'd just show up at the church," Lucas said. "Hey, it's going to be okay. No one has burned down the church. I'm sure of it."

Arizona sighed deeply and looked out the passenger window at the flat landscape of northern California. "It's so brown," she said, "and hot. Where are the palm trees?"

"There's one," Ki, squinting, pointed in the distance.

"I'm pretty sure we'll see more," Paddle addressed the blanket of despondency that was settling over Arizona.

"No ocean. No palm trees," Arizona muttered from the front seat. They rode on in silence for the next hour.

"Can we stop in Berkeley for lunch," Ki whined, "before we drive into San Francisco? I'm hungry."

"Yeah, turn here, turn here," Paddle chimed in.

"You're all working my last nerve," Lucas said over her shoulder as she swung the bus onto the University Avenue exit.

She squeezed into a parking spot just above the UC Berkeley campus, and they stuffed themselves on Indian food at a crowded, fly-riddled, hole-in-the-wall restaurant tucked behind a row of shops. Ki struck up a conversation with one of the locals who pointed them to Telegraph Avenue and Sproul Plaza, centers of peace, love, and protests, hand crafted goods, head shops, and a colorful array of characters decked in tie-dye and tattered jeans, long dresses and floppy hats.

Ki's head swiveled back and forth. Her mouth hung open as she took in the street scene. Sidewalk vendors hocked their wares. Guitars, harmonicas, and hand drums added to the chaos and the color. People danced in the street. A handful of children munched on watermelon curbside with rich red juice dripping from their chins. A turbaned Tarot reader in a makeshift tent waved as they passed, and a belly dancer spun about shrouded in brightly colored gauze as she balanced a sword on her head.

Paddle stared in confusion when a bearded youth in a leather headband and a sheet asked her if she wanted to buy a lid. She took a quick mental inventory of their cookware neatly stowed in the back of the bus.

"Do we need a lid for our pots?" she asked Lucas.

"He's selling a lid *of* pot—and no, we don't," Lucas said, rolling her eyes. The young man collapsed on the sidewalk in a fit of giggles.

At the far end of the street, Arizona was entranced with the circle of conga drummers on the Plaza and danced uninhibited to a native beat in an exuberant celebration of life. A black woman with a tambourine and a naked baby in her arms slipped a wreath of flowers on Arizona's head and said, "Sistah, you got rhythm."

Somewhere in the background, a rotund bald man standing on a box preached the word of God according to his unique understanding.

"This is the California I was looking for," Ki grinned.

"Mighty fine, mahn," a young man with cinnamon colored skin said as he appraised her, head to toe. She took a sip from a bottle that was being passed through the crowd and handed it to him with a wink before Lucas whisked her away.

Only with the promise of a return trip the next weekend and a surprise that lay up ahead, could Lucas pry the other three away from the lure of Berkeley street life.

"Man, that was the greatest," Ki said, her eyes wide with enthusiasm as the bus headed back down University Avenue.

"What's the surprise?" Paddle asked as they inched back onto the freeway.

"An art gallery," Lucas said. This met with groans from all around.

"We left Berkeley for an art gallery?" Ki huffed.

"Not just any art gallery, the Emeryville mudflats," Lucas said, pointing off to the right as she eased the bus off the road.

There, on the span of mud between I-80 and the Bay, was a collection of installation art that made them all gasp. Driftwood, cast-off metal, plastic tubing, abandoned bedsprings, washing machine parts and more, were magically converted into a maniacal looking band of musicians, a space ship, a rocking horse—all manner of fanciful musings transformed by the creative genius of artists with time on their hands, free material, and perhaps pharmaceutical inspiration.

"How did you know about this place?" Arizona called over her shoulder to Lucas as she sloshed through the mud to get a closer look.

"Remember Bubba, back at the garage in Reno?" Lucas gathered scraps of wood as she spoke. "His ex-wife, Iris, left him for a woman. They moved out here and joined a feminist art collective. That sailing ship over there is hers," Lucas tilted her head toward a wood and fabric replica of a sea-worthy vessel. "She sent pictures."

"Gee, that was friendly of her," Arizona chuckled.

Lucas fashioned the wood scraps into a miniature tee pee and secured it at the top with a piece of twine.

Paddle found a rusty iron hoop, rolled it over and set it on end behind the tee pee. With the Bay as background, she said, "I call it, 'Sunset on the Res.'."

Getting into the spirit, next to the tee pee Ki planted her creation, the PVC pipe to which she had affixed the head of a scroungey rag mop, very loosely resembling a palm tree. "Sunset on the Res. in Hawaii," she amended with a chuckle.

They hadn't noticed an elderly couple who had exited a Ford station wagon with Nebraska plates and had picked their way gingerly over the mud flats until the man cleared his throat and said, "Excuse me, young women, would you mind posing in front of your art? My wife, Edna here, would like a picture of some real California artists to send back to her sister, Mildred, in Nebraska." Edna waved her fingers at the girls and smiled brightly, her white permed curls frothing about her face like the foam on the Bay.

"Why, we'd be glad to, sir. Our pleasure," Arizona beamed. The girls made a semi-circle behind their creation and grinned hugely at the thought of winding up in Mildred's photo album as real, live California artists in the raw.

"Enjoy your visit to our beautiful state," Ki added with a wave, as Edna and hubby worked their way back to the wagon.

Back on I-80, Lucas turned west onto the Bay Bridge.

"Will you just look at all that concrete," Paddle mused as San Francisco came into full view.

"Oh, it's the most beautiful city I've ever seen," Ki gasped as she gawked out the side window.

"Where's the Golden Gate Bridge?" Arizona whined. "I thought we were going to cross the Golden Gate Bridge."

"It's on the other side of the City," Lucas explained. "We'll see it tomorrow. I want to get to the Church before rush hour traffic."

"I thought the ocean was on the other side of the city," Arizona continued in her tired toddler querulous voice. "Can't we see it today?" Lucas shot her a look in the rearview mirror.

Paddle traced the street map with her finger.

"Hmm, let's see—exit here and we'll be on Freemont Street. Okay, okay, we're good." A band of sweat had broken over her forehead as she hunched over the map. "Turn right on Market," she pointed with her elbow.

Lucas moved into the right lane of Market Street. Cars whizzed by.

"Uh oh. That should have been a left turn," Paddle moaned.

"No problem." Lucas crossed traffic like a pro and hung a left on California Street ignoring the squealing breaks, blaring horn, and raised fisted greeting of the driver behind her. Several blocks later, she stopped short at a red light.

"Hey!" Arizona shouted as she and Ki made an unexpected scoot towards the front.

All four sat open mouthed as the Powell Street cable car, held in place by faith and some elaborate and mysterious system, clanged its way through an intersection. Tourists, packed like too many tomatoes on a vine, clung to railings and waved precariously from the open car as it clambered on.

"Uh, okay, go up and turn on Taylor," Paddle said. She chewed on her bottom lip. Her eyes were glued to the map.

Lucas made a right turn onto the one-way street. "What's the address we're looking for?"

"The corner of Taylor and Ellis," Paddle said as she swiped the back of her hand across her forehead.

Ki peered over her shoulder and studied the map. "It's back the other way," she pointed out.

Arizona turned to look out the rear window where the street dropped off steeply behind them. "Oh my gawd," she whispered.

Paddle hazarded a glance out the front window of the bus only to see the street rise sharply ahead. She gasped.

"We're lost," Ki sighed heavily, "hopelessly lost in San Francisco."

"We've got a map," Paddle grumbled.

"Lot of good it's doing us," Ki said in a huff. "We're going to die on one of the steepest streets in the world. I just know our brakes are going to give out."

"Will you all just be quiet," Lucas hollered. "I can't concentrate."

With no further human sound from inside the bus, Lucas worked her way over to Jones, no less steep, but at least one-way the right direction. Going by internal radar as the map lay crumpled on the floor by Paddle's feet, she drove south.

"You just passed Ellis," Paddle mumbled, looking out her window.

Lucas stopped at a red light on McAllister in the heart of the Civic Center.

The girls were stunned into silence by the narrow streets between impossibly tall buildings spilling people onto sidewalks from their shops and offices as if evacuating giant anthills. Drivers created lanes where there were none, in their efforts to squeeze through the blockade of bumper-to-bumper rush hour traffic. Even lodged between immobile cars with irritable drivers honking their impatience, it felt as though they were moving at a fast pace, as though the city were a vicious river and they were trout swimming upstream.

"I think I'm going to be sick," Ki's voice wavered from the back of the bus. She pressed her forehead against the cool window glass and closed her eyes. Arizona handed her a pan from their makeshift pantry and returned to the window to gawk at life in downtown San Francisco.

The light turned green, and as if by divine inspiration, Lucas turned right, maneuvered her way through the maze of one-way streets and within five minutes pulled up in front of Glide Memorial Church. "Thank Goddess," she exhaled as she turned the bus into the parking lot across the street.

They sat for a moment, silent, spent, embarrassed by their collective cranky behavior.

"Well, that was fun," Lucas broke the silence with a chuckle.

Paddle was the first one out onto the street.

"It's freezing," she said more in surprise than complaint. She rubbed her arms vigorously and hopped from one foot to the other as the rest tumbled out the side doors of the bus.

"I told you we'd need jackets," Lucas reminded them as she sorted through a pile of clothes and blankets until she unearthed two woolen jackets, a poncho, and a heavy long-sleeved sweater.

It was close to six o'clock when they braced themselves against the chill of the marine layer that had begun to drift over the hills of the City and make itself at home. They tried the main door of Glide. Locked.

"Oh, great, I knew we should have called," Arizona moaned.

"Oh ye of little faith," Lucas chided.

They found an unlocked door at the side of the church and followed signs to the Office.

A young Black woman sporting a copper colored Afro and wearing a bright green Dashiki looked up, startled, from the desk she was tidying. Her coat and bag signaled the end of her workday.

"The office is closing. Can I help you?" she offered, looking at each of the four girls in turn.

Just then, a pallid looking man with yellow haystack hair and uncommonly big ears came through a door at the back of the office.

"Hey, Iaisha, I'll lock up tonight. I'm going to stay and work on that financial report." He was turning pages in a large binder and hadn't noticed the quartet.

"Milkweed!" Arizona hollered and bolted past Iaisha. The man grew even more pale as he looked up to see a woman with a long braid swinging wildly, clad in a purple poncho, hurling herself directly at him, arms open, huge grin on her face.

"Arizona Pancake!" he yelped. He scooped her up and twirled her around. Her foot caught on Iaisha's coat and sent it sailing onto the floor.

The others stood by mutely as this reunion played itself out. When Arizona had been returned to firm ground, she grabbed the man by the hand and led him over for introductions.

"This is Milkweed," she said, palms up in the air, as if that held special meaning. Blank stares all around. Paddle managed a weak smile.

"From the Morningsong Ranch," she added, "in Iowa."

Everyone talked at once. Where had the others gone? What had happened? Was the mean farmer down the road part of the problem?

Milkweed laughed, shook his head, and held his hands up in surrender.

"I can see I'm not going to get any reports done this evening," he chuckled. "Let me introduce Iaisha, my partner. She keeps the wheels turning here at Glide, among other things," he threw a gentle arm around the shoulder of the woman who had stepped forward and smiled warmly at them.

"So pleased to meet you. Are you from Iowa? What are you all doing here?" Her voice was soft and comforting like warm bread just out of the oven.

"Hi, Iaisha, I'm Lucas. We were actually looking for my friend, Luna. She works here. Do you know how I can find her?"

"Oh, sugar, I'm sorry, but Luna left last month for Maui. Said she was going to swim with the dolphins, or some such. I don't expect she's coming back any time soon," she gave a 'you know Luna' shrug.

A faint cloud of disappointment crossed Lucas' face then moved on. "We thought maybe she could put us up," Lucas said glumly. "I guess we should have called ahead."

Arizona cleared her throat and shifted her weight from one foot to the other.

"Well, you'll stay with us, of course," Milkweed offered. He glanced at Iaisha who nodded vigorously.

"We've got a big old Victorian over by the Park. Plenty of room," she smiled. "And the others will be so happy you've arrived."

"The others?" Arizona looked at Milkweed.

"Dandelion and Jewell, Ocean and Echo—oh, and they just had baby Squid a month ago. And..." he winked at Arizona and lowered his voice, "Coyote is with us too."

"Coyote?" Arizona said, all breathy, as if offering up a prayer.

Ki stepped forward and introduced herself. "Thank you for opening your home to us," she spoke the gratitude of the group.

"Let's get you home and fed," Iaisha offered, "then you can sit up and talk all night if you want."

Milkweed tossed his binder on the shelf, turned out the lights, and locked the door behind them.

Chapter 6

It was twilight when Lucas angled the bus into a parking spot around the corner from Lincoln Way.

"Well, this is service," Iaisha chuckled. "We're used to riding city transit just about everywhere. Gordon—uh, Milkweed's—pick-up sits in a rented garage for the occasional hauling emergency."

Milkweed unloaded bags and packs and boxes from the bus. Carrying their worldly possessions, they resembled a parade of vagabonds as they rounded the corner and trekked up the steep wooden steps of an expansive mauve Victorian that sat across the street from the Panhandle.

Paddle stood in awe on the bottom step. "Gosh, it looks like a castle," she whispered.

"It was my grandmother's, bless her heart," Iaisha turned to smile at Paddle. "Guess she knew I'd be having a big family one day."

Pandemonium broke loose when Arizona followed Milkweed into the dining room. "Hey, guys," she beamed a greeting to the familiar faces from what felt like another lifetime ago.

"Arizona Pancake?" Echo squealed and shifted baby Squid from her arms to the next nearest parent-figure. She jumped up, ran across the room and embraced Arizona in a twirling, giggling frenzy. Dandelion bounded through the kitchen door at the sound of Arizona's name and joined the dancing hug, as did Jewell. Coyote sat quietly at the large oak table, smiling shyly. He was coaxed into the group hug by Ocean, sporting Squid on one hip. Arizona's smile was as bright as a lighthouse beacon in the dead of night as she introduced her companions to her old commune family.

They feasted on spaghetti, salad, homemade bread fresh from the oven, and an oddly shaped bottle of Mateus. Conversation lasted past twelve brassy bongs of the grandfather clock when, with a huge yawn, Iaisha called it a night.

"Morning comes early for the Glide staff," she said as she led them to the spare room, where a double bed and two bunks were already made up for drop-in guests or leftover party-goers with too much of the grape in them to be safe on the roads.

The next morning, with time on their hands and no plans for their future, Paddle, Ki, Arizona, and Lucas sat around the kitchen table pouring over a street map of San Francisco. The smell of fresh coffee, bacon and yeast rolls filled the room as the commune family prepared for their day.

"This is our week at the O'Baby Co-op," Echo said, wiggling Squid into a tummy-sling while Ocean gathered up the diaper bag and other infant paraphernalia. "Anyone want to join us?" At the lack of enthusiastic response, he grinned, shrugged and said, "Okay, your loss. It's really fun. See you later."

"Don't feel like you have to do anything at all." Iaisha patted Ki on the arm as she passed by. "Come and go as you like, the house is yours. Spare keys are in the bureau drawer. Gordon? We're going to miss the bus," she called over her shoulder.

"Coming," he sang out on a trot through the kitchen, while slipping into a light jacket to guard against the seasonal morning fog. "I'm so glad you're here," he smiled. "Phone number is on the bureau if you need anything at all. See you tonight." With a wave, they were out the door.

Jewell rinsed and stacked the last of the breakfast dishes. "Don't you touch these, now," she gave a friendly warning. "This is Dandelion's job when he gets his tired butt out of bed, hopefully before lunch." She circled the table giving each girl a shoulder hug. "I'm so glad you're here. Now the family's complete." She did a little heel-click jump of joy.

"You'll have the house to yourselves, except for Dandelion, that is. Coyote is out beachcombing for driftwood. Come on down to Slice of

Heaven later and I'll cut you a piece of pecan pie to die for," she said as she creaked open the front door.

The four sat in stunned silence for a few minutes with only the hollow tick-tock of the clock from the other room. "Wow," Paddle commented on the whirlwind of morning activity.

By noon, the four had worked their way across Golden Gate Park to a meadow where a loosely-knit blues band from Grass Valley was wailing about cocaine runnin' 'round their brain. Ki stretched out in the sun and thumbed through a copy of the Berkeley Barb. "If we run out of things to do," she mused, "we could go over to Berkeley and be nude models. Twenty-five dollars an hour. Can you believe that?"

Paddle snorted.

"You're not in Wisconsin anymore, Dorothy," Lucas chuckled.

A bearded young man in a tall Lincoln hat and jeans that were mostly held together by an array of patches, wandered through the crowd calling, "Acid, get your acid here. Make your dreams come true. Trip of a lifetime." Ki glanced up.

"Don't even think about it," Arizona warned.

Over dinner that evening the family laughed and chatted amiably about their day.

"How many meals today?" Milkweed asked Iaisha for the total of people served by Glide's Feed the Hungry program.

"Two-hundred and thirty," she said, pleased. "We just need a few more hands to run more efficiently."

"I'd like to help," Arizona offered. "It's about time I do something useful, I guess."

"Be careful," warned Milkweed, "she'll promote you to head of the volunteer staff if you show up two days in a row."

"Actually, there is an opening..."

Iaisha was interrupted by Milkweed who gave her arm a gentle squeeze. He raised his eyebrows at Arizona. "You thought I was kidding," he smiled.

"I was looking through the class schedules for City College," Ki said. "I'm thinking I might want to look into The Beat Culture of San Francisco, The Art of Film Making, and Introduction to Wicca."

"The Wicca class is great," Ocean chimed in. "I took that last year. See if Crystal Moon-Rising is teaching it again. She knows her goddesses."

"How about you, Paddle?" Dandelion turned his robin's-egg blue eyes on her. "Anything in our fair city interest you?"

Paddle squirmed in her seat. "Tell you the truth, San Francisco is a tad too big for this small town girl. I feel kinda dizzy every time I go outside," she said. "All those tall buildings, and cars, and people..." Paddle emitted a breathy whistle at the thought of it all. "I remember seeing a Help Wanted sign over in Berkeley the other day, at a Mexican restaurant. Thought I might call."

"You'd leave us?" Ki gasped. "You'd just up and move to Berkeley all by yourself?"

"I was sort of thinking about Berkeley, myself," offered Lucas. "There's a lot happening on campus over there, with the anti-war protests and all."

"I could give my old landlady a call," piped Jewell. "See if she has a rental open. Put in a good word for you."

Excitement and new beginnings filled the kitchen and migrated into the living room as everyone gathered around the wood burning stove for tea and homemade biscotti.

That night, sitting under a dim clip-on reading lamp hooked to the headboard of the bottom bunk, Paddle penned a note.

Dear Ginny and Benji,

Whoa, you guys just have to save up your pennies and come out to visit us. You won't believe this place. I'm living in a commune in San Francisco, with real live hippies and everything. Soon, Lucas and I will be moving to Berkeley, hotbed of radical activity. Don't worry your head over those funny brownies you may hear about. I'll pass. As always, Paddle

Arizona tumbled from the top bunk as the alarm clock rang across the room the next morning. Lucas pulled her pillow over her head. Ki bolted upright, looked around as if dazed, then curled up under her covers again. Paddle's snores went uninterrupted.

Iaisha, Milkweed, and Arizona huddled around the breakfast table. "I was thinking prep today, and maybe serve tomorrow?" Iaisha ran her idea by them for integrating Arizona into the lunch leg of the food program.

The phone rang in the living room. "I'll get it," Milkweed offered.

"You can shadow Nell," Iaisha continued. "She's the queen of cooking for the masses," she chuckled.

Milkweed came back into the kitchen and sat down heavily in his chair. "Millie is sick, Bart is bailing his nephew out of jai—again, and Louisa promised the Methadone Clinic in Berkeley she'd stop by and pay Tisha's bill this morning."

Iaisha groaned, slumped forward, and sat with her head in her hands.

"Girlfriend," she fixed her gaze at Arizona, "it looks like you just got promoted to head server," she shrugged.

"I won't let you down," Arizona beamed.

As they were heading down the front steps, the next shift settled in over French toast and sausage, cocoa and orange juice.

"It's easy. Just take Nineteenth and transfer at Ocean Avenue. It goes right by City College," Jewell traced the route on the map with her finger. "Tell me more about the documentary you want to make."

Ki blew on her cocoa. "It'll be about the homeless. I want to talk to folks living in the Park, in alleys, under bridges, and in their cars." She stopped to fork some food into her mouth. "Go for the human dignity angle—there but for the grace, etc.," she said over a mouthful of toast. "Echo, this is the best French toast I've ever had. If you weren't married, I'd marry you," she teased Ocean's blushing husband.

"Well, sign up for the film class first. It fills up fast," advised Jewell. Across the table, Paddle and Lucas were debating the merits of firing up the VW bus or utilizing the transit system. They decided it was worth risking their parking place for the convenience of apartment hunting by car.

"School starts soon," Paddle said. "Probably everything on campus is taken by now."

"If you want to live on campus, we'll live on campus," Lucas declared with the confidence that only Lucas could muster. "Any particular street?" she inquired.

"Oh, sure," Paddle decided to play along, "how about Telegraph Avenue? I mean as long as we're going to do Berkeley, let's do it right."

"Right," Lucas affirmed, "the heart and soul of Berkeley—Telegraph Avenue. It is done in the mind of the Universe," she said solemnly.

"Yeah, uh huh," Paddle grinned.

"Great French toast, Echo," Lucas called over her shoulder as she took her dishes to the kitchen sink. Paddle followed, balancing her plate, cup, and glass. "Telegraph Avenue," she muttered, shaking her head.

"Later," they called to the breakfast dawdlers.

Dandelion yawned a greeting to them as they left the kitchen. He stretched languidly and then poured himself a cup of cocoa. "Hang tight," he called as the front door squeaked open. "Somebody should fix that," he muttered to himself.

At the far end of the wrap-around porch, Coyote assembled pieces of driftwood, seaweed, feathers, and other assorted found objects.

"That would look great next to the teepee," Lucas grinned at Paddle. Coyote waved to them without taking his eyes from his creation.

At noon, Paddle and Lucas pulled up in front of a dingy industrial loft in the flatlands of Berkeley.

"Why exactly are we stopping here?" Lucas asked. "This isn't Telegraph Avenue."

"It's a loft, it's available, and it's affordable," Paddle answered, ever the voice of reason.

They followed the dimly lit stairs to the second floor and stepped through the door that had been left ajar. A scruffy middle aged man with thinning hair stood facing the window. He looked over his shoulder and called, "C'mon in; I won't bite," and made a snorting sound that passed for a laugh.

"We called this morning, about the loft," Paddle began when the man turned around, a sickly grin on his face and his erect penis in the grip of his hand. Lucas grabbed Paddle by the elbow, spun her around, and dragged her out the door. They clambered down the stairs and emerged, indignant, into the bright midday sunshine. "Pervert," Lucas muttered as she fished in her pocket for the keys to the bus.

Paddle, looked pale and shaken, and said, "Do you think he does that sort of thing often?"

"I imagine so. The loft probably isn't even really for rent. Just some place to show off his miserable goods. Where do you want to go next?"

Paddle cast a look back at the loft and shook her head like a wet dog to rid her brain of that picture. "I'd like to see if the Help Wanted sign is still up at the restaurant," she said. "It's time for lunch, anyway. We could eat there."

They drove up University Avenue and onto the campus. Their heads swiveled to take in the sights. Lucas navigated a parallel parking spot on Dwight Way just around the corner from the Mexican restaurant on Telegraph.

The bustling wait staff, like the clientele, was an international mix of college students, hippies, and political activists that spanned the age, color, and sexual identity spectrums.

Lucas grabbed two menus and found a spare table by the window while Paddle went in search of an application. She watched from across the room as Paddle was stopped by a student who pointed to his empty water glass. Without hesitation, Paddle found a pitcher at the nearest station, filled the young man's glass, and exchanged a few pleasantries. A middle-aged Italian man with a gold chain around his neck and a plastic badge that said 'Manager' motioned to Paddle from behind the register.

After a short conversation, big smiles, and a handshake, Paddle joined Lucas at the table. "That's Gino," Paddle nodded toward the register. "He says this is just a formality; I can start tomorrow," she said with a grin that lit up her face. Paddle waved the application at Lucas, and then began filling out the form while Lucas read the menu to her.

After Lucas finished her Tofu Taco and Paddle had polished off her California Enchilada, Paddle turned in her application while Lucas located a phone booth and called Jewell's landlord friend.

"Oh, ye of little faith," she nudged Paddle playfully as they stood curbside just outside the restaurant.

"What?" Paddle scrunched up her face in confusion.

"You wanted to live on Telegraph Avenue?"

"Yeah"

Lucas pointed above the restaurant to the third floor corner window, where a red and white sign stated For Rent.

"You're kidding?" Paddle smacked her forehead in disbelief.

"The landlord asked if I thought we could find our way there in half an hour," she laughed.

They met Patrice in the entryway of what was once a grand hotel, now converted to rent-controlled apartments. Two overstuffed and well-patched leather chairs flanked a small table in front of the floor-to-ceiling windows in the lobby. A large-bladed wooden ceiling fan turned lazily overhead.

The formerly vibrant Oriental carpet, now worn to faded earth tones, was thin enough to reveal patches of wooden flooring beneath it. It ran down the center of the hallway that led to the rickety, antiquated, gated elevator. Oversized mirrors with chipped faux gold frames hung on either side of the collection of resident mailboxes affixed to the wall.

"I love it; especially the elevator," Paddle whispered to Lucas as Patrice slid the metal gate to one side. The elevator clunked and clattered its way slowly to the third floor where, at the end of the hallway, their new life was to begin.

That evening, back in the City, the family gathered over lasagna and steamed vegetables as they shared their adventures.

"The commute to work is going to be a breeze," Paddle chuckled.

"And it looks like a job in a bookstore's shipping/receiving department is coming open over on Bancroft," Lucas added. "The manager is an old Lefty; he says I can take off for protests and rallies if I make up the time later, and don't get arrested."

"I soooo miss Berkeley," Jewell sighed nostalgically.

"How was your first day on the food line?" Coyote smiled at Arizona who sat with heavy eyes, chin in one hand, elbow on table across from him, looking as though she could fall into a deep slumber with minimal effort.

"I just had no idea there were so many people without food." A tear slid down her cheek unchecked. "There was this old man, reminded me of my Granddad," she shook her head and stared at the lasagna steaming up from her plate. "Excuse me," she said, pushing her chair back from the table, "I seem to have lost my appetite."

Iaisha followed her into the other room. Ki looked alarmed. Milkweed said, "occupational hazard. She'll be fine. You should have seen her in action," he grinned. "They loved her. Heart as big as a barn. I think she's found her place."

"How were things at the O'Baby Co-op?" Ki asked Ocean who was nursing Squid and managing to spear broccoli florets left handed.

"They all seemed to be teething at once," she rolled her eyes. "I think it must be a conspiracy of some kind. Ow!" she shrieked. Squid let loose of the breast and wailed until his face was the color of a baby beet.

"You ever think about having kids?" Echo smiled at Ki over the racket. Ki was about to answer when Ocean thrust Squid at her and left the table. Ki held him awkwardly against one shoulder, a look of panic on her face.

"She just went for the salve," Echo reassured her. "Hey, look at that. You're a natural," he said as Squid grabbed a handful of her hair and settled into a mild whimper.

Ki tried for a smile, but it looked more like a grimace. She disentangled his fist from her hair and balanced him gingerly on her lap as if she were holding a wiggling puppy that at any moment might pee all over her.

"Did you get the classes you wanted?" Ocean asked, taking her seat and relieving Ki of a lapful of baby.

"The Beat Culture class was full, so I'm taking Tai Chi instead, along with Film, and Intro. to Wicca," she gave a tight smile to Ocean who beamed like the Madonna with Squid grinning around the other nipple, milk dribbling down his chin.

Iaisha served hot apple strudel topped with a glob of vanilla ice cream. Arizona rejoined them. Her eyes were red rimmed as she took her place at the table. "Gonna have to toughen up, I guess," she mumbled to no one in particular.

"I'm going to miss you guys," Paddle said, misty-eyed. "This is a real nice family."

Two weeks later on a Saturday morning, Milkweed slammed shut the gate of his truck and brushed off his trousers. "It's not going to be the same without you two," he said, hugging Lucas and Paddle in turn.

"Thanks, Milkweed, you've been such a dear heart," Lucas said.

"We'll have the family over for dinner soon," Paddle added. "Well, maybe two or three of you at a time," she amended.

"Call if you need anything at all. That's what family's for," he said as he climbed in his truck. *Ratchety, ratchety, ratchety* went the engine until it finally caught, and he pulled away from the curb with a wave.

"Well, I'd better change and get to work," Paddle started up the steps to the old hotel that was their new home.

"I'm going over to the campus for a while," Lucas called out. "See you this evening."

Paddle loved waiting tables and schmoozing with the customers just like she did back at Ginny's diner. She was rewarded with big tips that she gladly shared with the busboy and dishwasher, a semi-retired husband and wife team in their seventies. And as much as Paddle loved her work, even more she loved coming home to Lucas and their shared apartment.

"We shut down the Administration Building this afternoon," Lucas reported over dinner that night. The smells from the restaurant below wafted up and gave their chicken soup a very south-of-the-border influence.

"Why'd you do that?" Paddle asked.

"To put pressure on the Regents for having R.O.T.C. on campus," she explained, as if that would make any sense to Paddle.

"Lucas... "

"Yeah?"

"Are you happy? I mean that we moved here, and all."

"I'm delirious. Truly. I love Berkeley in the fall. It's the greatest." Lucas took her bowl to the sink, rinsed it, and headed into the bathroom.

Paddle's shoulders relaxed as she leaned back against one of the wooden St. Vincent de Paul Thrift Store kitchen chairs they'd picked up this morning. "Just checking," she said and smiled to herself. Paddle got up and wandered across the kitchen, stuck her head in the fridge and perused the contents.

"Jeff asked if we wanted to come by tonight," Lucas called from the bathroom.

"Jeff from the bookstore? Any particular reason? I kind of thought we'd stay in tonight," Paddle said, trying to keep any hint of whine out of her voice.

"Said he had something he wanted to show us." Lucas walked into the kitchen. Paddle pulled her head out of the refrigerator, turned around, and gasped.

"Wow," was all she could say as she took in sight of Lucas, hair brushed out, big gold hoop earrings, jeans that looked painted on, and a shirt that was missing the top two buttons. This was a version of Lucas she'd never seen. It was even better than the casino girl look. Paddle felt spit gather in her mouth and swallowed hard. She knew at that moment there was nothing she could deny Lucas—ever.

Paddle's stomach growled as they wound their way up through the Berkeley hills at sunset, past estates with trellises covered in purple vines, wrap-around porches with columns and arches, and manicured lawns that sloped down the hillside.

Lucas turned right at an ornate lamppost and followed a tire worn path along the ridge of the hill, through ferns and foliage past a large brown shingled house, to a cottage at the rear of the property.

Jeff greeted them with hugs after he got his eyes unstuck from Lucas' cleavage. "Come on in," he said and led them into a room where five or six people were crowded, munching food and passing a bottle of wine. Lucas introduced Paddle to her co-workers from the bookstore. Someone passed a plate of brownies, and Paddle grabbed two to still her hunger pangs.

Paddle noticed a funny smell hovering over the room, like that smudge bundle from her journeying however many lifetimes ago that was, and then again in the pick-up truck when she first met Arizona. A dark haired woman handed her a squished up little stub of a cigarette caught in a hairpin. Paddle wrinkled her nose. "No thanks, I don't smoke," she told the woman who giggled like that was the funniest thing she'd ever heard.

Paddle had just gotten herself wedged into a beanbag chair when Lucas held out a hand and said, "Come on. Jeff wants to show us his new sauna."

She grabbed Lucas' hand, but when she was upright she noticed that her knees had turned to rubber bands and she wavered a moment. When she got her balance, she followed Jeff and Lucas through the crowd, stepping carefully over legs, pillows, and bottles, outside and down a grassy path to a little freestanding wooden hut that looked sort of like an outhouse. A coat tree stood next to the door, and towels hung from brass hooks.

"You can hang your clothes here," Jeff said. "See you later." He winked, and vanished back up the path.

"Our clothes?" Paddle asked Lucas.

"Have I ever led you down the wrong path?" Lucas said, those muddy eyes shifting slightly in the dusk. Paddle's brain felt swathed in cotton batting, and her lips were going numb, so she didn't bother to answer.

They slipped out of their clothes and hung them on the hooks. Paddle wrapped her towel securely around her. Lucas hung hers casually over one shoulder as they entered the cedar-lined cubby. There was enough room inside the sauna for four friendly people, if you didn't mind sitting hip-to-bare-hip on the smooth wooden bench.

A pail of eucalyptus-scented water sat next to a small heater that glowed softly with red coals. Lucas sprinkled a handful of water over the coals and was rewarded by a moist, pungent hiss, as Paddle crawled up on the bench and drew her knees up to her chin. Rivulets of sweat trickled down her front and were sucked up by her towel.

Through the steam, she saw Lucas drop her towel on the bench and stretch her arms over her head. "Ah, this is life, Paddle," Lucas groaned in a way that made Paddle's body go limp.

Paddle closed her eyes and breathed in. The hot air prickled the hairs in her nose. Her tongue felt cool in her mouth. It took her a moment to place the next sensation. Lucas had slipped behind her, wrapped her arms around her, and was pulling Paddle right up close to her. Paddle's towel slithered to the floor, and she felt herself drift as the softness of Lucas' breasts cushioned her back and a bush of wiry hair tickled her buttocks. She couldn't have moved if someone had yelled *fire*.

Without a word, Lucas held her close and nestled a kiss behind her ear that made Paddle's heart want to jump right out of her chest. With her forefinger, Lucas slowly traced a little ski trail from Paddle's collarbone, down between her breasts, around her bellybutton, and ever so gently through the forest. Sweat poured down Paddle's back, and her breath caught in her throat.

"Uh—Lucas," Paddle stuttered as Lucas worked her way along the crevice. A shiver shook Paddle's whole body.

"Shhh," Lucas whispered. "Just lean into it," she said.

And Paddle did. She couldn't tell where she stopped and Lucas started. She was submerged in that murky water world that she'd seen so many times in the eyes of Lucas Plum.

The cedar door squeaked on its hinges and a burst of cold air clung to Paddle's skin as Raven stuck her head in. "Am I interrupting?" she asked.

"No," Lucas said, calm and in control. Gently she scooted Paddle forward, shifted her own body onto the seat next to her. "Come on in," she said.

Paddle collapsed against the cedar wall, numb, her body slick with a clammy sweat. From a distance, she heard them talking about a Grateful Dead concert, about a book order that had come in from the UK, and about some "fine stuff" Jeff had scored. Paddle concentrated as hard as she could on pulling air into her lungs.

The next thing Paddle was aware of was sitting on the couch back in the living room, fully clothed. Jeff handed her a glass of water which she accepted with shaky hands. How the blue blazes did she get there, she wondered. Stray sentences floated by her: "She ate *two* brownies? Oh my God," and, "I put her underwear in her purse, Lucas."

The only thing Paddle could see were Lucas' eyes, veiled, peering into hers, the water world all gone.

"You about ready to go?" Lucas said. "Good thing I'm driving." She grinned.

They were silent on the drive home. Shame knotted in Paddle's belly but she didn't know why, and she felt like crying.

"I think I'm just going to go right to bed," Paddle mumbled to Lucas as they entered the apartment. "I don't feel so good."

"Sweet dreams," Lucas called.

There was still coffee in the percolator the next morning when Paddle rolled out of bed. Her head felt thick and her tongue felt coated. It was Saturday, and she didn't have to go into work until the afternoon. She opened the cabinet door to get a bag of bagels and found a note taped to the bag: *Decided to drive down to Santa Cruz for the weekend. Be back Monday morning. Lucas*

Paddle was beginning to think the night before had just been one big weird dream.

"She wouldn't just leave after something like that, without saying anything at all, would she?" she demanded of the cactus on the window ledge. Her stomach lurched and she made it to the toilet just in time to heave until she thought her sides would collapse.

"Gino," Paddle said into the phone, "I hate to leave you in a rut, but I'm throwing up over here. I don't think I should come in to work today."

Gino told her to take care of herself and asked if she needed anything. Paddle felt a little guilty about stretching the truth. Her stomach was actually much better since throwing up, but she was feeling pretty tender, heart-wise.

"I'll be okay," she told him, knowing that was the truth, "but thanks. I'll see you next week."

Paddle watched the sun dance on the water as she rode the bus over the Bay Bridge. Again, her breath caught, as she looked at all the concrete that defined San Francisco. She nursed a secret worry that some day it would just sink right into the ocean from the weight, and selfishly hoped she wouldn't be on the bridge that day. Paddle felt a tingle of excitement—and a twinge of guilt—as she transferred to the bus that would take her home to her commune family. Ginny had always been her family.

Across the Bay, as the sun balanced on the water, Ki sat on the beach in earnest conversation with a walnut-colored middle-aged woman who looked much older than her years. A tape recorder caught the woman's story, while Ki described the woman appearance, the setting, and her own thoughts, in a spiral notebook. From time to time, the woman coughed convulsively and hocked yellow sputum onto the sand.

"My family owned a plantation, which I inherited, back in my country. The people, they worked for us," she poked her chest proudly with her thumb, causing another wracking wave of croup. When she caught her breath, she continued.

"I married young, and my son was born. Soon after, my husband died of the cancer." She seemed lost in memories for a long moment. Ki clicked the top of her pen. She stopped abruptly when the woman cast a sideways glance at her.

"I lost the plantation," she continued, "too much for a woman alone. When my son grew up, he wanted to study doctoring. A good boy; a bright boy. He got a—what do they call, schoolship?"

"Scholarship," Ki offered.

"Yes. We came here. We knew no one. We had only each other," she said, shaking her head slowly.

"What happened to him?" Ki probed gently.

"Murdered. For a few dollars in his wallet, my son lost his life." Her voice was empty of emotion. A liquidy cough rattled her chest.

"I cannot work, I have no skills. I couldn't pay the rent and I lost our apartment. Life here has been full of loss, and little else," she looked out over the water.

"Does your family know all this?" Ki asked, heavy hearted with compassion. She thought briefly of the empty bed in their lofty Victorian. Echoes of a long-ago conversation reverberated in her memory. Her mother stood at the kitchen sink, wiping her hands on her gingham apron. "Kiowa Su, you may not bring one more wounded animal into this house. It's beginning to look like a zoo. Now take it back where you found it."

"My family is all gone. The people at the shelter are my family now. Who would have thought life would turn out this way," she gazed forlornly at the sun as it slipped below the water and left an orange smear in the sky. The waves lapped at the edge of the sand.

"People walk by me as if I'm invisible. Thank you, miss, for stopping to talk to an old woman.

"My pleasure," Ki smiled warmly. She pushed the stop button on her tape recorder, closed her notebook, and stuck her pen in the pocket of her denim shirt. "Could I walk you back up the beach? It's going to cool down soon."

"No, I think I will sit here a while longer. Thank you."

Each step through the sand was an effort. Ki's body felt leaden and tears pushed at her eyelids. If this is my life's work, it could very well kill me, she thought.

She stepped off the bus a few blocks from home, and walked off the excess restlessness she carried from her interview with the Colombian woman. She jogged up the front steps and into the living room to find Arizona and Coyote cuddled on the couch in deep conversation.

Coyote blushed and looked down at his feet. Arizona grinned a greeting, and motioned Ki over to join them.

"Hey, I don't want to interrupt anything," Ki muttered self-consciously as she curled up in a chair next to the couch.

"Coyote just asked me to move in with him," Arizona beamed, "I mean, in his room, you know."

"Hey, that's great," Ki brightened.

"Guess you'll have that big old room all to yourself," Arizona said.

The walnut-colored face flashed briefly in Ki's mind.

"For now, anyway," Arizona teased.

The sound of a dish crashing against Italian tile caused all three to bolt from the room. Piling into each other at the kitchen doorway, Arizona looked at Iaisha, flushed with temper, a second plate raised above her head. Chunks and shards of china and bits of foodstuff were scattered about the floor. Dandelion stood plastered against the wall, pale and trembling.

"You will not bring drugs into this house," her voice quivered with rage. "You know the rules. I've wondered why you've been slacking off around here. Now I understand." She took a menacing step toward Dandelion who seemed to shrink in her presence.

Coyote slipped past Ki and reached out for Dandelion's arm. He led him from the kitchen saying, "Let's go take a walk, man. You have some things to figure out."

Iaisha lowered the plate and jammed it carelessly into the sink where it clanked against a milk-encrusted glass.

Ki scrunched her face up at the sound and turtled her head into her shoulders.

Arizona wrapped her arms around Iaisha and drew her close. Iaisha, heaving deep sobs, clung to Arizona in an oddly childlike way.

Later, as Ki helped carry the contents of Arizona's closet into Coyote's room down the hall, Arizona explained, "Iaisha's brother died of a heroin overdose a few years back. She found him."

Ki stopped mid-step. A wave of nausea passed through her, and she faltered momentarily.

Arizona touched her arm. "Hey, you okay? You want to sit down or something?"

"No, I'm fine," Ki shook her head to clear it. "Homelessness, drugs, hunger. I didn't grow up with things like that, you know?"

"Yeah, well, that's life in the big city. You'll get used to it," Arizona said as she pulled a large plastic bag of laundry down the hall.

"I hope not," Ki said over the top of a big box full of shoes.

Chapter 7

Autumn in the City didn't feel like autumn back home, Ki noted as she pulled her parka hood over her head against the steady drizzle. "It's just so gray," she mumbled to herself. The mournful sound of a fog horn off the coast added to the gloom. Another noise caught her ear and caused her to stop mid-step at the entrance to an alleyway. It was the sound of human suffering, a moan of pain or despair, or both. She glanced up and down the sidewalk—no one was in sight; it was up to her.

"Hello," she called tentatively, squinting into the dim alley.

"Help—me," a young male voice groaned. Just beyond the dumpster, a crumpled body lay with one bare foot at an odd angle.

"Oh my god," Ki gasped. "I'm going for help," she shouted.

"Don't leave—please help me," he cried out.

In a moment of compassion, Ki abandoned good sense and rushed into the alley. She knelt by the side of the young man. "I'm here," she said.

With a nearly seamless movement, he flipped over, grabbed her by the arm and yanked her to the ground, pinning her arms above her head with one hand and covering her mouth with the other.

Ki bucked and struggled. She tried to scream but only muffled sounds escaped. She saw the hatred and rage in his eyes although he said not a word. He lifted his hand and she gasped for air, only to have her windpipe blocked by the pressure of his forearm on her throat. There was a ringing in her ears and her vision blurred. Her legs kicked wildly but connected with nothing. Then, blackness all around.

On the Berkeley side of the bay, the fall semester was well underway on campus. A gray chill had settled in and the sky held the promise of rain. It was dark as Lucas rounded the corner, took the rattley iron-doored elevator to the third floor, and wiggled her key into the rusty lock of their apartment door.

The room was as gloomy as a bad mood. Paddle sat on their Goodwill couch, silhouetted in front of the window that looked out over Telegraph Avenue. The residue of a red neon light across the street tinted the gloom with a womb-like rhythmic pulse.

Paddle sniffed and blew her nose as Lucas closed the door gently behind her.

"Hey," Lucas said, more as a question. She flipped on the overhead bare bulb that served as their kitchen light.

"Better sit down," Paddle said, balancing a tissue box on her lap. She straightened her shoulders and took in a raggedy breath.

"What's up?"

"It's Ki," Paddle paused, drew another breath. "She was raped, Lucas."

Lucas, mute, mouth agape, shook her head slowly from side to side. Her body slumped gracelessly onto a wooden chair by the table. The chair groaned.

"In the Tenderloin," Paddle continued. "Some guy raped her in an alley, Lucas." Her voice broke and she dissolved in tears. "She heard someone cry out and she went to help, for God's sake," Paddle sobbed. She pounded the cushion with her fist.

Lucas came over, sat beside her, hung an arm around Paddle's rigid shoulders and drew her close. She leaned her head against Paddle's and let her own tears run freely down her cheeks.

"I've never known anyone who's been raped before," Paddle cried.

"Yes, you have," Lucas said quietly. Her shoulders shook with remembered pain.

Having missed the implication, Paddle asked, "What do we do now?"

"We go be with her," Lucas said. She stood, walked over to the hook by the door, and lifted the keys to the bus. Paddle grabbed her coat and they were out the door.

Traffic was jammed on I-80 South, and it took an eternity to reach the Bay Bridge. Lucas' jaw was clenched and her hands vice gripped the steering wheel as they inched their way over the bridge and into the City.

Iaisha met them at the door and ushered them into the kitchen where Ki was surrounded by the commune family. The teapot whistled. Ocean set cups on the wooden running board while Coyote and Arizona placed a basket of steaming muffins fresh from the oven on the table.

Lucas squatted down in front of Ki. She understood the blank eyed stare, the white pinched mouth, the aura of fragility and impenetrability that cocooned her friend.

"We're all here for you. You're safe now. We won't let anything more happen to you. You're home," Lucas crooned softly.

"I want my Momma," Ki said in a tiny voice. She blinked, and receded again inside herself.

"Have the police been called? Has she seen a doctor?" Paddle asked from the edge of the room. Nods and murmurs answered her.

"Should we call her folks?" Paddle asked.

Lucas placed a tentative hand on top of Ki's fist, balled tightly in her lap. She moved directly in front of her line of vision and spoke softly.

"Ki, would you like to call your Momma?" Ki gave a somnolent nod. "May I look in your bag for your address book?" Another nod.

Lucas dialed the number that woke the sleeping inhabitants of the Wisconsin farmhouse.

"Mr. Lafner, this is Lucas Plum. I'm a friend of your daughter's. I'm sorry to call at this hour, but Kiowa Su needs to talk to her mother," Lucas kept her voice calm. "Yes, I will." She waited a moment, and handed the phone to Ki. She helped wrap Ki's fingers around the receiver and lift it to her ear.

Ki talked for a long while with her mother. Arizona draped a quilt around Ki's shoulders and another over her lap. The others went quietly to the living room with mugs of steaming tea and warm muffins, which wafted the smell of comfort and well being through the household.

Much later, Ki wobbled into the living room on unsteady legs. Although her eyes were red rimmed, there was a presence that wasn't there before. She sniffed and pulled the quilt closer around her shoulders. Everyone held her in quiet regard.

"I love you all," her voice quavered, "but I've decided to go home where I feel safe." Tears rolled down her cheeks. A slight smile of relief played gently on her lips. "My Mom is flying in tomorrow to take me back to Wisconsin." She cleared her voice and looked around the room at each face in turn. "You've all been so wonderful to me. I'll never forget the good times, but—well, you know."

She opened her arms to receive the first of many hugs to follow as the family members said their tearful good-byes.

The first rain came unseasonably early in October. The sidewalks, roads, sky, and ocean were the same steel gray. People rushed around hidden beneath umbrellas.

"It's weird, you know," Paddle said as she reached for a seaweed covered cracker from a tiny serving dish at the Japanese Tea Garden in the Park.

"What's weird?" Arizona poured herself some more tea. "That we're here having a Saturday afternoon tea party in the rain?" she chuckled, raising her cup in a salute to her friend.

"I mean, without Ki. It's like our old gang doesn't exist anymore."

"Yeah, our new friends are great, but, you're right, it doesn't feel the same. She called the other night, you know."

"Who? Ki? How is she?" Paddle wrapped her hands around the warm teacup.

"Sounds kinda removed. Doctor said she didn't get any of those STDs and she's not pregnant."

"Geez," Paddle shook her head.

"Said to tell everyone she loved them and to take good care of each other," Arizona stared at her clasped hands.

"Hah," a chuckle bubbled up from deep inside Paddle and belched its way into the air. Arizona raised an eyebrow in alarm as she studied Paddle.

"Do you remember that water-logged wreck, sniffling on the riverbank 'cause her canoe took a trip by itself?" Paddle said and laughed again.

"Pathetic," Arizona smirked.

They reminisced about the trio's unlikely meeting last summer. Paddle grinned and Arizona shook her head.

"Then there was Lucas playing casino cash girl in Reno," Arizona recalled. "Boy, did you look surprised," she said.

"You just never know about old Lucas," Paddle chuckled.

"You want me to run you back over to Berkeley?" Arizona offered.

"Nah, that's okay. I'll take the bus if you can drop me off at the terminal."

They buttoned and zipped coats, unfurled umbrellas and stepped out into the downpour. The Park sparkled emerald green with the winter rains and rosebushes bloomed as if they had no sense.

It was late afternoon when Paddle unlocked the apartment door and stepped in. Water dripped from her coat and made puddles on the floor. She turned the old steam radiator on, and after it emitted a few burps, clunks and hisses, she felt warm air rise. She rubbed her hands briskly together as she walked over to the gas stove and set the teakettle on the burner, then noticed a post card and a sheet of notebook paper propped up against a loaf of bread on the counter.

On the front of the post card was a picture of an old woman wearing rhinestone-studded harlequin glasses and a bright red bouffant hairdo. On the flip side, it said, "Don't forget your roots." It was signed Ginny and Benji. Paddle chuckled. "I guess that's as close as she could come to saying she misses me," she said to the spindly cactus sitting on the window ledge. It was good enough.

She picked up the piece of paper and noticed it was in Lucas' scrawling handwriting.

Dear Paddle,

Thought I'd look up Luna. Berkeley is too cold and dank for my southern soul. Swimming with the dolphins sounds pretty good about now.

I'm leaving you a month's rent and the bus. Do with it as you will. I know we'll run into each other again—seems we're fated. It's been wonderful, hasn't it? Remember, it's not the destination, it's the journey. Hugs, Lucas

Paddle's knees buckled and she collapsed onto the floor. She sat, stunned, leaning against the kitchen cabinet. She noticed a shell of dried macaroni peeking out from under the table and a cobweb that hung between the legs of the chair. She looked around the empty apartment then curled up on the faded linoleum and cried.

Later that evening, wrapped in a blanket, Paddle sat on the couch and talked to Arizona on the phone.

"But how could she just do that?" Arizona was aghast. "You mean she really just up and left you? How thoughtless."

"You sort of have to know Lucas. She didn't exactly leave me, she just moved on—like a change of weather. That's what Lucas does—moves on." Paddle heard herself justify yet another devastating experience of being left in the wake of hurricane Lucas.

"So, what are you going to do? You should come back over here," Arizona answered her own question.

"I was sort of thinking that now I have all this restaurant experience and have even picked up a few Mexican recipes, maybe I'll go back and give Ginny a hand. I have some new ideas for the diner." Paddle knew as the words left her mouth they were true.

"You're leaving California?" Arizona gasped. "Really? How can you leave California?"

"Someone once said it's not the destination, it's the journey," Paddle said with a smile.

"Well, that's just the dumbest thing I ever heard," muttered Arizona.

"I think I've seen enough of our country now to appreciate where I came from," Paddle said, feeling very much like the grownup she sounded like. "Time to go home." Silence. "You still there?"

"Yeah," Arizona sniffed.

"Will you come visit me sometime?" Paddle coaxed.

"Sure," Arizona sniffed again. "Hey, Paddle?"

"Yeah?"

"I love you," Arizona sobbed quietly.

"I love you too," Paddle wiped at her own tears.

"Don't send me one of those dumb post cards when you get home, okay? Write me a real letter," Arizona said. "Promise?"

"I promise," Paddle said and returned the receiver to its cradle. She sat looking at the phone for a moment, lifted the receiver and then replaced it.

"Nah," she said with a huge grin. "I just want to see her face when I walk in the door and say, 'I'm home.'"

Chapter 8

Paddle sold the bus and bought a plane ticket home. "Hey," she said as she stepped into the diner, a silly grin on her face.

"Mary, Joseph, and Jee-sus!" Ginny screeched. She dropped her rag on the counter and ran over to scoop her wandering child into a big old hug. "Look what the cat drug in," she said through her tears. Daemon, taking offense, strode out the door, tail in the air. "Lordy, why didn't you tell me you were coming?" Ginny babbled on.

"The girl hasn't had a chance to say anything more than 'hey'," a kindly looking middle-aged man said as he approached. "My name's Pete," he offered a hand as Paddle disengaged herself from Ginny's hug. "You've got to be Paddle, right?" Paddle nodded.

"Pete's my fi-an-cé," Ginny drew out each syllable as she flashed the diamond ring on her finger.

"What?" Paddle gasped. "When were you going to tell me about this?" She grabbed Ginny in a congratulatory hug.

"Just happened last night," Ginny beamed a toothy smile at her man.

"Looks like you might be the answer to our prayers," Pete said to Paddle.

"You short a bridesmaid or something?" Paddle bounced her eyebrows at Ginny. Ginny turned a mottled shade of red, her eyes puddle up, and her bottom lip started to quiver. "Ginny?" Paddle said, truly alarmed.

Pete put a protective arm around Ginny's shoulder and gave her a little hug. "I asked Ginny to marry me and move back to Nevada with me where I have a horse ranch," he said in a calm voice, even though his face looked all pinched. "She agreed to the 'marry me' part," Pete continued, "but she didn't know what she was going to do about the diner." Pete cast a hopeful look at Paddle.

"And in I walk…" Paddle took up the story line.

"Oh Paddle, this would be the opportunity of a lifetime for me and Benji," Ginny said, wiping at the tears still flooding down her cheeks. "And, an opportunity of a lifetime for you, too, if you wanted it."

This couldn't have felt more like a plea if Ginny had been down on her knees. "Some day all this will be mine," Paddle recalled out loud, spreading her arms to take in the diner in its entirety. Ginny nodded, a hopeful lopsided smile on her face.

Mmhmm. Persons got to have a dream, she heard Lucas say in the far reaches of her mind. "I'll do it," Paddle said.

The following month, a small New Orleans trade paper ran a review on the Blue Hawk Diner, now under new management. The menu caught the reviewer's eye.

"An inexplicably diverse combination of Blue Fire Chili, Enchiladas a la California, Kiowa Stew, Milkweed Pancakes with Plum Sauce, and Berkeley Bean Soup draws the locals by the drove," he wrote.

Roots in My Garden

Emily felt the wet patches spread under her arms, like darkening half moons in the pale peach silk blouse. Her hands hesitated on the steering wheel. Her lips were dry and chapped as she ran the tip of her tongue slowly over them.

The Beamer engine purred at the curb like a well-fed cat, in a band of shade cast by a crepe myrtle that wasn't there in her childhood.

"You going up to the door, or what?" Robin smelled her nervousness. He fidgeted with the seat belt. He was the only passenger who made it stick.

"Or, we could just drive on and no one would be the wiser," he muttered as he tugged and rattled the clasp. "Fu...!" he said, throwing up his hands in a show of resignation, as if he might sit, trapped in his seat, for eternity.

Emily laughed in spite of her own mood, and shook her head. Robin never swore, he just sputtered out explosive sounds. You always got the point. She turned off the engine, reached over and unsnapped the clasp.

"Shi...!"

Emily rolled her window part way down and peered out at the wooden house across the street. Faded beige paint peeled and puckered, the porch sagged, the cement steps were chipped, and crabgrass ruled the lawn, peeking through in tufts at each sidewalk crack.

"It looks so old and run down," she whispered, more to herself. Her left hand now rested on the door handle.

"Honey, the house was probably old when you were born," Robin said. "It could use a coat of paint though, and maybe a new porch." He leaned forward and squinted against the sun.

"You don't suppose she still lives here, do you. What would I say? What if she doesn't remember me?" Her voice sounded tiny and insignificant, like an ash in a barbecue pit. "Or, what if I don't recognize her? Oh Robbie, I don't know if I can do this." Her body leaked energy, the way sand shifts to the bottom of an egg timer, and she leaned back heavily against the seat.

"Em, you don't *have* to do this. But, it's unlikely we'll be on the West Coast again any time soon." That was true. If it hadn't been for the chefs convention, instead of shivering through a week of San Francisco summer, they'd be sweltering back in Akron, Ohio.

It was the trip up the Napa Valley, to the Culinary Institute, that triggered this sudden obsession to find her roots.

Sensory memories of childhood came flooding back. The hot, pungent smells of wine country in the summer, the profusion of yellow mustard growing in the vineyards, small towns sprinkled along the highway— Yountville, St. Helena, Calistoga—hillsides spread thick with wildflowers, the piercing cry of a red-tailed hawk, all of these were deeply imbedded.

Better she should have spent the day shopping at Fisherman's Wharf with the other wives, he thought.

"You've come this far. You're a reporter..." he said, floundering to find something for her to hold on to. "Think story." Robin had never seen her buckle at a personal challenge. His wife, he mused—the Sherman tank, plowing under, over, or just right on through obstacles large and small.

Emily closed her eyes. Her lids fluttered slightly. Her lips were pressed together so tightly they appeared chalky.

"Hon, you okay?" Robin's voice was miles away.

"That a girl, Emmi babe, pedal, pedal!" Marge, who had been running behind the six year old, now stood gasping for air, grinning from ear to ear, arms thrown up in a victory "V". She pulled her inhaler from the breast pocket of her corduroy jacket and sucked the medicine deep into her lungs.

"You're No. 1! You're No. 1!" Val shouted from the porch.

"Will you look at that?" Mrs. Bernie, unloading groceries from the trunk of her Plymouth, turned and beamed at her as she flew by. Emily

flashed a dazzling smile, but didn't risk a wave. Not just yet.

She felt, at any moment, she might become airborne.

"Em, you're worrying me here..."

Emily opened her eyes to Robin's face inches from hers, peering closely at her, his forehead creased, and his mouth twisted in concern. He was patting her rapidly on the arm.

"Jeez, what are you doing? Will you stop with the patting already?" she said, irritated at being yanked out of her reverie.

"Sorry, babe, I thought you were having a seizure or something." He settled back in his seat, but continued to stare at her.

Emily's eyes puddled and her lower lip quivered.

"Oh, no, are you going to cry?" Robin asked, reaching into the back seat for the tissue box. "Em, talk to me," he pleaded.

"That was my last day here," she said quietly, looking down the street. "My two moms, so proud of me." Robin peered in the direction she was staring, as if that might help him see the pictures in her memory.

"I remember now," she said, sniffing. Emily took a tissue and blew loudly. "I'd just gotten that bike. It was a Schwinn, peppermint green and lavender," she smiled through tears wetting her cheeks. "When I got to the end of the street, I stopped, got off, and walked my bike around. She forgot to teach me how to turn," she giggled, hiccupped, and blew her nose again, "or how to start without a push."

I walked it all the way up the street to the house, and there they were, standing on the porch together, holding hands, smiling at me. I felt like everything was going to be okay then," she said through a fresh wash of tears.

Robin reached over and took her hand. "Then what happened?"

"The next thing I remember, Momma and I were backing out of the driveway, waving goodbye to Momma Marge. She was all by herself, leaning against that porch post, right over there, crying." Emily nodded her head toward the house.

"Ah, babe," Robin said, lifting her hand to his lips, kissing her fingertips gently.

"We were all crying. My bike was on a rack on top of the car. The back seat and trunk were full of our stuff. I remember my stomach felt like I'd swallowed my soccer ball, it hurt so much," she said as she turned to Robin.

"I miss my stars," she sniffed in a whisper of a voice. "Momma Marge put glow-in-the-dark stars all over the ceiling of my room. I wonder if they're still there."

"Honey, that was a long, long time ago," Robin said gently. His look of concern brought a fresh wave of tears, and she leaned against him, sobbing loudly with complete abandon now.

A frail looking elderly man walking a spotted puppy on a leash paused for a moment on the sidewalk, peered quizzically through the window, and then passed on by.

"That's the last time I ever saw Momma Marge, Robin, the very last time," she said against his neck, wet with her tears. Her shoulders shook in his embrace.

He rocked her gently, rubbing slow, soft circles over her back, hoping to soothe away the years of pain and longing the child of six had carried nineteen years into adulthood.

"She never tried to find you? Were there letters, or phone calls?" he asked when her breathing had become regular again. "That just isn't right."

"That's why I'm here, to get some answers," she said. Emily took a raggedy breath and slowly pulled away from him, re-tucked her blouse, and brushed her fingers lightly over the creases. She retrieved a comb from the glove compartment, ran it through her thick brown hair, gave her nose a blow, her eyes a final swipe with a tissue, and checked the damage in the rear view mirror. "Great, I'm puffy and splotched," she looked down at her clothes, "and wrinkled."

Robin smiled, leaned over and kissed her on the nose.

The door rattled on its hinges as she rapped with her knuckles one more time. Her head bobbed from side to side like a salamander, trying to see movement behind the door. The rectangular, beveled, seeded-glass windows in the upper part of the door allowed light, but not view. It occurred to her that she would have been too short to have noticed this before.

She glanced at Robin, slouched against the railing at the bottom of the steps. He shrugged and said, "Once more with attitude?" Emily grinned.

A sprightly face peeked around the corner of the house, startling both of them. A straw gardening hat perched at a jaunty angle and tied under the chin held fluffs of gray hair back from the face.

"If you're Jehovah Witnesses, I don't want any," she said cordially.

"Oh, no. No, I'm, uh—we're, uh..." Emily realized she hadn't thought about what she would actually say if Marge, or anyone else, was home. Her cheeks heated to crimson.

The woman climbed the side steps to the porch. She smelled of rich soil, sun, and hard work. She wiped her hands on her overalls, took a faded handkerchief out of her pocket and mopped her forehead.

"I'm Jessica Palmer." Jessica extended her other hand toward Emily and smiled warmly. She nodded at Robin, still balanced on the bottom front step. "Is there something I can do for you young folks?"

"I'm Emily Greenwald and this is my husband, Robin..." she was about to say, and I used to live here, but was stopped mid-sentence by Jessica's swoon. The woman turned pale as kindergarten paste. Her knees buckled and she flumped down onto the porch, eyes wide and mouth agape. Robin leaped off the bottom step and ran toward the car.

"Wait! Robin, I need help," Emily shouted in panic. She knelt in front of Jessica, took her hand and asked, "Ms. Palmer, can you hear me?"

"I'm getting the cell phone. I'll call 9-1-1," Robin hollered from the street.

The color began to seep back into Jessica's cheeks. She blinked a couple of times though she still looked dazed, and said, "Emily, you've come home." Then her eyes filled with tears.

Jessica brushed her eyelid with a soiled knuckle that left a slip of mud on the side of her cheek. "I'm sorry to frighten you, dear. I'm just a silly old sentimental woman. I didn't recognize you at first, you've grown into such a stunningly lovely young woman," she said, as she gathered her legs together and hoisted herself up with Emily's help.

"Robin," Emily called over her shoulder, "cancel 9-1-1." She turned to Jessica and said, "Are you going to be okay? Can I get you anything? Do you know me? Do you know my mother?" The words tumbled unrestrained.

"I'll be fine." She leaned for a moment against the house. "Just let me catch my breath. Yes, your mother is alive and very well indeed. Oh, my, we have so much to talk about," she said. Jessica removed her hat and fanned herself.

Robin returned to the porch and looked from Jessica to Emily and back again. "Ms. Palmer, shouldn't we at least get you checked out at the hospital?" His voice was wobbly and adrenaline caused his hands to shake.

"No, thank you dear, and please, call me Jessica. I think what we all need is some lemonade and a long chat," she said as she removed her dirt-encrusted gardening shoes. She bent over and banged them on the edge of the porch. Muddy clots flew everywhere.

Robin and Emily exchanged a glance.

"It's funny," she said, setting the shoes by the door, standing up and stretching her arms, torso, neck, "I was just out back doing battle with some blackberry bushes that were part of Marge's garden. I lost," she chuckled. Jessica opened the door and motioned them in. "I guess some roots are just meant to be permanent."

Jessica followed them through the front door into a large, sun-flooded living room with floor to ceiling windows. The walls were a pale shade of apricot, trimmed with bright white wainscoting, tied together by plush, light beige carpet into which Jessica's toes disappeared.

Emily's heart sank and her smile faded.

Jessica noticed the change and said, "You probably remember this room as being more of a yellow, with that hideous brown shag carpet, and big flowered curtains blocking out all this delicious sunlight. Am I right?" She grinned at Emily's sigh of relief and walked on through the room.

"And maybe even that ratty old over-stuffed thing that passed for a couch? It finally collapsed about nine years ago," Jessica called out from the kitchen.

Emily nodded. "It was over there, by the window, right? And there was a bookcase against that wall. Oh, look Robin, the floor vent!"

Robin smiled and shrugged. "Uh huh, that's a floor vent all right," he said, feeling like he'd missed a few chapters of whatever story they were currently re-living.

"I used to straddle it in the winter and the warm air would billow out my nightgown," Emily said, lost in a long-ago memory. "Momma Marge used to call me Your Royal Highness," she giggled.

Jessica returned with glasses of lemonade and a plate of cookies. "Come, sit, eat, drink, talk," she strung the monosyllables like beads on a necklace.

Robin strategically placed himself in the rocking chair opposite the couch where the two women had settled, a front row seat for the unfolding drama that lie ahead. The cookies were homemade, he noted, his chef's mind separating out the flavors and guessing at ingredients, ginger and chocolate—cardamom perhaps. Intriguing.

"I've been waiting for this day since you left, Emmi, and now I hardly know where to begin," Jessica said. "Things were such a mess back then. And you, you poor little tike, were caught in the middle of it all." She shook her head slowly at the memory.

"I'm sorry, Jessica, I wish I could remember you," Emily said, "I guess there's a lot I don't remember."

"Honey, there is a whole community of people who knew you and your moms. Marge and Val were very active socially and politically. You know that saying, 'it takes a village to raise a child'? Well, you were that child, and I was one of the many villagers in your young life, watching you grow up, learn to walk, then read—oh!" she gasped and threw both hands up in the air.

Robin lunged forward, prepared for another swoon.

"No, no, no," she said with a laugh, and waved him away. "I just remembered a box I found a couple years ago out in the shed. I'll be right back." Jessica jumped up and rushed from the room.

"A bit of an odd duck, isn't she?" Robin whispered to Emily, who grinned and shushed him.

Jessica returned with a flat box containing colored construction paper. "We used to have meetings here at the house, to plan events, political action, voter precinct walks and such." She handed Emily the collection of papers, weathered and faded, wrinkled around the edges, but clearly keepsakes.

"You used to sit quietly on the floor, right in the middle of all the activities, and draw pictures on the backs of the fliers. Quite the artist, you were." She grinned at the memory.

Emily slowly leafed through the red, purple, white, and green pages with scribbled pictures, shapes, block letter words printed in a careful child's hand—EMILY, MOMMA, HAPPY DAY.

Laughing, she passed them one by one to Robin. "What's this one?" he asked. "It looks like a horse in a flower bed eating out of a feed sack."

"You mean these have been here all these years?" Emily felt something lump up in her throat. "Momma Marge saved them in a box in the shed?" She hadn't forgotten her after all.

"Oh, Emily, she kept all sorts of things for years after you left. Nearly broke my heart to come by and see your toddler sized plaid tennis shoes sitting by the door. Do you remember them? From when you were about three?"

Emily glanced at the front door and smiled.

"And all those stuffed animals you used to have on your bed? They were in a big wicker basket right up until the day she moved from this house just five years ago!"

"The stars..." Emily said suddenly.

"Ah, yes, the stars. They'd lost their ability to shine some years back, but right up until she moved they looked down from your ceiling."

"She moved?" Emily's lip quivered.

"Let me back up and put all this in perspective," Jessica said, taking a bite from her cookie and a swallow of lemonade before settling back on the couch. She curled her bare feet under her.

Emily propped a pillow behind her back and leaned against the arm of the couch facing Jessica. Robin, fully attentive to the story that would fill in the missing pieces of Emily's life, rocked quietly.

"Val and Marge were a passionate couple. They played hard, loved hard, worked hard, and fought hard," Jessica recalled, chuckling at some private memory.

"They were together about six years when Val decided she wanted to have a baby. Things were different back then. Lesbians were using sperm banks, just like they are today, but the woman who was inseminated was considered to be the legal parent, by right of biology." Jessica paused and a look that was hard to read passed over her face. Her brows furrowed slightly and she cleared her throat.

"So, just to cover the bases legally, your moms drew up a document stating they would share legal and physical custody of any children that were born during this relationship, should they ever separate." Jessica noted Emily and Robin were hanging on her every word. She didn't know what Emily had been told throughout her life by Val.

"The whole community followed Val's pregnancy and celebrated your birth, and like I said, watched you grow from the crib to elementary school. Your Momma Marge was so proud of you. You two were practically inseparable."

"I remember her teaching me how to paint posters and signs for parades. And we'd walk to the store in the summer after dark to get popsicles," Emily chimed in, remembering now the minutiae of daily life.

"And the bicycle," added Robin, "don't forget the bicycle she taught you to ride."

"Oh, my, yes," said Jessica, "I remember hearing all about that. It was just before you and Val moved, wasn't it? Those were the best and the worst of times, I believe."

"Tell me about that time, Jessica. I just remember the tears, and all the changes—a new town, a new school, Charles and his family. Why didn't Momma Marge move with us?" Emily asked hoarsely. She reached over, took another cookie and began nibbling mouse bites all around the edge.

"Well, Marge was putting in a lot of overtime at work trying to keep up with the bills so Val could take a couple of classes at the college and only work part-time." Again, she paused. "I can see with my own eyes you're all grown up, but still. This isn't easy to talk about." She shifted positions, sitting up straighter, cleared her throat, and took another sip of lemonade.

"Can I get either of you anything else? More cookies?" she asked, noticing the plate was empty.

Both shook their heads no. Jessica cleared her throat again, and plunged ahead.

"Well, there'd been some tension for a while. You know, that happens sometimes. Life gets stressful and people either pull together or they start drifting apart to deal with it."

Emily nodded her head. She glanced at Robin and smiled. He winked in return.

"It seems that your Momma Val had met someone at school who just sort of swept her off her feet. It was a man. No one could have seen that coming. Marge came quite undone about it. It's what they call one of those irreconcilable differences. They tried therapy. They tried all sorts of things. When it looked like nothing could fix the situation, your Momma Val decided it would be best if she and Charles left the area."

Jessica kept her voice calm and neutral though her face tightened. She fiddled with her hands in an absent-minded sort of way.

"Marge finally had to agree it would be the best solution, although she was heart-broken. The only solace was that you would still be part of her life, even though the details were unclear about how to move you between homes—a minor inconvenience, supposedly. Would you excuse me a moment? There are some newspaper clippings I want to show you. I've kept them in my journal all these years, hoping for just this opportunity."

Jessica unfolded her legs and stretched slowly. There was a series of pops and clicks as her joints readjusted. She picked up the empty cookie plate as she left the room.

"How you doing?" Robin came over and sat next to Emily on the sofa. He put an arm around her and she leaned into his embrace.

"This is possibly more than I was prepared for," she sighed. "I shouldn't have eaten all those cookies. I feel a sort of nauseous."

"Who is this woman, anyway? She knows all this stuff about you, kept your childhood art, has newspaper articles about your life for God's sake. You don't even remember her?"

They could hear movement in the kitchen, cupboard doors opening and closing, the refrigerator door, plates, water running.

"You don't suppose she's forgotten we are here, do you?" Robin said, trying to sound light-hearted and at ease, though he was feeling neither.

Ten minutes later, Jessica came out of the kitchen balancing a large service tray with chunks of French bread in a basket, a bowl of spinach and cream cheese dip, a pot of tea and three cups.

"I was getting a sugar rush," she said, "figured we could use a little protein." She put the tray on the end table and left again, only to return with a manila file spilling out newsprint.

"Thanks, Jessica, but really, you shouldn't have gone to the trouble," Emily said through a mouthful of French bread. A straggle of spinach clung to the corner of her mouth. Robin reached a parental finger out and flicked it onto a napkin he held under her chin.

Jessica smiled at the pair. "If only Marge could see you now," she said, shaking her head. "You two are just terminally cute." She poured three cups of tea, passed them around, and settled into the rocker.

Emily's cheeks flushed at the compliment.

"Where is Momma Marge now? Would it be possible to see her, do you think?" Emily's excitement rose.

"I'm afraid not, dear. She's in Hawaii, scuba diving at this very moment, I'll bet," Jessica said. "What is the date today?" Jessica glanced about the room absentmindedly.

"I believe she's due back tomorrow night," she continued, not waiting for a response. "I have her flight information around here somewhere," she said, riffling through a rattan basket next to the rocking chair.

Emily held her breath. Fate was in charge of this one. "We're flying out of San Francisco International tomorrow night at seven," Emily said.

"Well, here it is. Heavens, I'm getting so forgetful lately. Good thing I wasn't supposed to meet the plane," she gave a short chuckle. "Yup, United Airlines, Flight 1030, arriving Saturday—that is tomorrow, isn't it? At five o'clock in the evening. Well, what do you know about that?" she said, looking at Emily.

A gurgle, like the sound of a rock being thrown in a deep well, came from Emily's open mouth. Tears pooled in her eyes.

"It'll be close, but we'll be there," Robin assured her.

Jessica's forehead wrinkled and her eyes squinted slightly. She put her fist to her chest and looked as if she was in pain. After a shaky breath, she handed Emily the file she had carried in a few minutes earlier.

"You might want to look through this. It will explain why you never saw Marge again," Jessica said quietly.

Newspaper clippings headed *The Battle of The Other Mother*; *Lesbian Takes Custody Battle to California First District Court of Appeal*, *A Community Divided*, fliers soliciting donations for the Mother/Daughter Defense Fund, posters, note cards brittle with age and emotion, faded and tinged with yellow, a picture of Emily, age six, on a thank-you note for Jessica's contribution signed by Marge, a poster calling for a Rally for Lesbian and Gay Equality—item after item, testimonies to Marge's attempts to keep Emily in her life.

"I don't understand," Emily said in a small voice as she scanned the folder of clippings. "You said they had an agreement on paper, before I was even born..."

"Yes, it's true. And she might just as well have wiped her..." she swallowed and made a face as if something bitter had been caught in her throat.

"The document had no worth in the courts at all. Now if you'd been a piece of property, a car perhaps, those agreements would have held up and an equitable settlement would have been made. But back then, the only person who had legal claim to a child was the biological parent," she explained, "and Val used that legality like a bludgeon."

Jessica held up a news clipping from *The San Francisco Chronicle*. "Court packed with supporters of lesbian rights. Judge rules there is no case," she read. "That decision changed Marge's life forever. Today, of course, the non-biological parent can adopt the child so that both parents share legal custody, but not back then."

"But, why wouldn't Momma Val even let me see her, or call, or write, or *some*thing?" Emily whined, feeling again the pain of the six year old. "*Why*, Jessica?" she demanded.

Jessica pulled out the article entitled, *A Community Divided.* "Honey, I'll never understand that myself, and Val wasn't talking to any of us, that's for sure. Maybe she just needed to start a brand new life. However, the more she pulled away, the harder Marge fought. Oh, it got nasty. There was even a restraining order so that Marge couldn't have contacted you without winding up in jail."

Robin was holding Emily's hand. "Geez," he said quietly, "and you thought all this time that she didn't care, that she'd forgotten you."

The tears were rolling slowly down Emily's cheeks. Jessica extracted the gardening handkerchief from her pocket and passed it to Emily who held it in a tight ball in her hand and continued to sniff.

"Nothing could be farther from the truth," said Jessica. "For years she mourned and grieved. Word of mouth had it that Val moved several times and we eventually lost track of you. Marge and I had been lovers for a couple of years. We lived here together. She kept your room like her own private shrine—truthfully, it got somewhat scary after a while," Jessica admitted.

"Earlier, you said she moved five years ago," Emily prompted.

"Yes. She had an opportunity to change jobs. Sort of burned out here—too many memories, I think. UPS made her an offer she couldn't pass up. That girl does love to drive a truck," she chuckled. "And, she looks so darned cute in that brown uniform." She smiled and shook her head, lost for a moment in her own memories.

"So, you two are no longer together," Robin asked.

"You know, I think that experience with Val sort of killed her desire to settle down. She'll always be family to me. I love her dearly. When she moved, I decided to stay on here, mostly for sentimental reasons." Jessica caught her bottom lip between her teeth and looked away for a moment.

"What?" Emily noticed the change of energy.

"Oh, I'm just worried I guess, about what she'll do when she sees you again after all these years. She had a bout with her heart last year. God, I'd feel awful if she dropped dead," she said bluntly.

Emily paled.

The back up of traffic on 19th Avenue in San Francisco had cost them half an hour more than they'd allowed. Emily glanced at her watch every few minutes, drummed her fingers on her knees, and heaved sighs of frustration as they neared the airport.

"Turn!" she shrieked.

Robin, startled by the sudden outburst, tugged the steering wheel to the right, and just missed the taillight of an SUV. The driver blared his horn and flashed Robin a one-fingered peace sign.

"Shi...! Will you get a grip?" he yelled at Emily. "You're going to get us killed."

"But that was the exit for returning rental cars," she said through clenched teeth. "Now we'll be late for sure."

"That was the rental pick-up exit. Relax, I know where I'm going," he said. Under his breath, he added, "I think."

"I'm sorry. I'm supposed to be navigating," Emily said. "Oh, Robin, we're this close—I just don't want to miss her," she whined.

"Look, honey, we've still got time. We'll check our bags, find our gate, then go on over to her terminal. If worse comes to worst," he reasoned, "we have her address and phone number. You've found your Mom, Emmi. The rest can unfold over time, if it has to."

"I hate it when you're right." She smiled wearily at him and punched him gently on the arm. "I think we better make the loop and try again." She noted the parking lot signs for incoming flights. This time as she breathed in, her chest didn't catch.

At 4:45 P.M., they entered the United terminal, dodging hoards of people, baggage carts, and wheelchairs. The overhead flight schedule blinked a delay just as Robin glanced up.

"Whoa," he said, catching Emily's hand and pulling her to a stop. "Flight 1030 from Hawaii, delayed," he read. "What the..."

"Oh, no," Emily groaned, "what do we do now?"

"Check in at our gate, see if they can give us any information," he said as he tugged her back into motion.

"Bad weather off the California coast," the agent replied, consulting her computer. "You'll have to keep checking the overhead for updates. No anticipated time of arrival just yet," she said, smiling, her voice artificially kind and practiced at reassuring hysterical flyers.

"Look, babe, there was a Starbucks back down the terminal. Let's go have a cup of coffee while we wait. There's really nothing more we can do, and it's between her gate and ours."

Emily's bottom lip protruded in a brief pout. She both admired and resented Robin's ability to be sensible in situations like this.

She gave in. "You're right. We still have at least an hour and a half before we board our plane. A Cafe Mocha with double whipped cream is exactly what I need."

They sat quietly, lost in thought, watching passers by through the plate-glass window. An hour passed and Robin stepped back out into the terminal to check the overhead. Delayed. Just as he turned to walk back into the coffee bar, the word Arrival flashed next to Flight 1030.

"No change," he reported, as he fitted himself back into his seat. The chair legs squeaked.

Fifteen minutes later at another gate at the opposite end of the terminal, a woman deplaned, backpack slung over one shoulder. She looked at the clock on the overhead flight schedule board and paused long enough to reset her watch and unzip her jacket. She rubbed her right elbow as though the sudden chill of the airport had attacked her bones.

"Damn," the woman muttered, unconscious of the fact that she could be heard by those around her. "I missed the connector bus." She scanned the long corridor, and then headed towards a coffee shop.

Emily leaned back in her chair, took the yellow folded paper from her blazer pocket and opened it. Printed in neat block letters were Marge's flight schedule and address. Taped carefully under that was a recent snapshot of Marge to help them identify her in a crowd. Jessica was right, she did look cute in her brown UPS uniform. Emily grinned.

She held the paper between her hands as if in prayer. In a way, she supposed she was pleading for divine intervention.

Robin checked his watch.

"Em, we really can't wait any longer," he said, gently.

Her lip quivered and she gave a furtive look at the swarm of people passing by. Tears rimmed her eyes, and when she blinked, one trickled down her cheek to the corner of her mouth.

Robin leaned across the small wooden table, cupped her chin in his hand and kissed her nose. He caught the tear with his little finger, and brought it gently to his own heart.

Emily folded the yellow paper carefully and slipped it back into her right pocket, located her purse, and followed Robin. Starbucks was teeming, as usual. She wondered vaguely if it would be politically incorrect to invest in coffee futures. They jostled past the long line of people out in the corridor waiting for their caffeine fix.

"Oops, sorry," Emily said over her shoulder as she bumped into a gray-haired woman in a windbreaker.

They took off on a trot, back to the gate that would take them home to Ohio.

"Good Lord, everyone is in such a hurry," the old woman grumbled. She looked down and noticed a folded piece of yellow paper by her foot. Bending over with a groan and a huff, she retrieved and opened the note. She blinked, looked back over her shoulder, and blinked again. "Jet lag," she pronounced loudly, to whomever wanted to listen.

She picked up her Cafe au Lait and navigated towards a small table near the window. Laying the paper down on the tabletop, she bent over it as she extracted a pair of fingerprinted, dog-chewed reading glasses from her jacket pocket.

After a moment of sitting slack-jawed, she reached into her backpack, pulled out a cell phone, and dialed. She took a sip of coffee while she listened to the ring.

Aboard Flight 2937, Emily peered out the window as the airplane taxied down the runway and became airborne. Robin tightened his grip on her hand as the wheels lifted with a thunk-clunk and receded into the bowels of the plane. She reached over with her free hand and gave the knot of their fingers a reassuring pat.

"You've been a good sport about this, Robin. Thanks. I sure do love you," she said.

Robin's eyes were squeezed shut. He forced a tight smile and said, "Love you too," then slipped back into the fear place he visited each time they took off or landed.

Her thoughts returned to Marge. So close, so very close. Emily reached into her blazer pocket for the picture of her mother, but found only a tissue.

"Hello?" Jessica said as she clicked on the lamp by the couch in the living room. The sun had shifted just enough to leave the room dim in the early evening. Or maybe it was her cataracts. She sat on the edge of the couch.

"Hi babe, I'm home," Marge said. It was good to hear Jessica's familiar voice after two weeks away. "Well, at least I'm at the airport," she amended.

"Oh, my god," Jessica squealed into the phone. "How did it go? Isn't she just the spitting image of Val?   Tell me everything. Did the kids get off okay?" she rattled on.

Marge, with a quizzical look on her face, lips parted, held the phone in front of her for a moment, staring at it, as if that might provide some clarity.

"Marge, Marge—are you there? Hello?" Jessica's voice was a tinny shout.

Marge held the phone to her ear again and said, "Yeah, I'm here, I think." She shrugged and rotated her shoulders backward, then forward. Her neck was cricking up on her.

"Jessi, what are you talking about?" Since disembarking the plane, life had taken a surreal twist.

"The kids! Emily!" Jessica shouted into the phone.

"Emily? *My* Emily?" Marge could feel herself pale and she leaned heavily against the plate glass. Sounds around her began to fade into an indistinguishable drone. She forced herself to take a deep, slow breath, and then another. Her lips were numb.

"Oh, no," Jessica gasped. "Oh Marge, tell me you saw them. Oh god, something went wrong, didn't it? You don't even know what I'm talking about, do you?"

Marge shook her head, as oblivious to the fact that Jessica couldn't see her as she was to the fact that all around her, strangers could hear her when she talked to herself or shouted into the cell phone.

"Marge? Honey, are you okay? Are you sitting down somewhere?" Jessica asked, beginning to panic. Stay calm, stay calm, she reminded herself.

"Uh," was all Marge was able to muster. A light sweat layered her skin. Out of nothing more than reflex, she reached for her heart. No pain. No tightness.

"Marge, sweetheart, Emily was here. She came home to find you, all the way from Akron, Ohio. They were leaving San Francisco an hour after you were due to arrive, so they planned to meet your flight. Marge, are you there?"

Marge found the yellow paper again and held it close to her heart. The world around her seemed to be slipping away. She recalled the words, "Oops, sorry," the young woman with the chestnut brown hair, a frail looking young man rushing along side her. Emily. Her Emily had come home.

A sob wrenched itself from deep inside her as consciousness seeped away.

Marge opened one eye half way. An auburn-haired angel of mercy wearing an EMT jacket hovered over her. Cute, Marge thought, opening the other eye. Single? she wondered.

"I'm Tanya Oliver—I'm an EMT. You've had a fall. Do you know where you are?" the woman asked as her doe-eyes melted away any thought Marge might have had of jumping to her feet and dusting herself off.

"Well, at last count I was sitting at a table with a Cafe au Lait..." Marge blinked a couple of times. "Why am I down here?" She turned her head from side to side noting many pairs of shoes, the underside of tables, a coffee-soaked napkin, and the bottom rungs of chairs.

"It looks like you fainted," Tanya said. "The man at the next table said you were talking on the phone, became pale, and just keeled right over."

Marge flushed with humiliation at her moment of public vulnerability.

"I think you're going to be fine—pulse, heart rate, pupils all check out." Tanya helped Marge to a sitting position, and handed her the cell phone Marge had taken with her on her short trip to the floor. "Just take it easy a while. Let me get you a cup of water," she offered. Marge nodded her acceptance.

Tanya hovered nearby as Marge got herself upright and into a chair, then she made her way to the counter. "Water, please?" she smiled her order to the server. The drama of the last few minutes had subsided and the coffee shop was back to its customary bustle.

Pieces of the last hour were falling back into Marge's memory. The dream of her lifetime, finding Emily, had brushed by her and vanished.

Tanya returned with a large cup of water, which she handed to Marge along with a warm smile. She sat for a moment opposite Marge, filled out some forms that Marge signed, wished her well, shook hands, and left.

Probably not single, Marge shrugged. Jessica. Oh, god, she's going to be in a panic, Marge thought as she dialed.

"Yes? Marge, is that you? Are you there? Marge?" Jessica's voice was tinged with hysteria.

"Babe, babe, slow down. I'm okay," Marge broke through the sobbing voice on the other end of the line.

"Marge, you just stay right where you are. I'm coming to get you. I'll be there in two hours," Jessica babbled.

"I won't be here," Marge said, suddenly knowing what she needed to do.

"What do you mean, you won't be there? Where else would you be?"

"Akron." Marge smiled serenely and took a sip of water.

All for One

Chapter 1

Miss Schreck's whistle blew shrill enough to make Bernina Fowler's teeth itch. Tall for her fifteen years, bowed and stooped, her sack-like clothes were challenged to follow the contour of her body, often resembling a lumpy bag of cats being hauled to the river. Gym clothes did not improve her condition. Her square face was framed by brown hair that hung lifelessly against each cheek, and her forehead sprouted a fringe of too-short bangs. Berni's chin receded, giving her face the appearance of a backwards landslide. She was moody, and prone to strange acts of aggression.

Just last Wednesday, Mary Day Warren sashayed up behind Berni—who was bent over the water fountain—and shoved her head-first, right into the spigot. Horrified, Berni spun around, her hand over her mouth, grimacing in pain and shock. Blood trickled between her fingers and dripped from her chin, soaking the front of her blouse. "Bernina Fowler," Mary Day said, "didn't anyone ever teach you how to drink out of a fountain? Look at you—you're a mess." She laughed, and waltzed on down the hallway.

Thursday, Berni missed school. The dentist put a temporary cap on her broken tooth. Sunday, Bernie slipped out of the house early, just before sunrise. She swiped the wooden Diamond match along the striker strip on the box, and Old Man Warren's cornfield went up in a blaze. From a distance she watched the fire spread as she sipped from the bottle of vodka she'd liberated from the Fowler's liquor cabinet.

Dani Jean Barnhall's eyes were focused on a smudge on the floor of the gym as she pondered its origin. DJ's (a nickname she had claimed for herself) shiny, thick black hair was cut as short as decency would allow. Her eyebrows, the same shiny thickness, arched like raven wings over almond shaped lavender eyes. Her lips were small but sensuous and prone to a quick smile showing perfectly formed white teeth. DJ's claim to fame was not athletics. She was, however, Fairlawn High's spelling champ. Anxiety often caused her to spell instead of speak, gaining her permanent nerd status among the student population. "I h-a-t-e this," she mumbled to Berni.

"Let's go, let's go," shouted Miss Schreck, "finish picking your teams right now or its ten laps." She caught Dani Jean looking at her—the message was either *rescue me* or *love me*. She wasn't sure. She had a sense about this particular girl—her heart ached for all of the girls who were left standing un-chosen. Her sister had been one such child, and the guilt of being a born athlete with naturally pretty features weighed heavily on the gym teacher. Still, she told herself that inculcating the ethos of organized play into the minds of her charges was a worthy pursuit.

"Oh, okay—Jewell." Patty Burke gave a deep resigned sigh.

With a beatific smile, Jewell Watson glided to the left end of the gymnasium. Jewell possessed an air of *noblesse oblige*, believing herself to be destined for fame and fortune beyond the confines of this hick town—an echo of her mother's unrequited dream. She had perfected the withering glance of Bette Davis, the enchanting head-thrown-back laugh of Kate Hepburn, and the arch-browed psychotic stare of Joan Crawford. Jewell wore only green. Her comfort with being different was inspiring.

"Todd, who will it be?" prompted Miss Schreck.

"Geez. I guess DJ," he said with no enthusiasm. DJ loped to the right. "T-h-a-n-k-s," she said, grateful only to get that over with.

Alone at the end of the court, Berni and Gem fidgeted. Gem Plotz sneezed and wiped the back of her hand across her nose. Her rat-like face was more a curiosity than an offense. Her frail shoulders hunched toward her earlobes and her arms seemed hinged to hang with palms forward. She tugged at her pale white-blonde ponytail and rocked back and forth, waiting to be chosen. Since puberty, her hormones raced with nowhere to go except to her active imagination—well, nowhere to go except to the music teacher, Mr. Zotto, whose hand would graze the slight swell of her breast as he'd reach across her to adjust the position of her cello, but no one knew about that. Or the day his hand rested on her bare leg and his finger found its way under the hem of her shorts. No one knew about that either. Gem flashed a toothy smile at Todd who quickly averted his eyes.

"Bernina," shouted Patty.

Berni glowered and shuffled to the left with not even a glance at her cousin who by default joined Todd's team.

"At least I didn't have to *choose* her," Todd muttered. Gem, her gait resembling a spider missing three legs, ambled past several snickering kids. She batted her pale eyelashes gratefully at Todd.

Later, in third period Science, Mr. Dean, the heartthrob of every pubescent girl at Fairlawn, leaned against the edge of his wooden desk, legs crossed at the ankles, looking to-die-for.

The sensual planes of his face had transformed into something resembling frustration. He held Friday's exams in one hand. With the pointer finger of the other hand, he tapped his lower lip lightly, wondering where to begin. As he held this pose, the room settled into the kind of quiet where you could have heard a dust mote land.

"Well, let's start with the good news," he said, gracing them with a wide-lipped smile that ended in an alluring dimple on either cheek.

"Our star pupils may come collect their 'A' papers, and as a reward, you may skip the half-hour lab at the end of the period. Your hall passes are attached to your papers. Nice work," he added as he called out their names.

Predictably, Gem, Bernina, DJ, and Jewell came forward one at a time, received their papers, and were blessed by a smile and a nod from Mr. Dean. They knew by now not to express joy or pride in their accomplishments. Except Jewell, who couldn't help dropping the deep curtsey she'd been practicing at home in front of the mirror. There was a subtle chorus of groans, snickers, and much rolling of eyes.

"Be kind," Jenny Slate stage whispered, "that's all they have going for them."

Jewel shot her a look and threw the end of her green shawl over her shoulder in a haughty gesture. "Peon," she hissed, as she sailed by Jenny's desk.

"The rest of you may collect your papers from my desk at the end of lab," Mr. Dean said, the corners of his mouth dropping as he shook his head slowly.

By the time the lunch bell rang, Gem, DJ, Berni and Jewell had already taken their seats in the cafeteria at the Dweeb Table, designated and shunned by the *in* crowd. The other students made an elaborate show of walking a wide sweep as they passed by, laughing and chatting with each other, avoiding any recognition of the exiled.

"I hope they choke on their tuna casserole," Berni mumbled.

"Hey, Berni, don't let them get to you. They're just jealous," Gem tried to soothe her, but her voice was hollow and her words lacked conviction. Not a minute passed when she didn't wish she could *belong*.

DJ was quietly moving noodles around her plate with her fork when Jewell came up with the worst idea they'd heard yet.

"Look at us," she said, gesturing at the gloomy girls inhabiting the end of the table. Berni slouched with elbows on the table and her chin in hand, her eyes glossy and unfocused. DJ looked despondent, and Gem picked at a pimple on her cheek. "We're acting like a bunch of dweebs. We *deserve* to be at this table."

Jewell leaned forward, lowered her voice, forcing them to lean in to hear over the clamor, and whispered, "I propose we go to the after school mixer. It's the last one before summer." She smiled brightly, sat back and looked into three pairs of horror stricken eyes.

"Look," she said, "If we want to belong, we have to stop acting weird."

"We're not acting," said Berni.

"And, who says we want to belong?" Gem asked unconvincingly.

"We've *never* gone to a mixer," Berni said, her voice tinged with pride.

"Hey, w-a-i-t," DJ spelled. "I think Jewell has a good idea. Can't hurt to try, can it? I mean, we'll all be together, and..."

"DJ, that's just the point," Jewell interrupted. "We're so stuck together we look like the blob from Planet Weird. No wonder they don't see us as real people.

"DJ, you're a phenomenal speller. Gem, to say you are a brilliant musician would be understating the fact. Berni, your mind for scientific fact and mathematical data is stunning. And I, well, when I'm walking the Red Carpet in Hollywood, you'll all say 'it was fate.' We're wonderful, unique beings who deserve respect." She cast a look over her shoulder. No eyes were on them.

"I say we each take a corner of the gym and stay there. Make them see us as individuals. What do you say? We can do it, huh?" Jewell was using her pep rally voice now. Her eyes sparkled with enough enthusiasm and optimism to slowly infuse the others, or at least to wear down their resistance.

After seventh period, they met briefly outside the gym to make a game plan. Corners were assigned, and they agreed to meet by the green Exit sign in half an hour to check in. It was hard to discern fear from excitement. One at a time, they filtered into the throng. Gem gnawed on her thumbnail. DJ kept running her hand through the short stubble of her hair, and casting furtive glances between Jewell and a clump of giggling girls along the sidelines. Berni blinked like a turtle with sand in its eyes. Jewell's smile was so wide it was scary.

Crepe paper looped and curled between the rafters, a mirrored globe spun lazily from the ceiling casting dizzifying shards of light over the gym floor, and the music blared. Girls danced together in groups or pairs. An occasional couple dotted the floor. The guys, posturing and joking, gradually gave up their posts holding up the walls and joined in.

Berni felt dizzy and sick to her stomach as she planted herself at the Visitors' end of the basketball court. The effects of the vodka that she'd found in her parents' liquor cabinet and secretly mixed with her orange juice at breakfast had long since worn off. Through the crowd, she saw DJ at a diagonal from her, squinting and with a silly smile plastered on her face as though she had a bad case of gas. Gem was flattened against the wall as though facing a firing squad, and Jewell— oh, no—Jewell was dancing, by herself, one of those interpretive things she did that reminded Berni of a mime with a seizure disorder.

Noise, movement, rhythm, the energy of youth was unleashed, tethered only by the four corners: misery, gloom, embarrassment, and resignation.

It was true, they just didn't fit. After five minutes, each of the four slithered away from her post to regroup outside the door beyond the Exit.

"Well, that was more fun than I ever remember having," Berni's voice dripped sarcasm.

Chapter 2

The Radical Outsiders Club was also Jewell's idea.

Inside the abandoned hobo hut next to the railroad track, DJ bent her slight body over four Dixie cups and carefully poured the sacramental grape Kool-Aid from the orange plastic pitcher as she had since age twelve. Her tongue worked itself at the corner of her mouth. When DJ took her seat, Berni stood with her back turned to the others, and took a small flask from her jacket pocket. She unscrewed the cap and poured a colorless liquid into her own cup, topping off the Kool-Aid, and then handed out the cups.

Dust motes twinkled in the dim light as it filtered through the missing wood slats and bathed Gem's splindly fingers as she unsealed the box of Ritz crackers. The waxed liner crackled in the silence. Berni grimaced and quietly clenched her teeth.

Outside the hovel, early autumn heat released a pungent fragrance of detritus: fallen oak leaves, mugwort, crushed dried grass. A mangy crow cawed in the boughs of a nearby fir. Inside, a granddaddy long leg spider dropped from the broken beam overhead, landed soundlessly next to the cracker box, and staggered slowly off the edge of the overturned washtub that served as the round table.

Jewell cleared her throat, signaling the beginning of their fourth year together, and lifted her cup.

"I now declare the meeting of The Radical Outsiders open." With her free hand and a flare for the dramatic, she tossed the end of the brown, feathered boa—her one departure from green, which she had insisted on wearing during these meetings since day one—over her shoulder. The boa was a long, ever-growing line of hen feathers gathered daily from her father's chicken coop, intermittently splashed with color from pheasant feathers snitched from her granddad's hunting bounty.

In unison, the other three cups were raised, four voices called out, "Never let life get the best of you." The gurgling sound of throats swigging down the cool purple liquid rippled through the room.

Thit, thit, thit, thit. The paper cups were smacked back down on the tub. Hands bumped knuckles as the girls grabbed crackers from the faded checkered napkin in the center.

Gem choked on her Ritz, making a sound like a duck laughing. DJ whopped her on the back. Berni rolled her eyes and said, "Really, aren't we getting too old for this? I mean, we're in high school now."

Jewell, who was reaching for the crackers, paused, threw a scathing glance at her friend, and said, "Need I remind you that you were not welcome in Yearbook Club? Gem was asked to leave Home Ec Club due to, well, hygiene issues. And they closed Debate Club mysteriously the same day DJ tried to sign up." She took a Ritz from the box. "I call for a reading of the minutes," she said through a mouthful of cracker.

The pitcher was passed and cups were refilled as DJ stood and struggled with a small spiral notebook in her back jeans pocket. The thin wire caught on a stitch of thread and took several minutes of tugging and twisting to liberate.

"You could carry a purse like a regular girl, you know," Berni *tsk*ed, as they settled back down on the matted dirt floor around the table. Puffs of dust rose and fell leaving a thin adobe patina on shoes and pants.

"We're all here because we're *not* regular girls," Gem reminded her. "Especially DJ," she added.

DJ glared at her.

Jewell, left elbow bent, hand on hip, the other hand raised straight up in a tight fist, signaled for the secret chant.

"All for one, one for all, no one harms us, short or tall," they intoned in bored voices.

"Sorry," Bernie muttered.

"Sorry," Gem said, with a glance at DJ.

"J-u-n-e seventh," DJ read from the minutes of the last meeting, "Berni explained to Polly Mullen that her name was a combination of her parent's names, Bernard and Nina, rather than hitting Polly for saying her name was stupid."

Berni's smile resembled a pipe cleaner turned up at both ends.

"Gem reported she was quitting cello lessons with that p-e-r-v Mr. Zotto." Gem carefully studied the floor. Her shoulders slumped and she seemed to recede in on herself. Her neck redden in shame. DJ continued, "Gem also reported that she is on the waiting list for Miss Bethel's class for exceptional students." She nodded toward Gem who blushed under the spotlight of having made the best of a bad situation.

"Jewell signed up to bring refreshments to the next meeting, and I took notes. Sincerely, DJ Barnhall, Secretary." DJ slapped her notebook closed and sat down.

The meeting progressed through announcements, new business, and refreshment sign-ups with DJ clicking her Bic pen and flapping her spiral notebook open and closed between each topic.

Berni, chin in hand, sighed deeply, and shook her head.

They were an odd lot, and they knew it. And they knew they had choices. An orthodontist and a good therapist would go a long way towards making Bernie socially acceptable. Longer hair and the addition of a few dresses to her wardrobe would help DJ fit in with the girls. Jewell could tone it down a few notches. And Gem—well, maybe in a few years her hormones would settle.

They could succumb to a life of miserable victimization at the hands of the so-called normal, they could pretzel themselves into some version of normalcy, or they could band together, embrace their peculiarities, and become experts at making lemonade out of life's potentially sour experiences. Intelligence, and Jewell's invincible spirit, was on their side.

Chapter 3

"Smile," Gem's father called from behind the lens of his Nikon.

"Bernina, honey, pull your hair back from your face. That a girl," Bernina's mother said, fussing about, hooking her own sweat dampened hair behind her ears.

Click. Click. Click. Click. Cameras captured the cap and gown photo op, the smiling faces, eyes squinting against the sun, or the future.

"Just one more," whined Gem's mother. "This time, Gem, *try* to keep your eyes open, although not as wide and scary as Jewell's," she said with a glance at her niece.

The girls groaned, shifted, adjusted caps, wet lips and froze for one more Hallmark moment.

"Wait—Jewell's cap is throwing a shadow right over Dani Jean's face. And Jewell's eyes are not scary," Jewell's mother admonished her sister as she charged forth, righted the offending cap, and backed away slowly, hands spread in front of her, as if not wanting to dislodge her work.

"J-e-e-z-u-s," DJ spelled through clenched teeth, which made her appear as though her jaw were wired shut.

Finally released, the girls rolled amoebae-like into the crowd of classmates for final good-byes before heading out into the world.

Having turned in their caps and gowns to Miss Schreck in the gymnasium, the girls slipped through the crowd to the free ice cream table. Shrouded in invisibility, they were not included in the outer world that swirled around them—squeals of delight, cries of freedom, tears of parting, promises to stay in touch, excitement about the next step, yearbooks being passed about for signatures and special notes.

"Plebeians," Berni muttered under her breath. "I can't wait to get out of here." She tugged at the edges of her shorts and stared at the ground in front of her. "Strawberry," she spat, not looking up at the woman behind the ice cream table holding a metal scoop dripping with water.

"Free at last, huh?" Jewell said to no one in particular in the cluster of students waiting for ice cream. "Move over world, Jewell is on her way!" she shouted, head thrown back, arms in the air. No one seemed to notice.

Gem's tongue lashed out too late to catch a glob of vanilla ice cream that slipped from her cone and landed silently in her lap. Her eyes darted about, hoping no one had noticed. No one had.

DJ, one hip braced against the ice cream table, watched her friends through soft eyes as she rimmed her chocolate cone with a lazy tongue. F-e-l-i-c-i-t-a-t-i-o-n-s, she spelled quietly. She felt like crying.

The girls found a spread of shade under an elm on the periphery of the milling graduates and settled into a companionable silence, licking ice cream from fingers, crunching cones.

Gem broke the silence, catching DJ's eye. "So, when do you leave for Guatemala?"

"Tuesday," she answered. "I'll fly into St. Louis, then on to Austin where I'll meet up with the others."

"You scared?" Berni asked. "I hear you can get real sick from the food and water down there. What do your folks think about all this?"

"Oh, they're just glad I'm going on a mission. Guess I'll be too busy to get sick, building houses and all. Anyway, I've got all my shots," DJ answered with more bravado than she felt.

"You going to be home all summer, Berni? When do classes start at Northwestern?" Gem turned toward Berni who was twisting a frayed strand of hair around her finger and imagining tainted food and brackish water.

"Huh? Oh, the Math Department's having a faculty tea for new students September third," she said, rolling her eyes. "It's mandatory."

"God, how droll," Jewell moaned. "I, myself, am due at a wine and cheese soiree at the Director's Frank Lloyd Wright style home in the Berkeley hills at the end of August."

"I can't believe you're going all the way to California to study theater. I mean, geez, they have acting schools nearer than that. Chicago, maybe? St. Louis?" Gem said. Her voice had an edge to it. She drew her knees up to her chest and wrapped her spidery arms around them. Her web of security was unraveling.

"Yeah, it's not like you know anyone out there," Berni chimed in.

"Oh, but I will!" Jewell flashed them a broad toothy smile. "That's just the point. People who know people live in California or New York. New York is too cold. Fame awaits me on the Gold Coast, dahlings." She sighed dramatically and threw kisses to an imaginary adoring public. Jewell lived life free of the complexities of reality that often plagued other people.

"Hey, don't forget to write when you land your first role. Maybe we can all fly in for your grand opening," DJ said with a grin. She had an uneasy feeling about Jewell and California.

"Gem, my dear cousin, you get the prize for *least* distance traveled," Jewell offered.

"Yeah, there *are* city orchestras *farther* away than Burlington, you know. Chicago, maybe? St. Louis..." Berni teased.

"The Burlington City Orchestra is a perfectly respectable place for a cello player," Gem said. "And unlike some," she arched her pale eyebrows, "I know my limits."

"Aw, oh, cut to the bone and dying a fast, painful death," Jewell said as she splayed herself out on the grass, eyes rolled upward, mouth agape, back of hand resting on her forehead for her final breath.

"You guys are too m-u-c-h," DJ said, laughing, shaking her head. Without warning, the tears that had been corralled earlier broke loose the gate. "I'm scared," she managed, in a small voice. "I'm going to miss you all so much."

Jewell, resurrected from the dead, bounded to her feet. With her hand on her hip and her other hand raised in a tight fist, she signaled for their childhood chant.

"Oh, god, not that stupid chant thing," Berni muttered as she pulled herself to her feet. She didn't look at DJ.

"Aw, that was kid stuff," Gem complained. "I don't want to."

"C'mon." Berni reached a hand down to Gem who unwrapped herself enough to stand.

"On your feet." Jewell nodded to DJ who was blowing her nose on a shard of tissue, remnants of which dangled out of her back pocket.

DJ shook her head. "You're *serious*, aren't you?" The corners of her mouth twitched upwards as she took her place in the circle.

"All for one, one for all, no one harms us short or tall. Never let life get the best of you!" they yelled and high-fived each other. Amidst the clamor, Jewell shouted, "Radical Outsiders forever!"

Gem looked around self-consciously, a tight smile belying her concern.

"You guys are n-u-t-s." DJ grinned.

"You bet your sweet bippy, baby," Jewell said.

That night, alone in her bedroom, Berni reached her hand into the bottom drawer of the chest by her bed, fished through her socks and underwear until her fingers closed over the neck of the bottle. She cast a quick look at the door and the curtained window before sliding the vodka out of its hiding place. She sat on the edge of her bed, untwisted the lid with a practiced hand, and took a slow steadying breath before tilting the bottle to her lips.

Chapter 4

E-mails found their way back and forth across country into the smoke-filled flat across from the Berkeley Co-Op, the upstairs apartment with the Mississippi River view, the Midwestern cinder block co-ed university dorm, and all the way to the thatch-roofed youth hostel in Guatemala.

Dear R.O.s,

It's hot, wet, and green down here in Guatemala. The mosquitoes are the size of robins. People are friendly. The food is great. Haven't gotten sick even once, Berni. And the hostel even has internet service. We framed in a house yesterday. I got a splinter—good excuse to visit the medic. Her name is Shauna, and she's real cute. One month down, eleven to go. God bless,   DJ

Dahlings,

California is just too divine! The school is in an old warehouse down in the flatlands of Berkeley. It's a ten-minute hitch from my flat. People are so friendly. Everyone smokes weed. Gem, don't be rolling your eyes—wouldn't hurt you to loosen up some. Isn't it fab that our DJ is building houses for the underprivileged? What a little butch. More later, gotta fly. Love, love, love,   Jewell

Hello,

My roommate hates me. She calls me Nerdnina. That's okay. I dropped her foam hair rollers in the toilet, accidentally. My professors appreciate me and are encouraging me to send a calculus proof in to a professional math journal. Northwestern is a nice school. You should come visit for Homecoming. DJ watch out for those skeeters, you could get encephalitis. Jewell, you should stay away from that loco weed. It'll stunt your growth. Gem, where are you? Yours truly, Bernina

Dear Jewell, DJ, and Berni,
Some of us have lives and can't spend a lot of time playing on the computer and smoking marijuana. I live with a nice family in a house that overlooks the Mississippi River. I ride my bicycle into town for rehearsal every day. Well, on Sundays we perform, not rehearse. The Conductor smiled at me last week. I hope he's not a pervert. Berni, be careful. You're going to "accidentally" get yourself thrown out of the dorm before the first semester ends. Sincerely, Gem

Thanksgiving, Christmas, and New Years passed. DJ extended her commitment for a second year in Guatemala. Jewell landed the lead in a student film about a young woman with anorexia. During the summer, Berni 's roommate requested a change of rooms. And, as the fall season painted the Midwest in dazzling colors, Gem fell in love.

Hey you radical women,
Greetings from the Guat. Who would have thought almost two years would pass before we planned a reunion? Sorry I missed the holidays last year. Nurse Shauna couldn't be left in the village alone over a holiday, could she now? (Ha, ha) Miss ya. I look forward to turkey, dressing, cranberry sauce, and all that pie. Mmm. Do I have a surprise for you! Please note new e-mail address. See you in Nov. Peace, DJ

Dearests,
So, I'll drag myself away from rehearsals, but I won't eat mashed potatoes or pie for god sake! I'm now a size six and I plan to keep it that way. Contract just around the bend for an Indy. "B" film. It's a start, okay? So much to tell! Ciao, Jewell

Hello,
It was nice of your folks, DJ, to invite us all over there for Thanksgiving. I wonder if we've changed. Jewell, you sound skinny.

You're not anorexic are you? I have been very busy assisting two professors, and tutoring some students. I still don't have any friends, but that's okay. I still have you. Yours truly, Bernina

Hi you guys,

Guess what? I'm seeing somebody. Yeah! ME! He plays the trombone in the orchestra. He looks like Barney Fife, but he's very talented. Oh, and it turns out the Conductor is a pervert— he's gay! Can you believe it??? See you soon, Gem

Chapter 5

"What are you doing?" Berni gasped. She fanned the air around her. "Put that out. Are you crazy? Someone will smell it." She darted for the window, which was stuck.

"Berni, relax!" Jewell said from a footstool next to the bed. "It's just a joint." She chuckled as Berni banged the window frame with the side of her hand. "Anyway, I'd be more worried about gin on my breath if I were you."

"Pass that over here," DJ said, stretching out an arm out. She leaned against a pile of pillows at the head of her bed. Her childhood room remained a shrine to her dreams. The walls were covered with posters of tennis stars, basketball pros, and ice skaters—all women.

Gem was rocking faster now in the high-backed wooden rocker. Squeak-squeak, squeak-squeak. Her eyes were magnified behind the thick lenses she wore. For Gem, that was an improvement.

DJ handed the smoldering paper-wrapped herbal bundle to her. "Here, take the edge off," she said. She coughed, then giggled, and then coughed some more.

"Don't succumb to peer pressure, Gem," Berni called over her shoulder. *Whack* went her hand against the window frame one last time.

Gem's big blue saucer eyes turned themselves on her cousin.

"Go for it, babe," Jewell said, as she reached for a brownie from the plate that Jeanette had sent upstairs with the girls after dinner.

Gem took a big puff of smoke and swallowed it with a mouthful of air. Jewell giggled and nibbled the corners off her brownie.

Berni was sitting on the floor now, back against the wall, inhaling whatever fresh air she could that wafted up from under the door.

111

"You could pass those brownies, you know," she said to Jewell.

"So, tell us your big news, DJ," Jewell said and handed the plate to Berni. DJ had a sappy smile on her face.

Gem had stopped rocking and, with wide pupils, was staring at her feet. "I've lost them," she muttered to no one in particular.

DJ cleared her throat. "Well, I've written to you about the village nurse, Shauna," she said, looking at each face. "We're in love. In fact, we sort of got married last Christmas. Well, at least we exchanged rings." The words tumbled out of her mouth. "I was going to write you all, but, it's not the kind of thing you put on a postcard," she said, looking from face to face.

"I for one am delighted for you and hope you're blissfully happy," said Jewell. "Half the students in my school are gay. I have no problem with this." She stood up, leaned over the bed and gave DJ a hug, knocking their heads together in the fervor of her embrace.

"Ow, geez! Thanks, I guess," DJ chuckled, rubbing her head. "I wasn't sure how you'd all be with this."

Berni, as if lost in a thick fog, shook her head and squinted her eyes. "You're what?" her pitch was an octave higher than usual.

"Love is a gift from God," Gem muttered from across the room.

"I'm gay, Berni, and I'm in love," DJ spoke slowly, patiently.

"Do your parents know this? Does the church know? I mean, how did this happen? This is—this is—completely unacceptable," Berni said.

"Berni, I've known since the second grade," DJ said. "I just didn't know what it was I knew, or what to do about it."

A strangling sound escaped Berni's throat.

"Hey, hey, what d'ya say, DJ and Shauna are gay," Gem chanted then laughed hysterically. All eyes turned to Gem who was finding herself most entertaining.

"Should we do something about her?" Berni asked Jewell who shrugged her shoulders and turned back to DJ.

"*Do* your parents know, DJ?" Jewell asked.

"Of course they don't know—they're acting as happy and gracious as ever," Berni answered for her.

"I was going to tell them," DJ paused.

"Like you were *going* to tell us?" Berni said, incensed.

"Look, you guys don't know this," DJ began.

"Oh, god, not more. I can't hear any more surprises," Berni said dramatically.

"My mom has cancer," DJ said quietly. A tear slid down her cheek and she wiped at it with the back of her hand. "She's starting chemotherapy after the holidays."

"What?" Berni, Jewell, and Gem cried in unison.

"Dad said she's not supposed to have any stress. I told him about Shauna and me two nights ago. I think he already knew, at least he didn't seem surprised," she said, pausing to blow her nose. "He said I should just go back to the village and not say a word about it to her, or anyone, because the stress of it could kill her."

The only sound in the room was Gem's intermittent hiccups.

"Geez, DJ," Jewell said, "I'm so sorry." She crawled up on the bed, laid her hand on DJ's leg and patted it softly.

Gem wobbled over to the bed, curled up at the end and began to weep. "That's the saddest thing I've ever heard," she sobbed.

Even Berni, who sat now on the edge of the mattress, sighed heavily and shook her head. "What are we going to do?" she asked.

In those six words, she cemented the bond they'd had since childhood. What happened to one, happened to all. No one suffered, or celebrated, alone.

DJ cried loudly now, without restraint, encircled by her sisters.

Chapter 6

Back in the Midwest, Berni shoveled snow from the front steps of her new apartment. At twenty-two, the prospect of spending her last college Christmas in an empty dorm was about as appealing as cold spaghetti. The Fowlers were spending the holidays in Florida checking in on Berni's ninety-seven year old grandmother who had slipped on a banana peel and broken her hip. Berni's first thought upon hearing the news was, *what a cliché*.

From the curb, a massive blue figure ambled its way up the sidewalk. The postman, swathed in layers of shirt, sweater, coat, and scarf, overlapping pairs of gloves, and a snow hat under his parka hood, fumbled in his pouch for a small stack of mail bound with a rubber band.

"Hey," Berni said, nodding a hello.

He mumbled something beneath the scarf wrapped around his mouth and nose, handed her the bundle, turned and waddled back down the sidewalk.

Berni leaned the shovel against the aluminum siding, stomped snow off her boots, and went inside. On top of the pile was a postcard from Jewell, with big letters on a hillside spelling out Hollywood. Berni smiled and shook her head. "This must be good," she mused as she turned the card over. "Jewell has never sent a postcard."

Dear Gem, Berni, and DJ,

June 1—come home. No questions, just be there, okay? Remember the old Hollenbeck place on the edge of town? I'm buying it. See you in June.   Jewell

Berni's hand fell to her side, her snowy mitten blurring the ink as the card dropped to the carpet. "Something is terribly wrong," she said aloud to no one. "Jewell wouldn't just move back home."

The postcard was lying on the dining room table when DJ walked in. The air conditioning felt great. Shauna had teased her mercilessly about her romantic attachment to being *nouveau poor* and living in the hostel, until she caved in. The condominium was a good idea.

She read the card as she walked toward the kitchen. "Hey babe, it looks like Jewell is going to become a real estate mogul. Did you read this?"

Shauna wiped floured hands on her apron, threw her arms around DJ and planted a big kiss on her lips. "Hi, gorgeous. Jewell sent a postcard?" She took the card. "Why do you suppose she's buying back home? Thought she'd gone all Hollywood on you. Sounds mysterious." She walked back over to the counter and punched down a rounded lump of dough. A warm yeasty fragrance filled the kitchen.

"That's Jewell for you, always dramatic. Guess the prices in California are too high. We're invited to help her move in." She pinched off a fragment of dough and popped it in her mouth.

"Honey, you know I can't get away in June now that I'm head of the immunization clinic at the hospital. You'll just have to do the grunt work without me," she said, faking a sigh of regret.

DJ came up behind her, wrapped her arms around her, and nuzzled her hair. "I don't know, babe, we haven't been apart for more than a day since we met." She breathed in Shauna's fragrance mixed with the scent of rising bread.

"I guess this is make it or break it then, huh?" Shauna turned to her and nibbled her earlobe.

"Mmm, I like the 'make it' part," DJ said, smiling as her body went warm and melty.

"Mom, Dad, we've already decided. Harley and I are moving to Chicago in June. He's been offered a position in the orchestra, and I can pick up some teaching jobs," Gem said with more enthusiasm than she felt.

"Gem, dear, listen to what you're saying," her mother simpered into the phone. "You're giving up your life, your career for some man you've known less than *two years*," she continued in a voice full of desperation.

"Emma, the girl's obviously in love," Gem's father offered from the extension in the bedroom.

"Thank you, Daddy," Gem said, truly grateful for the ally. "I know you two want me to have a career, and I will—I'm not giving up on that." Fortified by her father's support, she sounded more convincing now. "It's just that I can't imagine my life without Harley, and *he's* moving to Chicago."

"Has *he* asked you to marry him yet?" her mother's voice was sharp. "You know what they say about buying the cow when you can get the milk for free. Men just want…"

"Oh, there's the doorbell." *Saved by the cliché*, she said to herself, and smiled. "Gotta go. Call you later. Love you, bye." With that, she hung up, trundled down the stairs, and headed for the door. "Mothers!" she said through a loud expulsion of breath.

"Hi, Ginger," Gem said, greeting the neighbor who was standing outside the door holding several letters that she jabbed at Gem.

"It's the new carrier," Ginger said. "He can't seem to get it right. Here's your mail." She wagged the letters at Gem. "Bonnie brought mine over from across the street," she said in a voice full of exasperation.

"Yeah," Gem tried to match her level of irritation, "and they keep raising the price of stamps," she whined. For good measure she added, "It's so unfair." She took the mail from Ginger, who turned in a huff and headed back across the lawn.

Gem leaned against the banister and sorted through the mail. She left the household bills for the landlord on top of the television, and took her bills and a postcard back up to her garret. She folded herself into the overstuffed chair by the window and studied the Hollywood sign on the front of the card for a moment. She couldn't remember the last time she'd gotten a postcard from anyone.

"Hollywood," she harrumphed. Her cousin, the star. Jewell always had to do things big, always had to make an impression, be the center of attention as far back as Gem could remember. She thought about those stupid plays in the Watson's back yard when they were kids. Gem would be assigned the role of a dog, or a chicken, or even once, a tree.

She turned the card over. *June 1—come home*. Just like that. Snap her fingers and we're all supposed to drop whatever we're doing and cater to her wishes. Not this time! June first, she was moving to Chicago—with a *man*. She couldn't wait to tell Jewell.

Hello,

I was out shoveling SNOW in front of my NEW APARTMENT when Jewell's card arrived. I bet it never snows in Hollywood. I can't wait to see you all again in June. Jewell, what's wrong? Why are you doing this? Hope you all have a good Christmas. I'm staying here. My grandmother broke her hip. DJ, how are you doing since your Mom's death? I'm sorry you missed the funeral. Bernina

Hey Jewell, Berni, Gem,

This will be great! Your own home, Jewell? Color me jealous. Shauna can't get away, but sends her love. I'll be there with lavender bells on and all my butch muscle (smile). We're fine down here. Thinking about moving back to the States next year. I miss my Dad. He's pretty lonely without Mom. Congrats on your new apartment Berni— you were gettin' too old for the dorms anyway (chuckle). See you soon. Love, DJ

Dear Jewell, DJ, and Berni,

How very nice for you Jewell, that you're buying a house. I'm sure that shows how successful your career in Hollywood has been. As much as I'd like to celebrate your success and see everyone, I'm tied up in June. Harley and I are moving to Chicago. He has a very important job offer and just won't consider it unless I go with him. Isn't love wonderful? Maybe we can all get together again when DJ and Shauna come home for the holidays. Berni, why would you think something was wrong? Jewell lives a charmed life, right? My very best to all, Gem

A week later, Gem opened her e-mail to find a message from her cousin. She sat stunned, staring at the computer screen. Moments later she was on the phone with Harley.

Chapter 7

The moving van was an empty cavern parked on the cross street of Mill Lane, the ramp left hanging like a dry tongue. Inside the bungalow, Jewell sat on the plush blue sofa in a shaft of light, wrapped in a pale green floor-length satin dressing gown—regal as always—and directed traffic.

"That one goes in the bedroom," she said, pointing DJ down the hall. Bodies hauling boxes, furniture crammed in the living room, piles of clothes, and dishes stacked on the kitchen counter were the first breath of life the cottage had seen in more than a year. The doors and windows were thrown open to the early afternoon sun and breeze that helped chase away a lingering scent of mildew and neglect.

Crash. The splintering sound of glass fragmenting was followed by Berni's muttered, "Damn!" Jewell pressed her lips together. Glasses weren't important. Friends were important, friends who showed up. She reached up and readjusted the silk scarf that turbaned her head. Her scalp itched, her body ached, and she wanted nothing more desperately than a nap.

"Okay, I'll see you in a week," Gem said into the phone hanging on the wall just inside the kitchen. She turned her face to the wall, and made a small kissing sound into the receiver and giggled.

"Harley wishes you well," Gem said to her cousin.

"I hope I get to meet Harley before—well, I hope I get to meet him," Jewell said and covered her mouth for a yawn.

"You look like you could use some sleep," Gem said. "DJ, how's the bedroom coming? Got a place to sleep yet?" she hollered down the hall.

DJ strolled into the living room with a self-satisfied smile on her face. With her right hand, she grabbed her left elbow, making the first half of a human chair, and nodded to Gem who did the same.

"Oh, no!" Jewell cried in mock horror, "you'll drop me for sure."

With a square seat made by interlocking arms, DJ said, "Madam, your carriage awaits." They dipped low so Jewell could fit her slight form on to be hoisted off to the bedroom.

With an arm around each neck for support, Jewell squeezed her eyes shut and gritted her teeth against the wave of pain that seared through her and the nausea that clawed at her belly. Gem and DJ locked eyes briefly, took a deep breath and moved as gently as possible down the hall with their precious cargo.

Berni, leaning against the kitchen arch, wiped at a tear when they were safely past, and stopped her thoughts from wandering too far into the future. She had just finished putting pots and pans on the lower shelf of the cupboard when DJ and Gem returned from the bedroom. DJ motioned her into the living room.

Gem was perched on a box marked *books and scripts*. She traced the letters with her finger. DJ cleared off a corner of the sofa and sat with legs splayed. Berni moved aside a pile of towels and sat on the edge of a recliner. Hesitation had its own presence—it perched on the footstool in the center of their triangle. Jewell had always been the one who knew what to do next. DJ cleared her throat, readying herself to speak. The other two glanced at her, but no words were forthcoming. A muffled *tic, tic, tic, tic* from deep inside a box near the hallway was the only sound for a long moment. Gem bit at her cuticle.

"Okay," Berni barked. DJ and Gem both jumped, and hesitancy vanished in a pouf of invisible smoke. "The Watsons said she qualifies for Hospice care, so we know she has less than a year left." There. Someone had said it. Jewell was dying.

"Here's what I propose," she continued, very much in charge now. Gem dabbed at her bleeding cuticle with a dirty tissue from her pocket. DJ studied her boots, her face grim.

"We take turns, a month at a time. We'll stay here and be the caretakers until—well, until she needs more than we can provide." Berni sunk back into the recliner. Leadership had used up the last of her life force energy.

"I'll go first," DJ said. "I've wanted to spend some time with Dad,

119

and staying makes more sense than flying back and forth."

"I'll take the second shift," Gem offered. "It will give Harley and me time to get settled in Chicago." Her voice was matter of fact.

Berni opened her mouth to speak, but instead began shaking with deep grief-filled sobs. She pulled her legs up and huddled in a fetal position in the oversized recliner like a lost child.

DJ moved to the arm of the chair and sat stroking Berni's back, her own tears now falling helplessly down her cheeks. Gem stood close behind DJ with her hands on DJ's shoulders, offering comfort once removed to Berni. Her lip quivered and she sniffed repeatedly.

"Hey now," DJ said softly. "We're going to be okay, right? All for one and one for all, huh?" she said soothingly. With her free hand, she wiped tears from her neck.

"You both..." Berni struggled, "you both *have* someone. Someone waiting for you at home, someone to love you," she managed through her sobs.

DJ smoothed the ragged bangs from Berni's forehead and made soft shushing sounds as if coddling an overtired infant.

"You three are all I have," she wailed now, "and I can't afford to lose even one of you." Her sobs rippled through DJ and by extension Gem, linked together in misery and despair.

Chapter 8

"I don't know about this Tennessee Williams guy," DJ said as she closed the book. "You played Blanche, huh?"

"And a damned site better job of it than you." Jewell gave a weak chuckle. "The subtleties of the southern vamp are lost on you, girlfriend."

DJ grinned. She had read the whole play aloud, slipping in and out of character. It was the most fun Jewell had had in months.

"I've noticed something, my f-r-i-e-n-d," Jewell said as she placed her dry, pale hand on DJ's. "You haven't spelled anything for a really long time. What's that about?" she asked.

"Yeah. I told Shauna I used to do that. She said she hadn't noticed. That's when I realized I hadn't spelled anything since I came out to you guys that Thanksgiving." She blushed and glanced at Jewell through her thick eyelashes.

Jewell smiled and nodded. "You're only as sick as your secrets, right?" She gave DJ's hand a little squeeze.

"I guess," DJ said looking down at her hand covered by Jewell's. "In service of being really healthy then, I should tell you I had a crush on you when we were kids." She dared a glance at Jewell.

"Well, DJ, I'm honored," Jewell said, leaning her head back against the pillows on the couch. "Back then I was so self-involved, I thought everyone was in love with me. I'm sorry you had to go through that time all alone. We just didn't know."

"That means a lot, thanks. I didn't really understand it myself for a long time," DJ said. She stood up. "You up for a cup of tea?" she asked.

121

"You know, I think I need a nap. I'm dead tired," Jewell said. She noticed the crestfallen look that rearranged DJ's face. "God, DJ, lighten up—it's just an expression," she tried for playful.

DJ looked out the window for a moment.

"Okay, I'm sorry," Jewell said. "That was tacky. Look, why don't you swing by your Dad's for a while? I'll be fine here by myself. Really."

"Your Mom's bringing some homemade chicken soup over later." DJ gave an exaggerated smack of lips. "I'll be back for dinner. Need anything before I go?"

Jewell shook her head. She adjusted her turban, pulled the duvet up under her chin, and was asleep before DJ reached the door.

Daniel Barnhall was sitting motionless in the rocker looking out the plate glass window onto a patch of zinnias. The brightly colored flowers with their bushy heads brought him no joy. His face was a study of either deep thought or an empty mind. They looked the same on him.

DJ stood at the archway of the living room for a moment feeling as though she'd just walked into a Norman Rockwell painting. She would have entitled it, Widower Remembers.

Unaware that she'd just emitted a deep sigh, she caught her father's expression as he snapped his head around to face her. Grief.

"DJ, I didn't hear you come in," he said, rearranging his expression.

DJ walked over to the rocker, bent over and kissed him on his unshaven cheek.

"Hi Pop. Thought I'd keep you company a while so Jewell can catch a nap," she said, and settled on the sofa. "The garden looks real good," she said, and tasted her own tears somewhere in the back of her mouth.

"Hmmm," her father said with a slight nod. "So, how is Jewell today?" he asked. "What a shame," he said heavily. "Such a young thing to be facing this. Lucky to have friends like you girls to see her through..." his voice cracked.

"Dad," DJ said, suddenly feeling shy and awkward. She didn't know how to approach this.

Daniel regarded his daughter.

"Dad, you know I wanted to come home and be with Mom that last month. I would have. I could have gotten away. It just seemed..." she faltered.

"Did it seem as though I didn't want you here?" her father finished her thought. DJ dropped her head.

"Dani Jean, it all happened so fast. After the chemotherapy, she just sort of collapsed. Didn't want anyone to see her. She'd lost all that weight." His voice caught, and he took a deep, ragged breath.

"Couldn't handle losing her hair, her eyebrows, even her lashes. Said no one could understand. She just wanted to be remembered as..." Daniel's sobs shook his shoulders and his tears fell freely. He made a weak gesture with his hands.

DJ stood next to the rocker and put her arms around him. Her tears trickled into his hair. "Yeah, Jewell's having a rough time with that too," she said.

"And that whole thing about you and Shauna. You were so happy," he spoke through his sobs. "She just couldn't have handled it, honey. I couldn't do that to either of you." He turned his face up to meet hers. "I'm sorry, Dani Jean."

"I thought I'd die when I couldn't get back for the funeral," DJ said into her father's wet eyes. "What a time for an airport lock-down, huh?" she said with a weak smile. "Cards were just sort of stacked against us, it seemed."

Daniel extracted a white linen handkerchief from his pocket and blew his nose. He wiped his tears with a clean corner and shook his head slowly.

"I guess that's one of the reasons I wanted to be here for Jewell—kinda be part of it in a way that I couldn't for Mom," DJ said. An impulse hit her like a punch in the gut. DJ sat back down on the sofa, hard.

"Dad, I've got to go out for a while. You want me to stop by after dinner?"

"Let's make it tomorrow, honey. I brought some work home that I should try to get to tonight. And, I think I'll turn in early. Feel kind of spent, if you know what I mean." He turned a wan smile her way.

"Lunch tomorrow? My treat," DJ said. She kissed him goodbye and headed out the door.

It was five o'clock when she let herself back in through the bungalow's kitchen door. Her mouth watered at the aroma that filled the room, smells of comfort and childhood. A big aluminum pot of homemade chicken soup was sitting on the stove and a loaf of freshly baked bread, still warm, was wrapped in a cotton napkin on the counter.

She tiptoed down the hall and swung into the bathroom for a quick check in the mirror. She gave an extra tuck to the bright silk scarf wound around her head, and chuckled softly.

Her tap on the bedroom door was answered with, "I'm awake—come in."

The late afternoon sun streamed in through the windows, a shaft of light bathed the slight form in the double bed.

"You just missed Mo… Oh! My God! What have you done?" Jewell squealed, pulling herself to a sitting position against the head of the bed. Her mouth hung open.

DJ grinned. With one hand, she deftly pulled the corner of the scarf and unwound the turban to reveal a head shaved bald as a light bulb. "Thought you might like some company," she said grinning even more broadly.

Chapter 9

Jewell stopped believing in miracles some time ago, but her faith was returning as she sat against her plumped up Laura Ashley pillows and observed her cousin through adult eyes.

"The house isn't much," Gem offered, "but it's ours. Who would have thought I'd be living in the burbs, huh?" she laughed.

Gem's pale white hair from childhood was now strawberry blonde, and permed into a soft halo of curls that teased at her shoulders, which time, self-confidence, and a few years of physical therapy had pulled back, revealing a small but perky bust line.

"Who would have thought, indeed," Jewell echoed, but the comment was more a reflection of her observations. Over the years, Gem had picked up a trick or two about cosmetics. Her lightly penciled in brows arched with expression as she spoke. The blush of rose in her cheeks was only partially due to make-up.

"I'm really happy with Harley." Her voice was that of a child on Christmas morning.

All that energy was an infusion of life, and Jewell noticed hunger for the first time in days. She smiled and said, "What are the chances we could have cinnamon rolls and tea?"

Gem lit up. "You mean like when we were kids and I'd stay overnight? Aunt Euella made the *best* cinnamon rolls ever," she chattered on as she bounced off the bed and headed for the kitchen. "Hope packaged are okay. I still haven't learned to cook," she called back over her shoulder.

Jewell smiled. She didn't remember enjoying their childhood cousin-ship as much as Gem did. All those years wasted, she reflected.

Later, happily sated by liberally iced cinnamon rolls, green tea, and the yeasty aroma of baked goods comfortably filling the house, the cousins lounged on opposite ends of the bed.

"I used to envy you, you know," Gem confided, tracing patterns on the quilt with her little finger.

"I know," Jewell said.

"You always got everything you wanted."

"I did. It's true."

"You were the talented one, you were the pretty one," Gem's voice held a hint of whine.

Jewell remembered being the shining star. "Guess those days have changed, huh?" she said with attempted humor.

"What? Oh, God no. I didn't mean…" Gem stammered.

"Hey, it's okay," Jewell interrupted. "You had a hard time as a kid," her own eyes now fixed on the quilt. "I never knew what to say to you," she said in nearly a whisper.

"Yeah, being called rat-face wasn't a whole lot of fun." Gem could feel her eyes moisten. She would not cry and spoil her opportunity to say the words once, and for all. "But, Zotto—that was the worst." Gem tried to go on but she was stuck, hung up in a memory that put a shadow across her face, a face that had turned, if not beautiful, certainly distinctive and gentle over the years.

"I always wondered about that," Jewell reminisced. "I remember you transferred over to Miss Bethel because Zotto kept bumping you or something. I mean, I know you were sensitive and all, but…"

At the same moment, the cousins looked up into each other's eyes. Tears rimmed Gems, and a trickle of mascara began sliding down her cheek.

"Jesus," Jewell intoned, "that wasn't all he did, was it?" She slumped against her pillow and let out a long slow sigh. "Aw, Gem…" she reached out a hand to her cousin who sat shaking with silent tears.

Like a small child, Gem crawled up the bed and nestled her head in Jewell's lap and for the first time ever sobbed about the loss of her childhood innocence.

"I was so ashamed, I couldn't tell anyone," she cried as Jewell ran a soothing hand through the curls and made soft sounds of concern.

"It's going to be okay, Gem." Jewell patted her shoulder gently. "It's all going to be okay now, I promise," she said over Gem's

126

hiccups.

Gem's sobbing subsided. She blew her nose and shifted around so that she was sitting next to Jewell, sharing her pillow.

"How?" Gem said after a moment of silence. "How can it ever be okay?" she said and wiped at the smear of eye make-up with a tissue and regarded the brown wetness before wadding the tissue up and throwing it angrily across the room.

"Because that predator is still giving cello lessons to innocent little girls, is how." Jewell's eyes blazed. She could feel the old fight creep back into her bones. "Hand me my boa," she said, pointing at the ratty old string of feathers draped over one corner of her mirror. "I've got to think."

Gem, confused but obedient, walked across the room and liberated the boa. Loose feathers drifted to the floor along with a sprinkling of dust as Gem gave it a quick shake.

She wrapped it gently around her cousin's frail shoulders, and then sat back down on the side of the bed to wait out Jewell's silent pondering. Moments passed with only the tick of the clock marking time.

"Okay, here it is," Jewell said. "We're taking him to court!" She whomped a fist down on the mattress beside her, startling Gem.

"Huh?" Gem uttered, her jaw dropped.

"Well, not exactly *we*. I can't make it to the bathroom by myself. But *you* are taking him to court, by God," she proclaimed.

By the end of the month, with Jewell's coaching, Gem had gathered testimonies from three of Mr. Zotto's former music students. She had met with their parents, obtained an attorney who agreed to represent them *pro bono,* and was at this very moment filing the proper papers to have Samuel Zotto arrested on four accounts of child endangerment to get around the statute of limitations.

"Better than nothing," Gem said, as she perched on the side of the bed. "He'll wind up serving time for sure." She looked strong, powerful, and self-satisfied.

"Alright!" Jewell raised a weak hand in the feeblest high-five Gem had ever witnessed, but it was full of love and support.

"Couldn't have done it without you," she said grinning at Jewell.

"All for one and one for all. No one harms you short or tall, right?" Jewell said.

"I'm so glad Harley is in your life. Someone has to keep an eye on you, take over where I leave off." Her eyes moistened with affection.

"Jewell, don't say that," Gem's voice caught, and her own eyes welled up. She squeezed the small, dry hand gently.

"No use pretending, cousin dear. I'm not going to last a whole lot longer." Indeed, she seemed to wilt a little more as each day went by.

"When is Berni due?" she asked through a yawn a few days later.

"We're picking her up at the airport at six this evening," Gem said.

Jewell managed a soft smile as her eyes closed and sleep overtook her.

Gem leaned over and placed a kiss on her cheek. "I love you," she whispered. She hadn't known she needed it, but she realized Jewell had blessed her relationship with Harley, and she was grateful.

Chapter 10

"Oh, I know I should get back over there and visit that poor girl," Berni's mother said over her shoulder as she fussed about the living room, "but I just can't seem to bring myself to it. Does she look real bad?" she asked Gem who sat nibbling at the cheesecake Mrs. Fowler had foisted on them when they returned from the airport.

"Bernina, honey, I put your suitcase in your old room. You can unpack later," she called up the stairs. "So, *does* she?" she asked once more.

"Not much of the old Jewell left," Gem said softly. "Just skin and bones. I think she's been waiting for Berni to come home."

"Well, isn't that sweet," she answered mindlessly as she rearranged a doily on top of the television set. She picked at invisible lint on her skirt.

Berni clumped down the stairs, suitcase in hand. The years that had been kind to Gem, gently molding her into dignified womanhood, seemed to have neglected Berni. She hunkered her five-foot, eleven and seven-eighth inch frame into the barrel chair next to the couch. Her mother slipped behind her, and hooked her limp brown hair behind each ear, patted her on the shoulders and said, "Sit up straight, dear."

A vertical crease appeared between Berni's eyebrows as she unhooked the hair that fell flatly forward again. "Mother, I'm not staying here, remember? I'm staying with Jewell. That's why I've come back, to help out."

Her mother's petulance was diverted when Gem stood and said, "We'd better be on our way. Thanks, Mrs. Fowler, for the cheesecake."

"Bernina, will you be home for supper?"

"Mother..." impatience tightened her voice.

"Well, for goodness sake, I hope you plan on spending *some* time with your father and me this month," she said with a sulk.

As she stood, Berni accidentally knocked over a china figurine of a mother and child that sat on the coffee table. It hit the floor with a satisfying *clink,* and the mother's head tumbled under the couch. The irony was not lost on Berni.

"Oh, Bernina!" Nina's voice was full of exasperation, "Will you watch where you're going, please? Still just a bull in a china shop, aren't you," she *tsked.*

"I'll call you when I get settled in over there," Berni said, bolting out the door.

Berni heaved herself into the back seat and as the car pulled away from the curb, she muttered through clenched teeth, "God, that woman drives me crazy!"

"Berni," Gem turned a gleeful smile towards her, "I don't think I've ever heard you speak up for yourself like that." She reached an arm through the bucket seat opening and patted Berni's sturdy knee. "Way to go, girl," she said.

Berni's grin was lopsided and toothy. "Therapy," was all she said.

Later that evening after Gem had said her tearful good-byes, made promises to come right back if she was needed, waved and blew kisses, Berni stood next to the bed holding a tureen of warm chicken broth.

She nudged the spoon against Jewell's lips. "Just a couple spoonfuls," she said gently. The darkening circles under Jewell's eyes, eyes that seemed to fall back into their sockets, brought waves of grief to her heart.

Propped up and braced by a collection of brightly colored pillows, Jewell managed a wan smile as she waved away the soup.

"Berni," she rasped in a paper-thin voice, "do you remember when you said we were all you had?" She stopped to take a slow, shallow breath. "And you couldn't stand to lose any of us?"

"Yeah." Berni set the bowl on the nightstand and lowered herself carefully onto the edge of the mattress. She fixed her eyes on Jewell's nose, the only thing that seemed familiar about her face.

"Berni, when I'm gone..." she noticed tears streaking down Berni's cheeks. "Hey, it's okay," she said soothingly, reaching out for the large paw of a hand that lie fisted on the quilt. Berni wrapped her hand around Jewell's, sniffed, and cleared her throat.

"Yeah," Berni said, looking away for a moment.

"When I'm gone, I want you to have my boa. It would mean so much to me," she tried for a deep breath, "to know a piece of me was with you always."

At that, Berni's shoulders heaved and great sobs rolled up from her chest. "I've always loved you," she cried. "I'm going to miss you so very much." She turned and pulled Jewell's slight frame into a bearish embrace.

Aware of a muffled sound, she quickly released Jewell and gingerly settled her against the pillows. "Oh, God, did I hurt you?" She gently stroked Jewell's hair away from her face.

"No," Jewell chuckled, "you surprised me. I don't think you've ever put your feelings into words like that." For a moment, the old sparkle was in her eyes and Berni bathed in it.

"Therapy," she said with a grin as she wiped tears from her eyes. She grabbed a tissue from the nightstand and blew her nose. "And recovery," she said quietly.

"Recovery? Berni, I had no idea. I'm so proud of you." Jewell's voice sounded stronger now, almost conversational.

"Yeah, I was pretty miserable for a while there. Found myself going to the faculty parties just for the free alcohol. Teaching math is not as exciting as you might think," she said.

Jewell managed a chuckle.

"In recovery, we learn to take responsibility for our lives, to admit the things we can't change, and change the things we can..." she counted off, tapping each finger. "While I'm here, I need to make some amends."

"That's sort of like an apology?" Jewell asked. Her head swam with all the incidents from Berni's childhood that might merit an amends. It seemed she was always striking out in anger.

"Yeah, without making excuses. You remember Mr. Warren's cornfield?"

"The one that burned down that summer?" Jewell asked. "He figured it was a vagrant camping out in the field—they do that sometimes, you know."

"Nope," said Berni.

"Oh, Berni, you didn't! Sweet Jesus!" she gasped.

"I know that was real stupid. I was so angry with Mary Day. She was always putting me down, shoving me, laughing at me," her stomach churned with the memory.

"Mary Day was an idiot," Jewell said, rising to Berni's defense.

"True," Berni said, "But burning down her father's cornfield wasn't exactly an appropriate expression of my frustration with the little twit," she said with a sheepish smile.

Jewell considered the scandal that could result. "Berni, Mr. Warren could have you put in jail."

"He could. It would be his right. Hope he doesn't. But taking the consequences for my behavior will make me a better person in the long run." She shrugged off her fear.

"Berni, you're a better person in the short run," Jewell said, opening her arms for a hug, into which Berni moved with great caution. "Now, how about some of that soup?" she said.

Two weeks later, the sun filtered through the living room window and pooled at Jewell's satin-slippered feet. Berni had carried her like a fragile family heirloom to the sofa where she sat enthroned among pillows and blankets, and wrapped in her feathered boa. A light blush of color seemed to have returned to her cheeks and her spirits were high.

"So, what did he say?" she asked of Berni who was arranging a tray of tea and cucumber sandwiches on the coffee table.

"He said he's spent years paying for his daughter's arrogance. 'Takes after her mother, don't you know,' he said," Berni imitated Mr. Warren's deep bass voice.

"No way," Jewell said in disbelief. "He's not going to prosecute?"

"Huh uh. In fact, he thanked me for my strength of character, coming forward after all these years. And, I probably shouldn't tell you this..." she paused.

Jewell leaned forward. "Don't stop now, you're on a roll," she said.

"He said 'we recovery folks have to support each other.' You can't tell anyone that, okay? Promise?" Berni asked.

"I'll take it to my grave," Jewell joked.

"Geez, will you stop making death references?" Berni still paled at the gallows humor Jewell often used to cope with her pending death.

"Sorry," Jewell grinned at her childhood friend. She sipped her tea and reached for a triangular wedge of sandwich, noting the crusts had been removed, just the way she liked it. "Berni, I'm so glad you're here," she said.

Then, without warning, she lurched forward, grabbing her stomach with one hand, bracing herself on the table with the other. "Oh!" was all she managed, as a sweat broke over her body and a waxy pallor replaced the color in her cheeks.

"Jewell!" Berni leaped out of her chair, knocking slices of cucumber and wedges of bread to the floor. She knelt before Jewell, patting her hand, looking up into eyes squeezed shut in sudden pain. "Oh god, I'm calling the doctor," she said, struggling to her feet.

"No, wait," Jewell whispered. "It's passing." She reached out for Berni's hand. "Don't call the doctor just yet, Berni. Help me back into bed, okay?" Her voice was a wispy shaft of wheat blowing in the breeze.

With great effort, she leaned back against the couch taking long, slow breaths. Berni unwrapped the boa from around Jewell's neck. One end had fallen into her teacup and the feathers dripped a pattern of dots on the sofa next to her.

Berni peeled back the layers of blankets, and without effort lifted the wraith-like form and carried her gently to the back bedroom. Her eyes never left Jewell's face as she eased her onto the bed, fluffed the pillows, and tucked her in.

"Berni, I think it's time to call the others," Jewell said in a stronger voice now. "Then my family, then the doctor, and Hospice—if that's something you could do for me?"

All efficiency, Berni thought. It was like organizing a dinner party. Call the caterer, the florist, and oh, yes, the... In one ghastly moment, Berni realized she was feeling angry—angry, helpless, and out of control. Jewell was dying.

"Of course I will," she said through the flood of tears washing over her cheeks. "Oh, Jewell, I'm so sorry," she managed before sobs overtook her.

Chapter 11

The twenty-six candles illuminated the room, bathing each face gathered around the bed in a halo of light. Through heavy lashes, Jewell regarded those who surrounded her, believing them to be angels waiting to shepherd her to the next plane. Her smile was beatific as her last breath rattled forth, freeing itself from its cage of bones and skin.

Clasped hands tightened around the circle. Mrs. Watson wept quietly. Her husband gave her hand a gentle squeeze, his own tears falling softly. The Hospice nurse, a pagan at heart, said a prayer to the Goddess for safe passage as Jewell had requested.

Across the circle, DJ, Gem, and Berni regarded each other with tearful eyes and soft smiles, each lost in their own thoughts and memories.

"The circle is open, but unbroken," intoned the nurse. "We meet, we part, we meet again. Blessed be."

The next few moments were full of awkward hugs and mumbled words of support. Each one in turn stepped forward to place a kiss on Jewell's forehead.

Her mother lingered a moment, smoothing the hair back from the face of her daughter. "How very brave you were, my little girl," she whispered. She turned to her husband who held her close. "What do we do now?" she murmured.

"The kids have asked for some time alone with her," he said. "I think it's what she would have wanted." He thanked the nurse for her care and guidance through the last few months, and walked his wife down the hall to the living room. The coroner would have to be called, but all in due time.

Mrs. Watson was making a pot of coffee when DJ slipped into the kitchen, removed a package from the refrigerator, and a bag from the table. They nodded at each other. DJ winked then and flashed a mischievous grin.

"What are you girls up to?" she asked. Then, "No, never mind. None of my business."

"It's a club thing," DJ said and vanished back down the hall.

Gem pulled the well-chilled bottle of champagne out of the bag.

"This is so sacrilegious," Berni said as DJ closed the bedroom door behind her.

"Yup," DJ said, giving her an eye-crinkling smile.

"Irreverent to the end." Berni grinned as she unpacked the plastic cups.

DJ spread the Ritz crackers on a plate. "And here we have the holy sacrament," she said.

"Okay, now here's the truly bizarre part," Gem said, reading the list of her last wishes Jewell had left for them. "We've got to prop her up in the bed and wrap that stupid boa around her before we do the toast."

"You've got to be kidding," Berni protested.

"You ain't seen nothin' yet," Gem said with a shake of her head.

Gently, Gem and Berni lifted their dearly departed friend to a sitting position, propped up at the head of the bed with pillows.

POP! went the champagne cork and Berni yelped. "Sorry," she offered. "I'm just a little jumpy. I've never been to a party quite like this."

Berni, keeper of the sacred boa, wrapped it around Jewell's shoulders. "I can't believe she's making us do this," she muttered.

"No one is making us do anything," DJ said, as she poured champagne into the plastic cups and passed them around. Berni opened a can of Ginger Ale. The plate of Ritz sat on the end of the bed.

DJ cleared her throat. "I now call the last official meeting of the Radical Outsiders to order," she said. "We will dispense with the reading of the minutes, since it's been over a decade. I call upon Gem to lead us in the secret chant." She nodded to Gem who stepped forward and raised her glass.

"This is a toast to our sister, our leader, our friend," Gem said as tears began to trickle down her cheeks.

They all raised their glasses and turned to regard Jewell, regally draped in her boa, for the last time.

"All for one and one for all. No one harms us short or tall," they chanted. Glasses were clicked. The Champaign and Ritz were consumed, and there was a festive feeling to the room. The candles could have been lighting up a birthday party as easily as a wake.

With great ceremony, Berni carefully lifted the feathered boa from Jewell's shoulders, and together they eased her back down into the bed. The quilt was pulled up under her chin, and she looked like a sleepy child tucked in for the night—the forever night.

One at a time, the girls said their good-byes.

DJ traced the shape of a heart with her finger on Jewell's forehead. "You taught me that love is never wrong. Good bye, my sister," she whispered as she placed a kiss on Jewell's cheek.

Gem laid her hand gently on Jewell's cheek and said, "You helped me to know courage, to stand up for myself and be strong. I'll miss you, cousin," she said, placing a kiss on the top of Jewell's head.

Berni rested her hand on Jewell's shoulder and stooped over her saying, "You are such a beautiful soul. You helped me find words to express what I feel," she said solemnly. "And I'm feeling irritated that I have to keep track of that pile of chicken feathers you loved so much," she said grinning through her tears. She placed a soft kiss on Jewell's nose.

DJ, Berni, and Gem joined hands alongside the bed.

"Never let life," they chanted, "or death," Berni added, "get the best of you."

In The Light Of KerKhar

Chapter 1 – Abduction

"Eema, look—owl." Boha, wide-eyed, pointed as the bird of prey swooped into the meadow from a ring of redwoods, and landed like a shadow on the earth. "Owl in daylight means death," he murmured.

Eight-year-old Boha took his sister Eema's small hand in his and gave it a quick squeeze. Her pale skin, like the moonlight against his walnut colored hand, filled him with a sense of awe and protectiveness.

They had been foraging for mushrooms since sunrise. Eema, a sprightly four-year old, especially liked the white ones. They were as void of color as her very own skin and hair, and that comforted her.

The forage had been successful. The children carried between them a woven basket full of mushrooms, the kind Uncle had taught them were safe to eat, and wild strawberries.

"These too, Boha," Eema said as she tossed in a handful of dandelions. The bright yellow petals reminded her of the sun and made her smile, and the tender green leaves were tangy when Uncle boiled them over the fire.

Two pairs of bare feet padded slowly through the soft grass. In her free hand, Eema carried her favorite conch shell, the sole reminder of her mother. She was never separate from it.

From time to time, as she walked along, she'd listen to the ocean in its spiraling peach and cream-colored crevice, and would hum a water tune.

The sun still arched in the east as they came nearer their village. Eema heard the ocean just beyond the redwoods where her people lived. Kail, their cousin, stood at the edge of the forest, waving his arms wildly, and shouting something neither child could hear.

Without warning, Eema sat down on the ground, carefully placing her conch shell beside her, and spread both hands palm down, wiggling them deep in the grass until she could feel the earth.

Boha motioned frantically. "Eema, come. We go," he said, lifting the basket and backing out of the meadow.

Nevertheless, Eema sat rooted to the earth with a far away look in her pale pink eyes. Her delicate white lashes blinked slowly in deep concentration.

Boha glanced over his shoulder toward his cousin in the distance who was now pointing beyond from where they had just come and motioning them to return to the village quickly.

Boha scanned the meadow and saw in the distance a small cloud of dust rising from the earth.

"The earth, she shivers with cold," Eema said looking up into her brother's troubled eyes.

"Eema, Kail calls. We go—now." Boha took her hand and tugged, but the child sat firm.

Then he felt it—the vibration of the ground beneath his feet, barely discernible at first, then like a steady drum beat. At the far edge of the meadow, dust was being raised by something in motion. Panic filled his heart as he reached for his sister.

"Now, Eema. Run!" he shouted. As his palms moistened with fear, he lost his grasp on Eema's frail arm and fell backward onto the ground. Mushrooms, berries, and dandelions spilled from the basket as it bounced loose of him. Eema sat, as if entranced with the vibration of the earth.

Kail had turned, and was running back to the village, shouting. Overhead, a raven swooped and dove in the sky above the meadow, calling out *caw* and *kor*, then *ker* and *khar* as it wheeled above the children.

Three men on horseback, warriors from another village, made thunder on the ground as they pounded toward them. Boha had heard stories of men who stole women, children, and horses.

The ground shook, the raven screeched, and the rumbling hooves of the horses were upon them. Boha's brave heart shook in his chest and his legs were so weak he could not stand.

Eema gently picked up her conch shell and cradled it to her body. She looked at the oncoming warriors with curiosity as they approached and slowed to a trot. Their tribal language was not familiar to her ear.

The three pulled their horses up short and two of them dismounted. The warriors were dark and grisly, wild-eyed and smelled of bad meat. They approached the children, pointing and gesturing toward Eema and shouting between themselves. The raven circled with a whoosh of wings over their head screeching *ker khar*, *ker khar*, swooping lower and lower.

Boha tried to crawl to his sister, but his legs seemed filled with river mud and he began to cry.

The raven glided to the earth, landing between Eema and the warriors, flapping its wings wildly, calling out *ker khar*, *ker khar*, its claws ready to defend. The younger of the warriors slung a bow from behind his shoulder, readied an arrow and aimed at the raven. The arrow whined. Boha screamed and covered his eyes as the raven, impaled and bloody, bounced against the ground.

Eema, spotted with blood, sat transfixed, staring at the warrior. The young warrior would not meet her eyes. He looked at the ground, then at his companion who motioned him back onto his horse.

The older warrior approached Eema. He squatted before her and reached out a leathery finger to gingerly touch her translucent skin. With his thumb and forefinger, he held a strand of her colorless hair and studied it. Then he smiled gently into the child's eyes. As if she were no more than a feather's weight, he lifted her up and carried her to his horse.

"No!" Boha screamed.

The young warrior scowled, slung his bow around once more and aimed an arrow at Boha. The third warrior shouted something and the young man lowered his bow, spat upon the ground, and shook his fist at Boha.

Eema looked down at her brother as she was hoisted onto the pinto. The warrior mounted behind her and signaled to the others. The three reined their horses around and thundered off across the meadow with their captive, the mysterious child of light, who Raven called KerKhar.

The trees were a blur as the horses galloped inland. It was like flying except for the rhythmic bumping against the earth. With one hand, Eema held the conch shell tight against her tiny chest. The other clutched the stiff mane of the pinto. It felt like the boar bristles that Uncle used to pull through his hair before twisting it into long thick braids.

The mid-day sun shone brightly but her skin was cool as the air parted in their speed. The warrior held her firmly, his ruddy arms strong and sure as he urged the pinto beyond the meadow. The pungent scent of mugwort, thistle, and field grass filled her nose. The air was drier here, no trace of salt. Carrion birds circled slowly, soundlessly overhead.

Eema's stomach gurgled and she was aware she had not eaten since early that morning, and then only a handful of berries and a tender mushroom. As if the warrior had heard her thought, he shouted to the others and all three horses drew-up under a stand of trees that edged a steep ravine.

"Kha," the warrior said to her, thrusting a pouch toward her. The pouch was goatskin, like that from her village. Eema craned her neck to scan back across the plains. Nothing looked familiar.

Gently laying the conch shell in the hollow between her pelvis and the horse's strong neck, she accepted the pouch, raised it to her dried lips, and drank of cool water.

With her head tipped back, she watched Hawk circle in the distance. *Tell Boha I am safe*, she thought to the messenger bird.

"Kha," she said, handing the water pouch to the warrior. Deep creases appeared at the corners of his eyes and mouth. His smile revealed many missing or darkened teeth. His was not a pretty face, like Uncle's, but it was a kind one.

The younger warrior pulled his horse alongside and handed Eema a piece of dried meat the consistency of the moccasins she had left back in the village. All three tribesmen held big chunks of the meat in their mouths, and chewed it occasionally.

Eema's baby teeth could not break through the leather. The elder warrior took the meat from her, bit it into four pieces, and put one to her lips.

"Mmm..." he toned as he encouraged her to accept the food. "Maa," he said. Eema received the bite and held it in her mouth.

140

Strange and wonderful juices formed around her tongue and she smiled up at the elder.

"Maa..." she said, proud of herself. She now knew two new words, kha for water and maa for food.

The elder's weathered skin crinkled in a smile as he slipped the remaining pieces into the folds of her conch shell. With one turn of the shell, the meat disappeared. With another, it reappeared. For a moment, Eema remembered studying Squirrel one day as it hid a nut in the hollow of a tree. Storing food, Boha had called it.

As if by invisible command, all three warriors made a guttural sound, not unlike a bark, and reined their horses in the direction of the sun. They rode long and hard. The rhythm of the horse's hooves made Eema sleepy. Held safely between the powerful arms of the elder warrior, she drifted in and out of dreams. In her dreams, she saw Boha, waving his arms wildly, a look of fear in his eyes, and Raven, her protector, receiving the arrow that took its life. She heard the hypnotic waves of the ocean lapping just beyond her village, and saw Uncle with his catch of silvery fish that flopped in the back of his canoe as he pulled the boat onto the rocky shore.

A tear slid down her cheek and was absorbed by the arid summer day.

Chapter 2 - The Ipo People

They rode through the night. The moon with her full belly shone brightly and Eema knew she was under the protective watch of the Great Mother. Bright chips of stars twinkled through the treetops as the moist night air released the scent of eucalyptus and pepperwood.

The horses, at a walk now, picked their way carefully through the timber. Coyote called in the distance. Owl answered from afar.

Eema shivered. The elder warrior pulled a blanket from his pack and swathed her in the scratchy warmth. The blanket smelled of the earth, of warm puppies.

"All my relations," Eema whispered to the dark sky. No matter where she was, Eema knew she was at home. Or, perhaps, home was wherever she was.

Her nose caught the scent of wood fire and she sat up straight, straining to see through the night. The warriors rode steadily ahead toward a soft amber glow among the far trees. Eema was wide-awake now, and could sense the shift of energy in the warriors. Though weary, there was excitement in the words they shared as they neared their village.

The pinto, as if refreshed by the promise of rest and food, began trotting toward the familiar sight and smells of home. The other horses, ears perked, followed. The sound of their hooves was like hard rain on dry earth.

Hello, the elder shouted into the darkness. Two voices shouted back, *hello* and *welcome*.

A campfire was burning low at the entrance of the village. It threw dim light and shadows toward the collection of thatched tulle and redwood kotcas scattered nearby.

A young man with a slim body and a broad smile ran up to take the horses reins. *You caught moonbeam from night sky,* he joked, pointing at Eema.

The two young warriors laughed as they dismounted. Before dismounting, the elder handed Eema down to an older woman who had appeared from the closest hut.

No, the elder laughed, *bring something great value to Chief. We tell story at morning fire. To bed now, all,* he said, motioning them away.

Eema, held gently by the grandmother, heard the fire crackle softly and Owl call from a distant tree. Sleep now, Owl said, and she did.

Children's voices, footsteps, the smell of food wafting on the air, and the hushed sound of adults speaking a foreign tongue greeted Eema as she opened her eyes to the gift of a new day.

Thin shafts of light filtered through the thatching and a horse neighed nearby. She reached a sleepy hand out from under the blanket of furs that covered her and stroked the soft rabbit pelt. *Boha, I sleep with Rabbit,* she smiled as she sent a thought to her brother far away in another village.

Eema, her conch shell under one arm, peeked out of the kotca opening and, much like in her own village, saw women with mortars and pestles grinding acorns into meal to be blanched.

Strands of dried kelp tumbled out of a gray willow burden basket. Clay pots and steaming baskets held roots and bulbs not unlike those that Uncle's woman cooked over the fire. Eema's stomach gurgled like the brook after the first rains.

A small boy child rolled a hoop with a stick toward the opening where Eema stood. He wore a strand of abalone discs around his brown body, and little else. When the child saw her, he dropped his hoop and stick, and stood wide-eyed. Then he began to cry. Eema moved to comfort him but he ran to hide behind the skirt of a woman poking at the fire.

The woman turned, smiled, and motioned to Eema to come.

Mya, she said, tapping her own chest lightly.

Her smile was kind, her eyes a deep golden brown like the richest of owl feathers, and under the deerskin she wore, her belly was round with child like the full moon. Her necklace of bones, shells, seeds, and stones clinked merrily as she squatted down to comfort the boy child.

Must be hungry, frightened, so far from home, the woman murmured. The tone was comforting, though Eema did not know the words. She reached a gentle hand out and stroked Eema's cheek.

"Mya," Eema smiled at the woman.

The grandmother who carried her to dreamland last night appeared, carrying a bowl of woven reeds in her weathered hands, piled with acorn paste, field greens, and bits of meat. She sat down on the earth, scooped Eema into her lap and motioned her to eat. Her thick black braid tickled Eema's back.

"Maa," Eema said, smiling, as she placed her conch shell in her lap and ate ravenously from the bowl, smacking her lips, licking each finger to capture every tasty morsel.

The boy had been sent to fill the gourd dipper with water for their guest and stood again in front of Eema wide-eyed, open-mouthed. Eema remembered a story Uncle told of Coyote who crawled into the mouth of a man who stood about with his mouth open, and made words come out of him that angered the villagers. Eema giggled at the thought. The boy, startled by the sound, dropped the dipper. Eema placed her small hand over her mouth to stop the laughter and watched as a puddle of water soaked into the earth at the boy's feet.

Grandmother and the woman laughed and shook their heads at their timid one.

Just beyond the cooking fire, Eema saw the elder warrior approaching, followed by a man who must have been their chief, and his woman close behind. The woman's eyes were hard, her mouth a grim slash across her round face. She looked at Eema with the eyes of a snake, her head bobbing slightly from side to side as she came closer. Her thick black mane hung loose and to her waist. Her dress was of woven fur pelts and hung just past her knees. Her feet were covered in rawhide moccasins beaded in discs of turquoise and chips of serpentine.

The woman carried herself as though she was part buffalo. The image made Eema want to laugh aloud, but she feared startling the child again.

The chief was older than Uncle, but younger than the warrior who brought her here. He wore a breechcloth of many strips of hide woven together, a rabbit pelt hung at his side. His hair was tied back with twine and adorned with beads, shells, and feathers. On his chest hung strands of beads, bones, bright pieces of metal, and shells. The beads clinked and clanked with each step. Eema was mesmerized. His face was the round oval of the warriors, the women, and the child, unlike the more square-shaped faces of Eema's people.

The elder warrior was speaking with much excitement, waving his hands, looking at the chief, and then pointing at Eema. One of the younger warriors followed close behind the threesome.

My chief, I bring gift, child of light, moonbeam on earth. Raven calls "KerKhar." The elder squawked out the name as had Raven and the others laughed at the imitation.

Yes, raven Mito killed... stupid man, the chief jerked his head toward the warrior behind him. *Raven shape shifter, return, haunt village,* he admonished the young man.

The chief's woman narrowed her eyes at KerKhar as if to say already you have brought danger to our tribe.

The younger warrior hung his head yet managed to glare at Eema from behind the chief. His teeth were pointy like the wild boars and his silent snarl made Eema shiver.

The pregnant woman stood as the chief approached. Grandmother struggled to her feet, encouraging Eema to do the same.

"KerKhar," the chief said, his voice a low rumble like distant thunder. Eema understood that that word referred to her now—that Raven's death had renamed her in her new life.

As she would in her own village, with her conch shell under one arm, she clasped her hands in front of her and nodded her respect to the chief.

The sun shone through his eyes and KerKhar thought she could see his heart open with gentleness. Broad with smile, he bent and picked up the child of light with great care and tenderness. He cradled her small frame in his powerful arms and made a soothing humming song from deep in his throat. KerKhar felt safe, as if good Bear medicine protected her in the arms of the chief.

With large fingers, he plucked the conch shell from under her tiny arm, and held it to his ear. He smiled and nodded, then held it to

KerKhar's ear. She smiled and nodded in return, and slowly wrapped her fingers around the shell pulling it again close to her body.

"KerKhar," the word rolled from deep within him as he turned to face his woman with their new child.

The woman bared her teeth in an unfriendly smile and KerKhar thought she heard the rattle of Snake.

Chapter 3 - Turning of the Wheel

Life in the village was much like her old life, except no chores were expected of her. There were no morning herb and berry gatherings, no grinding of seeds, and no carrying of water.

KerKhar came to understand the language of the Ipo people by listening to stories around the campfire—tales of Coyote, Antelope, and Bear, tales of the medicine men and women, and stories about how the world came to be. She learned the names and the stories of the stars in the sky, the rivers and mountains in the distance.

Grandmother sat patiently with her for long days at a time, helping her tiny fingers weave the grasses, tulle, reeds, and redbud bark into coiled baskets with intricate designs.

As daughter of the chief, she was taught to count with mounds of acorns, shells, and counting sticks. Her favorite pastime was to follow the chief about the village, visit the family groups in the various thatched and redwood kotcas, play with the children, and watch as the women baked maize mush on flattened hot stones.

She watched quietly from the flat rocks as the other children splashed about in the creek that ran through her village, but entered the water only to cleanse herself at sunset, alone.

KerKhar spent as little time with the chief's woman as she could without offending the chief. Nothing good came of spending time in her presence. The woman was known to secretly pinch KerKhar on the tender part of her arm just below her shoulder. Or stick her foot in front of KerKhar's next step causing her to tumble to the ground, after which she would pick KerKhar up roughly and shake the dust from her, although never when the chief or Grandmother was near.

The days passed quickly. By the third moon of her life in the village, she was allowed to accompany Mya and her new papoose into the fields to collect acorns, buckeye, and hazel nuts to store for winter. They laughed and chased rabbits and ground squirrels. Sometimes KerKhar would think of Boha, but not as often. The sound of his voice was a fading shadow in her memory.

"Mya," KerKhar asked one afternoon as she watched the young woman rinse a basket of mashed acorns, "why chief's woman make anger with me?"

"Ah, chief's woman..." Mya said looking around to make sure they were alone. She leaned closer and spoke quietly. "She daughter of medicine man, so mate for chief. She shaman, bring babies into tribe, make powerful medicine, protect village from disease, evil forces. Not woman make anger," Mya warned.

"You tell no one," she lowered her voice to a whisper. "She barren, deep pain. Howl at moon like wounded mountain lion when blood spills, no baby grow inside."

Mya stroked the side of KerKhar's face gently. "You child she never have," Mya said as she ran another bowl of water through the mash.

KerKhar took this in, but felt no warming in her heart for the chief's woman. There were harvest celebrations to prepare for, rituals that the chief and his family would preside over, clothes to be sewn and beaded by the village women for the festivities.

Visitors from neighboring tribes, dressed in their finery and feathered headgear would arrive bearing food, baskets, tools, beads, pelts, and other gifts for the Ipo people. Stories were told around the fire, the peace pipe was passed, and children sang songs to the elders.

KerKhar rarely left the chief's side. The chief's woman, who sat on the other side of KerKhar, scowled and snarled under her breath and would poke and prod KerKhar when the chief's attention was held in conversation.

KerKhar never yelped or scowled back, she only snuggled closer to the chief who would occasionally lift her gently into his lap and hold her delicately as if she were made of moonbeams.

One afternoon when the oak trees were the color of fire and the air had begun to take on the scent of autumn, a traveler happened by the village on foot, leading a heavily laden pony.

KerKhar sat in the shade of a pepperwood just outside the lodge house waiting for the chief to finish speaking with the medicine man.

Mito stood with arms crossed, feet planted firmly, barring the way to the path that led to the lodge house.

"What want here?" he demanded of the stranger.

"I travel from coast and bring dried fish to trade," the man replied amicably, pointing to his many pouches and sacks. His voice was tinged with an accent that KerKhar's ear found familiar, and she studied his square face so much like her own.

The traveler looked past Mito and noticed KerKhar, pale as a lunar moth, sitting among the silver-green leaves.

"The child, I know?" he spoke to himself. Aloud, he said "*Gaii khwi*," in Hokan Pomo tongue, "white child, taken from..."

KerKhar sprang to her feet to greet the stranger, but Mito pushed her backwards harshly.

"No. Belongs tribe here," he rudely addressed the traveler. "Chief in counsel. You come." Mito motioned the stranger and led him back down the path, away from the village. He looked back over his shoulder at KerKhar and snarled a silent warning for her not to follow.

The stranger's voice had worked a sad magic on her heart and tears trickled slowly down her pale cheeks. She longed to ask the traveler if he knew of Boha or Uncle, but instead she walked as quietly as a whisper back to her kotca. With her conch shell cradled in her arms, she snuggled into the folds of her blanket and crooned a wordless tune until her tears dried.

That evening around the fire, after a fine meal of dried salmon and rockfish, Mito told of coming upon a stranger outside the village who had been set upon by the wolves, torn limb to limb, poor traveler. He told of how he had buried him in the ravine, weighing his grave down with heavy stone so his remains would rest undisturbed, and how the traveler's pony and goods were fair gifts to the community for him taking such care of a visitor who had fallen on disaster.

The chief was well pleased and didn't notice KerKhar shrinking deeply into herself.

Chapter 4 - Fall From Grace

Ten sets of seasons transformed the child of light into a young woman whose beauty had become legendary.

In the moon tent just outside the village, Mya and KerKhar sat, legs folded, opposite one another, and sipped a bitter herb tea. KerKhar shifted her weight slightly and felt the cloth that caught her menses become spongy with her rich, red blood.

"Time for you know ways of women and men," Mya said into the stillness. She reached over and took KerKhar's hands in her own and looked deeply into her eyes.

A tinge of color dotted KerKhar's pale cheeks, and she looked down, her white lashes fluttered gently.

"Spilling of seed?" she asked in a whisper. "Girls in village laugh. Is true?" The thought both repelled her and excited something deep within.

"Thing of beauty, KerKhar," Mya's voice was soft and dreamy, "Special man, make babies, protect."

KerKhar, remembered Mya's round full belly of last season, and looked down at her own flat stomach and the sprinkling of woman-hair just below. It's true, she has felt the stirrings and it has unsettled her.

"Rulu make babies in forest, many young warriors." KerKhar studied the side of the tipi as it swept gently to the top where it opened to the robin's egg blue sky. Her innocence caused Mya to laugh.

"Rulu's body not sacred for special man," she said. "Only *very* special man enter KerKhar's woman space." She released KerKhar's hand and shifted her weight backwards.

"Time take clothes to creek. Enough talk." Mya smiled and shook her head as she prepared to leave the tent.

"Moon so full. Floats on the water," said KerKhar several evenings later.

Mya smiled softly as she gazed at KerKhar, backlit by the golden orb. Such warmth she felt toward the young woman who felt so much like her own sister.

"If Pyan see KerKhar bathing in beautiful Mother Moon light, fall in love," she said as she rose from the water and offered KerKhar her hand.

"Not ready return to village, Mya. Night full of magic. We stay longer?"

There was a rustle in the brush along the riverbed. Startled, both women turned and strained to see into the shadows.

"Father, you startled us," KerKhar said as the chief stepped into the moonlight that had filtered through the redwoods and spilled onto the bank.

"You go, Mya. I stay with KerKhar," he said in his rich and resonant voice. He turned his back while Mya slipped from the water and wrapped herself.

"May dreams be of moon and magic," she said to KerKhar. "Good night, chief," she called as she padded down the path splashed with bright shards of moonlight.

"Come in water, father?" KerKhar called, her voice a song on the night air. "Cool, soft." She raised her arms and gems of water sparkled, fell like a gentle rain, and were absorbed back into the dark creek.

"I sit in moon bath," he said as he lowered himself onto the soft grasses and reeds of the creek bed.

When KerKhar was a child, he would often bathe with her at night when the other children were called back to the village. He taught her to swim like an otter, diving and plunging in and out of the current, holding her breath and weaving her way through the water, her long white braid bobbing behind. She was strong, sleek and agile. The chief smiled at the memory.

Now the corona of white hair lit by the moon was a shimmering aura about KerKhar's head. It flowed gracefully into the water where it floated like iridescent seaweed. Her skin was luminous, translucent.

Her rabbit-pink eyes shone with the depth of an old soul. No longer a child, she wore her womanhood with a power that pulled at his loins.

There was no denying the lust that moved him from the bank of the river, slowly, steadily, and into the still water, until he stood chest deep, facing KerKhar.

Her breasts were round and firm, and floated just beneath the water. As the chief was about to reach out, to stroke the gentle curve of her long neck, she giggled, a beautiful tinkling in the silent night, turned and dove under the water only to surface behind him with a splash of water aimed at the square of his back.

He laughed heartily, intrigued by her playfulness. His little otter. He turned, caught her arm and pulled her to him. As she had in childhood, she threw her arms about his neck and encircled his waist tightly with her legs. Laughing, she shook her hair back and forth spraying the air around them with beads of water.

As their eyes locked, awareness shot through her like a bolt of lightning. She was no longer a carefree child playing water games with the chief. The desire in his eyes frightened and excited her.

He spoke her name in a whisper as he lowered her onto his hardened manhood. She gasped, wild eyed, lost in feelings she did not understand as he poured his seed into her.

He was aware only of his need, a compelling force that wanted nothing more than to create an heir with this magnificent creature who had captivated his heart, mind, and soul since her arrival in his life, and now, his body.

KerKhar cried out, like a bird of prey piercing the night sky. She bit at his shoulder, feeling his shudder mingle with her own.

A shadow slithered behind a tree just off the bank and watched with virulent eyes, glowing red like the lava rocks in the sweat lodge. Her breath was ragged and foul. Her thoughts encompassed all the evil of the darkness that roiled about her.

Chapter 5 - Raven's Revenge

The stars were bright glittering chips against the blackness of night. Water ripples sparkled around them as the chief led KerKhar wordlessly back onto the soft, spongy earth. They stood, wet bodies reflecting moonlight, neither knowing what must be done next.

Finally, the chief said, "I must sit, think, wonder. Go now, have good dreams. We meet at morning fire." He wrapped KerKhar in a blanket, gently freeing the white mat of hair that resembled a butterfly chrysalis.

The moon had crested in its fullness and now hovered once again just over the water, a glowing orb that lit the path as KerKhar slipped quietly back to the village.

KerKhar smiled as she nestled herself under the blankets and pelts that covered her bare woman's body. One hand traced the curve of her new breasts and roamed slowly over her flat, taut belly. She remembered how beautiful, how full and ripe Mya had looked carrying her child, and she tried to imagine her own breasts and belly growing round and ripe like summer melon.

She dreamed of Snake leaving her skin behind on the warm rocks along the water's edge and woke the next morning full of portent and possibility.

"My life is forever changed," she said, as she dressed to join the morning fire circle. She was binding her wily tresses into the semblance of a braid when the chief's woman appeared like a black cloud at the entrance to the kotca, making the air thick and odorous.

"Sit!" the woman hissed through clenched teeth. Her eyes were black spheres of pure hatred and she moved in a slow, calculating way, like a coyote coming in for the kill.

There was no way to avoid her. KerKhar sat on the straw that covered the floor of her dwelling and averted her eyes.

The chief's woman squatted in front of KerKhar, so close that her fetid breath made KerKhar swoon.

"You bring destruction to village and death to chief if birth child into tribe," she said in a voice that sounded like a strangled whisper. "No destroy tribe."

KerKhar stammered in confusion.

"Silence!" screeched the woman. "Medicine woman know. Trickster spirit in KerKhar lure chief, spills seed," she spat her words at KerKhar. "Demon! Must leave tribe."

"Chief choose KerKhar bear child," KerKhar said, still not looking at the rabid woman. *How did she know?* KerKhar wondered.

"Enough!" the woman rasped. "Death to chief if child born," she cursed. "Death to child unless do as medicine woman say."

Terror and rage shook inside KerKhar like the rumbling of the earth. She would do nothing to put her chief at risk, or her child. They must be protected at all costs. KerKhar glanced briefly at the woman.

"By full moon," the woman's body swayed slightly from side to side as she spoke, "leave, forget Ipo people." Her voice was hypnotic now and KerKhar's eyelids became heavy.

"Go back own village," she paused, "make life with child," she said softly, almost compassionately. "When full moon," again, a pause, "medicine woman give you food for travel," she crooned now. "No harm to KerKhar, must leave, no choice."

"Only chief can send away," KerKhar managed though her throat had become parched. Her tongue felt sluggish and her mouth was like dried buffalo hide.

The woman leaned forward menacingly and spoke slowly. "No speak to chief," she warned, the venom returning to her voice, "tongue cut, fed to wild boars."

With that, the chief's woman spun around and strode out the opening. She did not stop or acknowledge those seated about the fire a short distance from the kotca.

The shaky feeling in KerKhar's stomach now convulsed, twitched and jangled her limbs. Silent tears sprung from her eyes and her heart pounded violently.

Lethargy filled her body for days after and she spent much of her time sleeping fitfully in the kotca, slipping out only under cover of darkness to relieve herself. She spoke to no one.

Mya kept regular watch and brought broth daily but could get nothing from KerKhar.

"Chief asks for KerKhar," she said one evening as she placed the bowl of broth beside KerKhar who lay on the mat with her back to Mya, "others think KerKhar ill, danger to village." Nothing but a small sigh escaped from KerKhar.

The sun and moon took turns moving the village through one day into the next. KerKhar's skin hung loosely on her small frame now. The breasts that should have begun to feel full and tender seemed withered and lifeless.

As the sounds of the village drifted into yet another evening, KerKhar listened to the night birds in trees beyond the circle of kotcas. Hawk's piercing screech, Raven's brazen chortle, and Owl's call rippled through the darkness. "All my ancestors," KerKhar whispered.

She reached out for her bundle, kept rolled up and tucked away just beyond her mat. KerKhar unwrapped her conch shell, the only connection to her childhood people.

"You must lead me home," she pleaded into the smooth, rounded folds that spiraled inward. Holding the shell to her ear, she listened to the ocean as she drifted into a deep sleep.

At the edge of the village where the harvested acorns were stored in a round wooden bin, the chief's woman placed a bundle of food, a special mush of acorn paste seasoned with poisonous foxglove and oleander for the depleted traveler. She smiled at the thought of a hungry and unsuspecting KerKhar breaking off pieces of rounded flatbread with field mouse droppings mixed with chunks of rotting carcass from a rabbit slain by a coyote.

Soon, she reassured herself. Soon her position would be restored in the tribe and she would have the respect she deserved.

Under the cover of darkness, she crept along the outer edge of the circle of kotcas until she approached the thatched hut of KerKhar.

Silently she slipped through the opening, and knelt beside the sleeping young woman for whom she felt no tenderness.

Her fingers, like cold talons, wrapped themselves about KerKhar's frail arm. She squeezed and shook until KerKhar twisted and sat bolt upright, squinting into the darkness.

"No sound," the chief's woman warned. "Is time, you go," she said. With her free hand, she pulled at the blankets covering KerKhar.

"Not well, not travel," KerKhar mumbled as she struggled to keep hold of her covers.

"Food, water in harvest bin. Days warm, take blanket, bundle," the woman whispered. "Go now or chief killed at sunrise," she threatened.

In the distance, KerKhar heard the cry of Raven break through the dark silence. She struggled to her feet, tears blurring her night vision. She wrapped herself in her blanket, slipped on her moccasins and rolled extra clothing around her bundled conch shell.

The chief's woman shoved her roughly through the entrance and walked silently behind her. They passed the glowing embers of the night fire and their bodies cast distorted shadows onto the thatched huts of the slumbering villagers.

Twigs snapped beneath their feet, small animals made scrabbling noises in the brush and an owl cried from the tops of a redwood nearby. KerKhar's heart was breaking and she sniffed loudly, trying to stifle the sob that threatened to free itself into the night air. The chief's woman behind her shoved her shoulder, and KerKhar scrambled to keep her balance. "Quiet," the woman hissed.

The woman lifted the lid from the round harvest storage bin and extracted the wrapped provisions.

"Best for tribe," she said, jabbing the bundle at KerKhar. "No look back," were her parting words as she disappeared.

"My chief," was all KerKhar was able to whisper as sobs overtook her. She followed the path past the sweat lodge and away from the village.

Raven called from a fir tree nearby, and with a whoosh of wings swooped like a black shadow into the village landing at the ring of the campfire. With one talon Raven retrieved a burning ember and lifted it high into the night sky, then winged to the edge of the village where the grasses were dry and brittle and dove with intensity and purpose, depositing the burning kindling amongst a pile of tinder.

First a crackle, and then sparks. Raven flapped thick wings fanning the ember. Flames shot into the darkness. Raven cackled and flew to the top of a redwood, cawing out her revenge as the fires spread quickly, engulfing the village, leaping to ignite the dwellings made of thatched dried reeds and bark.

KerKhar heard the sounds of fire, and then smelled the rancid smoke. Heeding the chief's woman's warning, she placed one unsteady foot in front of the other and did not look back.

Chapter 6 - The Journey

KerKhar moved steadily along the path, backlit by the eerie glow of fire. Far ahead darkness beckoned. Her heart and mind were numb, her body unaware of the distance covered.

She sipped brackish water from the pelt pouch that had been part of the food bundle. Sleep pulled at her yet she pushed on into the night.

Thick clouds hid the moon now and obscured the knots of grass, roots and fallen branches over which KerKhar stumbled. Beyond the forest, she heard a wolf bay. The lonely sound sent a shiver through her frail body. Under the folds of her blanket wrap, she held the conch shell, bundled in extra clothing, closely against her chest.

"You must lead me home," she whispered to the bundle.

Once more KerKhar's foot caught on a tangle of underbrush, and she fell with a muted thud onto the soft earth where this time she lay curled up against the night. Owl called consolingly from a branch overhead and settled in to guard the child whose consciousness had given over to exhaustion.

Just before dawn returned color to the sky, a raccoon lumbered out of the brush and surveyed the sleeping child and her bundle of foodstuffs. With one sharply clawed paw, the animal snatched the bundle and shredded the pouch that held the provisions. Eyes alert and nostrils twitching, he sorted through the poisoned mush and flatbread, only to turn an indignant nose and waddle back into the thick of the forest.

The last of the morning stars faded as a weak sun struggled among the tops of the redwoods, oaks, and bays and filtered through the early ground fog that swathed KerKhar.

As scrub jays, morning doves, and ravens called from tree to tree, squirrels skittered about in the brush, and the hooves of a doe and her brood of fawns snap-crunched their way through the forest detritus. KerKhar slowly unfurled her aching arms that had been wrapped tightly around herself, stretched stiff legs, and flexed sore feet.

She yawned hugely, and lay for a moment orienting herself with the position of the sun. Her head thrummed dully and there was a gnawing pain in her stomach.

"*All my relations*," she whispered a greeting to the new day, as was her custom. As she lay on her back gazing up at the trees, tears trickled from each eye down her cheeks and fell in drops from the small lobes of her ears. The nightmare visions played themselves in her mind—her kotca, the chief's woman snarling, shoving, the bundle, the sleeping village consumed in flames as she was exiled, carrying deep within her the chief's child.

What began as a low moan turned into a heartbreaking howl of agony. Birds fluttered from their perches at the keening, and small animals skittered away in fright. KerKhar grabbed her belly, rolled onto her side and let the tears fall, absorbed by Mother Earth, the only parent she could turn to.

As her sobs slowly subsided, KerKhar raised herself up on one elbow and noted the contents of her bundle strewn about. Hunger overcame portent as she reached for the round of flatbread that peeked from the shredded pouch. She gathered the acorn mush that spilled from its husk wrapping and, breaking off a piece of bread, scooped a large mound of mush into her mouth.

The mush was bitter as if not blanched well, and the foul-tasting flatbread crunched in her mouth in a peculiar way, but KerKhar was famished and eating for two now. She washed the food down with the remaining brackish water. What could she expect, she mused, when her provisions were packed by the chief's woman. She would fill the water pouch at the creek as she followed it west.

As KerKhar squatted to gather the remainder of her belongings, her head swam. She steadied herself with one hand on the ground, and breathed deeply.

"I turn myself over to your care, oh Great Mother," she offered to the earth. With effort, she stood upright and took a few wobbly steps. Her body ached but she counted on her youth to move her through the pain. With her free hand, she rubbed slow circles around her belly, which had begun to rumble and spasm as she walked.

The fog lifted and the sun was stronger now, warming her back as her feet found a slow rhythm to carry her forward. Her eyes scanned the forest floor for edibles—mushrooms, wood lettuce, greens—which she picked and tucked among the folds of her bundle.

As she bent to pick from a patch of miner's lettuce, her stomach seized and violent retches shook her body. The poisonous food spewed as she heaved repeatedly, dropping to her knees. Her stomach knotted once more and KerKhar let out a scream of agony as she fell to her side and curled her knees to her chest. Blood and fluids drained from between her legs as her body retched again. Drenched in sweat and shivering, KerKhar lie helpless, alone, among the forest debris, overtaken by a sense of loss so deep and profound as to make death seem welcome.

The sun continued its arc as KerKhar drifted in and out of consciousness. Her teeth chattered and her body convulsed from time to time, but the pain in her belly had subsided. A bloody clot clung stickily to her thigh, proof that if she survived, it would be for herself alone.

Protected only by the canopy of redwood and fir boughs from the midday sun, KerKhar half crawled, half dragged herself toward the sound of the creek, pulling her bundle after her.

Her throat was parched and dirt caked her sweaty skin. Scrapes and cuts marred her arms and legs as she struggled through the fallen boughs, twigs, bark, and needles. She closed her heart to all feelings and her mind to all thoughts beyond survival.

When she reached the creek, with great effort she hung her upper body over the edge of the bank and cupped the water with her hands. She splashed her face, arms, neck, and shoulders with the cool, clear water and brought handful after handful to her mouth, drinking deeply.

Completely spent, she fell into an exhausted slumber, one hand dangling in the creek, bobbing with the gentle current.

A sliver of moonlight shown through the treetops and soft noises of the night creatures greeted KerKhar as she rolled onto her back and opened her eyes. Crickets and bullfrogs singing, birds of prey calling from the branches, and small animal feet padding about brought her comfort. She remembered briefly how safe she had felt as a young child, out in nature among the insects, animals, and birds where she would serenade the golden poppies and talk to the clouds. A smile almost played at the corners of her mouth.

KerKhar noticed that her body felt less ravaged after her long sleep, though her joints were stiff and a dull pain thrummed at her muscles. She winced at the stench of her body as she pulled herself to a sitting position.

Trying very hard to hold back the memory of the last time she had bathed in the moonlight, she lowered herself into the shallow water near the edge of the creek. KerKhar peeled her rank clothing from her body and swirled them about in the water.

When she had wrung them out sufficiently, she tossed them onto the bank and slipped headfirst under the surface. The gentle current hummed in her ears. *I will carry you back to the sea*, it promised.

For a brief moment, KerKhar considered inhaling deeply. Instead, she broke the surface with a shake of her white mane and inhaled only the cool night air. She was rewarded with the cry of an owl standing watch from the top of a nearby tree. Climbing carefully onto the bank, she noted her white skin reflecting the moonlight. Being a child of light had lead to one tragedy upon another.

She stepped back into her damp clothes and reached for her bundle. Although the thought of food brought a wave of nausea, she knew she must strengthen her body for the long journey still ahead.

KerKhar emptied the remains of all the provisions packed for her by the chief's woman, and rinsed the foraged food she'd found in the creek to remove any contamination. As she nibbled at the sorrel and mushrooms she smiled up at the twinkling stars and the crescent moon arcing its way through the night sky. For the first time in many days, she felt a sense of peace.

KerKhar refilled her water pouch with clear, cool creek water, gathered her bundle, and following the creek west, set off to find her homeland.

As the moon set, the sun brought a golden glow to the waving field grass. KerKhar stopped to refresh herself with food and water, and replenished her provisions with late summer blueberries and wild strawberries that dotted the landscape.

She left the forest behind at daybreak, and faced a hilly meadow with stands of eucalyptus, scrub oak, and pepperwood. She sat in the tall grass, leaned back against an outcropping of gray rock, and listened to the songs of the morning doves and mockingbirds.

A mother doe and her fawn grazed quietly nearby, glancing now and then at KerKhar. A sob caught at the back of her throat, and a tear slid slowly down her cheek for the child she would never bear.

Quickly she put that thought away and focused instead on reuniting with Boha. Her brother would be a young man now, perhaps with a wife and baby. Again, the burning tears pooled at her eyelids and she blinked them away furiously.

Uncle. Yes, Uncle will cook for me, KerKhar told herself, *corncakes with sweet syrup...* She smiled.

With the sun to her back marking the east, KerKhar decided to part from the creek that seemed to veer south. Surely there will be water along the way, she reassured herself as she filled her pouch one last time and smeared rich brown mud over her bare forearms and legs where the sun had burned rough patches in her skin. She patted another handful of ooze on her cheeks, forehead, chin, and nose and sighed deeply at the cooling sensation. As an afterthought, she gathered moss, leaves, and grasses into a small pile, and mixed them with water and a handful of creek mud to fashion a head covering in the shape of an upside-down bird nest that soothed her reddened scalp.

Before rolling up her bundle, she removed the conch shell and held it to her ear. The rolling waves of the ocean greeted her, beckoned her home.

Crickets sang to her and flies buzzed lazily about her head as KerKhar walked on through the heat of the day. When the sun was at its highest point, she lay on the moist cool earth under the shade of a large oak.

Scanning the horizon, her eyes caught movement. Cresting a distant hill were riders on horseback. KerKhar scrambled for her bundle and staying low to the ground crept behind the trunk of the oak. Fear caught in her throat. She hadn't thought of traveling with a weapon to defend herself, and she looked around frantically for stones or sharp sticks. Finding neither, she wished herself invisible. Gone was the innocent child who knew no enemies, who embraced life and adventure with an open heart and mind.

KerKhar peeked around the massive trunk to see the party of four men on horseback, heavily laden with bundles, turn north just before the meadow where she hid. Her heart calmed only for a moment. *A trail—they have come from a trail*, she thought. Again, her heart pounded at the thought of a trail that would lead her to a village.

As soon as the men were out of sight, she ran in the direction from which they had come, and scanned the earth for hoof marks she could follow.

"There!" she called out, startling herself at the sound of her own voice. Like a child finding a treasure, she dropped to her knees and ran her hands over the fresh indentations.

Squinting into the late afternoon sun, she followed the path with her eyes until it disappeared over the crest of the next hill. Spurred on by hope, KerKhar walked until dark came upon her and the waning moon no longer shed enough light to follow the path.

"I go off trail, find a safe place to rest," she reasoned out loud, "travel at daybreak." Far away, a nighthawk screeched and Coyote sung to what was left of the moon.

KerKhar headed toward an outcropping of boulders a short distance from the trail, behind which she would be safe and out of eyesight. The ground was uneven and she tripped frequently, dropped her bundle once, and searched on hands and knees in the dark.

As she navigated around the largest boulder, her foot caught on a twist of root looping out of the ground. She heard a distinct *snap*. A sharp pain shot through her ankle and up her calf.

Her arms flailed about as she fell, disoriented by the pain and the dark, and landed on her back. Her breath left her body before her head cracked against a large rock. Her bundle bounced on the ground, and the conch shell tumbled loose and rolled behind the rock. What was left of her foodstuff was randomly scattered about on the ground.

At daybreak, she forced herself to open her eyes slowly, and saw only shimmering gray that obscured dull outlines of shapes. Willing her mind to remain calm, she did a mental check of her body.

Pain seared her ankle and she could not move her leg. Her back felt bruised, but she was able to move her arms slowly. Turning her head made her wince with pain, but to her relief, her vision was unimpaired.

A bank of fog had rolled in over night, and in the dim earliest hours of day, lay like a thick blanket over the meadow. She was chilled through to the bone and felt around at arms length for her pack. It lay just out of reach.

KerKhar raised herself onto her elbows and with her good leg shoved against the ground. Inching back slowly, with her leg throbbing wildly, she dragged herself just far enough to secure a grasp on what remained of her bundle. Struggling an extra wrap from the loosened folds, she pulled the cover over her shivering body just before she lost consciousness.

KerKhar knew time had passed, but not exactly how much. Her hair was matted with sweat and debris. She was parched and famished, and her skin hung loosely on her frame. The scraps of food had been consumed by scavengers who left only telltale paw and claw prints in the dirt.

With great effort, she pulled herself to a sitting position and noticed that though her leg was still painful, the swelling in her ankle had diminished. She sat very still, straining to hear any sounds that might indicate humans were nearby. She bent slowly, put her ear against the ground, and listened for the drumming of hooves that would carry along the earth's surface. She heard nothing but sounds of the meadow—the chatter of squirrels, the chirping of birds, and the humming of insects.

Weak from hunger, she lay on her side watching the blades of grass wave in the gentle breeze and wondered if this was the end of her journey. Her eye caught sight of the smooth pink round of conch shell protruding from behind a nearby rock. She longed for the sound of the waves washing the shore to comfort her and was ready to give over to tears when the distinct *slice* of raven wings soared so close as to lift the strands of her matted hair.

A soft object was dropped next to her hand with a thump She reached out to touch a fat, furry field mouse still warm from the kill, as Raven swooped upward leaving behind only a cry of *cor, kaw*, then *ker, khar* before vanishing beyond the trees.

Instinctively, KerKhar put her thumbs in the talon puncture marks on the mouse's belly and tore it apart. She brought the mouse to her mouth and sucked greedily, chewing meat and entrails, knowing only that she must live and Raven had provided her with the means.

Her mind was numb as she cleaned the tiny bones and scraped the inner pelt with her teeth. She said a prayer of gratitude as she laid the furry remains on the earth.

KerKhar noticed a patch of miner's lettuce nestled near the rock where her conch shell lay, and crawled slowly on her knees, keeping her ankle as still as possible. She picked handfuls of the round, slightly bitter leaves and chewed them thoroughly until her mouth watered with their juice.

She reached for her shell and turned it slowly in her hands. A small amount of morning dew had settled in its folds and she brought it gratefully to her lips as if it were bee nectar.

She smiled as she held the shell to her ear and was comforted by the sound of the surf. KerKhar hugged the shell to her heart for a moment, and then said, "We must go now."

She struggled to her feet, testing her tender ankle to see if it would bear weight. A fallen limb nearby lent itself as a crutch, and she slowly navigated her way back to the path she'd strayed from days ago.

With her conch shell wrapped once again in the remains of her bundle, now reduced to a dirty blanket and an empty water pouch, she made her way along the faded path.

The sun grew stronger overhead and KerKhar mopped her brow with her forearm leaving long wet trails of mud and grime. Her ankle throbbed dully. Her mind, which had remained quite numb for most of the day, slowly began to take in her surroundings through her senses.

She first noticed the *burping* of a bullfrog not far away. She squinted with the effort of matching the sound with what she knew—bullfrog—water!

"Water nearby," she shouted, turning about, scanning either side of the path beyond the trees. She heard the frog's distinctive belch again, and followed the sound to her left. Giddily hopeful, she swatted at a mosquito that buzzed near her head.

Straining, listening, she moved steadily toward the soft trickling sounds of a creek, nearly dried from the heat of late summer. The earth softened and moss grew along the tiny rivulet of water where an underground spring emptied.

KerKhar dropped her crutch and bundle and knelt beside the murky pool of water. She dug at the mud and sludge near the surface, making a wider berth for the cool, clear water that flowed beneath.

Gleefully, she soaked her hands and splashed water on her face and neck. She leaned close to the water and lapped like a thirsty animal until her mouth was refreshed and her throat was no longer dry.

"Great Mother," KerKhar prayed to the earth, "you provide food, protection, guidance for travel. Heart is full." With her spirits renewed, she covered her skin with fresh mud, and soaked and replaced her head covering. After filling her pouch with cool spring water, she struggled to her feet once again and followed the setting sun westward.

Chapter 7 – Homecoming

KerKhar foraged as she walked, adding to her provisions. She had given up fear of coming across travelers on this abandoned trail and followed the path long into the night. When she felt fatigue overtake her, she merely curled up by the side of the path and covered herself with her blanket to sleep until dawn brought a new day.

The sound of a gull woke her as the sun rose behind her in hues of orange, yellow and pink. The air smelled fresh and slightly salty as the morning dew sparkled on the grasses around her. Stiff from the moist night air, KerKhar stretched her arms and legs slowly and yawned.

A gull. It had been many years since she had heard the call of a gull. Memories began to stir deep inside KerKhar. The scent of salt in the moist air, the green grasses in the surrounding fields, the outcroppings of rock and boulders scattered over the hills—all were a familiar part of her homeland. Surely, she must be near. Her heart beat faster with excitement.

Infused with a new enthusiasm she ate quickly and gathered her provisions into her bundle. She tucked the conch shell securely under her arm and set off down the path as briskly as her injured ankle would allow.

She walked the better part of the day stopping only briefly for a bite of food and a sip of water. Late in the afternoon, she crested yet another hill and looked down upon a meadow strewn with dandelions and orange poppies.

Her heart leaped with joy. In the distance, as far away as her eyes could see, was the tree line of the redwood forest that sheltered her village, and beyond which lay the ocean.

Oh, to have wings, she thought as she watched two buzzards glide effortlessly above the meadow, *to fly straight to Boha and Uncle*. She smiled as she imagined their look of disbelief. Her lips, dried and chapped from sun and mud, cracked painfully when she smiled, but she paid them no mind.

It had been a long day, and KerKhar had covered a great distance. She would rest now by the side of the path, and reach her destination the following day. She drifted off to a deep and dreamless sleep watching the sun set ahead of her beyond the forest treetops.

In the morning, mockingbirds and meadowlarks greeted her with beautiful songs. As she readied herself to begin her walk home, her mind was filled with thoughts of a joyous reunion. Would she recognize her cousin Kail all grown up now? And Uncle—he too would be much older.

KerKhar abandoned the path she'd been following and cut across the meadow just to the north where a shallow creek ran westward. The water was not deep enough for proper bathing—that would have to wait until she reached the river that ran through the forest. However, she was able to refill her pouch and splash her hands and face with cool water. Her eyes felt scorched by the sun.

"Ahh," she sighed with relief. Her delicate skin was blotched and scaly from the sun, and caked with mud. The water made brown rivulets down her face and neck. Her hair was a dirty, matted gray, and was tangled inseparably with grass, twigs, and leaves. She chuckled to herself imagining how she must look as she brushed away some debris that clung to her clothing.

The ground was uneven in the meadow and KerKhar walked cautiously, aware that her ankle was still swollen and not as flexible as it once was. She stepped gingerly around a large critter hole in the earth, keeping her eyes fixed on the ground just ahead of her as she moved along.

Walking closer to the creek now, where the earth was less uneven, she fell into a slow but steady rhythm, moving almost hypnotically, unaware of how much ground she had covered.

The sun had peaked and begun its descent when KerKhar stopped again for food and a rest. She dropped her bundle on the ground, shifted her conch shell to her other arm, and stretched her back and neck. Her eyes roamed across the open field, which she recognized now as the field that bordered her village. She stood for a moment, stunned.

The past replayed itself in a whirl of images: herself as a small child at the edge of the village, facing the very spot where she now stood, the warriors on horseback, dust rising, riding toward her from where she had just come, and Boha screaming her name as the older warrior swept her up onto his saddle.

KerKhar blinked and shook her head to rid herself of the images. Her eyes now focused on two figures in the distance—one small, a child she thought, the other, farther behind him, a grown man, bent over a trap perhaps. She moved slowly, steadily toward the child decreasing the distance between them.

She could see him more clearly now, a young boy, in the field hunting with his bow and arrow. He had noticed her too, and was standing as still as a young buck.

KerKhar cupped her mouth with one hand and called out, but her voice was a strangled cry from lack of use.

The boy, stood wide-eyed, staring at the ghostly apparition—a wild-eyed colorless woman all tattered and torn, encrusted with earth from the grave—a spirit come to bring death to his village. He screamed and raised his bow and arrow in a threatening gesture.

Not wanting to frighten the child further, KerKhar dropped the conch shell and raised her arms to show she meant no harm, was not an enemy. She took another step closer, then another.

The older man who had been tending to something on the ground looked up and a flash of recognition caught in his heart. He saw the boy, arrow pointed, string drawn back, quivering with fear.

"No, son! No!" he hollered a moment too late. The arrow hissed.

"Eema..." Boha screamed. Her name clung to the feathered arrow as it flew through the air and pierced her lung. Tears blinding him, Boha ran toward his sister who had dropped to the ground where she stood.

Blood trickled from her ribcage as he fell next to her. He cradled her in his arms and wept over her, rocking her back and forth.

In a raspy voice she gasped, "Boha, I've come home." A faint smile parted her lips.

Through his tears, he saw the conch shell lying on the ground next to her, reached for it and gently laid it against the side of her head.

As her eyes glazed over, the sound of the surf ebbed and flowed in her ear. Her last breath was taken away with the flow, and returned to the source.

Waltzing With The Azaleas

Chapter 1

"You're not going to puke, are you?" Jessica cut her speed back to a crawl. Her variegated ponytail, Auburn Sunset and Grape Ice this week, swung abruptly over her left shoulder as she shot a look over at Cory in the passengers seat.

"I'm not going to puke," Cory mumbled. "I hate that word."

Jessica paced herself parallel to the curb, just in case. "You look sort of avocado."

"It's just the jacket."

"Well, then, why do you wear it?"

"Could we talk about something else?" Cory drummed his fingers on his knees. His cuticles were jagged from nibbling and picking. The old neighborhood crept by in a white coating of winter broken by slashes of barren trees.

He leaned forward, and with his bare hand wiped away the vapor that clouded the windshield on his side.

"Didn't your mother ever tell you not to do that? It leaves streaks," Jessica said.

"I was never allowed to ride in the front seat," Cory mumbled, brushing a tuft of hair from his forehead. "Turn right at the next corner. It's the blue house on the right," he instructed.

Jessica pulled up in front of a wooden two-story, with a large lawn that sloped to the curb. Hints of red brick peeked through the blanket of snow suggesting a sidewalk. "Do you think she's already there?"

171

"Not if we're on time," Cory said ruefully.

Jessica cut the engine. The temperature dropped immediately as the Midwest winter enveloped the car. She re-zipped her parka and struggled her hands into her mittens. Fighting a shiver, she said, "Tell me again why I'm here?"

"Because you're my best friend. And that's what best friends do," Cory said. He slipped his gloves on and reached for the door handle.

Jessica turned to look at him. "How many years since you've been back?"

Cory sensed she was delaying the inevitable with her prattle. "I was seven when Mother died," he said. "Aunt Lavinia took Catherine and me in, and leased the house. Life went on—more or less."

"You okay, really?" Jessica laid a mitten-swaddled hand on his arm.

"Yeah. No. But, thanks anyway," he gave a weak smile. "Let's go."

The frigid air sliced through Cory like a cleaver as he kicked at the snowy pathway, uncovering just enough brickwork for a foothold up to the porch.

"Holy Mary, Mother of God," Jessica squealed as she hugged her parka tight around her and followed in his steps.

By arrangement, the key was under the mat, although in this small burg it would have been safe to leave the door unlocked, even open, in good weather.

They stomped remnants of snow and slush from their shoes, powdering the dark blue porch. It reminded Jessica of foam on the ocean.

"I don't suppose they left the heat on?" she hoped out loud.

Cory jiggled the key, swung the door open, and stepped into the vast, dark cavern, a place you'd expect to see ghosts floating aimlessly. Jessica hesitated, wrinkled her nose at the dank smell, and then followed close behind Cory, pulling the door shut after her.

"I thought childhood houses were supposed to look smaller when you went back to them as an adult," Cory mused.

"Where's the thermostat?" Jessica asked. Cory pointed to the wall on the left.

He stepped to the right, into the hallway, and jumped at his re-flection in the built-in mirror. Suddenly he returned to the memory of another day over a decade ago in this same spot.

Chapter 2

The tree lights sparkled like handfuls of diamonds hurled into the night sky.

Five-year old Cory, cocooned in a fleecy white blanket, a passable imitation of an evening gown, stood before the hall mirror outside the living room and carefully draped shimmering strands of tinsel over his head, one by one, to create the perfect hairdo. He looked beautiful. He wiggled his toes in his mother's pink satin mules and smiled.

"Christ, Cory, is that my lipstick you've got smeared on your face?" Catherine swept into the room. She grabbed a fistful of tinsel hair. "Jesus, you're such a little freak. Mother!" she howled. Her white-blonde pony tail trailed like jet vapor as she took the stairs two at a time.

Cory looked at his reflection. A few remaining strands of tinsel slid down his small cherub face, hung unevenly from his shoulder, and then slithered like a silver snake down his leg to lie crumpled on the floor by his foot. Shame turned his cheeks crimson.

Devon Broadhurst descended the stairs as if carefully picking her way down a precarious mountain path. She paused half way down, leaned a leathery elbow heavily on the railing, and regarded her small son standing there like her worst nightmare. The words, 'Devil's spawn' floated into her mind, and she grimaced.

Devon wheezed and pounded her chest with her fist. "Cory, how many times have I told you not to touch Catherine's make-up?" It was rhetorical, she knew. She descended the remaining stairs, one heavy footfall after the next. Cory held his breath. She shook her head tiredly. Her scraggly black hair was plastered against her cheeks. "And, take off my Goddamned slippers."

A five-beat cough rattled her sunken chest, and she fanned herself with her free hand. "You look like a whore. What were you thinking?"

She didn't wait for a reply, merely wrapped her long, bony fingers around his scrawny arm and dragged his non-resistant body toward the bathroom.

Cory was doing an apt impression of Raggedy Ann. His mind was cotton batting, his feelings were numb, his body trailed along behind Mother. The pink mules sat abandoned on the cold hardwood floor of the hallway.

The white cream was in stark contrast to the cobalt blue jar, and the pungent scent of Noxzema filled the small room. Latching onto a tuft of his hair, Devon jerked Cory's head back and smeared his face with the cleanser. The fumes stung his eyes and made them water. She wiped his skin roughly with a handful of paper towels from beneath the sink. Her face was a study in disgust.

"I'm sorry, Momma," he whimpered, peeking up at lips clamped shut like a turtle's mouth, and eyes that were slits in her withered face.

He wasn't sure what he was supposed to be sorry for—the emphysema that wracked her lungs, for being a failure as a son, a freak, wanting to be beautiful—but he knew he was supposed to be sorry.

Devon dropped the pink-smeared towels on the sink counter. She slumped to her knees, grabbed Cory, and pulled him roughly to her bosom in a suffocating embrace. Her dressing gown smelled of cigarette smoke she'd sneaked in her upstairs bedroom. Tears fell from her red-rimmed eyes and soaked his hair as she sobbed, "Oh, Cory, Cory—what will become of you when I'm gone?" She rocked him back and forth.

Another series of coughs blew over the top of his head like tornadoes touching down, skipping, touching down. He hated it when she talked like this. She wasn't going anywhere. She couldn't. She was his mother.

Chapter 3

"Cory! Cory?" Jessica shook his arm. "Cory, what's wrong with you?" Her voice edged on hysteria.

"Huh, what?" Cory was doubled over, one hand holding his stomach. With the other, he grabbed the front of Jessica's parka to steady himself. His face was flushed. "I'm sorry, I'm sorry."

"Here, come on" She led him to the stairwell and pointed to the bottom step. "Sit," she said. "What are you sorry for?"

Cory's shoulders heaved, as a dam of tears broke loose. "I'm so tired of apologizing for myself," he sobbed, wiping angrily at the tears. "I'm not a freak!" he shouted into the hollow room.

Jessica sat on the step above him and peered down into his face, now blanched of all color. "No, Cor, of course you're not a freak," she said, stroking the back of his head. "Who are you talking to?"

"Ghosts," he sobbed, "the dead and the living."

Just then, the front door creaked on its hinges and swung abruptly open. A blast of arctic air attacked them from behind.

"Jesus, Mary, and Joseph!" Jessica jumped up, and spun around. With fists at the ready and feet planted firmly, she crouched, prepared to do battle with unseen forces.

"Cory, you in there?" Catherine poked her head through the opening. She glared at Jessica. "Who the hell are you?" she asked, stepping through the door, hands on hips.

Jessica slumped in relief as Catherine stepped into the room. She stuck out her hand in greeting.

"I'm Jessica. You must be Cory's sister." She took in the image of the Ice Queen—tall, with pale blonde hair pulled back in a severe

French twist. Her eyes were light blue and her face was as pale as her hair, the color broken only by a swipe of blood-red lipstick. She was wrapped in a long silver fur coat and wore high-heeled boots that weren't made for walking. Breathtaking, in a Greta Garbo, don't-touch-me sort of way.

"Guess I was expecting Darth Vader or someone," Jessica chuckled. She withdrew her hand that hung, unmet, in the air.

"Common mistake," Cory commented, rising from the stair steps. "Hey, Sis," he fumbled a hug around Catherine's rigid body.

She studied Cory for a moment. "You look emaciated," she said, with no particular emotion. "Don't homosexuals eat?"

Jessica, slack-jawed, and with eyebrows raised, willed Cory to utter a searing retort.

"Maybe we could stay focused on why we're here," Cory suggested, choosing his battles carefully. Jessica groaned.

"Ah, yes" Catherine made a sweeping gesture with her black kid gloved hand, taking in the emptiness of their childhood. "We're here to say goodbye. Really, Cory, couldn't we just have signed the damned papers at the broker's office and have been done with it?"

At the sound of the doorbell, all three turned and stared at the front entrance.

"Saved by the Southern belle," Catherine said as she went to the door.

"Whatta bitch," Jessica said after Catherine was out of earshot. Cory shrugged.

"Hello, hello? Y'all in there?" Dody Sawtell, the broker, called from the other side of the door. She gave the bell one final ring.

Catherine yanked open the door and motioned her inside.

Dody, a year or so older than Catherine, and a good forty pounds heavier, clambered into the room, stomping snow from her boots onto the hardwood floor. She tromped on by Catherine into the great room.

"Oh, my, this couldn't be young Cory, all grown up?" She gave him the once-over and batted her mascara-laden lashes. Her rubber soles made a squeaking sound as she passed Cory. She stopped briefly, regarded Jessica as one might a smudge on a glass, and walked on. Jessica stood like a shadow just behind Cory.

"Where did you find *her*?" Jessica whispered in Cory's ear.

Cory grimaced. "She's the only game in town, I'm afraid."

"And Catherine—my, aren't we just looking—healthy," she offered with a saccharine smile.

"Hello, Dody," Catherine's voice was hard and flat. "Can we just get this over with?"

"I hope y'all have had time to say your goodbyes to each and every little ol' room, as highly unusual as this is."

"I'm good," Cory replied. "Doesn't seem as important as it once did."

He shot a look at Catherine, who leaned heavily against the wall, arms crossed over her chest, lips pursed, and eyes in a squint. For just a moment, she looked like a teenage version of Devon that Cory remembered from an old high school yearbook. "You good?" he asked.

"Humph."

"Alrighty then," Dody chirped.

She looked around the empty space for a table on which to place her alligator briefcase. Cory's eyes fixed on the briefcase that contained the documents that would free him from his prison. Finding no appropriate surface, Dody spread the small, stapled stacks of paper along the length of the bottom step of the stairwell. With Kindergarten teacher precision, she laid a gold pen, imprinted with *Dody Sawtell, Title Officer* and her phone number, on the end of the step.

"I'll need your autographs on each line where there's an 'x.'" With a fuchsia-colored nail she pointed to an 'x' as a visual aid.

"I don't know whether to laugh or cry," Cory muttered. Jessica snickered.

Catherine slipped off her gloves, shrugged off her bulky coat, and slung it over the newel post so she could bend sufficiently to reach the bottom step. She and Cory each signed at their designated 'x.'

"That's it, then?" Catherine clicked the tip of the pen several times. "When do we get the check?"

Dody gathered up the pens and papers, filed them in her briefcase, and regarded Catherine. "Aren't we just as eager as flies on poo," she smiled with all the warmth of a mosquito. "The check will be at the bank first thing in the morning." She snapped shut the briefcase, and tossed the word "Ta," back over her shoulder as she strode past Catherine and Cory and out the door.

"I guess this is it then," Cory said, noting a catch somewhere in his throat.

"This was *it* fifteen years ago," Catherine retorted. "You were just too young to know it. I'll see you at the bank at nine in the morning."

"Are you staying at The Crossroads?" Cory asked.

"It's the only motel within driving distance of this Godforsaken place," Catherine said as she shrugged on her coat and gathered up her bag.

"Maybe we could all have dinner together," Cory said.

"I think not." Catherine slammed the door behind her.

"Holy shit," Jessica snorted. "Talk about Daughter Dearest."

"Yeah, well..." Cory was at loss for words to explain his family.

In Room 207 at The Crossroads, Jessica turned up the heat and then clicked on the television that was bolted to the wall. She bounced on the queen-sized bed closest to the bathroom. "Not bad," she judged, stifling a yawn. "Although I could probably sleep on an ice floe after today."

Cory clicked the television off.

"Hey, that was a rerun of *To Tell the Truth*," Jessica complained.

"How appropriate," Cory said as he sat down opposite Jessica on the remaining bed. "Can we talk?"

Jessica fluffed the pillows and leaned against the headboard. "Shoot," she said. "Are you missing David?" she asked, referring to the thirty-four year old man Cory had been dating for the last few months.

"We broke up." Cory kept his eyes focused on a spot on the flowered bedspread.

Jessica gasped. "You what? When were you going to tell me?"

"Look, I know you didn't approve of David..."

"It's not that I didn't approve, exactly," Jessica interrupted. "But, Cory, he was just so old! You two were in sort of different worlds. You've only been out for three years, and..." they sat in the uncomfortable silence that usually accompanied any talk of David.

"I know. You're right. He wanted to settle down, white picket fence and all that. I think he's having a mid-life crisis," Cory said with a grin. He glanced over at Jessica, then back down at the bedspread. "Jes," he cleared his throat and shifted his position. "I don't think I want to date gay men any more."

Jessica's mouth hung. "Cory, I hate to mention the obvious, but you've just obliterated the entire playing field of possibilities." She

179

shook her head back and forth slowly, trying to grasp any logic she might have missed.

Cory stood and paced the small room. "I've been thinking," he said as he passed the end of her bed, turned and headed the other direction.

"Uh huh, and…" Jessica prompted after a moment.

"I've been thinking for a long time," he passed by again.

Jessica stood, grabbed him by the arm, marched him to the end of the bed, and sat him down. She sat opposite him, knee to knee.

"A long time…"

"I don't think I'm really gay," he said quietly.

"What?" Jessica slapped both hands to her cheeks. "Why am I always the last to learn these things?" she sputtered. "Oh, Cory, it isn't me, is it? You haven't fallen in love with *me,* or something, have you? Please, say it isn't so," she said, horrified at the possibility. "I'm queer as a camel in a swim suit."

"Relax," Cory said. "I don't want to date girls." His voice dropped to a whisper. "I want to be one. I think I'm transsexual." He sighed heavily, his shoulders drooped, and he peered up at her through heavy eyelashes. He'd never said that word aloud. Jessica sat in silence. He watched as countless expressions washed over her face without so much as a single muscle twitch. She released the breath she'd been holding in a whoosh.

"Like TJ, who used to be a 'she' only the other direction?" Jessica asked.

Cory nodded. A trickle of sweat ran down his temple.

"I just haven't had the word for it before. I think I've known since I was a kid. As a teenager, when I'd shower, I'd imagine I had breasts. Then I'd look down and see this thing between my legs that felt like a foreign object," Cory paused. Jessica's eyes were wide, and her mouth was small and round.

Cory took a deep breath. "When I started dating guys," he continued, "all of a sudden my penis became this hugely important thing. It was all wrong, Jess. I've got the wrong body."

"So, you want to *be* a girl, you say," Jessica reiterated. Cory nodded. "So you can date straight guys?"

"I guess, yeah," Cory said.

"I don't know, Cor," Jessica looked away. "That's kind of hard to wrap my mind around. What will become of us?" She had a wary look on her face that made Cory uneasy.

"Nothing will change between us," Cory said, and knew as the words left his mouth that there was no guarantee.

At five minutes before nine the next morning, Jessica and Cory pulled out of the Dew Drop Inn and headed for the Farmers and Merchants Bank.

"Do you think Catherine will be there already?" Jessica asked.

"Oh, she'll be there," Cory said. "Trust me."

"You haven't said what you're going to do with all that money." Jessica glanced sideways at Cory. She pulled into the bank's parking lot and cut the engine.

"There's this place in Trinidad, Colorado," Cory said as he turned up his coat collar against the winter morning. "The doc there is a transsexual. She does the surgery."

"Oh my God." Jessica tried to keep her eyes above Cory's belt line. Failing that, she mumbled, "Shit." She looked out her window. "You sure about this?"

"I've never been surer of anything in my life," he said. "It will be about a year before I can have the surgery, so I'm going to let my money grow for a while, along with my hair," he giggled. "It's an inside joke."

They sat in silence for a moment, Jessica with elbows on the steering wheel, chin in hands. She cleared her throat. "Well then," Jessica finally said, "let's go get your future."

Catherine, wrapped in silver fur, stepped out of the F&M lobby onto the snow-shoveled concrete. She threw them a withering glance, turned and re-entered the bank.

"That girl's got a popsicle up her..." Jessica stopped short when she noticed Cory's stricken expression.

"After today, I'm afraid I'll never see my sister again," he said, staring at the spot where Catherine had been.

"Her loss, my friend." Jessica linked arms with Cory and trudged into the bank.

The finances were transacted in a blur of efficiency and within half an hour, the three were headed back out the door to the parking lot.

Jessica grabbed Catherine by the elbow and turned her around. "I've just got to ask you this for my own information." Catherine shot her an icy look. "Why are you so hateful to your brother? Really..."

Her exasperation was growing and her voice cracked with emotion. "I'm just curious. I mean, don't you know that he loves you?"

Catherine's face rearranged itself. She looked at Cory. For a moment there was a vulnerability Cory had never seen.

"When I look at you, Cory," she said in something just above a whisper, "I see our past. I see Devon, shrunken with cancer. I see a crazy little boy in girls' clothes. I see myself as a teenager, supposed to be able to figure out how to live my life with no one to turn to. I see that damned hell hole of a house that echoed with loneliness and hopelessness, that was full of sickness and stench."

Catherine closed her eyes. When she opened them again, the hardness was back. She wrenched her arm from Jessica's grasp. "That's not my life anymore. You're not my life anymore," she said to Cory. She turned abruptly and walked to her car.

Cory held his bottom lip firmly between his teeth. He would not let it tremble. He would not.

Chapter 4

Cory felt the sun filter through the gauze curtains behind him. His therapist regarded him thoughtfully from her wing-backed chair.

"So, you really said the word? No more euphemisms, like, 'I'm not comfortable in my body'?" Marguerite asked.

Cory beamed.

"And you decided Jessica would be the first friend you told," Marg said. "I suppose that makes sense," she nodded.

"Ever since we met in the Lesbian and Gay Support Group three years ago, she sort of took on the role of the loving big sister I never had. I figured I owed her the honor," Cory smiled.

"How did she take it?"

Cory shrugged. "It was a little hard to tell," he said.

"And how was it for you, to take that risk?" Marg asked.

"At first she didn't say anything. I thought, oh, so this is how it's going to be. The first in a line of losses." He kicked off his sandals and folded his legs yoga-style on the leather couch. "I wanted to cry or say, 'just kidding', you know, back pedal real fast?"

"But you waited," Marg said.

"Yeah, for a long time. Just as we were falling asleep, she said, 'Hey, Cor, whatever works for you is fine with me.'"

Marg smiled. "You've met with Doctor Chan regarding the hormone therapy?"

"Uh huh. We start next month. He suggested I start shopping now. Develop my style, you know. Maybe start letting my hair grow." He tugged at a tuft of hair tucked behind his ear and stared at the floor.

"What are you thinking about?" Marg said.

"Oh, I was thinking about that Christmas when I was five, and the tinsel hair—" his voice trailed off with the memory.

The following Saturday, Cory met Jessica at Hot Couture. He was wrapped in a pink-feathered boa, and was beaming at his reflection in the floor-length mirror.

"What in the name of sanity are you doing?" Jessica appeared next to him, punked-out with orange spiked hair and a clip-on nose ring.

"Stylin'," he winked into the mirror.

"Cor, you're going to be a girl, not a hooker." She led him over to the racks. "Are you a summer, fall, spring, or winter?" she eyed him from head to toe.

"Uh—"

"Fall," she decided.

"Fall? Sounds a sort of drab, doesn't it?" Cory worried.

"Think autumn leaves, golden stalks of corn, clear blue skies, pumpkins—"

"Pumpkins! Yes. Orange is good," Cory grinned, tweaking a pointy lock of Jessica's hair.

"You're sort of willowy. I'm thinking long skirt, silk over-blouse, maybe a vest, knee boots," Jessica offered.

"Sounds kind of Annie Hall," Cory grimaced. "I'm thinking something maybe more this decade. Tee shirt, Capri's, sandals—" he countered.

"Did you bring the padded bra?" Jessica asked.

"I'm wearing it," he said in a pout.

"Oh," she glanced at his chest. "Sorry. Guess you're sort of creeping up on them, huh?"

"Growing into them, Doctor Chan calls it," he corrected. Cory draped a russet colored short-sleeved tee, and beige Capri's with a russet and moss green floral pattern over his arm. "Uh oh, dressing room problem," he muttered.

"Unisex," Jessica smiled and pointed to a series of cubicles along the side wall.

Glad that he'd shaved his legs that morning, Cory pulled the Capri's up over his hips and slipped the tee over his 36A temporary bosom. The three-way mirror reflected back an attractive, trim, androgynous being. He stepped outside the cubicle where Jessica waited.

"Oh—my—God," she clapped her hands gleefully.

"But, do I look like a girl?" Cory worried, turning slowly.

"Well, you don't *not* look like a girl," Jessica said. "I think until your hair grows, you might want to try a wig."

"Where would I find a wig?"

"There's a cancer supply store on the other side of town," Jessica offered.

"You've got to be kidding."

Twenty minutes later, a sales clerk at Hair4U had lined up a variety of styles on the counter in front of Cory. The way she sized him up over the top of her glasses made him squirm.

"The weave on the inside of this one minimizes the itchy scalp that sometimes comes from hair loss," she gave a tight smile, and handed Cory a conservative bob in sandy blonde, closest to his own color.

Jessica snorted. "Sorry, allergies," she said as she pulled a tissue from her pocket and faked a sneeze. Cory shot her a look.

The clerk snugged the wig into position, fluffed it, and pointed Cory toward the mirror on the counter.

"Mmm, I've always wanted to go auburn," Cory said, gently fingering the shoulder-length wavy tresses on the stand to his right.

The clerk narrowed her eyes. "Most people don't want to do anything too extreme in these cases," she said.

Jessica, unable to contain her mirth, bolted from the shop, claiming an expired meter.

Cory regarded the clerk. "I'm feeling particularly bold these days. You know how it is," he smiled bravely at the clerk.

"Of course you are," she nodded as she slipped the blonde wig back on its form and eased the lush auburn curls over Cory's head.

"Yes," Cory whispered into the mirror.

"Well, then," she said as she rang up his purchase, "remember, we're *hair* for you," she twittered as she put the wig in a box and handed it over the counter.

"Thank you," Cory batted his eyes.

"Good bye—uh—Miss," the clerk said.

Chapter 5

Cory stretched her bare legs into the sunshine and wiggled her toes. Her back rested against the smooth bark of the elm tree. She was as mesmerized by the interplay of sun and shade as it danced on the grass in the breeze, as by the opalescent pink polish she'd painted on her toenails that morning. The color reminded her of her grandmother's favorite tea set.

* * *

The clink of the pink China teacups and Nana's smile filled Cory's heart with happiness and comfort as they sat on the patchwork quilt under the oak tree in the late afternoon sun. Tea parties with Nana, decked out in glittering jewels from her antique velvet jewelry box were Cory's favorite thing about summer.

"Here dear, try this strand of pearls." Nana looped the soft, eggshell colored beads about his delicate neck.

"Nana, try these beautiful red earrings," Cory said. He clipped to his nana's ears the garnet stones that reflected tiny beams of red onto her papery soft cheeks.

Nana giggled with delight. They clicked teacups. "To the beautiful people," she said, as they sipped their honey-sweetened ginger tea.

Car accident; *gone*; *won't be coming back*—pieces of phrases overheard. Momma stubbing out her cigarette; Catherine staring out the window. "What am I supposed to do now?" Momma asks of no one in particular as the smoke from her cigarette twists and curls like ghosts over her head. She sighs deeply.

* * *

"Earth to Cory," Jessica nudged Cory's leg.

"Huh?" Cory looked over at Jessica splayed out on the blanket, baseball cap shading her eyes.

"I said have you chosen a major yet?" Jessica sat up, yawned, and stared out across campus at the students crisscrossing the Quad like so many worker ants. "You are going on to the University, aren't you?

Cory scrunched up her face.

"Cor, you have to break out of the nest someday. You know that, don't you?" Jessica sighed. They'd been having this conversation all summer.

"I was thinking I could check out the Repertoire Theater here— they have a good season lined up," Cory offered.

"Ah, so this week you're going to be a theater major."

"You're being sarcastic."

"Last week, your professional goal was to become a florist. When do we get around to beautician? I mean, could you get any more cliché?"

Jessica shifted her position, sitting cross-legged opposite Cory on the blanket.

"Really, Cory, if you're going to practice being a girl, you've got to let go of the gay-guy stereotypes."

"It's fine for you to be a metal sculptor, but I can't be an actor? How fair is that?" Cory whined.

Jessica reflected on the myriad future paths her parents had indefatigably supported her through—artist, vet, entrepreneur, botanist, chemist—purchasing pastels, stethoscopes, ledgers, microscopes, as her interests changed by the year.

Jessica looked Cory in the eyes. "This isn't about a career, is it?"

Cory's eyes dropped to her hands, folded in her lap. She studied her cuticles.

"Yeah, I didn't think so," Jessica confirmed. "Talk to me, Cor."

"I'm, you know, concerned..." Cory's voice trailed off. She unfolded her hands, picked at her thumbnail, and folded her hands again.

"Concerned? Try again," Jessica urged.

"Okay, I'm scared," Cory blurted.

"Better. Go on."

"I mean, people know me here. They accept me as who I'm becoming. I'm not so naive as to think this is going to be an easy transition. And frankly, the thought of starting over in a new environment, having to pass—Jes, it fills me with terror." Cory's body shuddered. "Remember those two trans girls last year somewhere down south? They were dragged from their car and beaten senseless," she said.

Jessica reached over and took her hand. "You've been talking with Dr. Chan and Marg about this, haven't you?"

"Yeah. They say what I'm going through is normal," Cory gave a weak smile. "Well, normal for the situation, that is. And that with the hormones, my body is changing, and I'm appearing more credible as the months go by." She looked down. "Even my—well, you know—is getting smaller."

"So, what's the problem? You're gorgeous, dahling," Jessica said with a grin. "You get any more femme, I may have to ask you out myself."

"Don't tease, Jes. You know I'm not a lesbian."

"We could fix that," Jessica bounced her eyebrows a couple of times in response. Cory threw a handful of grass at her.

"And the voice lessons?" Jessica asked.

"I never was very macho, so raising my vocal register isn't all that challenging," Cory said. "The thing is, I don't feel like I'm being heard."

"Welcome to the wonderful world of women," Jessica said. "How are the walking lessons going?"

"I'm a long way from the runway, but I have a passable girl walk." Cory ran a hand up and down her hairless calf and frowned.

"Here's the thing, Jes. So, okay, I look, sound, and move like a woman. I'm pre-surgery. I find some incredible hunk. We go out. We like each other. Things get heavy. The hands start roving," Cory heaved a sigh, wadded the tissue she'd been twisting in her hand, and threw it as far as she could. "Even if I tape it down, there comes a point..."

"I don't know, Cor. I just don't know how to guide you through this one." Jessica sat with head hung, looking as morose as Cory felt.

"Wait," she sprung to life, "Remember last year when TJ left our group? Didn't he start something called Fifth Option?"

"TJ moved eighty miles from here. I lost track of him. Fifth Option?"

"Yeah, like lesbian, gay, bi, straight, trans," Jessica counted off on her fingers.

"Why is trans always last?" Cory asked.

"Don't get testy with me; I didn't name the group," Jessica said. "I know we could find TJ. He'd know about this stuff. Come on Cor," she urged. "What do you have to lose?"

"It's not what I have to lose that scares me. It's what I have to gain."

Chapter 6

"Hey, Cory, wait up," Josh called as he dashed out the door of the Arts Building.

"Hi, Josh," Cory blushed under the intense blue eyes focused on her. She felt naked and vulnerable as she took a raggedy breath in and tried to focus on the reality of the earth under her feet. "Can you believe that assignment? Create 'fear' using only blue. God."

"Yeah, I thought maybe we could work on it together," Josh's smile and those perfect white teeth stirred something in Cory that at one time would have passed for an erection.

"Oh, well, maybe. Uhm..."

"How about over coffee, if you're free? Or tonight? We could brainstorm over a bottle of wine." He stepped closer.

"Ah, well..." Her ears rang and her vision began to fade. Oh my God, I'm going to faint, she thought as she squatted and dropped her head between her knees.

"You okay?" Josh asked, kneeling next to her, one arm thrown protectively across her shoulders. "What can I do?" The alarm in his voice was like a sobering slap. She took a quick gulp of air and struggled to her feet, supported by Josh's hand beneath her elbow.

"I'm fine, really. Thanks. It's just—that time of the month," Cory stammered. She turned her face away in shame.

"Really? I mean, maybe another night then?" Josh studied the back of her head.

"Yeah, that would probably be better," Cory turned and offered a smile. "Thanks for understanding."

"Hey, no problem. I have sisters. You take care," Josh waved as he turned toward the Student Union.

Cory buried her face in her hands.

Two days later, Cory sat across from Marg. They sipped tea from delicate gold-rimmed cups with matching saucers.

"I've never heard of Chrysanthemum tea," Cory said. "Where's it from?"

"A friend brought it from Chinatown." Marg inhaled the fragrant steam that drifted from her cup. "Cory, we could sit and talk about tea until the cows come home, but I'm thinking there's something else on your mind." She sat her cup down with a clink.

Cory told her about the exchange with Josh. Her face flushed when she admitted using her period as a delay tactic.

"Interesting diversion, albeit biologically impossible," Marg smiled. "So, what's to lose by being honest with someone who seems to be interested in you—assuming it's the real you he values?" Marg asked.

"A potential friend, I guess. I'm not sure Josh knows about the real me. Seems like a high price to pay," Cory said, slumping lower in her chair. She swirled remnants of flower petals in her cup.

"And, what's to gain?" Marg asked.

"A potential friend. Someone who'd like me, even though..."

"I'd say that's about fifty-fifty."

"But if he's interested in me sexually, then gets all grossed out or something, I'm not sure I can live through that," Cory blurted.

"Cory," Marg leaned forward and caught Cory's eyes, "unless you plan on spending your life in the closet—a very tiny, lonely closet—you're going to have to live through these experiences." She sat back with a sigh. "If he rejects you because you're facing gender reassignment, he's not the sort of person you'll want in your life. Trust me."

The following Wednesday, Cory lingered by the door as students spilled out of the Art Building.

"Josh..." Cory called out as Josh bounded down the steps.

"Hey, Cory. How are you?" He turned and flashed a smile that made Cory's feet sweat. "You started on the project yet?"

"No, that's what I wanted to talk to you about. You have a minute?"

"Sure. You want to grab a cup of coffee at the Union or something?" Josh suggested.

"Okay." Cory took a deep breath as Josh slipped a supporting hand under her elbow as she took the two steps down to ground level.

They carried their cups to a small table in the far corner of the room where the general din was quieter.

It's now or never, Cory thought, as she took a sip of her latte and settled into the creaky wooden chair. She cleared her throat. Josh's eyes bored into her as he leaned slightly forward, elbows on the table.

"Um, Josh, there's something I'm not sure you're aware of that might make a difference in what happens next," Cory began.

Josh tilted his head attentively. "Sounds serious," he said.

"I'm getting ready for gender reassignment surgery," Cory said, not allowing her eyes to drop.

The corners of Josh's mouth twitched slightly. He blinked.

"I'm transgender," Cory said, daring Josh with her stare to have a reaction.

"Yeah, I know," he said with a slow smile. "But you still have to do the project."

Something between a chuckle and a gasp escaped Cory. "You know? And you're okay with this?" she asked with astonished relief.

"Cory, I think you're incredibly brave to take steps to get your life congruent. What integrity. I admire that. You're the kind of friend I'd like to have," he reached over, took Cory's hand, and gave it a quick squeeze, "if you'll accept me."

"Friend," Cory reiterated.

"Friend," Josh grinned. "So, what *are* your thoughts on portraying 'fear' using only blue?"

"Let me get this straight," Jessica's voice was strident on the other end of the phone. "You can't meet for breakfast because Josh is picking you up to take you to the Art Institute?"

"Well—"

"And you can't go to the movies because Josh is coming over for dinner?" Jessica interrupted.

"Jess—"

"And you're not available to go shopping with me today because you and Josh have to finish that friggin' art project?"

"Look," Cory said, "I know I've been spending a lot of time with

Josh lately, but he's my friend too."

"I'm thinking you're in denial, Cory. I just don't want to see you get hurt," Jessica said.

"You sure you're not jealous?" The sound of the receiver slamming into its cradle made Cory wince. She shook her head as she hung up her bedroom phone.

"Unbelievably possessive bitch," Cory mumbled, sorting through her closet for the black velour scoop-neck top she wanted to wear with her new jeans. She struggled into her black leather boots and checked herself in the mirror. "Yup," she smiled, "this'll make his eyes pop."

The doorbell rang at exactly four o'clock. Cory ran her fingers through her hair, gave her blouse an extra tug, moistened her lips with a swipe of her tongue and headed for the door.

"Wow," Josh gaped. "You look—amazing."

Cory smiled. "Come in," she said, holding the screen door open.

Josh handed Cory the grocery bag he'd been balancing on one hip. "I thought we'd do sort of a theme dinner in honor of the assignment," he said as she unpacked the goods on the kitchen counter.

"This is great," Cory squealed. "Cordon Bleu TV dinners, Blue Nun wine, blue cheese with blue corn chips. You are too much." From the bag she pulled out a bouquet of blue iris and went in search of a vase.

"Don't forget dessert," Josh said, reading into the bottom of the bag. "Blueberries," he grinned.

"Who knew art could be so much fun," Cory batted her eyelashes coyly. "Here," she said, handing him the corkscrew, "Let's start with the wine, chips and cheese."

"Gosh, Cory, it's only four o'clock. Shouldn't we maybe wait a while?" Josh said, sliding the sleeve of his sweatshirt back over his watch.

"Lightweight," Cory teased. "This is our inspiration. I say we go for it." She sat two wine glasses on the table, shook the chips into a pottery bowl, and placed thin wedges of cheese on a cobalt blue plate.

While Josh poured the wine, Cory slipped an Elvis CD in the player and found the cut that lamented a blue, blue Christmas without you.

"To art," said Josh as they clinked glasses. His gaze lingered at the scoop of her blouse.

"To the artists," countered Cory.

Over wine, chips, cheese, and more wine, they talked form and function of design, whether to go abstract in their statement or stay with realism. Words flowed easily as Cory poured her third glass of Blue Nun. Josh smiled lazily across the table. Hands behind his head, he arced backwards in a stretch that left Cory breathless.

"What?" he asked.

"What, what?" Cory responded.

"You have a funny look on your face."

Cory blushed. "That's my 'oh, my God, you're such an Adonis' look, I guess," she grinned.

"Uh, Cory..." Josh's face went blank, unreadable, like a mime's face

"Hey, let's get those dinners in the oven." Cory extricated her foot from her mouth, jumped up from her chair, and grabbed the table to steady herself as the floor tilted.

Josh was there in a flash, an arm around her waist, his thumb resting against the swell of her breast. "It's the empty stomach thing," he said. "You okay?"

Cory wanted to swim in the blue of his eyes. She turned to face him, slipped her arms around his neck, and drew him near. Her lips parted with want.

"Whoa," Josh stiffened, disengaged himself, and stepped back. "Cory, look, I don't think..." he stammered. "I really like you, and," he took both her hands in his and looked directly into her eyes. "You're attractive and all, but I mean, essentially, you're still a guy, right?"

Cory blanched. She pulled her hands free and wobbled towards the kitchen. Humiliation covered her like sweat, and tears stung her eyes.

"Oh, Josh, lighten up. It's just the wine," she struggled for a flippant tone. "C'mon. Let's fix dinner," she called over her shoulder. She clamped her lips tightly to check the urge to vomit.

Chapter 7

"Oh, my God, how can you drink this?" Cory choked, sputtered, and dabbed at her mouth with a postage stamp sized cocktail napkin. She set the aperitif glass of chocolate Port on the tiny round table between them. Their wrought iron bar stools were scrunched intimately into a quiet corner of Club Q.

"It's tres chic, my dear," TJ replied, practicing his newly adapted sophisticated-man style.

Cory grinned. "I think I liked you better when you were more, 'hey dude, let's grab a beer.'"

"That was *so* yesterday," TJ tipped his stool back slightly on its hind legs and regarded Cory over John Lennon lenses that rested mid-bridge on his nose.

"Would you not do that, please? I feel like you're talking down to me."

"My God, Cory, you've turned into a real bitch," TJ said, righting his chair and sliding his glasses back into their normal position. He sipped his aperitif. "What's up with you?"

Cory relayed the whole dreadful Josh debacle as couples of all persuasions moved with bodies glued together on the dance floor to a slow song. While waiting for TJ to respond, Cory snuck a peek at his chest. She wondered if he taped.

TJ looked down at the small glass in his hand. He sighed and shook his head slowly, as if recent history were replaying itself in his mind. "It's hard—the first time."

"That's it?" Cory leaned forward. "Does it get better? I mean, do you figure out a more graceful way to handle those situations?"

"It's going to sound like a cliché, Cory, but I think communication is the key. I mean, you sort of sprung yourself on the guy, right?"

"It was the alcohol."

"Bullshit. You had the hots for him. You chose your clothes to seduce him, right?" TJ's harsh words were tempered by the gentle tone of his voice.

Cory looked away in embarrassment.

"Hey, it's okay," TJ reassured. "It's normal that you're going to find guys attractive. And this guy even knew about you, right?"

Cory nodded.

"And he liked you as a friend?" TJ waited for another nod before going on. "So, what do you suppose would have happened if you'd told Josh that you found him sexually attractive, versus, say, pouncing on him?"

"He would have said the same thing, that he wasn't interested in me that way," Cory mumbled into her lap.

"So, that would have been disappointing. Would it have been as humiliating?

TJ's kind smile and the softness of his eyes made something catch in the back of Cory's throat. She took a raggedy breath in.

"No, I guess not," she said. "At least my dignity would have been intact."

The DJ cranked up the volume and bodies writhed to Madonna wailing about being touched for the very first time. Cory gave a sardonic smile. She could relate

As if reading her mind, TJ reached over and took her hand. "Look," he said gently, "there are going to be a lot of 'firsts' to adjust to, and people in your current life aren't going to know how to support you."

Cory nodded, knowing he was right. She swirled the remainder of her drink in her glass and looked at TJ.

"Why not do yourself a favor, and come to a Fifth Option meeting? We won't bite—well, unless that's what you're into," TJ grinned wickedly. "You don't have to figure this out alone; none of us did," he added.

Cory jotted down the time and place of the next meeting at Rod and Barbara's home, and promised to see TJ there. A real trans couple. Cory felt a certain amount of voyeuristic curiosity building. What had she been afraid of? Limited options? Never being able to have a relationship with a straight man? Fully accepting that she was now a transgender woman?

TJ, five foot six at best, and of slight build, stood to help her on with her coat. This transition can't have been easy for him either, Cory thought, as she stooped to allow TJ to assist her. Again, she was aware of that catch in the back of her throat.

The following Friday night, Cory stood staring into her closet. She sighed heavily. "What do you wear to a coming out meeting?" she asked of the dust bunnies that slept among her shoes. She pulled out the red power dress she'd bought on a whim at the thrift store.

"What was I thinking?" she said, as she shoved the dress back among her girl clothes. Cory settled on black skinny jeans, a rust-colored tee, and a light-weight black leather jacket. She clipped coral earrings set in silver on her ears and surveyed herself in the mirror. "It will just have to do," she said, checking her watch.

The lights shone brightly through the open curtained windows of the tract home on Harmony Drive. Cory parked across from the house and watched as people milled about, drinks in hand, engaged in animated conversation. "It's just a meeting, for God sake," she admonished herself. She wiped her palms on the legs of her pants, checked her rearview mirror, and glanced up and down the street before exiting her car. Freak show. Where did that come from? she wondered.

Cory gave a tentative knock, hoping the sound would be lost on the crowd inside and she could return home. A beautiful, statuesque woman in her mid-forties answered the door. Her hair was frosted chestnut, and she wore a stunning green brocade Chinese pantsuit.

"You must be Cory. Come in, I'm Barbara. We spoke on the phone." The woman took Cory's hand and led her into the living room. "Everyone, this is TJ's friend Cory," she gestured around the room. Cory felt her face redden as she plastered on a smile.

"Welcome, I'm Rod, Barbara's husband," a shorter version of a Tom Cruise look-alike said. "What can I get you to drink?" Cory shrugged. "A coke, I guess—thanks."

"Hey Cory, good to meet you. I'm Jake," a young man with a well-trimmed beard stuck out his hand. "I'm TJ's roommate. He had to work overtime tonight, and asked me to apologize for leaving you stranded."

He had perfect white teeth, hazel eyes under thick lashes, and small, square hands with manicured nails. Not at all hard to look at. So far, this was feeling like a gathering of the town's beautiful people.

Cory accepted her Coke, and found a place on the couch next to a—hmmm, either a very butch woman with a definite need of electrolysis, or a man who preferred dresses—she couldn't decide. Cory averted her eyes and hoped the meeting would be called to order soon. When she looked up, a person of indeterminate gender smiled and lifted a glass to her from across the room. Oh my God, she thought, that is the most gender-neutral person I've ever seen. She found it creepy that she really couldn't tell.

People took seats and the conversation quieted as Barbara called the meeting to order. Introductions were made and brief histories of their trans status exchanged.

"And when I began wearing dresses," Mark shared, "my wife packed up the three kids and moved out of state. My life consists of court battles and attorney fees. I can't even begin to think about the cost of surgery." Cory clenched and unclenched her jaw a couple of times to relieve the tension.

Ali grinned broadly as she said, "I have something positive to share. The new guy at the office asked me out for coffee." Cory noticed a churning in her stomach. *Be careful*, she warned silently.

Glenda shared that she'd been cornered in an alley outside the bar at two a.m. "This guy said, 'Your luck just ran out, slut.' I figured I was dead. His buddy was waving a broken beer bottle back and forth. If another couple hadn't come around the corner just then, well…" She took a raggedy breath, lowered her eyes, and said in a quiet voice, "I'm so glad you're all here, and that there's someone for me to tell this to. I'm so ashamed."

The meeting ended with the sharing of recently found resources, a good book someone had read, the name of a local therapist who was trans-friendly, and the reciting of The Serenity Prayer.

"Okay everyone, there's a ton of food in the dining room. Please help yourself," Barbara said. "Cory, will you stay for a while? I'd like to hear how this was for you," she added.

"Oh, thanks, Barbara, but I have to get up really early. I'm sorry. Can I call you?" They exchanged numbers.

Once outside, Cory ran to the nearest bush beyond the arc of the porch light and threw up.

Chapter 8

Cory drummed her fingers on the phone table as the third, and then the fourth ring sounded in an artsy loft across town. "Pick up, damn it," she said, exasperated. Five rings. Six rings. Cory was ready to hang up.

"Hello," a tired voice mumbled, followed by an unstifled yawn. "This had better be important, it's early."

Cory's voice caught in her throat like a patch of cloth on barbed wire.

"Hello, already," Jessica barked. "Who's there?"

Cory cleared her throat. "Jes, it's me, Cory."

Silence. Then, "Cory who?"

"Come on, Jes. I'm sorry, okay?"

"Sorry? That's supposed to make everything okay again? It's been weeks, Cory." Jessica sounded more hurt than angry.

"You were right, Jes. I came on to Josh and he dumped me because I have a dick. I'm sorry I didn't listen to you." More silence. "I miss you. I need a friend," Cory said.

"Yeah, for how long?" Jessica's voice was tight.

Cory hung her head and fiddled with the phone cord. "Forever," she said quietly.

Silence. Then, "Meet me at the Black Cat Cafe in half an hour. I need breakfast—your treat," Jessica added.

"Got it," Cory grinned.

Within thirty minutes, Cory pulled into the Black Cat's parking lot. Jessica was waiting out front with a 'don't talk to me' look on her face. They entered the café, slid into a booth, and gave their order to the waitress. They sat in silence waiting for their food. Cory traced her finger along the design in the Formica tabletop—she could play this game of paying her dues. Jessica studied the café as if this were her first time there.

When the food came, Jessica plowed her way through a stack of waffles, a side of bacon, two eggs over easy, a tall orange juice, and coffee, black. Cory picked at her English muffin and Earl Grey tea, silently observing the food-devouring phenomena across the table from her.

The cafe was all but empty. Crazy Mary, gray hair matted beneath a paisley scarf tied under her chin, sat cackling to herself over a cup of cocoa and a rumpled newspaper at the end of the counter. Cory recognized Kash, the new girl in town whom she'd met at the women's bookstore last week. She sat alone, staring out the plate glass window, her omelet growing cold from neglect. Cory tried to catch her eye, but failed.

After the waitress brought a third refill of coffee, Jessica finally sat back, patted her stomach, took a deep breath, released it with a sigh, and looked at Cory. "Okay, so I've missed you too," she said, then glanced out the window and frowned. The sky was the color of gunmetal. It had been raining for a week. Cory knew that Jessica hated winter. She knew a lot about Jessica.

"I thought you'd have a whole new bunch of friends from that support group you were going to," she continued. "So, what's up with that?" She folded her arms over her chest and looked Cory squarely in the eyes.

A smile played on Cory's lips. She felt as if she'd just been challenged to a duel to prove her loyalty and friendship. "The best thing that came from that group was a good reading list," she said, and gave Jessica a rueful smile.

"Everything you wanted to know, but didn't know who to ask?" Jessica grinned. "So, tell me," she said, leaning forward, elbows on table, getting into the spirit of things, "what were they like?"

"Well, they weren't like anything—I mean, they were all individuals. Everyone had a different story. One woman was living as a guy so she could be with her girlfriend, who was her former boyfriend, until the MTF surgery. The partner didn't want to be in a lesbian relationship."

Jessica rolled her eyes. "Are you making this up?" she asked.

"No, I swear," Cory raised her hand in the air.

The waitress swung by just then. "What can I get you, darlin'?" she asked Cory.

"Sorry, my mistake," Cory grinned, lowering her hand. Jessica chuckled.

"Another woman," Cory continued, "post op, was so beautiful. I mean, Jes, you couldn't tell. You know? And a middle-aged man—totally indiscernible. I gotta tell you, hormones and surgery can work miracles."

"So why did you stop going?

"One night they got in a big fight about fence-sitting. This gender-blender androgynous type didn't want to have to declare whether he or she was a guy or a girl," Cory said.

"And that's a problem how?" Jessica shrugged. "I mean, whose business is it anyway, unless you're going to sleep with him, or her. Hmmm, maybe on a need to know basis…"

"Do you mind?" Cory interrupted. "I'd gotten what I needed from the group—that there's no right or proper way to be a different gender. And, I'm not alone. And, I don't want to have friends just based on my gender—there's more to me than that," she finished with an emphatic nod of her head.

"Welcome home," Jessica said as she reached across the table and gave Cory's hand a squeeze.

* * *

"You seem pretty excited about the possibilities of surgery," Marg hooked a strand of gray hair behind her ear, leaned back in her chair, and settled in for the hour.

"Oh, Marg, you should have seen her," Cory's eyes were round with awe. "All the curves were real—I asked," Cory answered the unasked question. A blush tinted her cheeks.

Marg smiled and nodded. "Remember, each person's body is unique, and responds differently to the hormone therapy," she offered. "How are you doing with the walking lessons and the voice coaching?" she asked.

"As long as I stay focused," Cory rose and demonstrated by crossing the office and back, "I walk pretty much like a girl, don't you think?"

"Looks good to me."

"And even though I sometimes feel like Minnie Mouse, I'm managing to keep my voice in a register that's slightly higher than my normal voice is," Cory finished with a shrug and a grin.

"How's it going out in public?" Marg asked. "You passing?"

"The other night Jess and I went out for dinner." Cory sat forward in her seat, and excitement glittered in her eyes. "The waitress said, 'More coffee, ma'am?' She was talking to me. Cool, huh? I wasn't even wearing a dress."

"So, surgery is a few months off yet," Marg noted. "What's the next task ahead?"

Cory withered. She sunk back on the couch and sighed.

"Dating," Cory said, with the same amount of enthusiasm she might have had for swimming in a tar pit. "Ugh."

"We can't let the past be the template for the present, or we'd never move ahead," Marg said. Her voice was gentle, but serious. "I know you got your heart broken by Josh, but you really had more to lose there. He was your friend first, right?"

"Yeah," Cory agreed, "but casual dating has never really appealed to me, you know?"

"They say you can't learn to swim unless you jump in the water," Marg smiled.

"You're just full of platitudes today, aren't you?" Cory chided playfully. "Now *there's* a truly scary thought," she added.

"What's that?" Marg asked.

"Me, in a swimsuit." Cory rolled her eyes and faked a swoon off the couch.

"We've got splashdown," Marg chuckled.

Chapter 9

Cory held a perfectly white mushroom in the palm of her hand, marveling at its smooth surface, the unbroken underbelly. She counted out six and laid them gently in the plastic bag. As she reached for the smallest red bell pepper, it was whisked away by a large hand that appeared out of nowhere.

"May I?" The man attached to the hand offered her a different pepper.

Cory jerked her head up and locked eyes with a gorgeous hunk of manhood. He was tall and tan, with white teeth beneath a tantalizingly crooked smile, and wavy brown shoulder-length hair.

"I, I..."

"The other one had a blemish," he smiled at her. "I just put it back myself."

"Uh."

"I noticed how carefully you chose the mushrooms. Figured you'd want nothing but the best," he closed her fingers gently over the pepper that now rested in her hand. Cory gave him a weak grin.

In the background of the market din, a canned voice sang "Love Is All Around You." Cory gulped.

"My name is Kurt," he said. His hand, strong but gentle, lingered over hers.

"Cory. Cory, yes, that's my name," Cory babbled. She felt a blush start just beneath her collar bone and work its way up like a rising tide that would either strangle her or wash her out to sea.

Kurt released her hand and stepped back. Cory's inhale felt like glass in her lungs.

"Cooking something special?" he asked, those brown doe eyes lulling her.

"Vegetable soup. Dinner, actually." Before she could clamp down on the words, they spilled from her lips. "Are you free?"

Good God girl, she thought in a panic.

"Well," it was Kurt's turn to stammer, "uh, yes, I'd love to."

Too late, Cory thought fleetingly, I'm dead.

"Listen," Kurt continued, "why don't I grab a loaf of sourdough and a bottle of Chardonnay? Oh, do you drink wine?" he asked.

No, no, no, I don't, Cory said vehemently to herself.

"Yes," Cory said with enthusiasm, "that would be lovely."

"I'll meet you at the register," he winked and disappeared down the aisle.

Okay, just breathe, Cory instructed herself. No, call Marg. No, better yet, have Jess meet me out front with an emergency that needs my immediate attention. Cory wiped the sweat from her inner elbows on the sides of her shirt.

She swallowed hard around the lump in her throat and moved on to the zucchini bin.

Kurt was standing next to the check out line. He motioned her over and stepped into line. In his arms, he balanced a bottle of Chardonnay, a loaf of bread, and a potted plant sprinkled with coral colored flowers. She smiled in spite of herself.

"You bought me Azaleas?" Cory grinned.

"Oh," Kurt said, his expression crestfallen, "should I have gotten roses?"

"Actually, I love Azaleas. How could you have known?"

"You just don't seem like a traditional kind of girl," he smiled as he commandeered her cart, placed her groceries on the conveyer belt next to his, and pulled out his debit card.

"On, no, wait—" Cory protested, scrambling to separate her week's shopping from his dinner contribution.

"Humor me," he said, with a languid smile that started a flame in several parts of her body simultaneously. He ran his card through the machine, and typed in his PIN.

The clerk winked at Cory. "He's a keeper, honey," she stage-whispered.

As the groceries were being bagged, Kurt leaned close to Cory and

205

said, "I hope I didn't embarrass you. It's just that this is less than what I would have spent on taking you out to dinner. And, it will be such a pleasure to have a home-cooked meal." He stepped behind the cart and began to wheel it toward the exit, smiling at her companionably.

Cory felt at loss for words. It sounded so reasonable, coming from Kurt.

"Why don't I load these in my car," he said as they left the grocery, "and follow you to your house?"

"Okay," Cory managed. "Where are you parked?"

"The silver one, over there," Kurt pointed to the left. A shiny Mercedes convertible sat in the shade of a crepe myrtle. Cory's eyes went round.

"I'll pull up in front of you," she said. "Oh, and…" she placed her hand on his arm briefly and glanced at the groceries, "thank you. That was very generous."

"You're very welcome," he said, and headed across the lot whistling a nameless tune.

Kurt pulled out of his spot and followed Cory to the exit. She put her blinkers on to signal left, fully expecting Kurt to make a sharp right, disappear from sight with her week's groceries, never to be seen again. In her rearview mirror, she noted the Mercedes blinked for a left turn.

Alternative ending number two, she thought: He'll follow me home, carry the groceries in, strangle me with a pair of nylons, wrap my body in a sheet, and carry me to the dumpster. Then he'll take over my cottage. I wonder if he'll remember to water the plants in the window box, she thought idly.

Cory wove her way through traffic, the Mercedes a sleek shadow behind her, and pulled up in front of her brown shingle. Kurt drove on by.

"Ah ha!" Cory shouted. She banged her fists on the steering wheel. "I knew it. I'm screwed." She leaned heavily against the back of her seat and closed her eyes.

Kurt executed a neat U-turn and pulled up in the shade of a maple across the street from her. With boyish energy, he leaped from the car, grabbed both bags of groceries and the potted plant, and stood at the side of Cory's car. At the shadow cast by his body, Cory opened one eye. Kurt bent down, a look of concern contorting his otherwise flawless face.

"Listen, if you need a nap or something, I'll fix dinner," he offered as Cory climbed out of her car.

Idiot, idiot, idiot, she said to herself. "No, I'm fine, thanks," she said to Kurt. "Just, um, centering myself," she mumbled as she searched her bag for her keys.

Chapter 10

Cory gasped and coughed. Her windpipe felt crushed. Pain shot through her shoulder and red fluid blurred her vision as she struggled to see through swollen eyes. She noted the phone receiver lying loose in one hand, but could not make her fingers close around it. The piercing sound of a receiver off the hook filled the room like a flea bomb—then blackness.

From another world, the shrill sound of a siren cut through the oblivion. Cory struggled for consciousness as alternating streaks of red and blue lit the room around her in flashing syncopation. Gruff voices barked unintelligible words into the static of a radio.

A face leaned close but she couldn't make out the features. It was as though she was looking through cotton batting. Another stab of pain as a hand touched her belly, then darkness.

Swaddled in a sheet, Cory felt herself being lifted from the floor onto something hard and flat. Each bone in her body seemed to jam and smash against the next. Discordant words and fragments of sentences floated around and above her.

"ETA nineteen-hundred."

"ID is in her bag."

"Next of kin?"

"Address book"

"Who called this in?"

"Neighbor."

Then the night air, cooling her skin, which seemed on fire. A light strobed red, blue, red, blue. Nausea, then stark nothingness.

The wailing siren pierced Cory's head like a drill. She felt the stab of a needle in her vein as an IV was started. Her vitals were called out in a string of medic-speak. The ambulance swayed and howled like a drunken banshee. Once more, nausea overtook her.

A bright light shone in one eye as she managed to open her lid. She winced at the pain. A curtain swished on its metal hooks with the coming and going of figures as they moved around the small cubicle in a ghostly dance.

"She's conscious," a masked face hovered over her.

More fragmented sentences.

"Rape kit?"

"Not necessary."

"Why? Oh, my God."

Blankets were rearranged. Swabs that stung her skin rubbed her face and head, then her pelvis and legs. Cory groaned.

She was aware of someone holding her left hand. She struggled to turn her head and moaned with pain.

"Lay still, Cor," Jessica whispered near her ear. "You're going to be okay. I promise," Jessica sniffed as tears rolled down her cheeks. "You're in the hospital. They're going to take good care of you," she choked out feeble reassurance.

"J—Jess," Cory managed.

"Shhhh," Jessica kissed a small spot on Cory's head that wasn't scraped and bloody. "I'm right here. I'm not going anywhere. Just rest."

"Do you know how to reach his family?" one of the attending staff asked.

"*Her* family," Jessica corrected. "That would be me," she finished.

"Any news from the police?" Cory asked in a strained whisper three days later. She was settled in her bed propped up by mounds of pillows. Jessica tucked the edge of a quilt under her chin.

"No, seems he's gone underground, like toxic waste." Jessica squeezed Cory's hand. "Listen, you're safe. I'm here, and no one is getting in without going through me, little lady." Jessica did a quick John Wayne swagger. "Okay?"

Cory tried a feeble smile. "The doors are locked, right?"

Jessica nodded. "Cory, he's not coming back. There's a warrant out for his arrest, and that composite picture—it's on the news. They'll find him. It's just a matter of time."

"I'm so stupid," Cory croaked. "They say, 'too good to be true' for a reason."

"Honey, stop being so hard on yourself. There's no way you could have known. Try to rest. You need to save your voice for your appointment with Marg on Friday." Jessica touched Cory's cheek gently. "I'm going to clean up the living room, then I'll be in the spare bedroom, unpacking." Cory nodded, and turned her face to the wall.

"It looks like a bomb went off in here," Jessica muttered as she pulled the broom and dustpan from the closet.

Fragments of pottery, soil, and plant debris were strewn about. Delicate coral petals, like colorful tears, were scattered across the rug. Blood smeared the floor and crusted the edge of the coffee table. Stuffing spilled like vomit from the knife slit in the couch cushion. Jessica wrinkled her nose as she attacked the visible signs of her friend's night of horror.

Shards of glass made moving through the room hazardous. She righted a chair that lay on its side, and replaced the lamp that was wedged under the desk. A wine bottle, the jagged edges of its broken neck coated with a brown congealed substance, protruded from beneath Cory's favorite pillow cross-stitched with 'To Thine Own Self Be True.'

"God, Cory, what did he do to you?" Jessica gasped as she wiped a tear from the corner of her eye.

Chapter 11

Cory rearranged herself into the corner of the couch, and protectively hugged an extra pillow to her stomach. The lacey curtain behind her, rippled gently in the afternoon breeze. She took a sip of tea, cleared her throat, and tried not to decipher the look on Marg's face.

"Are you sure you're up for this, Cory?" Marg asked, as she removed her bifocals and laid them on small table next to her chair. She rubbed the bridge of her nose with her index finger.

"I'll never be up for this," Cory said, taking another sip of tea. "I'd rather run through the mall naked than recount that night. I feel like such an idiot, asking a complete stranger into my home."

"There will be time in the future to look more closely at your enthusiasm and decision making when it comes to this new world of heterosexual dating," Marg said with a gentle smile. "But for now, we're going to have to find a way to help you accept that what happened to you was not your fault."

Cory's eyes were fixed on a spot on the floor. She signed heavily.

"Okay, so you've gotten as far as leaving the grocery store. He followed you home, carried the groceries in, and watered the potted plant—an Azalea?"

Cory nodded.

"Odd choice. Then, he poured the wine while you started dinner, right?"

Cory's lips were pressed together like a rusty zipper. Again, she nodded.

"And," Marg prompted, as she slipped her glasses back on. The abrasions, bruises, and scabs on Cory's face and neck that blurred

211

behind Marg's nearsightedness came into sharp focus. She looked away, then back again.

"He sliced the French bread while I finished making the salad. I remember just a moment of fear when he put the knife down on the counter, then picked it up again. He ran his finger lightly along the edge of the blade. I was afraid he was going to cut himself, I think. It made my stomach queasy." A shudder rippled through Cory, and she hugged the pillow tighter.

"We had a nice dinner. He was charming and witty, and had lots of amusing stories about places he'd traveled. I was clearing away plates and he asked if he could put on some music. I pointed him toward my record collection—you know, those old vinyl 33s—the romantic tunes no one sings any more." Cory paused, accepted a refill of tea, blew on it gently, and took a sip. They sat in the quiet for a moment. Cory took a deep breath and continued.

"I remember my hands were soapy with dishwater. He asked me to dance. I told him I'd never learned ballroom dancing. He said, 'it's easy, just watch me', and he picked up the potted Azalea, held it in his arms and began waltzing around the living room. I thought I'd wee in my pants, it was so funny," Cory smiled briefly at the memory.

"Take a slow, deep breath, Cory," Marg instructed when she noticed Cory hadn't inhaled for several seconds. Cory sucked in an audible breath and exhaled loudly.

"Good," Marg said. "Go on," she prompted.

"He put the plant on the coffee table and motioned me to step into his arms. It was so exciting. For a moment, I thought we were going to be Ginger and Fred. I put my hand on his shoulder. He pulled me to him roughly. It surprised me and I tried to step backward, but I couldn't get away from him. His eyes looked angry, and his breathing was strange, almost like he was panting."

Cory stopped, shook her head, and said, "I don't know if I can do this." There were tears in her eyes, and in Marg's too, Cory noticed, when she looked up.

"I'm right here," Marg said. "You're safe. The worst has already happened. These are the feelings you blocked out. Take your time."

"I remember thinking, 'I'm going to die,' then my mind just sort of went numb," Cory said quietly. "He ripped at my blouse and was biting me on the neck. I think I remember trying to hit or scratch him, but he had my arms pinned. I could feel his erection shoved into my stomach. He moved back just enough to tear at my pants. He broke the zipper and jammed his hand down into my underwear. Then he made this horrible sound, like a dog hit by a car on the road or something."

Cory covered her face with her hands. Her shoulders shook as she sobbed loudly. Marg moved her chair near the couch and leaned forward slightly. She placed the tissue box within Cory's reach.

Moments passed as Cory wept unrestrained. Eventually, her breathing became more regular. She blew her nose and readjusted her position on the couch.

"And then?" Marg gently prompted.

"He grabbed my crotch hard. When he found himself with a handful of penis, he screamed in my face, 'What the fuck *are* you, anyway?' I was terrified and ashamed. He started hitting me with his fists. I fell over and hit my head on the corner of the coffee table. I remember curling up on my side as he kept kicking me and kicking me. He wouldn't stop. I couldn't breathe." Cory began to gasp for air. Her body went rigid and her hands were balled into fists.

"Cory," Marg said, "Look at me. Look at me now." Cory's eyes were filled with terror. "You're right here with me," Marg continued. She softly placed her hand over one of Cory's fists. "You're safe. I won't let anything happen to you." She continued the litany of soothing words until Cory's body softened and she slumped back against the couch.

"He hurt me," giant sobs raked through her body. Marg nodded, and waited. "That fucking bastard cut me, and kicked me, and hurt me," she cried loudly.

"That was a terrible thing he did to you, Cory. You didn't deserve to be hurt," Marg said.

"No, I didn't deserve that! He's crazy. He's sick. I hope he rots in prison," Cory shouted. "Or in hell. He's a bad man," she whimpered now, sounding young and very tired.

"Yes, a very bad man," Marg agreed.

Cory took a ragged breath, wiped her eyes with the back of her hands and looked up at Marg.

"How are you doing?" Marg asked.

"I think I could use a hug," Cory said.

Chapter 12

The crisp winter air made the hair follicles in Cory's nose stiff. She stomped slush off her snow boots leaving puddles of muck on the top step as she rang the doorbell.

Jessica appeared behind the frosted glass window in a long-sleeved, floor-length maroon bathrobe and fuzzy blue bunny slippers. She pulled a forest green scarf tighter around her neck before opening the door.

"Quick, get in here," she grabbed Cory by the sleeve and pulled her through the doorway. "Temperatures like this should be illegal," she declared.

Cory sneezed, blew her nose, and removed her gloves, coat, and boots.

"Here," Jessica plopped down a pair of sheepskin-lined slipper boots and helped Cory slip her feet into them.

"Thanks," Cory managed before another sneeze shook her frame.

"Follow me," Jessica commanded. Obediently, Cory trailed her into the kitchen, oven warmed and smelling of freshly baked banana bread. Jessica turned the burner on under the teakettle. "Fix you right up," she said. "Here," she handed Cory a knife and pointed to the steaming loaf of bread under a cloth napkin.

Cory sliced thick pieces of banana bread while Jessica steeped ginger tea in a pot and added a dash of cayenne and a shot of bourbon for good measure.

After a scraping of chairs pulled from the table, a moment of shuffling around, they settling in.

"So, this is it then, huh?" Jessica held Cory's eyes with a

penetrating stare. "Most people head to Florida for Spring break. You go to Colorado to get your wiener schnitzeled."

Cory grimaced. She took a sip of the brew Jessica had concocted. "Holy…" she choked on the cayenne floating on top. Cory cleared her throat and leaned forward, elbows on the table. "Yeah, this is sort of—it," she smiled tentatively.

"Cold feet?" Jessica asked.

"No. Just more information after the phone consult with the staff there. I've never had surgery. Still have my tonsils, never was really sick as a kid, no broken bones or anything." Cory managed a small gulp of brew.

"I could go with you," Jessica suggested. "I mean it's not like I have reservations in Ft. Lauderdale or anything." She stirred a teaspoon of honey into her tea.

Cory's eyes moistened. She reached over and patted Jessica's hand. "That means a lot, Jess, but this is something I have to do on my own. I'll need you on the other end of the phone the week after the surgery though."

"You got it, sister," Jessica smiled. "So what did you find out about the procedure—I mean, what exactly are they going to do? You going to get boobs?"

"I have boobs, thank you very much," Cory patted her B-cup padded bra. "I don't need facial reconstruction; my bones are actually delicate enough. And my body fat has redistributed itself this year, so I have hips and thighs."

"Nice hips, I might add. Good ass, too," Jessica added, grinning.

Cory blushed and swirled her drink in her cup. "So, they'll remove my testicles, use the skin of my penis and scrotum to line the vagina, and make a clitoris from the glans. I'll have sensation and everything." She glanced up at Jessica who sat wide-eyed and pale.

"Ouch," Jessica said.

"I'll be in the hospital for a week, and then I'll probably stay another week for a follow-up support group." Cory shrugged. "Then I'll be—" Cory searched for the word, "done, I guess. I was going to say safe," Cory admitted with a shudder.

"God, Cor, I'm so sorry about what happened to you." Jessica picked up her mug, blew on it, set it back on the table. She opened her mouth, hesitated a moment, then closed it again.

"What?" Cory asked.

"I'm not sure how to say this, Cory, but—"

"Geez, don't stop now," Cory said.

"Women get raped. I mean, I know the circumstances were different here, but I just don't want you to think that you're going to be safe just because you no longer have a dick." Jessica's cheeks flushed.

There was a long silence. Outside the kitchen window, icicles dripped with a *thip, thip* onto a cement slab. The grandfather clock in the living room made a sound like an old man clearing his throat, bonged twice, then continued its subdued *tick-tock*.

"I'm only telling you this because I love you," Jessica stumbled on, "and you don't know everything about being a girl yet. Like it or not, you've been raised with a certain amount of male privilege—even as a gay guy."

"First you try to poison me with this brew, then you scare the bejesus out of me. If this is love, I'd hate to be your enemy," Cory said. The corners of her lips twitched slightly. "Thanks," she said, smiling fully now. "No one else has had the courage to say that to me."

Chapter 13

Cory shifted on the couch. The rain continued to pour in a steady stream. The earlier hailstones lay clumped about like mushy oatmeal outside Marg's window.

"You seem restless," Marg observed. "Are you getting nervous about the trip?"

"No, not nervous. I'm not feeling much of anything, actually. Can't seem to make the plane reservations and rental car arrangements. I just feel sort of unmotivated." Cory glanced behind her and out into the gray afternoon. "Maybe it's the weather. I mean, I've been waiting for this my entire life, and it's been the focus of my therapy for a solid year now."

"Cory, this is such a huge step. It would make sense to have mixed feelings. It doesn't mean you won't go through with it, just that you need to proceed slowly—one step at a time, and all that," Marg smiled.

Cory sighed. "I suppose I could at least check out the flights leaving from O'Hare toward the end of April."

"Sounds good. You can tell me what you found out next week, okay?"

"Okay. And Marg—thanks. I mean, for everything. You just..." Cory wiped the tears that were running down her cheeks with the back of her hand. "Damned estrogen," she muttered.

"You're welcome," Marg said as she tossed the box of tissues to Cory.

Chapter 14

Cory rolled her suitcase up to the United Airlines gate and found a seat in an unoccupied row of plastic chairs facing the plate glass window. Her attempt at isolation was broken when a young woman in purple spandex and a lime green parka dropped a bagged pair of snow skis and a backpack into the chair next to her with a clatter. Why me, Cory wondered, noting the row of empty chairs on either side of her.

"Hi," the woman jabbed her hand in Cory's direction. "I'm Sunny Tuesday. Going to Colorado to ski," she chirped with enthusiasm. "You ski?" Her shaggy carrot orange hair clashed with everything in sight.

"Uh, no. Cory," Cory offered her hand for a quick pump. "Are those going to fit under you seat?" she asked feebly, nodding at the skis.

"Nah, they'll check them in the front cabin. That way I don't have to mess with baggage claim. It's a nightmare in Denver what with the tram and all."

Cory gulped. Tram? No one said anything about a tram. A ribbon of sweat broke out along her hairline.

"If you don't ski, why are you going to Colorado?" Sunny asked.

Cory blinked, swallowed, and took a deep breath. "To get my wiener schnitzeled," she said, as seriously as she could. When a tide of giggles worked their way up from deep inside her, she excused herself, got up, grabbed her bag, and wheeled it out of the gate area. "Well, that went well," she mumbled to herself between fits of giggles. Cory shook her head. What kind of name is Sunny Tuesday, anyway, she wondered as another spasm of giggles overtook her.

A woman shepherding two children under the age of five, threw her a look and placed a protective arm on each child's shoulder.

Settle down, Cory, she admonished herself, or they'll call Security. With two days before surgery, Cory saw no reason why she shouldn't treat herself to a drink at one of the airport lounges to calm her nerves.

She lifted herself onto a stool at the bar and tugged her suitcase up close against her leg. The lounge was dimly lit and the pink and green neon around the mirror along the wall gave an eerie reflection to the odd assortment of travelers at the tiny tables behind her.

Not having much experience with mixed drinks, Cory pondered what to order that wouldn't make her sound naïve. A gin rummy? No, that was a card game. Maybe a vodka and tonic. She'd heard of that at least. Cory glanced down the bar looking for the bartender. She turned back to find a clean-shaven, older man in a business suit had slid into the seat next to her.

"Buy you a drink, miss?" he asked, tilting his head and smiling pleasantly.

Cory spun around and flinched as the man's face morphed into Kurt's. She fumbled for the handle of her suitcase. Her heart pumped loudly in her ears and her mouth went Sahara dry. Unable to speak, she got off her stool and willed her wobbly legs to carry her out of the lounge.

Her face burned with heat and fear. Back into the flow of the crowd, under the glare of imitation light, she leaned heavily against the wall and counted her breaths—in, one-two-three-four, out, one-two-three-four—until the ringing in her ears was reduced to a faint hum.

This did not bode well for her life as a woman. Not well at all. Post-Traumatic Stress Disorder, Marg called it. A frigging handicap, Cory called it. Label it, she heard Marg instruct. Trigger, Cory responded in her mind. It feels like it's happening now, but it isn't. This is now, and that was then, and I am safe right now. There are people all around if I need help, she reminded herself as her breathing regulated and the heat drained from her face and neck. How was she ever going to meet the man of her dreams, she wondered miserably, as she contemplated a life of celibacy.

"United Airlines Flight 132 to Denver, now boarding from Gate 23," the nasal metallic voice intoned over the microphone attached to the check-in counter.

This was it, then. Cory took a long, ragged breath, straightened her shoulders, and lifted her chin in a show of bravery. Pulling her suitcase behind her, she stepped into the cross-hatched sea of humanity and wove her way back to the gate. With boarding pass in hand, she tried for the indulgent smile of a frequent traveler, and wondered, as she fell in line, how many other passengers would return from their travels with their lives inextricably changed.

Once on the plane, Cory folded herself into the cramped quarters of 16C and looked out the window at the ground crew slogging through the slush as they loaded the baggage into the belly of the plane. Feigning interest in this ritual made her feel less antisocial for avoiding the person struggling into 16B. A horrifying thought crossed her mind. What if her seatmate was the man from the lounge, and she was trapped for the next two and a half hours in her own personal hell? The plane was overbooked; there would be no seat changes available. Cory felt her temperature rise, her throat constrict. Reality check, she heard Marg say. Cory eased back in her seat and turned her head just far enough to scope out the person next to her.

"I'm sorry dear," an elderly woman with a halo of white hair said. "I can't seem to find the end of my seatbelt. I believe you might be sitting on it." She smiled warmly at Cory.

Tears of gratitude brimmed in Cory's eyes. "Sorry," she said as she lifted herself from her seat and extricated the runaway strap.

"Quite all right. My name's Martha," she held out her hand after strapping herself securely into her seat.

"Cory." They shook hands. "Are you coming from, or going to home?" Cory asked for the sake of conversation.

"Oh, going home—finally," Martha smiled. "I've been spending time with my son and grandson in Ann Arbor. Much as I love them, I'm pooped," she chuckled good-naturedly. "What about you?"

Just then a bell toned, and the flight attendant drew their attention to the front of the cabin where she demonstrated everything they would need to know to have a safe flight. Saved by the bell, Cory smiled with relief, silently grappling with the question: What about me?

The take off was smooth, and Cory thumbed idly through the in-flight magazine hoping to ward off conversation.

Moments later, the flight attendant took Cory's order for a Coke, and handed it to Martha, who passed it over.

"You were about to tell me where you are headed when we were interrupted," Martha said, an attentive smile on her softly wrinkled face. Her eyes were the kind of blue that inspired trust.

What if I just told the truth, Cory wondered. Would I cause this sweet old lady to have a heart attack? Would she be shocked and spend the next two hours trapped in silent horror next to a pervert? I'll never see her again—what's the risk?

"I'm going to Trinidad for surgery," Cory stated simply.

"Oh," Martha put a hand to her chest. "Most people who come to Trinidad for surgery are there for sex reassignment. It's well known in these parts."

Uh oh, Cory thought, and felt her throat tighten. She couldn't read Martha's face and there was no inflection in her voice. "That would be me," she managed.

Martha smiled warmly. "What a coincidence," she said. "My son, Sanders, led one of the support groups there before he transferred to Michigan. The head surgeon, Doctor B., is the best. Great staff, good aftercare, too. Small world," Martha mused. She reached over and patted Cory's hand reassuringly. "What a brave young woman you are."

The intimacy of sharing her life with a total stranger and finding acceptance and support there, was just too much for Cory. She melted back into her chair and tried to regulate her breathing, she mopped her brow with the damp napkin from under her Coke.

Noticing the saturated napkin, Martha fished in her purse and produced a travel pack of tissues, which she offered to Cory.

"It's all going to be okay. Everything will work out just wonderfully, you'll see," Martha said.

"I so want to believe you," Cory said, casting a sideways glance at Martha. "I haven't really felt scared until just this minute." She blotted at her upper lip and took another deep breath. "I miss my Nana," Cory said. "She's dead. I don't know why I'm telling you that. You remind me of her, I guess. She always made my world safe." Cory tried for a smile.

"You must miss her terribly about now. I'm pleased to be here for you," Martha said. Her soft blue eyes were like a balm.

The rest of the flight passed quickly with Martha securing a promise from Cory to phone her after her surgery, just to let her know how it went. Had it not been for a stay-over with an old school chum in

Denver, Martha said, she'd have insisted that Cory ride with her to her home in Pueblo, less than an hour from Trinidad.

When they deplaned in Denver, Martha herded Cory through the throng to the tram that took them to the baggage claim, and then pointed out the car rental kiosk.

"You're going to come through this just fine," Martha reiterated. Grateful for their new friendship, Cory hugged Martha fiercely.

A dapper looking older gentleman approached and stopped a respectful distance from the two. He stood smiling, watching their goodbyes.

"Martha, there's a man looking at us. Do you know him?"

"Malcolm!" Martha called out joyfully, as she fairly danced into the man's arms and received a kiss that was passionate enough to make Cory avert her eyes.

"Don't tell me this is your school chum," Cory teased, when Martha beckoned her over.

Martha, giggling girlishly, made the introductions. "Promise you'll call," she said as Malcolm hoisted her bag and took her elbow with his free hand. Then they were gone, leaving Cory in her aloneness.

A spring chill hovered around the Avis parking lot like a criminal in a dark alley. Cory broke into a cold sweat that had nothing to do with the weather. She slid into the driver's seat and slammed the Chrysler's door closed. The rental agent, Sam, according to his name tag, sat next to her and breezed through a tutorial on how to use the navigational system.

"Any questions?" he smiled.

"Is it too late to trade down to a compact, and can I get a handful of maps?" Cory said, befuddlement contorting her face. Being tracked and guided by a combination of satellite and computer creeped her out.

"Piece of cake," Sam reassured as he slid out of the passenger's side.

"Wait..." Cory panicked. "I don't think I can do this, really. Could you just put the address in for me, please?"

"Well, I could," Sam offered, his voice less amicable than before, "but how are you going to get back if you don't learn how to program this thing?"

"Triple A?" Cory grinned and batted her eyelashes.

"Let me walk you through it one more time, and then it's up to you. Okay?" It didn't sound like a question.

With South Bonaventure Avenue, Trinidad, programmed in, Sam waved Cory out of the parking space. "It should take you around three hours. Drive safely. Don't panic. If you miss a turn, you'll be directed back onto the route. There's no such thing as lost with GPS."

Miss a turn? Cory's stomach churned.

"You are now on I-70 West," the voice from the console verified as Cory left Denver International Airport.

"So far, so good," Cory said, checking her rear view mirror. She took a deep breath and released it slowly. Her shoulders began to relax. The computer voice was soothing, cultured, the kind of voice that inspired confidence. Cory wished she could engage it in conversation to pass time. The very least she could do for her own amusement, would be to give her guide a name. Penelope.

"My fate is in your hands, Penelope. I'm counting on you," Cory said. "Would you look at that," Cory's voice was awe-filled. Snowcapped mountains, each one slightly larger than the one before it, lined up like giant dominos ahead. A sheen of haze, like perspiration on the skin of the sky, subdued the plum color of the mountain range. "Makes you feel sort of insignificant, doesn't it?"

"In one mile, turn left onto I-25," Penelope answered.

"Gotcha," Cory said. She made the turn and the four mountain ranges shifted to her right. "Oh, my gosh, there's another one," Cory gaped at Pikes Peak in the distance. "This is so amazing. Isn't this amazing, Penelope?"

"You are now heading south on I-25." That would be Penelope's last contribution for the next two hundred miles.

Cory passed towns with names like Castle Rock that sported an oval shaped outcropping of rocks jutting from the earth, and Colorado Springs, where a huge jet, posed between the highway and the Air Force Academy, stood sentry over travelers like a futuristic bird. Overhead, an airplane towed a glider across the bluest of blue skies. "Breathtaking," she whispered. Her head swiveled as she took in the sky and the mountains. "We're not in Kansas anymore, Penelope," she chuckled. The blare of a horn on her left, called her swiftly back into her own lane.

Cory turned on the radio. A sappy country tune played on the local station as she passed the industrial town of Pueblo. *No matter how fast I drive, it's a long way to go for your love,* she sang along with the chorus. She clicked the radio off.

"Miles and miles of more miles and miles," she said. The slush-covered plains stretched endlessly to the east. Cory wiggled in her seat. She was getting butt fatigue, and her stomach was sending out hunger messages.

She realized she'd been in a perpetual squint for the last hour or so, and rubbed the corners of her eyes with her thumb and index finger. The mid-day sun was bright overhead, but brought no warmth. The mountains to the west cast narrow shadows as she approached Trinidad.

"Turn left onto Benedicta Avenue. Go one-tenth of a mile," Penelope directed.

"Yes, Ma'am," Cory swung into the heart of downtown Trinidad with its nouveau-chic-Western motif. Splashes of primary colored awnings shaded coffee shops, curios, and bookstores.

"What do you think, Penelope? Quaint, huh?" Cory smiled.

The cobblestone street sang its own tune under the tires of the Chrysler. Trolley tracks ran past the First National Bank. It was a tidy town with tree lined streets and old gas-light style lampposts.

"This would be a nice place to visit someday, Penelope. Maybe we'll come back when—"

"Turn left onto St. Vincent Avenue," Penelope interrupted.

"Sure thing," Cory responded.

Penelope led her right up to the hospital. "You have arrived at your destination."

"You have no idea how true that is, Penny, my friend," Cory said as she turned off the ignition. The chatty bravado waned and Cory slumped weakly against the back of her seat. "What have I gotten myself into," she said in a small voice.

Chapter 15

"Trust me Jess, I couldn't have called any sooner. The pain meds have only just worn off," Cory said, breathing shallowly against the wooziness.

"I've been going crazy here, Cor. So, are you okay, really? I mean, do you have an *innie* now?"

"Yup. Pretty convincing, too, the doc says. Or it will be, once the swelling goes down. I'm so sore, though, that a life of celibacy is sounding good," Cory said.

"That will pass," Jessica laughed wickedly. Then, more seriously, "God, Cory, I don't know what to say. I mean, this is such a big, friggin' deal, you know?"

"I know."

"I suppose you're going to take Martha up on her offer to stay over for a couple of weeks." The words were tinted with an emotion that Cory read as jealousy.

"Nah, I want to get home to my best friend. I am going to stay an extra week for the support group."

"Okay, but you've got to tell me everything they say so I can be a good support person once you're home."

"Jess—"

"Yeah?"

"I love you."

"Great—just what I needed. A straight girl in love with me. Get home soon, okay?"

Cory hung up the phone. "That girl is an emotional brick," she said, shaking her head.

On the third day, Nurse Ann popped her head through the doorway. "Everything okay in here?" she asked. Cory nodded, and then winced in pain as she attempted to turn onto her side.

"The doctor will be by to see you this afternoon. You up for a visitor?" she asked. "She says she's your 'Colorado family,'" Ann shrugged her shoulders.

"Blue eyes, white hair?" Cory asked, with a smile so big it made her cheeks ache. "Kind of grandmotherly?"

"That's the one," Ann said with a mischievous grin. "I'll show her in," she said and winked.

Cory's eyes were glued to the doorway. She blinked as the entrance began to fill with pink balloons—twenty-four in all, dangling long green ribbons. The message on each balloon was, 'It's A Girl.' A hand pushed its way through to clear a space where Martha's face appeared with a beatific smile. She looked like the center of a gigantic rose.

Cory roared. She grabbed her stomach, as everything south of her belly button hurt like crazy. She laughed until tears soaked the neck of her hospital gown. "Ow, ow," she groaned, rocking back and forth, and laughed some more.

"Oh, my. I seem to be causing you more pain," the center of the rose spoke. Martha popped her head back out, pushed the bouquet of balloons through the door, and fumbled them into the room. She tied them to the back of a chair near the bed stand and bent to give Cory a warm hug.

"Martha," Cory said, wiping her eyes, "I couldn't be happier to see anyone. Thank you so much for coming. How was your visit with Malcom?"

"The sex was great," Martha beamed. Cory blushed. "He sends his regards," she added. "How's our girl?"

"I don't even know how to put it into words," Cory said. "I feel—I don't know—real, I guess. Also scared, vulnerable. I don't quite know how to be in this body yet. Does that sound odd?"

"It sounds like the exactly right answer," Martha squeezed Cory's hand. "I know you're anxious to get back home, but you're welcome to spend some time with me before you leave."

"Thanks, Martha. Could I maybe have a rain check on that?"

"Of course. Maybe you and Jessica will vacation out this way some day," Martha said with a warm smile.

"I think she'd love that."

"I've been instructed not to stay too long and wear you out. I'm afraid I've already crossed that line," she said as Cory tried to hide a yawn behind her hand. Her limbs felt heavy, her mind fatigued. "You need your rest. Promise you'll stay in touch."

"You know I will. I'm so thankful I met you." Cory reached up to embrace Martha. "And, thanks for the balloons. You sure know how to celebrate," Cory grinned.

"Take care, dear," Martha waved and blew a kiss, as she slipped through the doorway.

The pain seared, throbbed, played a game of cat and mouse throughout Cory's body as she dropped into a fitful sleep.

At the end of the week, Cory checked out of the hospital. The swelling was down, and the pain was manageable. The skin grafts were 'healing nicely,' the doc said, though Cory couldn't bring herself to look just yet. She had also recommended that Cory spend the next week before leaving Trinidad in the aftercare support group.

"Did you miss me?" Cory asked of Penelope, as she programmed in the address of a cross-town motel. Penelope's green light blinked spasmodically on the console. Cory grinned. "Thought so," she said. "You can't imagine what I've been through." Cory rolled her eyes.

There had been a dusting of snow overnight. The tire tracks on the tarmac reminded her of ski trails crisscrossing down a mountainside as she backed out of the parking lot.

"Do I look different? Do I really, really look like a girl?" she asked Penelope.

"Turn right at the next corner; proceed six blocks," Penelope responded.

"Yeah," Cory said, "I think so too. I think it's a noticeable change." She smiled at herself in the rearview mirror.

Safely delivered to the motel, she unpacked then turned on the shower. "Oops," she said, remembering it would be a while before she could immerse herself in water. Sink-bathed, and fed, she readied herself for the afternoon group, and headed back out the door.

Cory pulled into the hospital parking lot and sat with the motor running. The heat that poured out of the vents did little to warm her clammy hands.

"I'm scared, Penny," she admitted. Gingerly, she slipped her hand between the legs of her cashmere slacks and gave a gentle pat. "Yup, still gone," she reassured herself.

Winding her way down the corridor, Cory found the conference room and stood peering through the glass door, unable to take the next step.

"The worst is over," a tall, forty-ish, stunning redhead said, laying her hand on Cory's shoulder. "Step into the next part of the rest of your life," she smiled, swung the door open, and gestured Cory into the room. "I'm Gwen, the facilitator for this meeting." Her eyes were green like forest moss, and there was a sprinkling of freckles across the bridge of her nose. There was an earthy scent to her, like a freshly turned garden.

"Cory," Cory wiped her sweaty hand on the leg of her pants, and then offered it for a shake.

"Well, Cory, since you're the first one to arrive, how about being my greeter?"

"Uh, okay. What do I do?" Cory shifted from one foot to the other.

"First you relax," Gwen smiled. "Then as people come in, welcome them, introduce yourself, and point them to the nametag table. There's coffee, tea, and water on the second table," Gwen called over her shoulder before she disappeared from the room.

Cory breathed in, slowly and deeply, and released it with a long *sssssssss*, a relaxation technique Marg suggested she use.

"You too, huh?" a young man in jeans and a Bronco sweatshirt said, startling Cory. "I've been sitting in my car doing that for about five minutes. I don't think it helped, I just feel lightheaded," he grinned.

"Hi, I'm Cory," Cory offered her hand. "Welcome."

"Thanks. I'm Rob—used to be Roberta. I'm from South Carolina. Are you on staff here?" he asked.

"Oh, gosh, no. I just came early. Gwen put me to work—she'll be back soon—I hope," Cory looked back over her shoulder. Three more people stepped tentatively through the door. Cory felt the warmth of compassion spread through her heart, like a candle under a chafing dish.

"Hi, come on in," she smiled. "I'm Cory—welcome; there's tea, coffee, and water—oh, and grab a nametag too." Well, this wasn't so hard after all.

As she shook each person's hand, Cory smiled in recognition of the journey they had all made here. Her heart felt tender and open with a sense of belonging. There was pixie-like Erin from Pennsylvania, early twenties; down to earth Arthur, wearing overalls and a flannel shirt, thirty-something, from a ranch in Wyoming; and Charlie, formerly Charlene, tall, late twenties, with a soft smile, sea-green eyes, and hair the color of late autumn wheat. Charlie was from the Midwest and looked wholesome enough to cast in a milk commercial. He nervously fingered the top snap of his flannel shirt, a gesture Cory thought oddly endearing.

Gwen returned balancing a tray of chocolate chip cookies, warm from the oven.

"Good job, Cory," she beamed, noticing people milling around, talking to one another. "You're a natural." Cory blushed.

"Welcome, people. My name is Gwen. Let's settle in and get to know each other, shall we?"

Two hours passed quickly, with more intimate, intense sharing than Cory had ever experienced in a group—let alone a group of complete strangers. They talked about their hopes and dreams, their new bodies, their fears, and the losses—all the losses.

"I lost my family when I made the decision to have the surgery," Arthur shared. "They were more or less tolerant as long as they knew I was still biologically their daughter. Like maybe I was just playing dress-up. They just sort of lost it when I was determined to get myself in alignment," he cleared his throat.

"I like that term, getting ourselves in alignment," Gwen commented.

"I'm an art major at South Carolina U," Rob drawled. "My momma and daddy are amateur photographers. We had more pictures of 'little Roberta' hangin' on our walls than the Louvre has paintings, I swear." He shook his head. "When I came out as trans in my teens, my folks burned all the pictures of me. Left a whole lot of blank walls." His grin touched a knot of feeling in Cory. Well, piss on them, she thought.

"I grew up Amish," Erin said. "I've been banned from the church. I still get occasional letters from my sister, Laura, but she'd be in big trouble if my parents or the church ever found out," Erin sighed heavily. "It's hard to lose your family, and your whole community." She wiped a tear. Rob laid an arm gently around her shoulders.

"I used to shadow my dad around the farm, work on restoring the Vet together, plow the field," Charlie shared. "I'd ride on the back of the tractor, holding on to his shoulders. Man, that was the greatest," he smiled nostalgically. "I knew I was in the wrong body when I started my menstrual period. My mom shrieked with joy, called my aunt and my sister, and told them her girl had just become a woman," Charlie grimaced at the memory. "Now *there* was a fate I'd hoped to avoid. Men don't have periods," he said softly. "There were no more tractor rides after that."

There was an uncomfortable shifting about. "God," Cory said, as her own story clawed its way up from the sludge to be told. "I was beaten, stabbed, and left for dead by a man who planned to rape me," Cory told the group. There were murmured words of recognition and support as she unfolded her story, slowly, as if it were wrapped in layers of burlap. "Thing is," she said, "I'm not sure I'll ever be able to trust a man, intimately." She lowered her eyes. "Even now," she added.

"Well, I feel wrung out and hung up to dry," Charlie said after the group. "How about you?" He turned a milk-and-cookies smile on Cory.

"Yeah. I usually only share things like this with my best friend, Jessica," Cory admitted as she gathered her belongings.

"She must be pretty special," Charlie said as he helped Cory on with her coat. "Hey, could you use some dinner or something? I mean, I'm not ready to be alone just yet," he confided.

"Uh, well—" A kaleidoscope of emotions shifted about in her, colorful fragments of fear, pleasure, and curiosity.

"Oh, hey, no pressure," Charlie stepped back tentatively. "I mean, I just thought if you were going to eat anyway."

Cory looked into his eyes and saw herself reflected there.

"You know, I *was* going to eat anyway, and I would like company," she smiled.

They strolled the downtown streets as the sun was setting. "How about this rib house?" Charlie suggested.

"You can't imagine how relieved I am to find out that you're not a vegetarian," Cory said.

"We carnivores have to stick together," Charlie said, as he ushered her into the restaurant.

"Oh, my God, this is *so* not hospital food," Cory grinned as she gnawed indelicately on a barbequed rib. Red goo oozed down her chin. Charlie dipped a corner of his paper bib in a glass of ice water, reached over, and swabbed Cory's chin.

"Oh, man, that was such a gender slip," he said, chagrinned.

"I think it was sweet," Cory smiled. "You can wipe my chin any time." Oh, way to flirt, Cory groaned internally.

Charlie chuckled. "I think we could both use some dating practice. How about it? We have another week here."

Cory's eyes widened. It felt like an elephant had just tripped over her collarbone and landed on her chest. "Date?" she wheezed. "Was this a date?" her voice squawked. "I haven't had such a stellar dating career," she admitted, memories of a middle-aged gay man, a straight art student, and a serial killer lurked in her mind.

"Hence, the practice. I figured it would be safer to start 'in house' than out there in the real world." His smile was as warm as the hand he laid gently on top of hers.

"Ew," he lifted his hand quickly.

"Oh, come on; it can't be that bad," Cory said, alarmed.

"Barbeque sauce," he said, reaching for his napkin.

Chapter 16

"I don't know, Cor," Jessica's voice was like ice water on Cory's enthusiasm.

"Wait—hear me out," Cory sputtered.

"Cory, you just met this dude. Do I have to say the 'K' word?" Jessica said.

"Jess, he's nothing like Kurt, I promise." Cory paced the carpet in her motel room kicking up static, frustration sparking like a downed transmitter.

"If you tell me Penelope approves, I'm hanging up," Jessica said.

"Penelope hasn't even met him yet," Cory said, smiling. She knew Jessica was rolling her eyes.

"What do you even know about this guy? He is a guy, right? I mean, now?"

"He's a guy. He's a sweet Iowa farm boy, studying Vet Science at the University. Real down to earth. You'd love him, Jess, I know you would," Cory said.

"He sounds like one of the Waltons," Jessica said. "Tell me he doesn't have a double name, like Billy Bob."

"Charlie. His name is Charlie. It used to be Charlene."

"Of course it did," Jessica sighed.

"We've been going out every night after group. Jess, I can talk to him for hours. There are no secrets between us. We really connect, you know?" There was a moment of silence. "Jess, you still there?"

"Cor, when are you coming home? You are coming home, right? I mean, classes start in a week."

"Tuesday morning," Cory interrupted the tirade she knew was

coming. "Can you pick me up at the airport? Ten-thirty?"

"Gosh, it will interfere with my bikini waxing, but I think I can manage it," Jessica said, her voice dripping sarcasm. "Of course I'll pick you up. Baggage claim, okay? Bye."

"All sentiment," Cory sighed at the dial tone humming in her ear.

"How did it go with Jessica?" Charlie leaned over and nuzzled a kiss just below Cory's ear as she eased herself into the booth next to him. "Did you tell her I'm looking forward to meeting her?"

"Didn't get quite that far," Cory sighed. "Some things are better said in person. Did you order?"

"Oh, man, she hates me, doesn't she?" Charlie moaned. The waitress set two glasses of house red in front of them..

"She doesn't hate you; she doesn't even know you."

"She hates the idea of me then," Charlie said.

"Well, yeah," Cory conceded. "She's been sort of my main go-to person for years. But when she meets you, she'll soften. I know she will," Cory tried to convince herself.

Vera, their waitress, set a large vegetarian pizza in front of them. "Can I get you kids anything else?" she asked.

"Got any advice on winning over my girl's best friend?" Charlie asked.

"Honey, a good lookin' boy like you—you'll have to bat her off with a stick," Vera smiled. She unloaded a handful of napkins on the table and vanished, leaving Charlie grinning like an idiot.

"Made my day," he chuckled as he slid a slice of pizza onto his plate.

Sated on carbs and slightly tipsy from the wine, they walked the cobblestone streets of downtown Trinidad, hand in hand. Cory's grip tightened. For a moment, it felt like she was clinging to life itself. The air was crisp and the stars shown in bas-relief against the black sky.

"Look at that," she pointed to the beautiful serpentine temple in the distance.

"That's the Ave Maria Chapel," Charlie said. "And down that street, past the First National Bank, that's where the trolley runs."

"How do you know so much about Trinidad?" Cory asked.

"Internet search," he said. "I'm going to write a story about this some day. Do you realize how unique what we've done is?"

"Sometimes I'm not sure it's real. I still have to check, you know?"

Cory's blush was hidden by the darkness.

Charlie wrapped his arm around her and pulled her close. They stood, gazing into each others eyes with an intensity that raised Cory's temperature to red alert. "How will it end? The story, I mean?" she asked, as she slid her hand around the back of his neck and stroked his corn silk hair.

"That depends on you," Charlie said, and kissed her softly on the lips.

The sky was the color of gray ash as Cory drew aside one corner of the curtain. The window looked out onto the bleak motel parking lot, nearly empty except for the two cars outside Cory's room, a battered RV several spaces over, and a moldy looking pigeon scratching about in the cinders.

"What time is it?" Charlie asked around a yawn. He stretched, rolled over on his side, and pulled the covers over his head.

"Seven," Cory smiled at the long, lean lump in the bed. She ducked her head under the covers. "Don't go back to sleep. We have group in two hours."

Charlie drew her close.

"I want so very much to make love with you, Cory," he whispered, his palm circling her breast.

She buried her face in his neck, kissing the morning stubble and breathing in the scent of him. "We will," she murmured. "We just have to give it time. No rush, we have a lifetime," she said as she trailed kisses up to his lips. She felt safer than she'd felt in years.

"Promise?" he asked, holding her chin tenderly and gazing so deeply into her eyes, her soul caught fire. "I know we're new, to ourselves and each other, but Cory, this just feels so right. I don't want to lose you," he said, his eyes glossy with tears.

"Not going to happen," Cory smiled. "We talked about this last night. You'll come up for graduation in June; I'll fly down for Christmas. We'll make it work. By September when you graduate, we'll know what our next step is." She stroked Charlie's chest and trailed her finger gently along the surgical scars from his breast removal the year prior. "We can do this," she said with determination.

"Our first hurdle will be telling the group," Charlie sighed. He brought Cory's hand to his lips and kissed each knuckle. "We're in big trouble already. You know we're going to get Gwen's 'give it a year' lecture; Erin will cry; Rob will mutter something unintelligible in that southern drawl..."

"...Arthur will groan, click his boot heels together, and pull his cowboy hat down over his eyes," Cory laughed. They lay quietly for a moment, lost in their own imaginings. "I'm really going to miss everyone," Cory said softly. "It's like having a house full of the brothers and sisters I never had, and getting ready to leave home."

"I need a stack of pancakes before I deal with the siblings. What do you say to breakfast?" Charlie tweaked her nose and kissed her forehead.

After breakfast at a diner with a western theme, Charlie paid the bill and Cory waved goodbye to the moose head hanging over their table. The morning was bitter cold as they drove back to the hospital.

The smell of fresh perked coffee filled the conference room. The chairs creaked as the group settled in for the last meeting. Suddenly, the floor had taken on a new fascination. Eye contact was fleeting, the energy in the room subdued.

"Okay, we may never see each other again," Gwen began, "So this is the time to say all those things you'll wish you would have said two months from now."

Silence seemed to have taken its own chair and was busy dominating the group.

Erin finally interrupted. "I'm afraid to go home," she said just above a whisper.

Rob mumbled something that sounded vaguely like "home is where the heart is." Arthur shifted in his chair and pulled the brim of his hat over his brow.

"That's a start," Gwen encouraged. "Let's talk about going home. What's your biggest fear, Erin?"

"I'm afraid no one will love me," she said, as tears rolled slowly down her cheeks. Cory felt a fire rage somewhere deep inside. *You're not my life anymore*, she remembered Catherine saying.

"Well, that just sucks," Arthur said, leaning forward, elbows on knees, peering up from under his cowboy hat. "You're a lovely, kind, generous little lady. You're brave and honest. Anyone should be proud to be your friend, let alone your family, and downright thrilled to love you," he said, uncharacteristically effusive.

"The people who meet you now, will love the real you, not the you who tried to be what everyone else wanted. That has to be worth something," Cory offered. Erin wiped her eyes with the back of her hand and gave a weak smile.

"And you're starting off with five people who love and support you, whether we see each other again or not. We're always there in each other's hearts, right?" Charlie added. Erin nodded. Cory reached over and gave her hand a gentle squeeze.

"I know it doesn't make any more sense than a skunk wearing Patchouli oil," Arthur said, "but I'm afraid if people find out I'm a post-op trans, I'll lose my credibility as a cowboy—at least in my neck of the woods. That's not all I could lose. Some of them rednecks can turn on you like a surly snake."

"You even going to be able to ride a horse for a while?" Rob grimaced, folding his hands protectively over his groin. Good-natured laughter bubbled around the circle.

"You're the real-thing cowboy, Arthur, that's what people are going to know about you," Cory said.

"Safety issues are real," Gwen added. She glanced briefly at Cory, who slunk almost imperceptibly down in her chair. "You're all going to have to exercise a great deal of discernment as to who you trust and why you disclose to someone."

Charlie cleared his throat, shifted in his seat, took a deep breath, opened and then closed his mouth. He glanced at Cory who had that deer-in-headlight look on her face, but nodded anyway.

"Yes?" Gwen prompted.

"Okay—Cory and I are in love, we're going to go back to our own homes, finish school, then probably get married, and move to the suburbs," the words spilled out like stuffing from a pillow.

Charlie looked around the circle. Four mouths were shaped in big 'O's, like donut holes. Cory's lips were pressed tightly together. It was so quiet you could have heard a dust mite sneeze.

"Well," Gwen said, breaking the silence, "Cory, do you want to add anything to that?"

Cory, red-faced from her own embarrassment, said, "We didn't really talk about the suburb part."

"You dawg, you," Rob punched Charlie playfully on the arm. Erin burst into tears, Arthur clicked this boot heels together and said, "Hot damn."

"We know about the one-year rule," Charlie turned toward Gwen, "and by the time we're ready, it will be just about that."

"It's a wonderful thing, to fall in love," Gwen smiled. "The idea of waiting a year is really more about giving yourselves time to get to know how you're going to relate to other people, so that you don't just latch on to the first safe person who accepts you, out of fear," Gwen said, looking at Cory and Charlie in turn, then to the group in general.

"But we really do love each other, Gwen," Cory chimed in. "We've talked about this, and it's what we both want. I have no interest in even meeting other men," she cast a look at Charlie, who grinned and blew her a kiss.

"I know you love each other," Gwen smiled sadly. "Just remember, that rules are made for a reason, usually based on life experience. That said, I wish you well."

The conversation shifted to pragmatics of life back home, reestablishing connections, work, and school. There were promises to keep in touch, tears, hugs, even talk of a reunion. They said their final goodbyes as Gwen herded them out of the room like a momma hen with her chicks.

Back in the motel room they had shared for the last two days, Cory folded a pair of slacks and zipped her suitcase closed. Charlie made a last sweep of the closet and drawers, cabinets and counters.

"Man, I always leave something behind," he muttered, as he checked the bathroom.

"That would be me," Cory said, forlorn as a wilted flower. As she sat on the end of the bed, a scene replayed itself from the further reaches of her mind—in another motel room, during a different winter, saying to Jessica, *I don't want to date one, I want to be one.* How many lifetimes ago was that?

Charlie moved the suitcase to the floor and sat down beside her. "Wish I could go visit Martha with you, but my flight arrangements are pretty much set in stone," he smiled, and draped an arm around her shoulder. "I'm glad you decided to do that before you leave."

"Oh, you'll meet her someday, I have no doubt about it," Cory grinned, thinking about her spry friend. "And Jessica, too," she added.

"You're going to work on softening Jessica up some before June, right?" Charlie said, intimidated by their tight connection, and Jessica's abrasive style.

"What was it Vera said? You'll have to bat her off with a stick?" Cory laughed. There was an awkward moment of silence.

"I guess we can only put this off so long," Charlie said, and pulled Cory into a tight embrace. Their tears mingled as they kissed, sweetly, deeply.

"Call me when you get home," Charlie said, wiping his eyes. "Don't walk me to the car, or I won't be able to see to drive, okay?" He kissed her quickly, shrugged on his coat, grabbed his bags, and walked into the cold Colorado morning without looking back.

With the guttural cry of a wounded animal, Cory curled up on the bed and wept.

Chapter 17

Cory slipped her glove off and banged harder on the metal door frame. No answer. She blew warm air on her fist, rubbed it with her gloved hand, and was about to try again when she was interrupted by a thirty-something, gorgeous specimen of man making his way around the shrub that separated the two lawns. He was athletically built, had a shock of red hair, and moss-green eyes that grabbed hold of Cory's and wouldn't let go.

"Hi, are you Cory?" he proffered a solid man's hand.

"Yes," she hesitated.

"I'm Brian, Martha's neighbor." As they shook hands, a tingle worked its way up Cory's arm. "She said to expect you, keep a look-out for you," he said.

"Has she stepped out?" Cory asked.

"More like carried out," Brian offered. "The medics came a couple of hours ago."

"Oh my God, is she okay?" Cory panicked and tightened the grip on the hand she still held. Brian's eyebrows shifted toward the center of his forehead as he dropped his glance to their hands, fused in the cold. Cory followed his eyes. A band of red crept up her neck like a dickey, and she dropped his hand.

"Yeah, I just talked to her. They thought it was her heart, but everything seems to be all right now," he offered a lopsided grin that made his left cheek dimple. Cory knew the tip of her little finger would fit that indent perfectly. "She was worried about not being here to greet you," he said.

"That's so like Martha," Cory said, smiling in relief. She was fascinated by the specks of brown that brought out the mossy color of his green eyes, and the way his upper lip reached two small peaks, like a mini-mountain ranges. She'd never touched red hair.

"Come on, I'll take you," Brian said, commandeering her elbow and leading her across the lawn.

"What? Where? " Cory felt like she'd follow this man anywhere, but would prefer to know where he was headed first.

"The hospital. Martha's ready to be picked up," he chuckled. "Where did you think I was taking you?"

Cory shrugged, her cheeks flamed. She lowered her eyes, feeling suddenly vulnerable and exposed. *Give yourself time to get to know how to relate to other people*, Gwen's voice echoed in her mind. I feel like a crushed-out teenager, Cory thought. What's wrong with me? I just left the love of my life, and I'm drooling icicles over a total stranger.

Brian opened the passenger door of the rust-fringed blue Chevy and Cory slid in. Penrose Hospital was minutes away, across I-25. They turned onto Lake Avenue and parked in the lot next to the ER. Cory opened her door, and stepped into a patch of slush. Her foot slipped, and she made a three-point landing in the cold muck. Brain stood at the front of the car searching for his passenger.

"Help," Cory called weakly. Brian rushed to the passenger side, reached out a hand, and hauled her to her feet.

"Lord love a duck," he chuckled, "you're everything Martha said you were." With his gloved hand, he swiped at her coat and pant leg, sluicing off the dirty snowmelt.

Struggling to regain some dignity, Cory brushed the hair out of her face, and straightened her coat collar.

With a firm grip on her elbow, Brian led Cory across the drive and through the doors of the ER.

"Well, for goodness sakes, what happened to you?" Martha greeted her from a plastic chair where she sat swaddled in a blanket.

"That was supposed to be my line," Cory grinned as she threw her arms around the older woman, and inhaled the maternal scent of her. "Are you okay?" she fussed with the blanket, tucking it in where she'd dislodged it with her hug.

"Oh, I'm fine—checked out and ready to go home. I just like to throw some excitement in to my days," she grinned wickedly. "I see you've met Brian," her eyes twinkled mischievously. "Quite a hunk, isn't he?" she stage-whispered.

Cory swallowed hard, counted to five before answering. "I suppose, if you like that sort of thing," she averted her eyes. Brian, legs stretched out, hands folded in his lap, occupied a chair across the aisle. Occupied it well, Cory thought. His arrogant expression suggested he was used to being admired.

Martha stood, folded her blanket, and laid it on the back of the chair. "Let's go home. I can't wait to hear about your adventure," she said, slipping her arm through Cory's. Brian stepped between them, taking each one by the elbow. "Trust me, this is a better idea," he grinned.

Brian ushered the two women into Martha's cozy, sun-warmed kitchen. It smelled like cinnamon rolls, and Cory inhaled deeply. Martha put the copper teakettle on the burner of the white enamel gas range. "Will you stay a while?" she addressed Brian.

"Thanks, Martha, but I'll leave you two to catch up. Cory," he held out a tentative hand, "it's been real," he grinned.

"Mutual," she said, giving his hand a gentle squeeze. "I'm so glad you're in Martha's life."

"Mutual," he said with a wink, and backed out of the door.

"That young man is enough to bring back hot flashes," Martha said, fanning herself. Cory laughed.

"So tell me all about Charlie," Martha said, setting a plate of cinnamon rolls on the table and filling two mugs.

"Charlie—" Cory began. Oh yeah, Charlie, she thought, rerouting her thoughts. Her face reddened with embarrassment.

"Are you okay, dear?" Martha asked.

"It must be the hormones," Cory said, tugging at the neck of her blouse. "I'm so confused, Martha, I was actually flirting with Brian. I mean, shame on me," she said harshly.

"Don't be so hard on yourself, dear. I flirt with Brian from time to time. He just brings that out in a girl," she smiled. "Come on, sit down, have some tea and a roll, and tell me all about it."

Two hours later, Cory glanced at her watch. "Oh, Martha, I have to go soon," she sighed. "Part of me wishes I could cancel my flight, cancel my life, and just move in here with you. You're the best," she said. Cory got up and gave Martha a bear hug. "I never exactly had a Mom," Cory confided.

"I'm sorry to hear that, dear. Please, come visit any time," Martha said.

"You'll be getting two for one, you know," Cory teased. "Jessica is the sister I never exactly had, either."

"I'll expect you, Jessica, and Charlie to come visit real soon. Wait until I tell Sanders. He's way too used to being an only child," she chuckled.

Martha helped Cory on with her coat and fussed with her collar. With a last ferocious hug, the two women parted. "Love you, Martha," Cory called as she opened her car door.

"Love you too, dear," Martha called out. "Drive carefully."

Cory programmed Penelope for the Denver International Airport. "In one block, turn left onto I-25," Penelope instructed.

"I've missed you, too. I'll talk fast," Cory said, clicking on her turn signal, "we don't have much time."

The sky was dark, deep, and clear, when Cory reached the outskirts of Denver. Stars blinked and glittered like her Grandma's diamond necklace, and Cory smiled.

"I guess this is it, Penny," Cory said as she pulled into the rental lot. "I'll never forget you. We'll always have Trinidad. Here's lookin' at you, car," she said, in her best Bogart impersonation.

Chapter 18

"Delayed," Cory groaned and rolled her eyes. "Delayed how long?" she asked the agent behind the counter.

The woman's forehead was creased with impatience and fatigue. "Snow in Chicago has everything backed up," she said, for probably the hundredth time that evening. "Check the overhead. We'll let you know as soon as there's word," she gave a smile that held no joy.

Cory selected one of the phones clustered in a maze of metal partitions and dialed Jessica's number. The answering machine clicked on, and a surly voice stated, "Talk to me."

"Jess, I'm stuck in Denver. Snow in Chicago. Don't know for how long. I'm so sorry," Cory sighed. "I hope you check your messages when you wake up. I'll call you as soon as I know anything more." She hung up with a sense of dread, knowing how Jessica hated last minute changes. "It's out of my hands," she explained to the phone as she eased it back into the cradle.

Cory collapsed in a cold, plastic chair, exhausted. The cinnamon roll had worn off hours ago. Motivated by hunger and boredom, she meandered back down the concourse in search of a restaurant, and found them all closed. Airport food, especially at night, didn't really appeal to her, but neither did a low blood sugar attack that would make her woozy and unable to pull off even the simplest of transactions.

The green light over the lounge bar cast a cadaver-like sheen as Cory stepped up to the counter. There were no other patrons. She battled a wave of déjà vu and looked back over her shoulder as she hoisted herself up on a stool. The little round tables behind her sat empty and forlorn.

243

"Evening," the bartender said, placing a small white napkin in front of her. "My name's John. What'll you have?" he smiled.

"Food. I need food, John," Cory leaned her elbows on the bar. "Do you serve food here?"

John placed a short bistro menu in front of her. "Bless you," she said, and scanned the menu hungrily. Cory ordered a pastrami sandwich and a glass of red wine, and John went off to work his magic in the tiny kitchenette.

Cory spun her stool around and watched the few weary travelers pass by. A fatigued looking young woman pushed a fussy toddler in a stroller and dragged an oversized suitcase on wheels behind her. She shot Cory a look. Cory sent her an encouraging smile. An older man in a blue uniform swabbed a large dust mop that looked like a giant dead moth back and forth.

"Here you go," John placed the sandwich and wine on the counter. "Bon appetite," he said with a wry smile.

Cory sank her teeth into the spicy meat with a grateful sigh.

"Excuse me, miss," a man said from behind her.

With a mouth full of sandwich, Cory froze. She couldn't swallow, couldn't cry out. Trapped. John had vanished. Eyes wide, she looked at the image behind her in the mirror that lined the bar. Business type, mid-thirties. Her shoulders tightened, and she felt like any moment she might choke.

"I think I left my book here a while ago—a paperback. Right where you're sitting. Did you happen to see it?" he asked, catching her eye in the mirror.

Cory shook her head no.

"Okay, sorry to bother you," the young man said. He turned and left the bar.

Cory spit the mouthful of soggy bread and masticated meat out onto her plate, and wiped the sweat from her brow with her napkin. She took a gulp of wine, then another. A few deep breaths later, her shoulders relaxed. How long will it take, she wondered, as she stared at the unhinged woman reflected in the mirror. On wobbly legs, she left the bar and her sandwich behind.

Cory paced the gate area. She pressed her face against the plate glass and stared into the dark nothingness. A young man, head pillowed on his backpack, was stretched out along the baseboard of the window.

His snoring was circular, nonstop, frenetic. It made her want to kick him. She rubbed her eyes and settled into a chair.

A middle-aged woman wrapped in a royal blue blanket thumbed through a magazine, cheater glasses resting mid-bridge on her nose. Now and then, a bronchial cough rattled the air around her. She shifted in her plastic chair, blew her nose, and went back to her magazine.

Cory dozed fitfully. Forty-five minutes later, she woke with a crick in her neck just as a bedraggled, but uniformed woman stepped behind the check-in counter, and spoke into the microphone.

"Flight 329 from Chicago will be landing in a moment. We'll begin boarding as soon as the incoming plane has been prepped. That should be about twenty minutes," she stifled a yawn. "We thank you for your patience."

Cory offered up a silent prayer as she dragged herself back over to the wall of phones. After the beep, she said, "Jess, 7:30, baggage claim, Frontier, Flight 748," she paused, "God, I can't wait to see you," she finished with a catch in her throat.

Northward bound on a moonless night, Cory reclined her seat as far as it would go, and tucked the blue micro-fiber blanket under her chin. Gravity and fatigue tugged at her eyelids.

A gentle hand on her shoulder shook her awake. "Miss, we'll be landing in ten minutes. Please bring your seat upright," the flight attendant smiled warmly. Cory blinked, disoriented. She'd been dreaming of the group, but instead of Gwen, Martha had been leading the discussion. Except Martha was really Nana. Reality fought its way through the dream fog as she realized she was about to embark on her new life, with her real self finally brought forward. She shook her head to clear her thoughts. Excitement and fear battled for position.

Cory scanned the crowd as she made her way to the baggage claim. Hoping that Jessica woke in time to get the message, she reached for her bag and yanked it off the carrousel with a solid clunk. She pulled the retracted handle out and turned to exit the throng of travelers.

"Yikes!" she said as she stood nose to nose with Jessica, crowned in green dreadlocks, wearing overalls and a pumpkin-orange turtleneck sweater under her fatigue jacket.

"God, Cor, you look awful…" Jessica grinned, "… tired, I mean— awful tired," she amended.

Cory grabbed her, and hugged her hard. "I've missed you so

much," she chuckled softly into the mass of hair twisting away from Jessica's face.

"Cut it out," Jessica wriggled out of her grasp. "People are going to think you're queer."

"Martha sends her love," Cory said as she rolled her suitcase behind her. "She wants all three of us to come visit soon. Jess, you'll love her..."

"All three of us?" Jessica interrupted. She turned around and looked at Cory. "Is there something you forgot to tell me? Like what's-his-face is hiding around the corner, waiting to join us? He'll have to walk; there's not enough room in my car for another person and their luggage," she said, her words running together.

"Whoa, my jolly green friend," Cory said. "No one is going to jump out at us around the corner. Charlie is back in Iowa. Martha just wants to meet the two people I love most in this world, okay? Someday. Not this week, not this month."

Jessica hitched her chin, squared her shoulders and walked on, appeased for the moment.

"You know you're going to have to meet Charlie at some point, right?" Cory slipped her arm through Jessica's and flashed her a convincing you're-my-best-friend smile.

"Not this week; not this month," Jessica grumbled as she led Cory through the parking lot.

Chapter 19

"So—can I see?" Jessica bounced her eyebrows.

"Geez, Jess, no," Cory flushed. "Is nothing sacred?"

"Hey, I'm just curious. No biggie. Well, at least not any more," Jessica chuckled. She sat crossed legged on the futon and slurped her tea.

"You have no idea how good it is to be home," Cory said, looking around her colorful studio. Batiks hung from the ceiling; stained glass caught morning sun through the window; overstuffed multi-colored pillows flumped against the walls and scattered rugs from Mexico lent bright splashes of color to the dark wood floor. On her way to the kitchen, she cranked the wall heater up another notch and it pumped out warm, dry air. It wasn't cinnamon-cozy like Martha's, but it was all right.

Cory poured steaming water from the bright yellow enamel kettle into her mug and dunked a ginger teabag. She placed four brownies on a cobalt blue plate and put them on the wooden crate-turned-table in front of Jessica.

"What, are we on a diet?" Jessica grumbled.

"There are more in the kitchen. Help yourself," Cory said as she nestled three pillows together near the heater.

"So now what?" Jessica asked as she devoured a brownie.

"What do you mean?"

"I mean, what's next in your life? You'll be finishing your AA this summer. You going to fly to Iowa, join Charlie and the other Waltons, and plant corn or something?"

"I thought I'd see if Alise will hire me on at the gallery downtown.

I thought you and I would hang out after work and on the weekends, like usual. That's what I thought. You have a problem with that?" Cory lobbed a pillow at Jessica.

Jessica's grin was flecked with brownie crumbs. "Think you could talk Alise into showing one of my metal sculptures?" Jessica swiped at her chin with her napkin, and then took a swig of tea.

"First, I have to get the job," Cory said, then amended, "No, first, I have to call Marg and make an appointment."

"You've been back a week and haven't called her? What's that about?" Jessica eyed Cory. "Used to be we couldn't have a conversation that didn't somehow involve Marg says this, or Marg says that."

"Yeah, odd isn't it. I'm just not feeling as dependent on her as I was back then."

"Back then, before you were..." Jessica struggled. "I mean..." she glanced down at Cory's crotch, "you know."

"Let's just say pre-op for that period of time, okay?" Cory picked up another brownie. "Anyway, I'm thinking I might be done with therapy for a while."

"I hope you're not thinking I can guide you through any snags you might come up against with what's-his-name," Jessica mock-shuddered.

"His name is Charlie, and no, I'm not thinking I'd turn to you for advice about our relationship. Sheesh," Cory shook her head. "I do owe it to Marg to have a final meeting though."

Chapter 20

Cory took her traditional seat on the couch in front of the large window. The lace curtains were drawn back to reveal the bare branches of winter and the pale shimmer of afternoon sun. The room seemed smaller to her.

"Did you move the furniture around or something?" Cory asked.

"Oh my," Marg smiled, "we've come to that point in our journey," she said cryptically. "I've experienced this before with clients who do a huge piece of work, go away for a while, and return. It's as if you've outgrown the container," she explained. "Sort of like coming back to a childhood home after growing up—it often seems smaller." She settled into her overstuffed brocade chair.

"When I went back to my real childhood home, it seemed huge, cavernous in fact," Cory remembered. "I guess in some ways, this has been more a home for me to grow up in."

"As in most homes where we grow up, there comes a point at which we leave—we launch ourselves into the world. I sense that time has come for you, am I right?" Marg's gentle, implicit permission made the next step feel like a graduation for Cory.

"I have been thinking of stopping for now. Do you think that's premature? I mean, I know I have all these changes coming up," Cory faltered.

"Hopefully, you'll always have changes coming up in your life, Cory. That's how we grow. You know I'll always be here for you, right? Anytime you need," Marg assured her.

Cory felt her throat tightened with emotion. She blinked back tears. They sat for a moment in silence, honoring the relationship that had become important to both of them.

"Can I tell you about this wild adventure I've been on?" Cory grinned finally.

"I'd like nothing better," Marg said.

They spent the remainder of the fifty minutes in conversation about the surgery, the group and all its colorful members, Charlie—especially Charlie—Penelope, Martha, and Brian. What Cory chose not to talk about was her fear, that prickling feeling of dread in her stomach, like the clench before diarrhea every time she thought about having sex. Instead, they did a kaleidoscope review of their work together over the last two years, and parted with a hug and a promise that Cory would call anytime she needed.

Cory stepped out into the afternoon chill. If she had been Mary Tyler Moore, and, if she had been in Minneapolis, and if she had been wearing a beret, she would have tossed it into the air in celebration of her new self.

Chapter 21

"Buy you a beer, darlin'?" the stocky redhead asked, sidling up next to Cory. His face was puffy and his eyes bleary. He ran a grimy nailed, pudgy finger down Cory's arm in a too-familiar way that made Cory want to recoil. But she didn't.

"Sure," she said instead.

Something cowboy played on the jukebox and a fog of cigarette smoke hovered over the bar. Couples leaned into each other on the dance floor, hands wandered over bodies, sloppy kisses slid over faces. You could smell sex in the stifling heat of the summer's night. She downed half her beer. Her stomach clenched. It has to be someone unimportant, insignificant, she reminded herself.

"Vern," he introduced himself, his boozy breath creating a palpable fog between them. Cory wrinkled her nose and stifled a cough. He was old enough to be her father. Cory felt a sneer forming on her face and worked her muscles to turn it into a smile.

"Carol Payne," she said, nodding. "Pleased to meet you." She cast a glance at her half-empty glass.

"Two shots," Vern called to the barkeeper and moved the beer glasses aside.

She rewarded him with a grin. "Now here's a man knows what a woman likes," she forced herself to say. She knocked back the shot.

"So, what's a sweet girl like you doin' all alone in a dive like this?" he slurred.

Fair question, she thought. How do you tell a man that you're looking for a cheap quickie to try out the new equipment so you're not going into a long-term relationship a total virgin? And, God forbid, what if it doesn't work?

"Looking for company, like everyone else, I guess," Cory said, offering a closed-lipped smile that hid clenched teeth.

"In that case," Vern said, leaning his bulk suggestively against Cory, "let's blow this joint. I've got something back in my room that we can light up and have us a party." He laughed and nodded vaguely toward the door.

Vern slapped some bills on the bar, slid off his stool, stumbled onto his feet and wavered there a moment. "Par-*ty*, par-*ty*," he chanted, and then belched loudly.

The streetlight filtered in through the broken slats covering the one dirty window of Vern's shabby studio over the hardware store. The stench wrapped itself around Cory's neck and threatened to squeeze. Without turning on a light, Vern grabbed Cory's hand and dragged her onto the bed made lumpy by an assortment of crap that Vern threw randomly on the floor.

"Got anything to drink?" she asked. What she needed was anesthesia mainlined into her veins, but whiskey would do.

"Got beer," he said, "and some dynamite weed. Be right back." He fumbled in the refrigerator, then the cabinet drawer and returned with two beers and a joint as fat as a slug. He handed Cory the bottles while he groped for a book of matches from his pocket and lit the joint. Vern inhaled deeply, coughed around the edges, and passed the joint to Cory.

Cory took a deep swig of beer, then imitated Vern and inhaled the pungent smoke. She held it in until she thought her lungs would burst and exhaled it in a coughing fit worse than the time she swallowed her gum.

"You got some capacity," Vern said with admiration.

Cory took another hit, smaller this time, followed by a long swig of beer and set her bottle down on the nightstand, toppling an overfilled ashtray onto the floor

"Come here, you sexy thing," Vern said, grabbing a handful of her shirt.

Cory tried to focus her eyes on a crack in the ceiling and held her breath against the stench of Vern's mouth. Vomit in the back of her throat threatened to choke her. She shoved Vern away from her and sat up, panting, her arms crossed tightly in front of her.

"I can't. I just can't do this," she said.

Chapter 22

The tops of the gallery's double Dutch doors were open to the sidewalk, and the flush of spring that had turned the grass green and filled in leaves on the trees, diffused the air with the scent of early wildflowers. Sunshine poured through the plate-glass and warmed the Italian tile floor where Cory stood. She wiggled her toes in her sandals as she considered the best placement for the new painting that she held in her hands. She turned slowly, eyeing the possibilities.

"Can you handle things while I slip out for coffee?" Alise asked, hand on the doorknob. Cory nodded. "Bring you anything? A mocha, maybe?" Cory nodded again. The Tibetan bells on the door jingled as Alise pulled it closed behind her.

Cory leaned the painting against a freestanding wall, stepped back and did a visual critique. It had to be perfectly placed. It was, after all, Josh's first show—Josh of 'paint fear using only blue' fame. She smiled at the memory.

Absorbed in thought, she didn't hear the door open behind her, and turned only when a shadow cast itself on the wall she was considering.

"Good morning. May I—" Cory was interrupted by a delivery man wheeling in a poorly taped rectangular box.

"Delivery for Cory Broadhurst," he said as he removed the dolly from under the box. He handed Cory a clipboard with an attached receipt to sign. There was no return address.

"Who would send their art wrapped no better than this?" Cory said, cringing at the sight of the dilapidated box, addressed in a child-like scrawl of magic marker, frayed tape loosely holding the ends together. She pulled a box cutter out of her back pocket and sliced the flimsy tape, ripping at the cardboard, which gave way easily, to reveal the contents.

"Oh, my God—Charlie!" she screamed and threw herself into his opened arms. "What are you doing here? This is insane," she said, looking at the remnants of box and tape at their feet. "You weren't due until June," she babbled, kissing the corners of his goofy grin.

He hugged her tightly and spun her around in a circle. "Couldn't wait," he said. He held her at arms length and appraised her. "I swear, you are still the most beautiful woman in the world, and I'm crazy in love with you. Close your eyes and hold out your hand," he said.

"I can't take one more surprise today," Cory said, but obediently closed her eyes. She felt a disc in the palm of her hand and opened her eyes to a single diamond set in gold.

"Marry me," Charlie said simply.

The blood slowly drained from her head and she felt a swoon coming on, which was interrupted by the jingle of Tibetan bells as the door swung abruptly open and then closed with a bang.

"Bad timing?" Jessica's sardonic voice broke the spell. She took in the scene—a man grinning like an idiot, standing amidst torn cardboard, holding Cory's hand in which rested a ring. "Charlie, right? You're early," she said.

"This could have been possibly the most romantic moment of my entire life," Cory sighed.

Charlie smiled awkwardly and offered Jessica his now free hand.

Jessica stood, one hip cocked, glanced at the ring then at Charlie. "Might this be premature?" Her voice sounded schoolmarm-ish.

Cory's foot tapped out a little rhythm of impatience. "Allow me to introduce you two—Charlie, Jessica. Jessica, Charlie. Now is when you shake hands like adults," she set her jaw.

"Aw, crap," Jessica muttered and stuck out her hand. "Sorry; you just caught me off guard," she said.

"I seem to be doing that a lot today," Charlie grinned and clasped her hand warmly. "You wouldn't believe how scared I've been to actually meet you," he said.

"Good; let's keep it that way for a while," Jessica replied. Her tough-girl act was belied by the quirks at the corners of her mouth.

The bells jingled again as Alise returned. "Ah, you made it," she gave Charlie a hug. "I'm Alise. We finally meet," she smiled.

"I called ahead to see if you could get the day off," Charlie answered in response to Cory's look of confusion.

"You knew about this," she turned to Alise, "and you didn't tell me?" Cory's jaw dropped in disbelief.

"I have the day off too," Jessica chimed in. Cory shot her a look. "Of course, I have about a month's worth of laundry to do," she backpedaled.

"I would be honored to take both of you lovely ladies to lunch, before we drop Jessica off to do her laundry, that is," Charlie grinned.

"Cool," Jessica said, wedging her way in between them and linking arms with both Charlie and Cory. "Let's go."

Charlie held the door open at By The Sea, and pulled out chairs for Cory and Jessica when the waitress led them to a table by the window. Jessica shot him a look as if he'd just sprouted a head of purple hair.

"So, what are your plans?" Jessica asked pointedly as she took a bite of spicy crab cake followed by a forkful of coleslaw.

"You have the appetite of a truck driver," Charlie said with admiration. "That's your second order."

"Strong metabolism," Jess said, gulping her Sam Adams.

"Plus, she works out and does Tae Kwon Do," Cory added. "Don't let her dainty presentation and genteel manner fool you, she could take you down in a minute," she chuckled.

"Back to you, Chuck. What are your intentions here, if you don't mind my asking," Jessica said.

"Chuck?" Charlie said, amused. "No one has ever called me that."

"Up until now," Jessica burped and patted her chest. "Your intentions?"

"Well, I graduate in June, and I've been looking at the Vet school up here as a possibility," Charlie smiled across the table at Cory. "I'd have to work for a year to establish residency—probably at the animal hospital. I thought maybe Cory and I would live together to make sure we're compatible before we hitch our wagons, so to speak."

"You haven't even 'hitched your wagons' yet?" Jessica sounded incredulous. "Interesting visual," she added as she speared a thick cottage fry doused in catsup. "Most people 'hitch their wagons' before they even think about compatibility or marriage for God sake. Unless you're still sore from the surgery, or…"

"Jess," Cory interrupted, "'hitch your wagons' means get married."

"Oh," Jessica took another swing of beer. "Talk amongst yourselves," she waved at them, sliding out of the booth, "I've gotta pee."

Charlie shook his head. "Is she for real?"

"She grows on you," Cory smiled. "I've been scanning the rental ads since we talked last week. You're serious about this?" She reached over and took Charlie's hand.

"I'm serious about this," he said. "Should we be looking for something with a granny unit?" he jerked his head toward the ladies room.

"Oh, horrors, no," Cory chuckled. "She'll settle down, really."

Chapter 23

"This place is just as I'd imagined it," Charlie said, patting an overstuffed, magenta pillow next to him on the futon. "Your apartment is an extension of the beautiful work of art that you are."

"I'm so glad you're here," she said, yawning as she laid her head on his shoulder. "I wish you could stay longer."

Charlie wrapped his arm around her and drew her close, kissed her forehead, her eyes, her nose, and worked his way down to her mouth. He stopped suddenly, glanced at the door, and said, "Locked?" Cory nodded. "I keep thinking she's going to pop in any minute, or come crashing through the window or something."

"She really does have a month's worth of laundry to do," Cory said as she parted her lips to allow the tip of Charlie's tongue to dart playfully into her mouth. Cory felt the world begin to tilt on its axis, and a pleasant, melty sensation spread through her loins.

"Funny," Charlie said, "Jess thought 'hitching your wagons' meant, well, you know, sex," he said under his breath. Color rose in his cheeks.

"Yeah," Cory smoothed a hand over his hair, touched his cheek, and kissed his chin. "I mean, I guess she has a point about compatibility," she said. "We couldn't really have sex before we left Colorado."

Charlie shifted so his he was leaning into Cory, his weight on his elbows. He looked into her eyes and saw his own reflection swim in their depth. "Um, do you think we—I mean, we couldn't then, but maybe now we should..."

Cory's stomach shook with suppressed laughter. "'Hitch our

wagons'?" she grinned. "Wow, this will be a first," she squirmed. "Are you healed enough?"

Charlie paused a moment, a look Cory couldn't read passed quickly over his face and was gone. "I think so. How about you?" He propped himself on one elbow and was exploring the curves of Cory's body with his free hand, playing with buttons, un-tucking fabric, jiggling her zipper.

Cory felt a wave of nausea and shoved a memory back into the dark corner of her mind. "Uh-huh," she wrapped her arms around his neck. "I think so. I guess there's only one way to find out," she said as she pulled him to her. "Let's go slow, okay?" she whispered in his ear.

Two hours later, Charlie flopped over on his back. "Not bad for the first time out of the gate," he grinned wickedly as they lay sprawled, spent, on the futon.

"Not bad?" Cory punched him playfully. "I think that was a blue ribbon run. We should celebrate," she suggested.

"I thought we just did. I need to at least catch my breath," he teased.

"I mean our engagement. You know—champagne and caviar or something. Just the two of us," she added when Charlie glanced over at the phone sitting on an overturned orange crate.

"You have some place special in mind?" Charlie asked.

"Chez Moi," Cory responded. "I have an eclectic selection of foodstuffs left over from various potlucks. I'll put the champagne in the freezer. You run a bubble bath."

Over a candlelit bath in the old claw-foot tub, they spoke of love and their future. "This is real, isn't it?" Charlie smiled slowly. "It's what I've been waiting a lifetime for," he said.

"This is as real as it gets," Cory said. "I didn't know if I'd ever have this experience once I started on my journey, you know?"

"I do know. I really, really do know," he said, as he lifted her foot out of the bubbles and placed a gentle kiss on a water-wrinkled toe.

Down the hall, the kitchen phone rang. "Whoever that is can wait," Cory said sinking back into the warm water and the look in Charlie's eyes, as the machine picked up.

An hour later, Charlie pulled the champagne out the freezer and found glasses in the cupboard. Cory, wrapped in a plush white bathrobe, winked at him from across the room as she pushed the Play button on the answering machine. 'Pop!' went the cork.

"Cory, this is Gwen, from Trinidad's After Care Program." There was a pause. Cory smiled expectantly. "I know this is going to hard to hear, but Erin's parents called me yesterday. Cory, Erin killed herself. I don't have all the details yet." Charlie dropped the glass he was holding. It shattered on the tile. "The parents asked that I let the group members know," Gwen continued in a monotone, "but they don't want to be contacted. They said this is a very private time for them, and asked that you all respect that." Cory's legs no longer supported her and she reached for the chair. Missing that, she landed on the floor. Unable to take in any more, Cory didn't hear the end of Gwen's message, only the beep signaling the end of the call.

Charlie sat beside her, propped against the cabinet, in silence, his clammy hand holding Cory's tightly. Shards of glass glittered from the floor near the sink as minutes passed with a muted 'thick, thick, thick,' of the clock in the living room.

Cory opened her mouth to speak. Her jaw trembled, and she closed it again. They sat, under the 60-watt bulb, for what seemed an eternity. Cory glanced up at the champagne bottle on the kitchen counter. "I can't…" she said, struggling with the words. "I know," Charlie replied. He struggled to his feet, held out a shaky hand and helped Cory up. He led her down the hall to the bedroom. There would be time for words tomorrow.

The next day, Sunday, started with a low cloud level, the gloom outside matching the gloom inside as Cory made a series of calls to group members.

"It's Rob," she handed the phone to Charlie. Charlie sighed and with a husky voice said, "Hey my man, how's life in the south? We've missed you—yeah," he said in response, "I wish it could have been under different circumstances too." They talked back and forth for a while, Charlie nodding thoughtfully. He was silent for a few moments, and then said, "We're good—aside from this, I mean. I popped the question, she said yes. Okay, I will," he said and glanced at Cory. "You too."

His eyes were moist as he hung up the phone, pulled Cory to him and kissed her gently on the lips. "From Rob," Charlie said, smiling weakly. "He said to tell you life is for the living, and he loves us."

Chapter 24

The weekend storm had cleared, and sun shone brightly through the living room window. The scent of fresh mown grass wafted in through the screen door. Cory had taken the day off, deciding to follow the 'life is for the living' theme, and was moving about the kitchen clattering dishes onto the counter. Charlie sat, legs folded yoga style on the futon, and slowly turned the pages of the album he'd brought from home. "I look like a dork," he groaned.

"Everyone looks like a dork in a cap and gown. It's like enforced geekdom," Cory chuckled and handed him a glass of orange juice. "Don't want you going hypoglycemic on me," she said. "I wish your Mom could have been there."

"Yeah, well…" Charlie ran a thumb over the picture of his Dad, next to him, with an arm draped over Charlie's shoulder, grinning like the proud parent he was. "She could have been. At least Dad was there," Charlie said, with a break in his voice. He took a sip of juice and set the glass down.

"I'm incredibly proud of you." Cory leaned over the back of the futon and placed a big sloppy kiss on his cheek. Charlie grinned in spite of himself. "Do you think they'll come visit after we've settled into the new house?" she asked.

"Don't know. What time are Jess and her new girlfriend coming?" he said.

"Ten. Be kind, okay? Britta is sort of…" Cory searched for the right word.

"Odd?" Charlie supplied, catching Cory's hand and bringing her around to sit next to him.

"Intense, I think would be fair. Look, she's the first girl Jess has dated in years." Cory got up, went into the kitchen nook, and pulled out the coffee grinder and beans. She measured out eight cups worth of beans and pushed the button on the grinder.

"Guess she finally got it that you're not available," Charlie said under the metallic whir.

"What?" Cory said, pausing, "Couldn't hear you."

"Nothing," Charlie said, closing the album. "I'll set the croissants out. You want me to make Mimosas?"

"Let's wait until they get here. You could start the bacon," Cory said just as the doorbell rang. "Scratch that," she amended. "Go for the Mimosas. I'll get the door."

Jessica opened the front door as Cory left the kitchen, and led a wispy, pale-faced young woman by the hand into the hallway.

"Jess, good morning," Cory gave her a hug. "Britta, welcome," she offered her hand.

Britta was sheathed in black; the lower half of her head shaved, and from the crown sprouted a tuft of strawberry blonde hair. Her eyes were dilated, and rimmed in ebony. Her cheeks were concave, her lips were thickly layered in white, and she slowly lifted an anorexic hand that Cory was hesitant to shake for fear of wounding her.

Cory clasped the fragile hand gently. It felt like a spider web.

Jessica rubbed her hands together briskly. "Smells great in here," she said. "Where's the little man?"

"In the little kitchen, making those great smells," Cory bantered back. "Come on in. Honey, the girls are here," she called to Charlie.

"What's this, a throwback to the old days?" Jessica whooped when Charlie stepped out of the kitchen wearing a white lace apron and sporting a spatula.

"Bacon grease," he punched Jessica playfully on the arm. "Hi there," he addressed Britta, "I'm Charlie. Hope you brought your appetite."

As if through a haze, Britta struggled to focus her eyes on Charlie's smiling face. Failing that, she dropped her attention to the floor and waited for further instructions from Jessica who obliged and guided her into the kitchen.

Charlie glanced at Cory who shrugged her shoulders and mouthed 'be kind.'

Charlie poured the Mimosas while Cory finished the bacon and scrambled the eggs. "Jess," she directed, "could you get the cinnamon rolls out of the oven for me?" They moved like a well-oiled machine, each navigating around the other efficiently in the tiny kitchen. Britta was propped at an angle, against the doorframe, like a branch that had been snapped from a tree.

Once plates had been filled, they assembled on the living room floor, propping themselves with pillows and creating makeshift tables out of whatever surfaces were available.

"So, Britta," Charlie turned to her, "tell me how you and Jess met." His smile ricocheted off her blank face.

"We met in Philosophy 200," Jessica said. "Britta is an Existentialistic Nihilist," she beamed.

"Great," Charlie managed. "Cor, breakfast is great," he reached over and patted Cory's knee. "Great," he repeated, and fixed her with a 'get me out of here' look.

"What do you hear from the realtor? Wish somebody had left me an inheritance. Can I have your place when you move?" Jessica asked through a mouth full of cinnamon roll.

"They're considering our offer," Charlie said. "We should know by the end of the week." Cory added, "I can recommend you to the landlord. It's not like we're interchangeable."

Jessica chortled. "I should say not. Can you imagine me living with Chuck?"

"Now there's a truly scary thought," Charlie said playfully.

Britta hiccupped and the three turned in surprise having forgotten she was present. She blotted her white lips with her napkin, and then returned to moving her food around on her plate with a fork.

"Could I get you something—different?" Cory asked, concerned that perhaps Britta was a vegan or a vegetarian and Jess had overlooked that detail.

"She doesn't eat much," Jessica said. "So yeah, put in a good word for me with the landlord. I can't believe you're willing to move to the burbs," she rolled her eyes. "You've really changed, Cor."

"Duh," Cory said, and the three of them broke into laughter.

"That was awkward," Charlie said later as he dried the dishes. "I don't think Britta said a word the whole time. Strange girl. What is Jess thinking?"

"I think she's afraid I'm leaving her," Cory frowned, "so she's responding in her Jess-sort-of way—you know, extreme."

"She's replacing you with a zombie? Real flattering," Charlie grinned. Cory grabbed the towel from his hands, and snapped him on the backside with it.

"Last time I abandoned her, she dropped me like a hot potato. I had to grovel for forgiveness, and ply her with lots of food." She leaned her head on Charlie's back and breathed in his scent. "I'm not abandoning her, I'm moving across town for God's sake. And I'm not selling out. I just want to live in a nice house." She sounded petulant even to herself.

Charlie turned and planted a kiss on her nose. "It used to be you and Jess against the world, you know. Things change," he pulled her close.

Cory laid her cheek against his shoulder. Suddenly serious, she said, "Sometimes I wonder if we deserve to be this happy."

Chapter 25

"Please, tell me you're kidding," Cory said into the phone the following morning. With her free hand, she stirred a pot of oatmeal on the stove. The smell of French Roast filled the kitchen and the toast popped just as Charlie came into the room. He pantomimed taking it out of the toaster and Cory shook her head.

"I know Belize is beautiful, and you can live there for practically nothing," Cory said. She thrummed her fingers on the side of the stove as she listened.

"I don't care that she lived there half a year after she dropped out of high school," she rolled her eyes at Charlie, "Jess, you can't just up and move to Belize with Britta. That's nuts." She flailed about for a good argument. "Besides, I was counting on you to be my brides—uh."

Charlie leaned back in his chair and snickered.

"Forget Britta," Cory snapped. "Jess, I need you as my bridesperson. I don't know how I could get through this without you by my side."

She turned the heat off under the cereal and glanced at Charlie, who sat with hands folded, and stared out the kitchen window. Her heart clenched with love for this man.

"Jess, you have it all wrong. This isn't like before." Cory clattered the lid on the pot and slumped against the counter. "We need to talk. Get your butt over here for breakfast—right now," she said, and slammed the receiver back into its cradle.

She turned to Charlie, "Pull out the waffle iron," she said, "this is war."

Twenty minutes later, the three sat around the small table in a pool of sunlight. Jessica, eyes downcast, sniffed runaway mucus. Her face was splotchy and her once punked-out hair had lost its oomph.

"You look like someone just hung your cat," Charlie said as he passed her the box of tissue. As she reached for the box, Charlie noticed a dried smear of blood from one of three deep scratches across her wrist. He looked away.

After a loud honk into a handful of tissues, Jessica took a ragged breath. "I haven't forgotten what happened the last time you got all involved with a guy," she said, still staring at the table.

Cory scooted her chair closer and took Jessica's hand. "I was younger and stupid, okay? That was a terrible way to treat a friend. Jess, this is a different time in our lives. *Our* lives," she gestured, taking in all three of them.

"We want a family," Charlie said, "and our kids are going to need an auntie to keep us from ruining their lives."

Jessica jerked her head up with a quizzical look. "How can—I mean, you can't—uh—can you?" She blinked and swiped at a tear.

"Adoption," Cory said. "That's not the point. Jess, you are part of my life, and by extension, part of Charlie's as well."

"You're stuck with me kid," Charlie bobbed his head, trying to elicit a smile. "Jess, we're just moving across town." Charlie lifted her chin so she had to look him in the eye. "We'll see you as often as we do now. Well, not exactly…"

"What Charlie is trying to say is, nothing is going to change between us," Cory said. "I love you. You're my chosen sister, you know that." She pulled Jessica into a clumsy hug. Charlie joined the hug.

"Now, will you please break up with Britta?" Charlie chucked her on the chin.

They were interrupted by the jangling of the phone. "I'll get it," Charlie said, disengaging himself. "Hello?" There was a brief pause. "Sure, hang on," he covered the mouthpiece and said, "It's someone named Brian for you."

Cory jumped up and ran over to the phone. "Brian," she squealed. "Are you in town? Great to hear from you…" she stopped mid-sentence. Her face went ashen and her eyes pooled. Charlie pulled a chair up behind her and motioned her into it. "No. Thank you. I wish it had been under different circumstances too," she said, the phrase an echo of only days ago. "I'm so sorry. Yes, she certainly was."

Cory finished the conversation and fumbled the phone back into its cradle. She stared out the window. In barely a whisper she said, "Martha's dead." Jessica moved behind her and stroked her head as Charlie wrapped his arms around her. "Aw, honey," he crooned.

"I had hopes, you know," she said over Charlie's shoulder, "that Martha could be sort of like the mother I never had."

"She *was* the mother you never had—for a little while," Jessica offered. Cory nodded. Charlie winked appreciation at Jessica. They stood together, a little splotch of sadness on an otherwise sunny day.

"So, are we going to have waffles, or what?" Jessica asked.

Chapter 26

"I guess it's a moot point," Jessica answered her unasked question as she wrapped newspaper around a pottery goblet and fit it gingerly into the packing box.

"What's that?" Cory looked back over her shoulder from the top of the stepladder. To Charlie she said, "Here, hon," and handed him a platter from the cabinet shelf.

"Whether or not we were going to meet Martha before the wedding," Jessica said. "I mean, it's sad. She was going to be your matron of honor." She folded and tucked the flaps of the box.

Cory sat down on top of the counter for a moment and shook the kinks out of her arms.

"Who's giving you away?" Jessica asked.

"No one is giving me away. I don't belong to anyone," Cory said with a look that dared anyone to disagree.

"I'm not wearing a funny dress," Jessica declared.

The rest of the day was spent hoisting boxes, driving back and forth across town, working together as a team. That night over pizza, Jessica said, "Honey Dew Lane. Could you get any more burb-ian?" She took a swig of her Sam Adams. "I saw your neighbor peek from behind her curtain. Wonder what she's thinking."

"She's probably thinking a nice couple with a peculiar friend is moving in next door," Cory shot her a look. Charlie chuckled and threw another log in the fireplace. The room smelled homey and lived-in already. He stretched out on the tan carpet, plumped a pillow under his head and sighed with satisfaction.

"Are you going to tell them? Your neighbors?" Jessica wiped pizza sauce from her chin with her sleeve.

"It's not like it's a secret," Charlie answered, "but I don't know that it's really any of their business."

"If someone asked directly, I'd give them an honest answer. I think," Cory added.

"Sure. Like someone's going to say out of the blue, 'Hey, did you used to be a guy?'" Jessica chuckled.

"One hurdle at a time," Charlie said, as they cleared the pizza box and beer bottles from the living room floor. "Are you coming back over to help unpack tomorrow?"

"Sounds like I'm not staying the night," Jessica said with a grin. "I'll be here for breakfast," she called over her shoulder on her way down the hall and out of the front door.

The next morning, Cory stood in front of the bathroom mirror brushing her teeth while Charlie finished in the shower. At the front of the house, the doorbell rang.

"Good God, it's eight o'clock on a Saturday morning. Jess isn't due until nine," Cory grumbled as she rinsed, spit, and slipped on her robe. She peeked through the security hole before opening the door, and groaned.

On the other side of the door was a middle-aged woman with a saccharine smile plastered on her face. She wore a jogging suit, and her honey blonde hair was tightly bound on top of her head, exposing her brown roots. She rang the doorbell again and Cory jumped.

"Good morning," the woman chirped as Cory opened the door. She shoved a loaf of something covered in a cloth napkin forward as she sized up Cory. "I'm Mrs. Geraldine Fortney..." her voice raised at the end, as if she questioned that fact. "My hubby, Sam, and I are your neighbors across the street," she pointed with a brick red nail, in case Cory had missed the behemoth structure taking up more than its share of the block. "We just wanted to welcome you to the neighborhood," she rattled on, "and to say how glad we are to see a nice young couple move in." She took a breath.

"Thank you, Geraldine. How nice of you," Cory was about to introduce herself.

"You just never know who's going to move into a neighborhood these days," Geraldine launched out in a new direction. "Just last month a homosexual couple looked at the place."

Cory could feel her eyes begin to squint and she fought the urge to back up and slam the door in the woman's face.

"I told Sam we'd have to go to church twice a week and pray real hard for an acceptable buyer for this house, and look—here you are," she spread her hands in glee, her smile stretched even farther.

"What? Oh, okay honey," Cory called back over her shoulder. "I'm sorry Geraldine, my husband is calling. Thank you for the lovely loaf of, uh... We'll talk again," Cory backed up and began to ease the door closed.

"That's perfectly okay, honey. You just go take care of that man of yours," Geraldine waved bye-bye as the door clicked shut.

"Holy shit," Cory muttered as Charlie came down the hall, towel clad and smelling of soap and new beginnings.

"I'm sorry," Charlie stopped and tugged his towel closer. "I guess I should have put a robe on?" his expression was quizzical.

"Oh, no, love, not you. The neighbor—a real whacko," Cory said shaking her head.

"At least she brought food," he said, taking the loaf from Cory and peeking under the napkin. "Mmm, banana bread—still warm, too," he smiled appreciatively.

"If she'd known who we were, I'd be checking it for arsenic," Cory said. "Charlie, our across-the-street neighbors are raving bigots. I'm not so sure I feel all that safe at the moment." She leaned heavily against the wall.

A sound at the door made both of them jump. "Don't answer it," Cory whispered. They stood, staring wide-eyed, as the doorknob turned. Jessica shoved the door open and stepped into the hallway.

"Geez," Cory hissed with exasperation, "since when don't you knock?"

"Well, excuuuuuse me," Jessica said. "You two look like you were expecting a burglar or something." She dropped her backpack on the floor and headed for the kitchen.

"Worse," Cory said. "A bigot." Cory recounted the experience with the neighbor over banana bread, eggs, and coffee.

Jessica raised her eyebrows. "She said what?" She choked on the bite of bread she was chewing. "I ought to ride my Harley back and forth across her well-manicured lawn..."

"You don't have a Harley," Charlie interrupted.

"I ought to get one then," Jessica said. "Or maybe I'll sneak over late at night and rip out that azalea bush by the front door."

Cory paled. Butter smeared down the tablecloth as the knife slipped from her hand and fell onto the floor. "Azalea bush?" she said in a whisper.

"Oh, shit," Jessica muttered. She jumped up, ran around the table and threw her arms around Cory, whose body was shaking. "Cor, let it go. That was a long time ago," she said in a soothing voice, resting her head against Cory's. "You're safe now," she added.

"No, no I'm not safe now. There's a crazy woman across the street that could hurt me," her voice wobbled. "Charlie, I can't live here," her eyes flashed desperation.

"Whoa, babe, slow down," Charlie took her hand and looked into her eyes. "Take a breath. We've got you covered. You're safe right this very moment. Jess and I won't let anything happen to you," he crooned. Cory's hand was cold and Charlie rubbed it briskly to restore the blood flow.

"PTSD," Jessica said, "Post Traumatic Stress Disorder," she explained at Charlie's look of confusion. To Cory she said, "I think you'd better call Marg."

Chapter 27

"I feel like a failure," Cory said, her voice thick with emotion as she stared at the carpet. She pulled a pillow from the end of the couch and held it close to her stomach.

"Cory," Marg's voice was gentle, yet firm, "look at me please," she urged. "Thank you. You got triggered. You realize that, right?" Marg maintained her soft gaze. "The azalea reminded you of the harm Kurt did."

"But, this woman really is dangerous," Cory defended.

"Her mindset is dangerous," Marg agreed, "but there's no reason to believe that she will cause you physical harm, no reason to believe you have to leave your home."

Cory remained unconvinced. "She doesn't know me. If she knew who I was, I'd be in danger. You should have heard her."

"Take a breath, slow down," Marg urged. "What she believes is that you're a happily married young woman who has purchased her first home. That's true, isn't it?"

"Yes, but, I don't know that my goal in life is to 'pass'," Cory said. "I want to be able to be myself without worrying about my personal safety."

"Do you remember a long time ago," Marg settled back in her chair, "we spoke of all the 'firsts' you'd be facing in your new life? And that you couldn't hide from life to avoid them? That you'd have to learn from them what you could?"

Cory nodded.

"What you choose to disclose about yourself, after getting to know someone, is entirely a separate matter. Right now, what she knows about you is true and accurate, is it not?" Cory nodded again.

"I'm not suggesting this woman will ever be someone you'll call a friend, but here's an opportunity to get to know her over time, and perhaps by doing so, expand her world view a little." Cory's shoulders relaxed and her jaw unclenched. "Possible, don't you think?"

"It wouldn't have made a difference with Kurt," Cory said.

"No, it wouldn't have made a difference with him," Marg acknowledged. "Try to separate the two events in your mind. I'm not talking full disclosure," Marg said, leaning forward. "As you get to know her over time, you might take a small, safe risk and see how that goes."

Cory looked doubtful. "Maybe. I guess I can at least see that she's not the same as Kurt," she conceded.

"Cory, you're a wonderful woman, and anyone would be all the richer for knowing you," Marg said.

"How did it go with Marg?" Charlie asked that evening. He handed her a glass of Merlot, sat down next to her on the sofa, and threw an arm around her shoulder. Cory snuggled in close, took a sip of her wine, and released a long sigh. She stretched her legs out and rested her feet on the ottoman.

"I guess we don't have to put a For Sale sign on the lawn just yet," she smiled. "Maybe they're not all like her," Cory said.

"Maybe..." Charlie said with a wicked grin, "we could put a For Sale sign on *her* lawn."

"This is truly scary," Cory teased. "You're starting to sound like Jess."

Chapter 28

Outside, colorful lights lined houses and wrapped trees. They twinkled and cast their hues onto the snowy crust covering Honey Dew Lane. Bright chips of stars glittered overhead against the black night. Inflated plastic Santas, snowmen with derby hats, reindeer, and all manner of holiday bric-a-brac covered the lawns. Icicles, real and electrical, dripped soundlessly from the eaves.

Inside, Cory steadied the chair as Charlie leaned precariously to top the tree with their first ornament purchased as a couple.

"John and Peggy, Mrs. Alexander from down the street, and, I don't know—maybe five or six more people," Cory counted the neighbors expected for the annual holiday party at Geraldine and Sam Fortney's house—or, The Fort, as Sam liked to call it.

"How long do you suppose Jess will pout over not being invited?" Charlie asked. He climbed down, stood back and admired his work.

"I don't know why she's pouting at all—she hates the Fortneys," Cory said.

"Good food, open bar—my guess," Charlie leaned his head to the side. "It's crooked, isn't it," he said, looking at the tree topper, an antique angel with spun glass hair and feathered wings. "Why didn't you tell me while I was up there?"

"I like it crooked," Cory smiled and wrapped an arm around his waist. "It's like the angel's smiling down on us, blessing our first Christmas together." They kissed, celebrating the moment.

Charlie broke away with a quick pat on Cory's behind. "Get your coat," he grinned. "We might as well get this over with."

"I'm thinking it might not be so bad," Cory said. "We have some pretty interesting neighbors," she pointed out. "Did you know Mrs. Alexander's parents were Holocaust survivors? She just finished a book about her life. And Mary Drew used to be a daytime soap star. How cool is that?"

Charlie chuckled as he helped her on with her coat. "I'm proud of you," he whispered into her hair as he kissed the top of her head. "And Marg would be proud of you, too."

Across the street, they were greeted with Bing Crosby crooning 'White Christmas' through speakers hung from an evergreen. The sound of laughter and raucous conversation drifted out of the door as the Fortneys welcomed their neighbors.

Cory kept one arm linked through Charlie's as they wandered among the guests, smiling and exchanging small talk. A fireplace crackled warmth and good cheer in the background.

"Damned Democrats think they can get that gun legislation through—over my dead body," Sam was trumpeting to a captive audience. "Sweetheart, it's Christmastime," Geraldine said as she led Sam away, releasing the grateful quartet he'd cornered. "And, look, Cory and Charlie are here..." she embraced each in turn, and Sam slapped Charlie on the back.

The food was divine, and the champagne flowed freely. Sam gathered the throng around the fireplace, "A toast to the holidays, to good neighbors, and a prosperous year ahead," he said, raising his glass. Cory and Charlie clinked glasses and exchanged a kiss.

"Isn't that sweet," Geraldine said, smiling at the pair. The tone around them had dropped to quiet conversation with neighbors sitting and standing in small, intimate groups. Sam stood next to his wife and threw a hearty arm around her shoulder.

"So, tell us, Charlie," he said with a champagne slur, and a nod toward Cory, "how you and the little woman here met."

Cory's teeth clenched and she stepped closer to the fire, warming her hands behind her. "Yes, dear," she smiled, unhinging her jaw, "tell the people how we met." She looked around and saw a crowd of eyes focused on them. A film of sweat broke out on her upper lip.

"Well, you see..." Charlie slid his arm around Cory and pulled her gently to him, "we met in a support group following our gender reassignment surgeries." He paused and noted the polite smiles and attentive nods. He cleared his throat and continued, "Cory having been a man originally, and I having been a woman, that is." He brushed a quick kiss across Cory's cheek and she leaned her head against his shoulder. "It was a match made in heaven—well," he corrected, "actually in Colorado, at the hospital."

The cemented smiles began to crack as the story seeped into each guest's information processing center. There was a palpable sense of collective breath held.

"Hah!" chortled Sam. He whopped his leg with an open palm. "That's a good one. You really had us going there for a minute, Charlie." The spell broken, the guests laughed heartily, milled about, refilled their drinks, and chatted noisily.

Cory's feet tingled with sensation after experiencing a few moments of the numbness that comes with being out of body. "I can't believe you said that," she whispered.

"I figured it was just easier to tell the truth," Charlie winked at her. "Merry Christmas."

Photo by Trudy Vandell

Author Bio

Jo Lauer is a psychotherapist by day. She is the published author of numerous articles, essays, and stories, and is the author of *Best Laid Plans: A Cozy Mystery*. She lives with her stuffed raven, Loudly, in Santa Rosa, CA.

You can find out more about her by visiting her website at: www.jolauer.com.

www.ingramcontent.com/pod-product-compliance
Lightning Source LLC
Chambersburg PA
CBHW062139170626
46813CB00002B/752